Linus Pierpont Brockett, Benjamin Gregory

Walter Powell

of Melbourne and London, merchant, philanthropist, and Christian

Linus Pierpont Brockett, Benjamin Gregory

Walter Powell
of Melbourne and London, merchant, philanthropist, and Christian

ISBN/EAN: 9783337393007

Printed in Europe, USA, Canada, Australia, Japan

Cover: Foto ©Andreas Hilbeck / pixelio.de

More available books at **www.hansebooks.com**

OF

MELBOURNE AND LONDON,

Merchant, Philanthropist, and Christian.

" Diligent in business, fervent in spirit, serving the Lord."

EDITED AND LARGELY REWRITTEN FROM REV. BENJAMIN GREGORY'S

"MEMOIRS OF WALTER POWELL, MERCHANT."

BY L. P. BROCKETT, M.D.,

AUTHOR OF

"MEN OF OUR DAY," "WOMAN'S WORK IN THE CIVIL WAR," ETC., ETC.

NEW YORK:

GEORGE ROUTLEDGE & SONS,

416 BROOME STREET.

1872.

PREFACE.

THE union of remarkable business ability, deep religious fervor, and intense activity in Christian work, though more frequent now than forty or fifty years ago, is not so common that we can afford to lose the benefit of any conspicuous examples of it. In a country where "the haste to be rich" has infected so large a part of the community, and where professing Christians are prone to forget their holy calling, in their zeal to accumulate wealth, it is refreshing to the soul to read the history of a man who, while "diligent in business, was also fervent in spirit, serving the Lord." Few men have been endowed by our Heavenly Father with such rare business capacities as Walter Powell, and fewer still use them, as systematically as he did, for the glory of God.

Who can tell how much good has been accomplished by the memoirs of these eminent servants of God? Hundreds of thousands have read the biographies of Norman Smith, of Nathaniel R. Cobb, of Samuel Budgett, of Amos Lawrence, of Harlan Page, and of William Wilberforce; and that they have exerted a powerful influence in moulding the characters of men now on the stage of active life, whose noble beneficence and deep devotion are the glory and joy of every branch of the one household of faith, is acknowledged by these very men.

In presenting to the Christian public another example of the fervor of a living Christian faith, manifesting itself in abundant good works, we feel that we are contributing our humble mite to the promotion of that cause which was ever uppermost in the heart and life of Walter Powell.

The work, in its present form, makes little pretension to originality. "The Thorough Business Man: Memoirs of Walter Powell, Merchant, of Melbourne and London," by Rev. Benjamin Gregory, is its basis, and from that work we have drawn very largely. But while Rev. Mr. Gregory believed, and perhaps wisely, that it was necessary for his English and Colonial readers that he should interweave his narrative with elaborate discussions of questions of commercial ethics and political economy, we fail to perceive a similar necessity for American readers, and have ventured to relieve the simple story of his life from these extraneous matters. We have also given somewhat less prominence to the special customs and forms of the Wesleyan Methodist Church in Australia, as not necessary to the completeness of the narrative, and not differing in principle, though they might in name, from the corresponding sub-organizations of the Methodist Episcopal Church here. Though a zealous Methodist, where Methodism was needed, Walter Powell was too broad and comprehensive a soul to be regarded as the exclusive property of any one division of

Christ's kingdom on earth. He was first and foremost of all, a CHRISTIAN, and to all the children of God, as members of the household of faith, his heart and hand were ever open.

The introduction and the chapters in which we have endeavored to urge upon Christian business men in our own country the blessedness of such a life as his, and its sublime influence in the promotion of the cause of Christ upon earth, are all which are not in a greater or less degree drawn from Mr. Gregory's work. That the Giver of every good and perfect gift, from whom come alike the intellectual gifts and the moral power which bless humanity, and to whose grace was due this conspicuous manifestation of the Christian life, may bless this simple narrative, to the upbuilding of His cause, is the sincere prayer of the editor of this work.

L. P. B.

BROOKLYN, N. Y., *September*, 1872.

CONTENTS.

CONTENTS.

INTRODUCTION.

In introducing to our readers the man whose life is narrated in the pages of this little volume, we have far other aims than simply to increase the already large list of biographies of a religious character, by the addition of the memoirs of a man whose only claims to commemoration were his piety and benevolence. We have already a sufficiency of these biographies of obscure men, without adding to their number. But Walter Powell was no common man. Reared from infancy in the newest and wildest of the British Antipodal Colonies, amid severe hardships and great moral perils, with no early education, except that derived from a mother's teaching; transferred, in the very prime of manhood, to the scarcely more settled and civilized Australian town of Melbourne, exposed to the great temptations and vicissitudes of the early gold mining period; voyaging repeatedly to England and America; establishing in the midst of great excitement and constant changes, an extensive business, on a basis so firm, that no financial panics were able to disturb it; and when his house had become the leading one in the Colony, withdrawing from its personal supervision, and establishing in London a still larger one, whose transactions were extensive in every quarter of the globe. Amid this extraordinary business activity, conducted often under the pressure of impaired health, this man found time

and opportunity for intellectual and æsthetic cul·
ture so extensive and generous, that he became,
even in their favorite studies, the peer of men
whose scientific attainments had been gained in the
halls of the great universities, and under the most
favorable circumstances. He became a popular and
eloquent public speaker, and could have gained, had
it been worthy his ambition, a seat in Parliament.
And yet he died in the very prime of life, at the
age of forty-five years.

But it is not for his great business abilities, nor
for the height of intellectual or æsthetic culture
which he had attained, self-taught, that we have felt
that his memoirs should be written, but because
amid all this commercial activity, and this incessant
study, underlying it all, and forming the solid and
substantial basis of his character, was an active,
ardent, working piety. He had consecrated himself
to Christ, in the dawn of his youth, before his extraordinary commercial prosperity, and he was not
the man to draw back from that consecration; in
the time when business was most overwhelming, he
was most active in the service of his Divine Master,
and this activity was never relaxed until he was
called up to the service of praise on high. His religion was not a Sabbath-day worship, whose benign
influences did not extend into his week-day life; on
the contrary, it permeated every business transaction; it showed itself in his solicitude to do rightly
and justly by his customers, and his determination
to exact what was just and right from those with
whom he dealt; it caused him to be honored and

respected as a man of the stanchest principle, by all who had dealings with him ; it illustrated the truth so often doubted and denied, that the highest Christian principle is consistent with commercial success.

Thoroughly interwoven with this spotless Christian life, was that almost unbounded liberality which was so beautiful a trait of his character. To all good causes, his hand was ever open, and his charity was not a mere impulse ; large as it was, it was systematic, and adapted skilfully to accomplish the ends he wished to promote. Whether it were the founding a Home for the poor emigrants, flocking in such numbers to Melbourne, erecting chapels, establishing a Book Concern and a public library, sustaining missionaries, aiding students for the ministry, helping the Lord's poor saints, succoring those who had been disastered in the financial vicissitudes so common at Melbourne, organizing schools, or rendering assistance to the families of the unfortunate, his gifts were always judicious, and though, sometimes, he submitted to serious personal privations, rather than let the poor, or the cause he so much loved, suffer, yet he rarely, and perhaps never, gave unwisely.

A life of such enterprise and commercial activity, so beneficent and fruitful in good works, and withal so self-denying and untiring in its Christian zeal and devotion, surely deserves to be put upon record for the encouragement of those who would fain tread in his footprints, and seek to follow his example, even as he followed that of his Divine Master.

It is worthy of notice that while memoirs of

scholars, statesmen, military and naval commanders, clergymen, physicians, jurists, and philosophers abound, there are comparatively few of merchants, and most of these are occupied with their mercantile career alone. Why should we not record the struggles and successes of one, who, while diligent in business, was also assiduous in laying up treasure in heaven?

We rejoice to know that in our own time there is a constantly increasing feeling of obligation on the part of Christian men of wealth, our bankers and merchant-princes, that not only their money, but their lives and personal activities, should be consecrated to Christ, and that from banks and offices, from warehouses and manufactories, from stately mansions and beautiful villas, as well as from the humbler dwellings of the poor, there are now marshalling a host which no man can number, fully armed and equipped for the service of the Captain of their salvation; ready for any sacrifice of time and money, and personal ease and comfort, so that they may do the will of their Master.

In the great day of accounts, when the good and evil which men have done on earth during their lives, and the influence which their work and example has wrought after their death, shall be summed up, we believe it will be found that Walter Powell's eminently Christian life, amid the cares and trials of a business career, has been productive of great good to many thousands whom he never knew here, but who will be among the stars in his crown of rejoicing in the Paradise of God.

CHAPTER I.

Though a stranger to England until his thirty-fourth year, Walter Powell first drew breath at Tottenham, near London, in May, 1822. His father had been a member of a highly respectable firm of merchants in London, still existing as Messrs. Henry Powell & Sons, Fenchurch Street, City; but the rapid increase of his family, and the commercial revulsions which followed the Napoleonic wars, had induced him to withdraw from the firm, and attempt some shorter route to wealth. He had removed to Southern Wales, and there attempted to accomplish his desires by several experiments in manufacturing; and these failing, either from lack of experience and skill, or from an insufficient market, he had declined to accept a position as head manager of a large and lucrative business, and determined to emigrate to the distant and then newly opened colony of Van Diemen's Land, or, as it is now called, Tasmania. Several of his friends had already gone thither, and Mr. Powell resolved to follow. It was during the farewell visit of the family to friends in London and vicinity that Walter Powell was born.

"At that time," says Rev. Mr. Gregory, "the colony of Van Diemen's Land was in its infancy. Although that beautiful island had been discovered so long ago as 1642, yet the first settlement upon it was made in 1803, nineteen years before Mr. Powell's immigration. Even then a spot so favored by Nature, yet so long abandoned to the occupancy of savages of the lowest type, was utilized by the British Government only as one of the cesspools of civilization, being chosen as a convict station for criminals of the worst class, a second time transported—first from England, then from Botany Bay. Barbarism and crime held joint tenancy of a land framed by the Creator to be the home of a happy Christian civilization. For ten years all communication between it and the rest of the world was interdicted, with the exception of Great Britain and New South Wales. In 1813, however, the ban was removed. The first free settlers endured great hardships, being often unable to procure any other food than a little kangaroo flesh and a few sea plants, humorously called "Botany Bay greens." Even refuse blubber, washed on shore from the whalers after the oil had been extracted, was eagerly added to their scanty commissariat. The British public, however, gradually became aware of the superior claims of Van Diemen's Land to the consideration of emigrants. They heard of the unrivalled deliciousness and healthiness of its climate, peculiarly favorable to the constitution of an Englishman, enjoying insular freshness, in a latitude corresponding to that of Southern Italy. They read of the richness of its soil, suited to almost every production of our own fields and gardens, the varied picturesqueness of its landscapes, an Arcadian or Palestinian combination of plain and mountain, meadow and woodland, and brooks of water which run among valleys and hills, with the setting of a magnificent coast, broken by sheltered coves and ample harbors, that of Hobart Town being one of the largest in the world. The island is, in fact, a kind of antipodal Devon. "Somersetshire," says Sir C. W. Dilke, "cannot surpass the orchards of Tasmania, nor Devonshire match its flowers."

It was not till 1818 that emigrants in any considerable numbers sought this distant land of promise. At the time of Mr. Powell's immigration, the entire population of the colony, according to the census just before taken, amounted to seven thousand one hundred and fifteen.

If the first layer of Tasmanian society was a coarse concrete of crime, the second was composed mainly of adversity and adventure. Resolute men, whose prospects in their native land were blighted, and whose way was built up or swallowed up, betook themselves to the goodly land which Providence had "espied" for them across the desert-deep. Amongst these came a few men of business who preferred colonization to clerkship. Of this class was the father of Walter Powell. He settled on the Macquarie plains, described as "a splendid alluvial valley, which for fertility and beauty of scenery can scarcely be surpassed." * He built for himself a mud-house of some pretensions, which, being double

* Stoney's "Residence in Tasmania."

the height of the ordinary dwellings, and betraying the weakness of its constitution by a very marked obliquity, was humorously called a Pisa house, in allusion to the famous Italian leaning tower. There misfortune dogged him. Soon after his arrival at his forest home, he was prostrated by a severe and long-lasting attack of rheumatic fever, the penalty of unwonted exposure and exertion. Whilst stretched helpless in bed, bush-rangers broke into his cottage, and stripped him of almost all he had. This outrage, followed by the loss of a very valuable horse, brought the family to the verge of ruin. The mother, an accomplished lady, tried to raise a little money by opening a school for the children of the scattered and struggling emigrants. In her letters to her friends in England, she confesses that the beautiful country and climate formed their only solace. Thus Walter Powell grew up amongst the worst hardships and dangers of a pioneer-settler, and the bitter mortifications of moneyless gentility.

The aborigines showed towards the new-comers a skulking and ferocious enmity, setting fire to their homes and stacks, and making themselves altogether very dangerous neighbors, especially to those who, like Mr. Powell, lived at a distance from the towns. The relations of the natives and the settlers had at first been of the most friendly kind. The Tasmanian savage was, while unprovoked, a good-humored, simple-hearted creature. His friendship seemed likely to be more troublesome than his enmity. Like the aborigines of New South Wales, the natives of Van Diemen's Land were fond of squatting in the neighborhood of the emigrants. But runaway convicts, and others whom the governor had been compelled, from want of provisions, to send into the woods to find their own food, had perpetrated upon the poor creatures the most diabolical atrocities. This naturally aroused in them a fierce determination to extirpate the new-comers, whom they began to regard as deadly enemies. The only mode of warfare which their rude weapons and savage strategy allowed was sly and detailed murder. They constantly lurked about the settlers' homes and fields, crouching, cat-like, in the bushes. When discovered, they always appeared to be weaponless, having acquired the art of dragging their spears along the ground; for they could use their toes as deftly as their fingers. They seemed to belong to the order *quadrumana*, their feet and hands could exchange functions at the moment's need. On the whole, they were formidable enemies, making up by cunning and extreme dexterity in the preparation and use of their rude missiles, for the inferiority of their tools and the want of fire-arms. Their spears were straightened by their teeth, till they poised as perfectly as an English fishing-rod, and both these and their clubs they could send quivering through the air with terrible force and precision. Even their women, in procuring opossums and crayfish for food, had become incredibly expert, both in diving and climbing. The savages found a leader in the person of a clever villain, who went by the name of Mosquito. He was a native of Sydney, who, having been condemned to death for the murder of a woman, had by perverted pity been reprieved and transported to Van Diemen's Land, where, by simulating repentance and reformation, he obtained his liberty, married a black woman, and organized a desperate attack upon the whites.

These planned outrages commenced in 1823, a few months after Mr. Powell's arrival. The state of things was such, that the settlers in remote parts of the island were perpetually in bodily fear for themselves, their wives, and their children. In the words of Mrs. Meredith, "A residence in this country was one long series of alarms, suffering, and loss, with the daily imminent peril of a fearful death, when every bush within spear-throw was a source of danger; and to stray beyond the door-sill unarmed was nothing short of *felo-de-se*." * Backhouse states that "there were few families in the island who had not sustained some injury, or lost some member, by the treachery of the aborigines.

But far more savage than the savages were the bands of escaped convicts, who haunted the forests like demoniacs, devoting themselves to robbery, outrage, and murder. Being men who in the lowest depth of penal discipline had found a lower deep, had baffled the utmost resources of punitive discipline, and had become as intolerant of their own lives as they were reckless of the lives of others, they had by desperate daring escaped the teeth of watch-dogs and the shot of sentinels, and found themselves provisionless in the gloomy woods, har-

* "My Home in Tasmania," vol. i., p. 190.

dened, hopeless, maddened by hunger, reduced to cannibalism, and often preying upon each other. No wonder that they did not spare either savages or settlers, when they had them at their mercy. A neighbor of Mr. Powell, Mr. Alison, of Stramshall, on the Macquarie river, who had emigrated at the same time, and had in earlier life commanded a ship under Nelson at Copenhagen, sustained a fearful encounter with three of these men, who left him for dead on his own door-step. "Scenes had been enacted or talked of in the presence of children which made them, when grown to manhood, hate the land of their birth, and fly to other shores."* Add to all this the frequent bush-fires, and the sudden, devastating floods to which the Tasmanian rivers are peculiarly liable, from the nearness of their sources in snow-capped mountains; and one may form some idea of the multiform dangers amidst which Walter Powell's boyhood was passed. The lovely island was not yet Tasmania, but still Van Diemen's Land. The then existing state of things corresponded to the doleful associations which the very name conjured up to our boyish fancy—chains, and hopeless drudgery, and work under the whip, amidst hateful companionship.

Yet the memories of his childhood exercised a very traceable influence upon Walter Powell's character. Having few playmates or schoolfellows, he grew into close companionship with nature. He became an intense watcher of the habits of insects

* Dilke's " Greater Britain."

and forest birds, spending hours in an admiring
study of their various modes of life. His chief associates were the graceful emu, stately as a swan,
comely in going as a he-goat or a king; the gentle,
soft-eyed kangaroo; the colloquial and consequen-
tial cockatoo, with lemon-colored head-dress, and
vivid plumage, many-hued, glancing in the sunshine.
Animal forms which seem to us so queer and abnormal, the wombat, etc., were those with which his
childhood was most familiar. He loved to wander
amongst the stately gum-trees, rising like cathedral
columns, straight and round, for a hundred or a
hundred and fifty feet without a branch, and
crowned with feathery foliage; and the superb tree-
ferns with stems twenty feet in height. One of his
favorite recreations was capturing these pompous
cockatoos, as they levied contributions on his father's
corn.

One of the earliest forms of self-help which the
young Tasmanian developed was the manufacture
of his own playthings. There were no toy-shops on
the Macquarie plains; yet, wherever the European
emigrant may pitch his tent, the game of marbles
must sharpen the eyes, and exercise the finger skill,
and bring out the acquisitive rivalry of his active
lads. Walter and his brothers, having no smooth
"stonies" or polished "alleys," were fain to make
to themselves common *taws* of clay, rounded by the
hand and hardened in the fire. One day, while su-
perintending the latter process, Walter, then only
five years old, watched his work too closely, and one
of the heated pellets flew out of the fire, and hit him

in the wide-open eye, depriving it, for life, of all power of vision.

Walter's only schoolfellows and playmates were his brothers and sisters, and the two or three settlers' children who came to his mother's school; and the fields and woods were his playground. He had no education but that which his parents could find time to give him, before he was thirteen years old. Both being well educated, and very solicitous for the well-being and advancement of their children, his schooling was, to its small extent, thorough and refined. The very disadvantages and dangers of his position, through the goodness of God, and the sensitive watchfulness of his parents, had a salutary effect on the formation· of his character. As none but *convict servants* could be procured,* his moral surroundings, outside the nursery, were of the most perilous description. But this redoubled the carefulness of his mother to compass him daily with moral supports and restraints. The education of young Walter's heart, of course, mainly devolved upon her. She impressed upon him high moral

---

* At that time, the " assignment system " was in full operation. So soon as a shipload of criminals reached the island, most of them were *assigned* to the various settlers, mainly as domestic servants and farm laborers. The principal objects of this arrangement were, to save the Government the expense of their keep and supervision, to utilize their labor for the advantage of the colonists, to break up the old criminal associations, to bring the prisoners into healthy contact with the orderly and industrious population, and thus give them the best and earliest chance of self-recovery. Their masters were required to find them shelter, clothes, and bedding, plenty of wholesome food in regulated rations; and they found their own fuel in the woods.

principles and sentiments in the most permanently effective, because the most pleasant and interesting, manner. Almost everything was done at home which could be attempted to awaken thought, to cultivate the affections, and inspire him with a reverence for principle and piety. This was his safeguard against all that was coarse and corrupting in his inevitable associations. There grew up in his heart a most reverent affection for his mother. Filial love seemed his strong anchor to hold him to purity and truth. It was, throughout life, a cause of gratitude to him that he had escaped the contaminating influences which encompassed him during his most impressible years. He heartily welcomed the abolition of the system of transportation, although the colony suffered materially from the withdrawal of the troops and the great diminution in Government expenditure. Yet he was every inch of him a *lad*, a thorough child of the bush; and, like many other fine-natured boys, was a strange combination of thoughtfulness and daring, docility and passion. His sense of wrong or insult blazed out into uncontrollable wrath. On one occasion, this impetuosity of indignation very nearly proved fatal to himself and to another. Of course, the use of fire-arms was part of the primary education of a young Tasmanian emigrant. He and his brother had gained permission for a day's shooting on a neighboring estate. The keeper, (as he is there called, the overseer,) not being apprised of this, met the boys, and saluted them with a Greek fire of blasphemy and insolence, a genuine specimen of convict billingsgate. The high-spirited lads, instead of soft answers and speedy explanations, being, most likely, stung to the quick by the questioning of their word, retorted on the rough ranger in his own tone. They had with them two splendid dogs, loved by the boys as almost members of the family. The keeper having spent his ammunition of abuse, and finding that the boys were not to be silenced or terrified by his tongue, divided between the dogs the contents of his double-barrelled gun. Walter, maddened with rage and pity, immediately levelled his own piece at the keeper's head, and snapped the trigger, with full intent of avenging the death of his innocent dogs. Happily, the report which drew the keeper's attention to their presence had come from Walter's gun, and his piece was unloaded. To the end of life, he reckoned it amongst his special mercies that he was thus saved from actual homicide.

But though he passed in that young country a free, a buoyant, and a plucky childhood, his father's straitened means, and his mother's strained anxiety to provide for her large household the rough comforts of a settler's home, awoke in him a precocious forethought, and a longing for the productive toils of manhood, that he might be helpful to his parents, and rebuild the shattered fortunes of the family. This feeling took such strong possession of him, as even to supplant his passionate love of nature and wild woodland freedom, inspiring him with a deep preference for the bustling activities of city life. Withal, his sensibilities were vivid, and his combativeness abnormally developed. The principles of muscular Christianity seemed to be, in his case, a part of natural religion. He instinctively acted on that adaptation to the young of the morality of the Sermon on the Mount, which underlies the teachings of the " Tom Brown " school of theology: " If a boy smite thee on the one cheek, hit him on the other also. And if he compel thee to run a mile, make him run twain." Had he lost his life in such encounters, a martyrdom which he more than once narrowly missed, he might have claimed canonization. In fact, he bore throughout life the stigmata of this bluff saintship.

He formed the fixed resolve of retrieving the fortunes of the family by all-conquering energy and industry. In giving heart-room to this noble ambition he laid the foundations of virtuous success. Thereby he entertained an angel " unawares."

How different were the surroundings of his early childhood from those of a city or country boy in his native land! His genuine independence of character, his marked individuality, and the strong simplicity, which is the very antithesis of tameness, were, doubtless, traceable, in part, to the associations of his woodland home. Self-reliance, circumspection, boldness, and frugality, were some of the valuable lessons learnt in the mud mansion on the Macquarie plains. If he had not before him the dread of the pedagogue's ferule, he must keep a sharp lookout against the spear of the *blackey* and the bludgeon of the bush-ranger.

But this free, out-door life was of too brief continuance. His eagerness to be helpful to his parents did not long remain ungratified. At that time, 1834, respectable youths, who could write a fair hand, keep simple accounts, and be trusted with sums of money, were very scarce in Tasmania. Hence, when only twelve years old, Walter obtained a situation as clerk, in the office of Mr. Francis Evans, merchant, in the port of Launceston, the northern capital of the island. Launceston is beautifully situated at the confluence of the North and the South Esk, which form here the fine tidal river Tamar. It was even then a thriving town of great bustle and commercial activity, though bordered by the solitudes of the primeval forest. Its population at that time was over two thousand; it quadrupled during the eleven years of Walter Powell's residence there. One who was then living at Launceston has a vivid recollection of his appearance at that time, since, in a small and new community, every respectable arrival is an object of keen interest and inspection. He is described as very thin and thoughtful-looking.

Here his position tended rather to deepen than to dissipate his habitual reflectiveness. Being the only business *employé* of his unmarried master, who was frequently away from home, and took little interest in or notice of his taciturn boy-clerk, his sole companionship was that of a man-servant, who had "left his country for his country's good." The only incident which broke the monotony of his desk work here was the accusation of having embezzled a missing five-pound note. Without waiting to deny the charge, he ran home to his mother; who, returning with him, was met with an apology, and the information that, in her son's absence, the misplaced sum had reappeared.

His conduct on this trying occasion showed a marked advance in self-control from the day when he levelled his gun at the gamekeeper. Even yet he was not perfect, according to Lord Bacon's acute comment on the inspired maxim : "A soft answer turneth away wrath."—"This teaches, first, that an *answer* should be *made*." Doubtless Walter could not trust himself to speak. The recollection of his narrow escape from the guilt of murder must have acted as a salutary check. His steadfast resolve to devote himself to relieving the difficulties of his parents, and repairing the fortunes of his family, sealed his lips under this exquisite provocation ; and surely nothing can be more calculated to ignite a high-spirited and high-principled youth than the sudden charge of theft. The instinct which impelled him at once to seek shelter in the counsels of his mother was equally honorable to both.

He was condemned to this uncompanioned drudgery for three years. At the end of that period, the death of a rich relative closed his master's office, and Walter was transferred, with highly favorable testimonials, to a store in the same town, that of Mr. Bell, who had recently resigned a government appointment, in favor of that which all the early colonists regarded as much more lucrative, the business of an auctioneer.

Here he practised at the desk those lessons of laboriousness which he had learnt in the forest clearings, where, if anywhere, the proverb holds good—

> "He that by the plough would thrive,
> Himself must either hold or drive."

He kept steadily in view the object of his ambition : to rise in the world, and to raise his parents with him, by sedulously cultivating those habits which alone, he knew, could entitle him to hope for that result. Yet, in the intervals of business, the wild spirit of the woods came back upon him, impelling him to feats of daring, agility, and strength. He bore to the grave several marks of serious injuries received in the performance of these risky exploits. A broad scar across his left temple was the memorial of one of his perilous hazards of field and flood. He was expert and fearless as a climber, leaper, swimmer, and diver ; in all the headlong gymnastics which seem so befitting a young borderer of the unclaimed wilderness. To one of these adventurous attempts was, doubtless, traceable his extremely precarious state of health throughout the remainder of his life, if not his comparatively early death. Although a spare stripling, his muscularity was highly developed, and he had acquired unbounded confidence in his own agility and nerve. As he was obliged to pass a great part of his time with those from whom he could gain no mental or moral improvement, he learnt from them all they had to teach—physical efficiency and animal courage and skill. Among the servants of Mr. Bell's establishment, was a sort of unprofessional Blondin, whose achievements Walter was very ambitious to equal or outdo. One of these was to leap out of a swing-boat, such as are seen at fairs, whilst at its highest pitch of velocity. Walter, having often seen this done, not only with impunity, but with ease and grace, concluded that what man had done man could do. He took the spring, but missing the exact second, was caught by the returning oscillation, twisted violently, and thrown to a great distance. The result was not only a severe shock to the nervous system, but an injury to the spine, inducing severe attacks of palpitation, and a decided stoop in his heretofore erect figure.

These traits and incidents prove plainly that his characteristic considerateness and steadiness did not grow out of a tame temperament or natural timidity and self-distrust. One can scarcely help asking to what extent this occurrence contributed to the formation of his character. It can scarcely be called a casualty, being rather the penalty of over-hardiness. Whilst it aggravated his natural fieriness of temperament into a morbid irritability, which became a sad trouble to himself, and, for a time, to those about him, it must have tended to tone down his overweening self-confidence, and could not but serve as a perpetual *memento mori*.

Mrs. Bell records several incidents illustrative of his sensitive integrity, and the prompt, impulsive, and almost imprudent generosity, which contrasted finely with the rigid regularity and close economy of his personal habits. One day, Mrs. Bell, looking out of her window, saw Walter conversing with a person, who, on shaking hands at parting, slipped into his palm at parting a sum of money, which Walter instantly flung from him with flushed indignation. On inquiry, she found that the individual had asked Walter to do him a business service, the true nature of which was first betrayed by the offer of money. The first payment he received in Mr. Bell's office was devoted to purchasing for his mother a sack of flour and a chest of tea. On another occasion, receiving a letter from his married sister, describing the distressing difficulties of herself and husband, as pioneer settlers at Port Philip, he at once laid out the whole of his savings in procuring for them a dray and a pair of horses, and in defraying the cost of shipment. Nor was his sympathy confined within the circle of his own relationship. A poor man lamenting to him the straitness of his means and the largeness of his family, Walter suggested the possibility of improving his circumstances by starting as a " dealer." The man replied hopelessly that the *start* required ten pounds; a sum which, in his state of hand-to-mouth dependence, he had no prospect of ever possessing. Walter, seeing that his well-meant advice had served only to make the poor fellow more painfully sensible of his utter helplessness, immediately gave him the ten pounds, although his own salary was but one hundred pounds a year.

In addition to many fine fruits of his mother's high moral culture, he had given several signs of religious thoughtfulness. Mrs. Bell was a member of the Wesleyan Church, and her husband devolved on her the duty of conducting family worship. She was wont to read a portion of Scripture, and offer a short, extempore prayer. When the young clerk joined the establishment, she so far yielded to the diffidence of her sex as to leave him unapprised of this godly usage of the family. On learning the fact, however, from the servants, he earnestly solicited the privilege of attending, which the lady, despite her natural diffidence, was not able to refuse. This seriousness was further manifested by his evincing a preference for the more direct and searching ministrations of the Methodist chapel, to which he gradually attached himself, although he was a member of the choir at church, and was much cherished on account of his superior musical gifts.

Here, then, is a young man of eighteen, the foster-child of the forest, whose brief boyhood has passed in gentlemanly poverty, who has proved the hardness of straitened circumstances without their debasing humiliations, with whom correctness of conduct is not only the impress of the high *morale* of his secluded homestead, but also an element of good breeding, a bright badge of caste, amidst the helotry of crime. He has learnt self-help and self-reliance from the necessities of his position, self-respect and self-control from the glaring miseries of those who wanted both; he has acquired physical fearlessness amidst a normal state of danger, and from the enforced companionship of men who had little else to teach; he is by temperament high-spirited, and feels in his veins the blood of an English gentleman; he is lovable, attractive, musical.

He has in him "the makings" of a noble character. One cannot fail to feel some interest in this frank, generous youth, whom filial love has chained to the desk ever since he was twelve years old. What will become of him? Will he make the best of himself, the best of life, the best of both worlds?

CHAPTER II.

THE severe shock to his system and the serious spinal injuries which young Powell's mishap in his attempted gymnastic feat had induced, were long concealed through fear of their effect upon his mother; but the time finally came when farther concealment was impossible; he was very ill, and his life was imperilled from the injuries he had received, and his whole nervous system was so shattered that it rendered him excessively irritable and petulant. He went home in the hope of benefit, but, restless and unhappy, soon returned to Launceston, it was feared, to die.

His habits up to this time had been correct: he was well-disposed, energetic, persevering, free from the vices common to young men, liable, indeed, to occasional outbursts of temper on comparatively trifling provocation; but, on the whole, a moral and well-bred young man. But as he stood face to face with death, and began to look beyond the narrow bounds of time, he began to see with far clearer vision than ever before, how imperfect and worthless was his own righteousness; how entirely inadequate to his salvation were his best deeds, and that unless Jesus would undertake for him he must be lost forever. He was not ignorant, theoretically, of the way of salvation. Though at his boyish home there were no churches or religious meetings, he had ever since his residence in Launceston been a regular attendant upon the services of the Established Church until a few months previous, when he had begun to go to the Wesleyan chapel with Mrs. Bell; not impossibly drawn thither, also, by his regard for Miss Annie Bell, her daughter, who afterward became his wife. He had also been uniformly present at family worship, and had listened to Mrs. Bell's fervent prayers for his conversion.

Now, however, for a long time he was unable to visit the house of God. There was just then beginning in Launceston that great revival which lasted eight years, and which was so all-pervading in its influence for good in Tasmania; a work of divine grace in which all, high and low, the moral and exemplary free settler, and the most depraved and vicious convict, were pressing into the kingdom of heaven. This revival was confined to no denomination; all experienced its blessed effects. Perhaps the most simple yet graphic descriptions of its power and extent, are to be found in two interesting volumes written by members of the Society of Friends, who had been sent out thither by the English Yearly Meetings, and were eye-witnesses of the work of Divine grace.*

From any personal participation in this blessed

* Backhouse's "Narrative of a Visit to the Australian Colonies," and "Life and Labors of George Washington Walker," both admirable works.

season of refreshing, young Powell was at this time
cut off by his illness. But God, who is rich in
mercy, had thoughts of love towards this poor frail
lad. It pleased Him to bring him into His kingdom and make him one of the pillars in the House
of God.

After a long struggle with wasting disease and
racking pain, he began to improve, but very slowly
at first, and still suffering from severe prostration
and great depression of spirits. At that time Rev.
Nathaniel Turner was the superintendent of the
Launceston Circuit, a man of the most apostolic
character and devotion, to whose trials, labors, and
successes thousands of all denominations could bear
testimony. He had labored first as a Home Missionary in England, and in 1823 had accepted an
appointment to New Zealand, where in the following year he planted the first Wesleyan missionary
station at Wesleydale, in the midst of the Maories.
After he had lived and toiled amongst them for
more than three years, his house was attacked and
burnt by a party of natives, his goods stolen, his
dead child disinterred, and he and his wife and
household, barely escaping with life, fled by night
to the *Keri-Keri*, where, after lurking for a while,
they were picked up by a ship bound to Sydney.
Mr. Turner subsequently labored in the Friendly
Islands, where he remained until 1831, when his
health broke down under excessive toils. After
resting a few months in New South Wales, he removed to Tasmania, where for five years he preached
the Gospel with great success. In 1836, he re-

turned to New Zealand, and devoted three more years to his old enemies, the Maories, and was then retransferred to Tasmania. Here his ministrations were remarkably successful.

It was to this devoted servant of Christ, that God had committed the great privilege of bringing Walter Powell to see the plague of his own heart and the efficacy of the blood of Jesus to save him from sin. He came to him while he was still looking death in the face, prayed with him, conversed with him, showed him the value and worth of his soul, that soul for which Jesus had died, that soul from which the blood of Jesus alone could wash away sin.

While the young man trembled with awe and terror at God's power, at the unutterable value of his own immortal spirit, and its imminent peril of being forever lost, Mr. Turner led him to Christ; taught him that God so loved not the world alone, but Walter Powell individually, that He had given His beloved and only-begotten Son, that *he* should not perish but have eternal life; that the gift of Christ was personal to him, if he would only believe; and opened to him the way of faith more perfectly.

Walter Powell received this blessed message as a revelation from God, and walked forth from his sick room a changed and converted man. From henceforth, he was not his own, but Christ's. A change deeper and more searching than that which death is able to effect, a change pervading and permeating every fibre of his being, his intellect, soul, and body, had passed over his spirit, and made him a new man in Christ Jesus.

But though converted, he was not yet perfect. The traces of the old hot nature, the restlessness of impaired health, the temptations to sin, in thought, word, and deed, were still present with him, and, to the end of life, he must struggle with the remains of indwelling sin.

It was a great blessing to Walter Powell that the revival of which we have already spoken, which pervaded all the Australasian Colonies and continued, in Launceston at least, for eight years, was still in progress, when "this miracle of healing," this restoration of the body from apprehended death, and rescue of the spirit from the bondage of sin, took place. He was prepared to enter upon its holy services and its sacred feasts with delight, and the searching discourses and exhortations then delivered, led him to an habitual and rigid self-examination and self-discipline, which, though in a man of different temperament it might have induced undue depression and despondency, was, in him, the foundation of a substantial and very consistent and uniform Christian life. His self-examination and self-discipline did not terminate in *self;* while it revealed to him his errors and faults, and led him to be sometimes perhaps unduly severe in rebuking his remissness, yet it drove him to the only true source of help and pardon.

The eight years' revival at Launceston was of a genuine and genial kind. The Tasmanian standard of morals amongst the "free population," as the non-convict inhabitants were called, was quite as high as that of the mother country; the average intellectual culture was decidedly higher. The free settlers seem to have regarded external decorum as an indispensable badge of distinction between them and the criminal population, and they were mostly of the intelligent and orderly middle-class, men with less capital than brains and energy. Everybody's *antecedents* had to be closely scrutinized before admission into respectable society. But the moral and religious condition of the convict population was appalling, and the free population seemed intent on compensating themselves for their abandonment of country and kindred and the disadvantages of their new position by the rapid realization of wealth. The style of preaching adopted by the missionaries may be gathered from Walter Powell's diary. He kept a record of their texts, often adding an outline of their sermons. These were admirably adapted to the circumstances and spiritual requirements of their audience; *e. g.*, "Sow to yourself in righteousness, reap in mercy, break up your fallow ground: for it is time to seek the Lord, till He come and rain righteousness upon you." "Because thou hast forgotten the God of Thy salvation, and hast not been mindful of the rock of thy strength, therefore shalt thou plant pleasant plants, and shalt set it with strange slips: in the day shalt thou make thy plant to grow, and in the morning shalt thou make thy seed to flourish: but the harvest shall be a heap in the day of grief and of desperate sorrow." (Isai. xvii. 10, 11.) "Whoso covereth his sin shall not prosper, but whoso confesseth and forsaketh his sin shall find mercy." "How shall we escape, if we neglect so great salvation?" "I came not to call the righteous, but sinners to repentance."

Mr. Backhouse gives the following specimen of this wise adaptation of the style of preaching to the circumstances of the hearers: "We had a meeting in the Wesleyan chapel, in which the people were reminded of the time when, by attending to the convictions of the Holy Spirit upon their own consciences, they perceived their lost state; and that their hearts were occupied by sin, when they were also brought to repentance, and found peace through faith in Christ; made a profession of religion, and brought forth fruits of righteousness. This process was then compared with that of their taking possession of the land they are occupying, and clearing it, by felling and burning off the timber and the scrub, the natural and unprofitable produce of the earth, and fencing and cultivating the land. They were then desired to reflect upon the condition to which such land soon returns, if neglected; and to consider how soon, according to their own knowledge, it again becomes covered with forest and scrub, so as only to be distinguishable from 'the wild bush' by the remains of the fence. From this they were urged to remember that, without a constant care to keep their own hearts under the influence of the Holy Spirit, they, in a similar way, would soon again become unprofitable, and overgrown with sin; notwithstanding they might retain the appearance of a fence against evil, in some remaining profession of religion. This appeal was not without effect. One man acknowledged to us, that he was already sensible of some measure of relapse into the sinful state that had been spoken of."

Such were the subjects which these earnest men pressed home upon the consciences of colonists and convicts, whom they had followed to the ends of the earth for the one purpose of bringing them to God. Sabbath after Sabbath they assaulted the " strongholds " of immorality and indifference. Every successive sermon fell like the blow of a batteringram upon the embattled mass of prejudice, insensibility, and evil habit. It could not but be that a vibration was communicated to the dead wall, which at length threw it off the perpendicular, and brought it to the ground. But it was not only the message, but the spirit and the manner of these devoted ministers, which told so effectively upon their hearers. They themselves never lost sight of the fact, and they never allowed the audience to forget it, that they had forsaken Fatherland, and tracked the outcast, the exile, and the emigrant, with but one object ; and that not the extension of a system, but the salvation of souls. Hence there was a fearful reality in their warnings, an impassioned ardor in their appeals, a tempestuous enthusiasm in their pleadings for Christ. They seized the hesitating sinner with an awful urgency, and put forth the utmost pressure of persuasion. They were like the tender-hearted angels, sent to snatch Lot and his family from the sulphur-storm of Sodom; who when Lot lingered "laid hold upon his hand and upon the hand of his wife, and upon the hand of his two daughters, *the Lord being merciful unto them;* and said, Escape for thy life; look not behind thee, neither stay thou in all the plain; escape to the mountain, lest thou be consumed."

But Walter Powell, though thoroughly changed, struggled slowly into the clear light of the Gospel. There hung about him for some months a perceptible gloominess and sadness. This was, doubtless, partly owing to external causes. His health was still feeble and precarious. Many family matters tended to depress him. His father's business career was made up of flattering successes and disheartening failures—fat years eaten up by lean. Then followed, in quick succession, the death of father, mother, and favorite sister. The "shaft fell thrice." Then the tide of commercial prosperity began to ebb apace. The stream of emigration to the new colony of Victoria, which, at first, had given a strong impulse to the trade of Tasmania, now began to drain the island of the sources of its wealth. The market for the staple commodities, wool and grain, became unprecedentedly depressed; many of the principal houses failed; many more were in extreme difficulties; all were despondent and perplexed. Above all, the disease which had so nearly proved fatal, left behind it an extreme nervous irritability; which, superinduced upon his natural warmth and quickness of temper, was the occasion of incessant self-conflict and self-reproach. But the deepest source of his despondency was his difficulty in realizing Christ as his present and perfect Saviour, the ground of his happy relations with God, and the fountain of all spiritual strength. At last, however, the darkness passed, and the true light shone; and he began to live a life of faith on the Son of God, who loved him, and gave Himself for him.

Immediately on his connecting himself with the Church, he began that system of proportionate giving by which he, for the rest of his life, " honored the Lord with " his " substance, and with the first-fruits of all " his " increase." Mrs. Bell again relates: " Shortly after his union with the Church, he commenced reading the Bible through consecutively. On reaching the twenty-eighth chapter of Genesis, he was struck with Jacob's dedication of a tenth of all the Lord might bless him with to His own service. He told me that he had determined to do the same."

The commercial difficulties of the colony, at this period, touching as they did Walter Powell's employer amongst the rest, brought out finely the nobility of the young convert's nature. " Giving diligence," he added to " his faith virtue." A co-inmate of the house testifies: " He put forth his utmost energies. He worked like a slave in the quantity, though not in the spirit, of his work. He would toil far into the night. He even went so far as to insist on the reduction of his own salary, as he saw that the business could not justify its present amount." He devotedly attached himself to the impaired fortunes of his principal, quietly replying to the admonitions of worldly wisdom, "I know that my employer is my friend, and that his intentions towards me were liberal; he took me when I was at a loss for employment, and I shall not leave him till I see him re-established." He undertook at the same time the work which had heretofore been divided between two.

"Well done, *good* and faithful servant; thou wast faithful in a few things." This was the man who, when wealth came, knew how. to make the best use of it.

CHAPTER III.

AMIDST this expatriated community, who were either working out their terms of penal servitude, or straining every energy to build up a fortune in as short a time as possible, young Powell was strenuously working at and working out his " own salvation with fear and trembling ; " was building up a Christian character, and steadily and successfully educating himself for effective service in the Church of God, and for the nobler society and offices of heaven.

Immediately upon his conversion, Walter Powell made it the one aim, anxiety, and ambition of his life to attain " the measure of the stature of the fulness of Christ "—in feebler modern phraseology, to be a thorough Christian. What appliances did he use to accomplish this object ? To what extent was he successful ? What exact type of Christian character—so uniform in its basis, so multiform in its individual manifestations—came out from his special personality, acted upon by the special culture to which he was voluntarily subjected ? Happily, we have ample materials for answering these questions. Simplicity and earnestness put him upon a shrewd, business-like mode of conducting the affairs of his

soul, and suggested the obvious expedient of keeping a journal.

This journal, in eleven folio volumes, admits us to
his deepest confidence, and, allowing for occasional
breaks, makes us familiar with his spiritual history
and his daily occupations during the latter half of
his life, the twenty-three years stretching from January 7th, 1844, to November 13th, 1867. To those
who knew Mr. Powell as a business man, this intense and persistent self-scrutiny seems prodigious.
Let those call it morbid who can match its healthy
and robust results. Doubtless, in conjunction with
all his other labors, it shortened the earthly life
which it intensified and refined. It was part of the
reality and energy of his character. It is invaluable as enabling us to watch the unfolding of his
spiritual life and to carry forward the context of his
spiritual history. It shows, first of all, the decisiveness of his Christianity, how manfully he braced
himself for the noble gymnastics of godliness, and
the secret discipline of holy life. It proves the
sincerity with which he had renounced a self-pleas-
ing life, the steadiness with which he pulled up
stream heavenwards, taking his bearings and noting
his progress with keen-sighted accuracy. He could
not bear a slovenly, indefinite mode of conducting
the most important of all his affairs, the interests of
his soul. He carefully notes slight relapses, sets
himself to stub out "roots of bitterness," which
"springing up" might "trouble" him, detects the
swerving or the slackening of his will, any clouding
of his conscience, or overcasting of his religious joys.

His diary shows how day after day lays in another touch, and tones or fixes the coloring of his character.

On the first Sunday in 1844, he commenced this "Journal," describing to himself its object on the fly-leaf: "With the view of recording events which may prove interesting in the future, and of correcting those failings and errors which may be hindering the writer's course." This diary was, in fact, simply an expedient of conscientious self-inspection and self-culture. The purpose which we hope it will now serve, that of instructing and stimulating others, and marking the gradual building up of a Christian manhood, obviously never entered the writer's mind. The light in which he regarded it is seen from such entries as the following. After an unusual hiatus, he writes, "Since the above lines were written, I have to lament my indifference to my journal, in having allowed nearly six weeks to elapse without recording many interesting events which have occurred during that period. May the Lord help me to persevere in constantly examining my heart, and noting my experience, and may my path be that of the just." Again, "More than a month has flown since I last wrote in my journal. It may be said in reference to this duty, as has been said of prayer, 'What various hindrances we meet!' and the old motto might also in this case be justly applied, 'Where there is a will there is a way.'" Again, "I know not how to write in this neglected journal. If it were not for the goodness of God, which leads me to repent, I could not bear the thought of committing the present state of my mind to paper. Oh give me a disposition and perseverance to record Thy dealings with me continually!" The entries manifest all the "simplicity and godly sincerity" which befit such mementos. We must quote a few of the earliest:

"Sunday, January 7th, 1844.—I arose late this morning, and felt great condemnation in consequence; for we hold a prayer-meeting on Sabbath mornings, at six o'clock, for the purpose of supplicating God's blessing on our labors as Sunday-school teachers. I, by my slothfulness, lost this favorable opportunity. The more I teach children, the greater impossibility I find in doing it effectually without first obtaining wisdom and simplicity from God. After being engaged in the school till twelve, I called on R. B——, who was so reduced as not to be able to speak without first wetting his tongue. He could not confidently say that God had pardoned his sins; but he hoped so. May his faith be so increased as to attain unto 'the *blessedness* of the man whose transgression is forgiven and whose sin is covered!' In the evening, after service, the Society entered into solemn covenant with the Lord, and the sacrament was administered by the Revs. N. Turner and H. Gaud. People and ministers appeared solemnly and deeply affected. May the impressions not be like the morning cloud!"

"Monday, 8th.—Attended the love-feast this evening, and was refreshed. We all felt that 'as iron sharpeneth iron, so doth the countenance of a man his friend,' and went on our 'way rejoicing.'

I called again, with two friends, on R. B——, who appeared drawing very near to death. Our hearts were, for the first time, gladdened by his declaring that he *believed* God had forgiven him. We prayed with the dying man. He expired still professing faith in his Redeemer."

"Tuesday, 9th.—The quarterly watch-night was held."

"Wednesday, 10th.—A few of the younger brethren were constrained to offer the Rev. N. Turner a token of our gratitude. Reading Archbishop Jeffries' Charges 'Against Custom and Public Opinion.'"

"Tuesday, January 16th.—Attended as clerk, Mr. Bell's sale of land. Was struck with the covetousness which exhibited itself in my heart, in wishing to obtain that which could have proved of no use to me. Thomas Blackleach roused me from my dream by reminding me that we should soon have to part with all earthly possessions. I know that my life is especially uncertain."

The following entry illustrates the simplicity and sweetness of his child-like confidence in God. A lonely ride through the bush, in 1844, when the bush-rangers were perpetrating the most horrible atrocities to which suffering and despair could drive escaped convicts carried away by demoniac passions, required no little courage.

"Wednesday, 17th.—Was at Longford, having set out on the Tuesday evening. I felt great confidence in the God of Providence while riding, for I knew that the hairs of my head were all numbered. I felt that ' a horse is a vain thing for safety.' "

The next extracts indicate his decision of character, the often-foiled but never-intermitted struggle to be wholly the Lord's. Alluding to a popular and fashionable amusement of which he had heretofore been passionately fond, he writes :

"January 19th.—I am truly grateful that I feel no disposition to mingle in those things which do not belong to my peace. I felt grateful to my Redeemer that, although my feet were once swift in following a multitude, they now are turned unto the way of His testimonies. Felt at the class-meeting that an hour in the service of God is worth a whole life spent in those occupations which would monopolize the name of pleasure. Must lay to heart a remark of our leader that we can teach far more by our conduct than by precept. Oh that there were more of good silent practice ! "

On this point, a gentleman, who lived in constant intercourse with him at that time, writes thus : " We both had to work hard, and had long hours. We neither of us allowed ourselves to seek pleasure for pleasure's sake. Dancing, etc., we regarded as worldly, and partaking of sin ; therefore to be avoided by those who had to work out their salvation. I can only recollect going out with him on one excursion partaking of the nature of pleasure-seeking, and this was bathing with three or four others. He only could swim. I was impressed then with his sweet unostentatiousness, under circumstances offering to a young man temptation to pride and display."

"Sunday, 21st.—I continue reading Harris's 'Mammon.' I intend, by the grace and blessing of God, to put some of its advice into practice, feeling convinced that no man can serve two masters; and how possible it is to worship idols, and not know it. Mr. H. Reed * preached this day, or rather discoursed, on the duties of parents, children, and servants."

"March 27th.—The part of this month which has now passed away forever I cannot look back upon with satisfaction. Through the press of business, my mind has been constantly in a state of nervous excitement, and even to this my little journal I could not settle down steadily enough. How hard it is to continue steadfast in any pursuit! Yet the men who have risen to eminence are those who were persevering. I find that my little journal was nearly falling to the ground for want of this virtue. So difficult it is to bring the mind to examine past circumstances. They appear to have little interest in one's eager anticipation of the future. Lord, help me *so to number my days*, that I may apply my heart unto wisdom."

"April 22d.—In the evening attended the prayer-meeting. Was strengthened, but afterwards much condemned, for yielding to bad temper towards some members of the family."

"April 23d.—Received a letter from my best

* His future London partner.

earthly friend, cautioning me, with much Christian kindness and love, against yielding to my moroseness of disposition. I know the grace of God is alone sufficient, and to Him must I apply for the utter expulsion of this unchristian tendency."

"24th.—At a sale. Found the conversation, jokes, etc., of a most corrupting nature. Oh that I may ever watch and pray for that grace which will enable me to withstand, when the enemy comes in like a flood!"

"Sunday, 28th.—This morning, I grieve to say, was partly lost through slothfulness. I made a resolution, and prayed for Divine grace to enable me to overcome this evil habit. Felt very happy in teaching the children."

"Monday, 29th.—How soon do the impressions of the Sabbath vanish! Ought it to be so? Will it always be so? Oh no; blessed be God! I feel desirous that they may never be effaced, and yet I have this day yielded to temptation, and fallen into sin; but the Lord graciously restored me at the prayer-meeting, so that I could say, 'Whom have I in heaven but Thee? and there is none upon earth that I desire beside Thee.'"

"April 30th.—Employed two or three hours this day in finishing a little work, entitled 'The Maid of the Hathy.' Although rather high-colored, it is still much to be admired, and eminently useful as showing the delusiveness of this world. Give me, Lord, the *enduring* riches!"

"May 11th.—I regret that I have neglected the duty of posting up this journal. But as this small duty tends to an examination of my conduct during each day, and I am fully conscious of the necessity of examining my deceitful heart, I will, by God's grace, press forward, and, feeling the insufficiency of my own efforts, continually pray for ' the Spirit of power, of love, and of a sound mind.' "

" Sunday, 12th.—I did not rise early enough to attend our teachers' prayer-meeting, and my heart condemned me for suffering sloth to overcome me."

" May 16th.—In most of my duties I find it hard to do one thing at a time. I find the like difficulty in reading. Instead of cleaving to one book, I open several, and thus my mind, in place of instruction, reaps confusion. But these things must be overcome. *All, by watchfulness and prayer, will be set right.*"

" May 17th.—Attending sale at Evandale. While there, neglected an opportunity of showing a sinner the wickedness and danger of swearing. I felt my mind darkened, and was sorely grieved ; but, at the class-meeting, I was enabled to cast my whole soul upon God."

" 21st.—Attended a sale, and was surprised to find, notwithstanding my seasoning to such scenes, that I got much excited while bidding for some of the property."

" June 17th.—Have been encouraged by reading the Life of Samuel Hick, and, at the same time, greatly humbled in comparing his fidelity with my own unfaithfulness. An unlettered blacksmith, the means of bringing many souls to the Saviour and of stirring up believers by his example and exhortations; having 'bowels of mercy' and kindness to the poor and afflicted, a burning zeal for his Master, and a persevering love for the souls of men; undaunted in every branch of Christian duty. O Lord, make me like him?"

"18th.—Longford. Spent the whole of the day in reading, writing, and walking. I find the calm, peaceful, silent country very soothing and salutary. One feels a strong disposition to get away from the bustle and 'strife of tongues;' from 'the filthy conversation of the wicked.' Yet, while we steadfastly set our face against these things, we must not seek by solitude to evade duty and flee from the cross. Lord, help me to take up the cross and despise the shame."

"June 22d.—Found my mind much weighed down during the latter part of this day, but was revived by reading a few remarks of the Rev. John Fletcher, whose life I am reading. I was tried about my *conversion*—was it a *true* one? *Have* old things passed away, and *are* all things become new? I believe I can say, with sincerity, Yes. But a new question arose, and I must place it before my minister on the first opportunity. I must also not neglect to lay the matter before the Lord. It was this: What has been the character of your repentance? Was it scriptural? Did you not, *first*, resolve to serve God from a dread of future punishment? *Yes.* Have you not, since you were justified by faith, often sinned against God; and, when you did so, did not your sorrow for sin arise, *partly*, at having fallen from grace, and partly from a dread of

God's displeasure; and ought you not to sorrow *only* from a sense of having grieved your Saviour, after the sacrifices He has made? By these thoughts my mind was much exercised, and my own opinion is that the genuine spirit of repentance is well expressed by Wesley's hymn,—

> " 'Which grieves at having grieved its Lord,
> And never can itself forgive.'

Repentance, as it seems to me, is well exemplified in the Prodigal Son. He acknowledges his sin with grief, avows that he is no more worthy to be called a son, and requests to be received as a hired servant. Oh for the true poverty of spirit, the feeling described by Ezekiel! 'Then shall ye remember your own evil ways, and your doings that were not good, and shall *loathe* yourselves in your own sight for your iniquities and for your abominations.' "

Yet the "*first* resolve" of the Prodigal sprung out of the sharp sense of misery and immediate danger: "*I perish.*" The discovery of danger awoke the consciousness of guilt; and the lower feeling was not lost in the higher until reconciliation was complete. Thus faith, and even assurance, is necessary to the perfection of true penitence; it cannot take that refined and lovely form in which Walter Powell justly recognizes "the bright consummate flower" of evangelical repentance, until it bursts into bloom under the glow of God's forgiving love; as Ezekiel again teaches: "That thou mayest remember and be confounded, and never open thy mouth any more because of thy shame, *when I am pacified toward thee* for all that thou hast done, saith the Lord God." But what earnest Christian has escaped the temptation to doubt the reality of his past experience?

"June 25th.—Spent the afternoon with Mr. Eggleston, and consulted him as to the best method of studying the Holy Scriptures. He advised me to form a Biblical Commonplace Book, with an Index of doctrines, duties, promises, etc., and to arrange all passages, as I come to them in continuous reading, under their respective heads. For example, to have a leaf headed 'Atonement,' and to place under that word all passages referring to that truth of Revelation; others headed '*Sin*,' 'Repentance,' 'Envy,' 'Resurrection,' etc. I know that this will require much wisdom, but I must do my best, keeping in view that promise, 'If any of you lack wisdom, let him ask of God, that giveth to all men liberally and upbraideth not, and it shall be given him. But let him ask in faith, nothing wavering.'"

CHAPTER IV.

As it is our purpose to trace through all its earlier stages the formation of Mr. Powell's character, both in its spiritual and secular aspects, we shall be pardoned for introducing some further extracts from Mr. Powell's journal illustrating this point. The solid foundation of heart piety and faith in God on which he was rearing the edifice of his life, the careful scrutiny which he exercised over every act, thought, and word, and the resolute determination to overcome the errors he discerned, account sufficiently for the strength, breadth, and elevation of his subsequent experiences. There is a wonderful charm, an instructive lesson, in these resolute, simple-minded efforts of an ailing, overworked clerk of two-and-twenty summers, to realize in his own life the Christianity of the New Testament. For Christianity is a *life* in both senses of the word—a *principle* of life and a *course* of life. Many religious men of business, members of Christian Churches and generous supporters of Christian Institutions, lavish of their money in the promotion of the public interests of the Gospel, would willingly make almost any sacrifice to lose a certain uneasy sense of incongruity between their secular and spiritual course. There is but one way in which the Christian and commercial life can be brought into perfect harmony; and that is the way which Mr. Powell had adopted, in obedience to the Master's own instructions: "Seek ye first the kingdom of God and IIis righteousness."

Had not Walter Powell acquired in youth this habit of unflinching self-investigation, he must have encountered disheartening difficulty in the attempt to form it amidst the whirl and weariness of after life. Benjamin Franklin attributed whatever he enjoyed of the serene happiness which flows from moral healthiness to the "little artifice" of keeping a diary, in which he noted down his failures on any point even of minor morality. The like "little artifice" was of equal service to Walter Powell in the cultivation of spiritual-mindedness. It was thus that he acquired and preserved that keen and delicate sensitiveness of conscience which he manifested throughout his business life. As surely as "idle people give themselves most trouble," so surely is a self-sparing temper a self-disturbing temper. To spiritual health it is absolutely necessary that we should live by rule, and consequently that we should have a rule to live by, and statedly compare our daily life with this rule. Without it our whole spiritual constitution must and will become relaxed. Self-neglect is as fatal to the soul as to the body. We see, as we glance at young Powell's journal, how frankly he admits, and how resolutely he fights, the failings to which he had found himself most liable, and how sedulously he treasures all the instruction he can gather from whatever sources.

"Longford, Sunday, July 7th.—Mr. Eggleston preached in the evening, from, 'How shall we escape, if we neglect so great salvation?' He showed the greatness of the salvation offered, its infinite cost, the glorious nature, human and Divine, of Him who procured it for us, its perfect sufficiency and effectiveness, the almighty agency by which it is made available and actual in individuals. He then pointed out the hopelessness of escape if it be neglected; this being the only possible opening; since had there been any other conceivable way of escape from the loss of the soul than by such a death of such a Being as Christ, that could never have been resorted to. He exposed the folly and madness of indolently and insolently trusting to God's mercy, whilst neglecting its highest possible manifestation, and doing 'despite to the Spirit of Grace.' He plainly and powerfully proved that neglecting this salvation entails final destruction, since no other way of escape is possible; and that life everlasting is the certain consequence of our freely and fully accepting it. May I more and more feel the value of, and evince my gratitude for, this *great salvation!*"

"12th.—While I am not unmindful of the great salvation my Saviour has accomplished, I am astonished at the unbelief and indifference I find still existing within me. If my eyes are not constantly lifted up unto 'the hills from whence cometh my help,' I shall be rapidly carried back to the horrible

3

abyss of stupid negligence, as to my eternal interests, from which I have escaped. I must put on the *whole* armor of God in order to withstand my foes. But I am thankful that Christ has said, ' My grace is sufficient for thee, My strength is made perfect in weakness;' and the blessings I most want are suspended on simple conditions: ' Ask, and ye shall receive.'"

Alas! many another earnest Christian is, like young Powell, "haunted by the self of other days, which seems to rise up as a spirit of darkness, and cast a spell upon him, and fix him with its eye."

"13th.—Having heard of the unjust or, rather, unkind treatment of a beloved friend in a trifling matter, I found Satan quite ready to fill me with feelings and thoughts neither accordant with the Apostle's language, ' Charity suffereth long and is kind,' nor with my Saviour's direction, ' Pray for those who despitefully use you.' Oh may I always bring my feelings to the test of Scripture, and may every thought be brought ' into captivity to the obedience of Christ !' "

"Wednesday, 17th.—The Rev. W. Butters preached on the necessity of Christian watchfulness. I mournfully proved the importance of the admonition; for, on going home, I entered upon a discussion relative to a trifling subject, and so gave way to anger as to grieve the Spirit of God. May the Lord have mercy on one so unworthy, and grant that I may again feel the unclouded light of His countenance !"

How could young Powell know that he had

grieved the Spirit of God? By the perceptible abatement of the "consolations of God," of which he was habitually conscious.

"August 10th.—Went to Ross in order to stay a short time with Mr. Jackson, a most Christian-hearted man, earnestly aspiring after the mind that was in Christ, and endeavoring to walk as He also walked."

"29th.—Joined a class formed by the Rev. W. Butters for the mental improvement of the young men connected with the Wesleyan Society."

"Sunday, September 1st.—Again visited at their homes the children of my Sunday-school class. After the evening service partook of the Sacrament of the Lord's Supper. Lord! may I live more *to* Thee, *for* Thee, and *in* Thee."

Sometimes, instead of noting his experience, he would wisely solace and enliven himself by para-phrasing some passage of Scripture; for amidst all his struggles he was buoyant enough to "relish ver-sing." These lines often show no contemptible power of versification, but are chiefly remarkable for cleanness of workmanship and vigorous com-pression.

"Sunday, 8th.—Felt painfully my weakness and ignorance in endeavoring to teach my class in the Sabbath-school. O gracious Lord, have mercy on me, their teacher, lest, after instructing 'others, I myself should become a castaway.'

"In the evening, Mr. Eggleston preached on the Rich Man and Lazarus. He called attention to the fact, that the rich man was not a miser or morose, otherwise the friends of Lazarus would not have laid him there; nor had his treatment of Lazarus pressed on his awfully awakened conscience; nay, had there been no kindly relations between him and Lazarus, he would have been the last person to ask to leave Abraham's bosom to alleviate his sufferings. He would not have even dared to mention his name, for that name must have inflamed his tongue. The rich man's fatal sin was that of his brethren; he had not so *believed* Moses and the Prophets as to be *persuaded* to *love* the Lord his God, with all his heart, and mind, and soul, and strength; and his neighbor as himself. He had neglected to consider that 'that which is highly esteemed among men is abomination in the sight of God,' the fact which our Lord especially designed to illustrate. (Luke xvi. 15.)"

"14th.—During this month I have been reading the Life of Dr. Adam Clarke, and have been particularly struck with his great industry and perseverance. His labors were so gigantic, that a person of average energy might be appalled at their vastness. He *redeemed the time.* He secured thousands of hours, which are generally wasted. Oh that his example may be followed by me!"

"Sunday, September 15th.—The anniversary of the Sunday-school in which I am an unworthy teacher. Mr. Eggleston's text was, 'But godliness is profitable unto all things, having promise of the life that now is, and of that which is to come.' He described the character of true godliness, and the extent of its operation; its vitality, its necessity; its *profitableness* for the present life, as conducive directly to bodily health, tranquillity, harmony and healthiness of soul. He contrasted the profitless and *expensive* amusements and indulgences of the world with the solid happiness *given* to the godly, 'without money, and without price.' Having proved its *cheapness*, its soundness, its utility, as to *the life that now is*, he dwelt on its incalculable advantages as the only means of securing the life *that is to come.*"

"Saturday, 21st.—During the past week I have been led to examine myself minutely, but I fear very imperfectly, from the fact of my memory being confused, and from a dull, trying pain which always dwells in my head, in a greater or less degree. Nevertheless, I have been able to discover, that if my hours were differently arranged, I should have much more time to attend to those duties which would enable me, to a far greater extent, to discharge my obligations to God and man. I grieve to find myself such a slave to habits thoughtlessly acquired. I do not retire to rest at the proper time; consequently I do not rise early enough to commune with God, and then take the necessary bodily exercise. The result is, I am each hour striving to catch up the arrears of work left by the preceding, and thus body and mind are unduly, unnecessarily, and injuriously strained, burdened, and excited, and unfitted for the vigorous discharge of the duties incumbent upon me ; and I am not able to maintain that serene, steady, faithful, thoughtful, fervent walk with God, which befits the believer in Jesus. I sincerely trust, and pray with great anguish of heart, that this my mourning for past transgressions may not be in vain, but that my conduct may show that, by His grace re-enforcing my resolutions, I have been enabled to break through this cruel bondage of habitual procrastination. Lord, have mercy upon me, and upon all in the like slavery, for the Saviour's sake!"

"Sunday, November 15th.—Was enabled to rise before five, and attend the prayer-meeting."

"Sunday, January 5th, 1845.—Renewal of the Covenant and Sacrament. On looking back upon the past year, I cannot but be grateful to the Father of all my mercies. My progress in the Divine life is very unworthy of my privileges. Twice have I been raised from the bed of sickness, with a resolve to forsake all and follow Christ, and yet here am I at the present almost fainting in my Christian course. I humbly trust that, if spared through another year, I may find it one of ardent devotion, of yearning compassion for my fellow-sinners, of dedication of all to Christ, and of conscientious stewardship."

"15th.—Have been reading the 'Life of the Rev. Theophilus Lessey.' The wealth which he acquired was of the right kind. Convinced that no man can serve two masters, he early forsook the service of Mammon, foreseeing that the only wages that the god of this world can afford is 'death.'"

"March 4th.—I have reason gratefully to record this day. It is one the importance of which eternity alone can fully disclose—my *marriage-day*. What a happiness that we both are endeavoring to walk in the way of life, and, I believe, each anxious for the other's spiritual welfare! We became convinced of our fallen condition through the same instrumentality. May the gracious God enable us to love each other as He in His own Word commands us, and by that Word may our whole course of life be guided! Mr. Butters conducted the service most impressively. My sister Rose and William and Frederick were also present, and my bandmates Bonner and Denny. As to myself and dear wife, we feel determined to work for God, and devote our all to Him. We feel that we are stewards, and as such are required to be 'faithful.' We are convinced of our own helplessness, our utter need of the teaching and guidance of the Holy Spirit. We know that our Redeemer requires us to economize our means, to exert all our energies in His cause, to take up our cross daily and follow Him. These requirements would drive us to despair, had not our Lord promised all-sufficient grace."

Walter Powell's principal had given the highest proof of his confidence in the virtues and the business qualities of his young clerk, by accepting him as his son-in-law. He states—" Although so young, the public impression of Walter's integrity and judgment was such as to be often of no slight service to me. Whenever any disputes arose in the course of business, a word from Walter was like 'an oath for confirmation—the end of all strife;' the objecting party would at once yield, saying, 'If Mr. Powell says it is so, I must be wrong.'"

"Sunday, 16th.—Mr. Eggleston preached from James i. 25 ; on the law of God, its threatenings, promises, requirements, privileges, and its direct bearing on every department of human life—the necessity of *looking into it* with intense regard and unwearied application, like the cherubim, bending over the Mercy-seat, beneath which the law was hid, ' desiring to look into ' it through that medium. He warned us against *uninterested* hearing and reading of the Word of God."

These notices of the preaching of the Wesleyan missionaries show that they were not mere ranting, red-hot revivalists. They reasoned out of the Scriptures. It was the moral momentum with which they threw out these plain truths, and the explosive intensity of their own personal conviction, which made prejudice "pass away with a great noise," and insensibility "melt with fervent heat." They did not let the Word fall softly on the pulpit cushion, or pass over their audience like a cooling cloud, which tempers the burning beam to the weary traveller, but does not startle the loiterer with menace of a thunder-storm.

"April 27th.—I have had to keep a jealous eye over my own heart, during the last month, lest covetousness should gain a foothold in it, and I should become ensnared in things that *perish in the using.*"

"Sunday, June 22d.—Mr. Reed preached on repentance in believers, from the several addresses to the Seven Churches. He showed that our situation was in one respect like that of the Church at Pergamos; for surely in this land ' Satan's seat is,' since for deeds of crime this country has been scarcely ever equalled. He urged the consequent necessity that Christians should be pre-eminently zealous, watchful, and holy. ' Lord, how long ' shall this state of things continue ? ''

There is one point touched on in the preceding extracts which it may be well to glance at for a moment. Young Powell's journal shows that his own single-mindedness, as well as the rules and teachings of the religious community to which he had attached himself, decided for him a question which confronts every earnest Christian at the outset of his religious course; namely, the practical bearing of certain gaieties upon the daily cultivation of spiritual-mindedness. Relaxation is a necessity imposed upon us by the Creator, and is therefore an obligation. The need and the duty of frequent, thorough recreation are in proportion to the strain which a man's pursuits put upon his energies. The hard worker must have effective amusement, and no man works so hard as he who combines with an eager devotion to business assiduous mental and spiritual cultivation. Hence no practical and experienced men have ever condemned amusements which really accomplish their purpose—to " renovate the spirits, and restore the tone of languid nature " —without any over-balancing evil, physical, moral, or spiritual. Mr. Powell felt bound to avoid diversions which have a strong tendency to become dissipations, and thus defeat the real object of an amusement, being prejudicial rather than conducive

3*

to bodily, intellectual, and spiritual health. The Puritan worthies of the seventeenth century condemned dancing, and yet noted down in their diaries their games of billiards, side by side with their spiritual struggles and successes; and with perfect consistency, because, in their day, dancing had become unsafe and unseemly in its associations, and in its customary mode of indulgence was connected with and provocative of unquestionable evils; whilst billiards were not, as they now too often are, associated with drinking, gambling, and late hours. We have seen that young Powell's journal frankly thanks God that he had lost all taste for these exciting and enfeebling "pleasures."

Unquestionably many professing and some real Christians do countenance, by their presence and occasional participation, the practice of this amusement; but we must believe that in their case the conscience has not been brought to its true point of sensitiveness, and that they have failed to recognize that the true question for the follower of Christ is not, " Can I indulge in these amusements without serious spiritual injury to myself ? " but, " Will the indulgence in these pastimes glorify God or benefit my fellow-men ? "　There may be no very harsh incongruity between such usages and a Christianity which consists in little more than an external observance of the Ten Commandments, modified by the conventional code of social and commercial morality, with the addition of neighborly good-heartedness and an easy-going attendance on the public services of religion ; but the case is altogether different with such a man as Mr. Powell, who made the cultivation of Christian holiness the great purpose of his life.

As to all other questionable amusements, he showed the wisdom of the child of light. His business-like mode of going about the affairs of his soul taught him to postpone the common question, "What is the *harm* of such and such diversions?" to an earlier and more pertinent inquiry, "What is the *use* of them? Are they the safest and most effective recreations?" But for all those gaieties which Christian prudence induced him to forego, he found amply compensating substitutes in music, for which he had both taste and capacity, and of which he was passionately fond, in books, in swimming, in the public services of religion, and in "sweet counsel" with like-minded Christians.

CHAPTER V.

THE Wesleyan Methodists of England and the Colonies, though acknowledging the same founder and the same doctrinal views with the Methodist Episcopal Church in the United States, yet differ from them in many minor details. The Wesleyans have Superintendents but no Bishops ; Circuit Superintendents but no Presiding Elders. They have the Class-meetings and the Class-leaders, the Love-feasts, the Watch-night (which they observe quarterly instead of annually), and they have also the Band-meeting, the Covenant-service, and the Prayer-leader's Plan, which the exigencies of their position have developed, and which differ somewhat from American developments of Methodism.

The *Class-meeting* and its *Leader* are institutions too well-known in this country wherever this powerful denomination has planted its churches, to need any particular description here.

The primary organization—preceding often the organization of a Church—of the Methodist body, it gathers for a weekly religious exercise a dozen or more members of the Church, or probationers, of both sexes, and under the guidance of a judicious leader, a man of experience and religious activity, requires of them individually some account of their Christian life for the week. This exercise, interspersed with singing and prayer, is one of great value and importance to the spiritual growth of the entire membership of the Church. It secures a more thorough watch care over young, fickle, or wayward members than is otherwise possible; and promotes the spiritual growth of all. The *Band-meeting* of the Wesleyan Church of England and the Colonies is a still smaller organization, and where the Bands include the entire membership of the Church, a still more efficient one. It consists of three or four members of the Church of the same sex and of nearly the same age, who unite together for religious exercises and mutual watch-care and Bible-study. The relation of band-mates is very intimate and cordial, and in most instances productive of the very best results.

The *Prayer-leader's Plan* is another institution of English and Colonial Methodism, which under certain circumstances is productive of great good and to which the rapid spread of Methodism in the Colonies is largely due. A carefully prepared plan of the various wards or districts of a town, or of the neighboring villages and hamlets, is drawn up, and *Prayer-leaders* are selected and appointed from the most active and efficient of the younger members of the Church, to conduct cottage prayer-meetings in designated neighborhoods. The Prayer-leader is not allowed to deliver an address unless he is enrolled amongst the body of lay-preachers or exhorters. He is amenable to a periodical (usually a monthly) meeting of his associates, which is presided over by the minister, and is required to report all cases of religious interest which have come under his cognizance with a view to their being brought under immediate pastoral care. Walter Powell, as we have seen and shall see, was identified with each of these sub-organizations in turn, and also became a lay-preacher or exhorter, developing remarkable power and fervor in his addresses. He had joined a *Class* and become a member of a *Band*, at his first connection with the Church; not long after, he was appointed a Prayer-leader, a Sunday-school teacher, and eventually a Class-leader, and as we have said, an exhorter. Of the special religious services we have named, the *Love-feast*, a revival with some modifications of the *Agapæ* or *Feast of Charity* of the Primitive Church, is a monthly or quarterly gathering of the members of the different classes and other probationers for the recounting of their religious experience, and to each of those present a piece of bread and a draught of water is offered during the meeting, in token of hearty fellowship. The *Watch-night*, formerly in England and America and still in the Colonies, a quarterly and originally a monthly service, is a season of protracted prayer, accompanied with singing from 8.30 P.M. till a little after midnight, usually with special reference to a revival. At its close a few minutes are spent in silent prayer; after which a triumphal hymn is sung and the benediction pronounced. The *Covenant-service* is also an annual solemnity held on the first Sabbath of the year. After a full and clear exposition of the covenant relation between God and His people, a solemn form of personal consecration to God is read aloud by the minister, and followed and assented to in silence by the members of the Church; suitable hymns are sung, and the Sacrament of the Lord's Supper administered. The frequent allusions to these services in Mr. Powell's journal seemed to render this much explanation necessary. Besides the cottage prayer-meetings, band-meetings, and class-meetings, there were larger and more central gatherings for prayer. It will be seen from Mr. Powell's journal, that one weekly meeting for supplication was held on Sunday mornings at five o'clock. These early assemblies were coeval with the origin of Methodism, but seem little adapted to the tyrannous usages of our over-trading and over-feeding age. No doubt Walter Powell, in his self-severity, often sat down to the account of spiritual slothfulness what was really attributable to physical exhaustion. But abler men than he have fallen into the like error; for instance, that earnest and devoted Christian, Dr. Arnold, of Rugby, who reproached himself for an indisposition to rise at the moment which he had fixed, not taking into account the exhausting labors of the previous day. Walter Powell, however, was right in condemning late retiring, when he felt early rising to be a duty.

But to return to the journal. Allusions to the above-mentioned services abound in Walter Powell's diary. We subjoin a few illustrative extracts:

"May 22d, 1844.—Met with my band-mates at

seven A.M., and was strengthened and encouraged in my Christian course. Praise God for such means of grace!"

"Nov. 22d.—Class in the evening. Very profitable. Brother S. confessed to us a grave fault for which he had that day been solemnly rebuked. Seven years ago, he and other friends had been wont to visit regularly an individual who had, in his youth, drunk deeply into deistical opinions, endeavoring to win him to the truth; after some time they became discouraged and wearied out, and Brother S. lamented that latterly, even in meeting him, he had refrained from conversing with him on his spiritual state. He had just been bitterly reminded that he had not worked while it was day, by seeing the passing funeral of this very man. Surely neither past nor future work will atone for neglect of present duty."

"Monday, July 1st.—Went to Launceston by coach, and attended the love-feast in the evening. I was grateful to my Heavenly Father to hear so many testify of His loving-kindness. It must have been a source of encouragement to all, to see in how many instances the Lord used the most humble instruments and the simplest means to effect conversions. Oh, if I were faithful and improved each moment, the Lord would also use me. A simple word spoken in earnest, and with a view to glorify God, was the means of turning to righteousness some that addressed us. God is Love! He proves it; manifests it each succeeding day. He is a well-spring of everlasting happiness to those who acquaint themselves with Him. He will guide them by His counsel, and afterward receive them to glory. Faithful is He that has promised."

"Tuesday, 2d.—This evening the quarterly watch-night was held. I trust we all felt the influence of the Holy Spirit acting upon our hearts. Oh that I may not have to mourn the non-improvement of such a solemn season! May the voice which sounded then, sound now; yes, let me ever *feel* Thy voice! May I "attend the whispers of Thy grace." Mr. Lassitter showed powerfully how foolish it is to content ourselves with *hoping* for rest in Christ, when it is our privilege to be *conscious* of it. He brought forward the absoluteness and decisiveness of Scripture on the point of a personal consciousness of rest in Christ. Mr. Crookes followed, and spoke of the declension of the Society during the past quarter. He touched on some things which he supposed might possibly be the cause : want of unity, prayer, and faithfulness in the ministers themselves, and also in the members. He exhorted us not to rest in our present state, but that night to set out afresh. Grant, gracious Lord, that the prayers, the cries, the tears, which come up before Thee, may be answered ! "

" 6th.—Attended my class-meeting : was sensibly strengthened and quickened. I felt doubly grateful, for God's unbounded love in bringing one soul more into the glorious liberty of the children of God, a person of the name of S——, who, a very short time since, ' walked according to the course of this world.' "

"February 2d, 1845.—I again met in class, having missed one week, in consequence of my visit to Longford. I spoke my mind to my excellent leader in reference to the great unwillingness I felt to perform my duty in reproving sin. He urged me to apply to the Giver of every good and perfect gift for wisdom to direct me, and further said, that in order to perform this duty properly, we must have great love for the souls of men, and that whilst we feel the least approach of sin, and repel it with the greatest abhorrence, and are keenly zealous for the honor of our Father-God, we must manifest grief rather than anger, when we see or hear His laws broken."

"Wednesday, December 3d, 1844.—Went to the weekly service, and heard Mr. Crookes on 'Love not the world, neither the things of the world; if any man love the world, the love of the Father is not in him.' Considering how my mind has of late been drawn away by worldly objects, the address came seasonably. Lord, help me to keep my heart with all diligence."

"6th.—Attended class, and obtained a clearer view of my glorious Saviour than I had for some time realized."

"Sunday, 17th.—Led the morning prayer-meeting at seven. I was installed into the important office of prayer-leader this month. I trust I shall see my need of walking humbly with God, and that He will fit me for my duties. How awfully responsible is the Christian profession, in all respects! By our conduct, we are either urging men to the kingdom of God, or proving stumbling-blocks in their way. Deliver me from blood-guiltiness, O Lord !"

"Monday, October 23d.—The quarterly watch-night. Mr. Butters closed the meeting by a touching appeal for the prayers of the Church on behalf of himself and colleague, telling us that were we only aware of their conflicts, perplexing doubts, and anxious fears, we should more frequently intercede for them at the throne of grace, that God would eminently fit them spiritually, morally, mentally, and physically for their great work. May the Lord answer !"

"Tuesday, 24th.—The quarterly love-feast. I was induced to offer a few remarks as to God's gracious dealings with me during the past quarter. I considered it to be but acknowledging a debt of gratitude to God. Had I listened to the numerous suggestions which presented themselves to my mind of my sinful and unworthy conduct in the past, I should have sat in shame and silence; but I remembered that I had not to trust in my own righteousness, but in that of my gracious Saviour; and though I could not but acknowledge my unfaithfulness, I could not forbear testifying of His love."

CHAPTER VI.

REMOVAL TO MELBOURNE.

In the autumn of 1845, Mr. Powell, then twenty-three years of age, was obliged to begin life afresh. The new settlement of Victoria, which had at first perceptibly improved, now diverted to itself the trade of Tasmania. Business at Launceston was for a time at the lowest ebb. Mr. Bell, Mr. Powell's father-in-law, and who was also his employer, found that his business had dwindled till there was little hope that it would be sufficient for the support of two families. It became clear that Walter Powell must, like his father, become an emigrant. Since trade would not come to Launceston, he must seek it at the point toward which it was evidently setting, and that point was Melbourne. He resolved, then, to migrate with his wife to the newest of the Australian colonies, a newer and wilder country than that to which his father had come twenty-three years before; but one of more rapid growth and greater business promise.

Eight months before, he had married with a fair prospect of a modest and hard-earned competence among the friends he had known from childhood. But, alas! for human calculations and forecastings. He found himself now compelled to take his young bride to this new and bustling colony, where everything was in the roughest possible condition, and comforts, as yet, were few. Yet, "as an eagle *stirreth up her nest*, fluttereth over her young, spreadeth abroad her wings, taketh them, beareth them on her wings: so the Lord alone did lead him." This seemingly adverse current, which bore him from his sheltered moorings, was but the rising tide that taken at the flood led on to wealth. For the present, however, honest bread-getting was all he could aspire to. His poverty was almost as absolute as when at twelve years old he entered the office of an auctioneer, with the brave resolve to retrieve the fortunes of his family. Walter had now the responsibilities and the counterbalancing supports of wedded life. But the most disheartening aspect of his affairs was his shattered state of health. He had not long before been utterly disabled by a succession of sharp and threatening sicknesses. All this, however, brought out the strength and beauty of his character. Under date June 10th, he writes, "Still in ill-health and unable to take any active part in the business. I feel this to be a severe restraint, but my chief duty is submission. Oh that my own will were entirely swallowed up in that of my Heavenly Father! My withdrawal from business has been attended by a marked providence—the Lord has heard the cry of the distressed, and sent one to fill my situation, who is in needy circumstances, with a wife and large family." In the same spirit he records his arrival in Victoria:

"Melbourne, Nov. 22d, 1845.—Our affairs in

Van Diemen's Land having taken an unfavorable turn, and the Pillar of Cloud appearing to move away from our little homestead at Launceston, on the 8th instant we embarked for Melbourne, where I trust He will be with us, whose favor is better than life. I said, 'If Thy presence go not with us, carry us not up hence.' After lying at George Town and in the river, wind-bound for a week, we bade farewell to the land of our childhood on the evening of the 15th, and on the 17th landed at William's Town. Lord, grant that since Thou hast extended such mercy to the unworthy, I may live and work for Thy glory. 'Tis true, I find within me 'an evil heart of unbelief' ever ready to depart 'from the Living God;' but I have learned the Apostles' prayer, 'Lord, increase our faith.'"

Thus at this anxious turning-point in his temporal affairs, his chief, his almost absorbing solicitude was to keep his heart *right with God.* How faithfully did his Heavenly Father fulfil to him His engagement—" But seek ye first the kingdom of God and His righteousness, and *all these things shall be added unto you !* "

The Melbourne of 1845 was not the spacious, stately, crowded, golden city, which now invites so many immigrants. It was then but nine years old, and was still in the roughest and most rudimental state. Four hundred miles from the nearest settlement, in the midst of immense grass plains, with an exuberant fertility of soil, and a delicious climate, its population was then about equal to that of Launceston, Tasmania, numbering some seven thousand.

During Mr. Powell's residence there it increased more than fifteen fold. In 1861, Melbourne had 108,224 inhabitants.

In those early days, house accommodation of any sort was very scarce, and the best of it extremely comfortless. But Mr. Powell and his young bride quietly adjusted themselves to their lot. Providence did not betray their trust. Their fellow-townsfolk being all in the like struggling and transitional condition, rudeness of residence and the humblest forms of self-help involved no forfeiture of social consideration. The best-born there sustained an amount of manual labor and bodily exertion almost incredible to men of like position in the mother country, and delicate ladies were their own cooks and maids-of-all-work. In short, hard work was the order of the day; all who had no taste for that were out of place in the embryo capital of Australia Felix. But Mr. Powell's principles and habits were exactly suited to such a state and stage of society. Regularity, perseverance, punctuality, self-denial, and economy, combined with unwearying industry, crushed into smoothness that rutty road to honorable affluence. And, best of all, his journal shows that in these new and testing circumstances he was still resolved to conform his life to what Wesley terms "the accuracy of the Christian model." Happily he found at Melbourne that which is almost ubiquitous, that of which the acknowledged mission is to go where it is most needed—the faithful quickening ministrations and the kindly fellowships of a genial evangelism. Here, too, amidst the keen competitions of a new community intent on rapid money-making, and the importunate anxieties of a business in process of formation, he showed himself ever ready for the service of his Church. And his Church was not slow in claiming whatsoever service he could render. A few extracts from his journal will show that a violent change of circumstances did not divert his attention from the great object of life.

"Sunday, January 25th, 1846.—Was appointed Secretary to the Collingwood Sunday-school. Eighty-one children present, who conducted themselves in a reputable manner."

"April 19th.—Visited Geelong for the purpose of holding a meeting to advocate the cause of total abstinence. The meeting was held in a store. Fifteen persons took the pledge. I trust that this small beginning of this branch of the Australia Felix Temperance Society will not be blighted; but that it will grow and flourish until this beautiful district, which is now deluged with drunkenness and its attendant evils, will be altogether rescued from this fatal vice, and the moral aspect of society will become as lovely as that of nature around us."

"September.—Religion without charity, that is, love, is a mere parade, an empty show. When we part with love we part with God. Let me recapitulate, and ever keep before my mind the various characteristics of this most God-like grace:

"1. Charity suffereth long.
 2.   "   is kind.
 3.   "   envieth not.

4. Charity vaunteth not itself.
5.   "   is not puffed up.
6.   "   doth not behave itself unseemly.
7.   "   seeketh not her own.
8.   "   is not easily provoked.
9.   "   thinketh no evil.
10.   "   rejoiceth not in iniquity.
11.   "   rejoiceth in the truth.
12.   "   beareth all things.
13.   "   believeth all things.
14.   "   hopeth all things.
15.   "   endureth all things.
16.   "   *never faileth!* "

"This grace of the Spirit can be cultivated into beautiful perfection by every one who is born of the Spirit. The poor sinner who has wallowed for long years in evil may, by repentance and faith, have the seed of this virtue deep planted in his heart. The Holy Spirit both sows and nourishes this precious heavenly seed. Am I, a professor of the religion of Christ, without love? Deliver me, O Lord, from this great transgression! During the past week I have been laid aside. I esteem it a mercy from my Lord, yet I have not improved this providential retirement from the business of the world as I might have done; but I bless God that I am not satisfied with my present Christian experience, and am resolved, by His grace, to distrust myself and lean only upon Him. I have been prevented from fulfilling my duty as superintendent of the Sabbath-school, but have prayed to the Chief Shepherd that

4

He would remember it in tender mercy, and pour
His Spirit upon the children and the teachers."

We incidentally gather from the last entry that
he had been raised from the secretaryship to the
superintendency of the Sunday-school; and from
subsequent records, that he had been appointed to
several other Church offices.

"November.—I know not how to write in this
neglected journal. My present situation is perilous,
and unless I cry at once 'to Him who is mighty to
save,' I shall become a miserable backslider in heart
and life. And this to be the state of my mind when
occupying important offices in the Church of Christ!
To stand on the Plan as a Leader of Prayer, when I
feel almost destitute of the spirit of prayer; required
by the Church to superintend a Sabbath-school, to
guide young children to Christ's gentle arms, to
lead them to His loving lips, when I myself need
to be led by the hand; appointed to the solemn
office of Class-leader, to direct, advise, comfort, and
animate my fellow-Christians, when my own soul
needs the direction and the counsel of those whom
I am appointed to instruct. Ah, Lord! Thou
knowest my extreme barrenness and spiritual destitution. 'Restore unto me the joys of Thy salvation, and uphold me with Thy free Spirit; then will
I teach transgressors Thy ways, and sinners shall be
converted unto Thee.'

"I solemnly resolve, by the grace of God, to

"1st.—Rise early, for the purpose of searching
the Scriptures and prayer, and to study useful books.

"2d.—To pray more for the conversion of my

relatives; for the outpouring of the Spirit upon our minister and the people here, and the Church generally; to seek a revival of His work in my own soul, and to ask for its extension to every creature under heaven.

"3d.—To be not slothful in business; to be constant and punctual at the means of grace; and to earnestly seek each day to grow in grace, and in the knowledge of my Lord and Saviour.

"4th.—To pray that I may enjoy, at all times, the witness of His Spirit with mine that I am His child.

"Knowing that I am incapable of any good thing without His grace, I humbly implore Him to empower me to carry out these resolutions, so far as they consist with His blessed will. O Lord, give me a disposition to record Thy dealings with me continually."

"October 20th, 1847.—My old band-mate, Thomas Denny, has been staying with me a month. I have been weighed down with cares of the world. This ought not to be. These cares choke the good seed. Oh that my care may be cast upon my Saviour! I can testify to the goodness of God in marvellously helping me in temporal matters; helping me when I knew not where to look for help, and inclining the hearts of many to assist me. My soul, in all thy ways acknowledge Him, and fear not. He will direct thy paths."

"November 23d, 1847.—Our little daughter left us, after a joyous earthly existence of twenty-three months; joyous because she was docile, and rendering a ready obedience to all our wishes. It has been our aim to train her up for God, and we have not shrunk from enforcing obedience by correction; knowing that the foundation of every virtue is *obedience*, and that ' even a child is known by his doings, whether it be pure, and whether it be right.' We can testify to the advantage of checking the first manifestations of a rebellious nature, and of teaching a child so to ' love ' as to ' honor and obey.' We have been rewarded by the sweet affection of our child. We hoped to have seen the day when she would give her young heart to her Redeemer. But she was His. He has opened the kingdom of heaven for her, and she is now singing the song of the redeemed. Her Heavenly Father used simple means in taking her to Himself—an ordinary child's fall. The Lord had need of her. A short time before her death, He poured consolation into our hearts in a wonderful manner; so much so, that our sorrow was turned into joy. We felt the Holy Spirit acting on our hearts like a refiner's fire, and were enabled to hold loosely all earthly things."

" 25th.—Was blamed by Mr. Lowe for not allowing my name to be added to the list of exhorters. I told him my motive for refusing was now removed. I had declined because I was conscious that the world was getting into my heart, and I had feared lest, by being thus brought prominently before the public, my inconsistencies might be brought to light. But now, O Lord, my helplessness and ignorance I offer not as an excuse for declining any service which Thy Church requires from me. If called by

Thee to labor, Thou wilt fit me. 'Not by might nor by power, but by My Spirit, saith the Lord of hosts.'

> " 'Give me Thy strength, O God of power,
>   Then let winds blow, or thunders roar ;
>   Thy faithful witness will I be,
>   'Tis fixed, I can do all through Thee.'

"But, O Lord, if Thou seest that I am not fitted for this awfully responsible and glorious work, then interpose Thy hand. I still possess peace with God through our Lord Jesus Christ. Glory be to God!"

"Sunday, 28th.—Scarcely able, from bodily feebleness, to walk to my school; but the work must be done. O Lord, let me always labor for Thee! May the salvation of souls ever be uppermost in my thoughts! May I never lose Thy regard! Anything but this. O Lord, save Melbourne! Convince its inhabitants, by Thy Spirit, of sin, of righteousness, and of judgment!"

The Sunday-school which Mr. Powell superintended soon became very large. It was situated at a considerable distance from his house, so that its toils formed no light addition to the labors of the week.

Thus sedulously and passionately did young Powell strive to walk in the narrow way, and to conform his inner and his outer life to God's Holy Word. Doubtless he made fewer allowances for himself than the Saviour made for him; and perhaps the anxious patient sometimes felt his own pulse until it throbbed and faltered beneath the pressure; but he was steadily growing into a robust and buoyant piety. *Building* himself *upon* his most *holy faith, praying in the Holy Ghost,* he kept himself *in the love of God.*

CHAPTER VII.

MR. POWELL had long cherished a natural desire to visit the unremembered land of his birth. Having received warm invitations from his maternal aunt, he resolved to gratify this longing. He also hoped that the enforced rest of a long voyage, and the tonic virtue of change of air and scene, might effect that restoration of his shattered health, which medicine and brief intervals of anxious inactivity had failed to accomplish. A good inspiration acting on his native energy and promptitude, awoke in him the resolution to make one bold struggle to attain a less dependent and straitened position than that of a clerk. He determined, if possible, to obtain, through his maternal connections, an introduction to some wholesale houses in England.

In pursuance of these objects, Mr. and Mrs. Powell embarked for England on the 7th of April, 1848, in the " Fox," commanded by Captain ——, a devout man, who every evening assembled the passengers, and as many of the sailors as the cuddy would hold, for thanksgiving, prayer, and the reading and exposition of the Word of God. As the Antipodal May corresponds with our November, our travellers suffered much from extreme cold during the earlier weeks of the voyage. No care could save the gorgeous Australian birds which they were bearing as presents and mementos from the birth-place of their children to the country of their kin. The ice-king also levied heavy contributions on their commissariat, a hundred and ninety-two capons having perished in four days. Mr. Powell himself, being in very low health, was utterly unable to bear up against the rigor of the season. He could not so much as make the accustomed entries in his journal; a duty which was, however, undertaken by his wife, though she, too, was near her confinement, and "wretchedly ill." Their route was by the "formidable Horn." They endured the tedious discomfort of a voyage of four months and eleven days, seeing, for the most part, "naught but the restless plain." For weeks the wind was not only piercing, but baffling and adverse. They beguiled as they might the weary weeks; watching the white foam fly off their bow; "chatting about all that we have left, and all that we are going to;" recalling day by day the home occupations inter-mitted for so long a time.

They did not fail to note the few incidents which relieve the monotony and cheer the confinement of a long sojourn on the sea; *e.g.*—

"April 25th.—A whale forty feet long came within two hundred yards of the ship. The morning was sufficiently clear to enable the captain to take an observation, which made us yet one thousand eight hundred miles from Cape Horn."

"Sunday, May 7th.—Had a few glimpses of the

sun. Early this morning quite a sensation was created by the sudden cry of a sail, seen undoubtedly by several on board. It proved, however, to be a mere illusion, a marine mirage; being but the reflection of our own ship. Had Divine service in the cuddy. The captain read an excellent sermon in the morning, and in the afternoon two of James's Pastoral Addresses, and another good discourse in the evening. Wind still contrary."

"May 10th.—Still contrary wind, barometer very low, foreshowing high winds. We were called on deck last night to see a lunar rainbow."

"July 4th.—Have seen a great number of dolphins. Caught one of them."

"Sunday, 5th.—Divine service. Texts suitable. In the morning, 'What I say unto you I say unto all, Watch.' In the evening, the history of Jonah."

"27th.—Spoke the 'Ben Lomond,' a fine ship of a thousand tons. She had spoken a French brig, which gave her the news of another French revolution."

"Sunday, August 7th.—Could not have Divine service, as we are passing through the Channel between two of the Azores. At three P.M. we were close to both of them. The land is high, and at first sight the hills seemed rocky and barren; but, on a nearer view, we found them richly cultivated. We could distinguish a windmill, a church, a castle, and several houses."

Two events, however, served materially to break the tedium of that protracted voyage. On the 23d of May, at midnight, whilst the ship was staggering about Cape Horn, driven by an adverse wind into dangerous proximity to it, and, unable to round the Falklands, was feeling and forcing her way through the seething Straits of Magellan, in a wild snow-storm, Mr. Powell's first-born son entered this tempestuous world. The birth was quite an event in the ship's history, and was duly chronicled in *the log*.

The other enlivening event is thus recorded, after many entries of "contrary winds" and "calms," and "very heavy weather."

"June 26th.—This evening, with a fair wind, we entered the beautiful harbor of Bahia. The coast scenery is picturesque and lovely in the highest degree. The bay is spacious. The light-house stands on an elevated point, at the termination of a noble range of hills, stretching as far as the eye can reach. On nearing the city, one's dreams of fairyland seem almost realized. The green hills, bathing their feet in the white foam; the strange but graceful trees; the novel and yet handsome buildings of an immense city, containing about two hundred thousand inhabitants, and terracing a lofty hill, form a view of surpassing magnificence and beauty. A commanding fort stands in the centre of the harbor. We were not long here before we were boarded by an officer from a splendid Portuguese frigate, of sixty-four guns, which lay at anchor, offering us any services we might require, and inviting the captain and passengers on board the frigate. They confirmed the startling intelligence of another French Revolution."

4*

To one who up to the age of twenty-six had never beheld a town larger than the little capital of Tasmania, Bahia must have been an imposing spectacle.

"June 27th.—The passengers went on shore. The scenery formed a rich contrast to the silent plains and sombre woodlands of Australia. The cocoa-nut palm, the bread-fruit plantain, and the orange-tree, covered the hills in delicious luxuriance. The bay was studded with fishing and trading vessels of all shapes and sizes; ships were tacking out and in, and some hundred and fifty vessels anchored near the town. The various consulates are handsome buildings, ranging along the hill, at the point of which the light-house stands. But 'the lower town' is extremely dirty; the wharf is a narrow, shabby landing-place, and along its extent are built rows of dirty stores, from two to six stories high. The negroes perform every description of labor. Some are selling refreshments, toys, etc.; others carry water and heavy burdens. Every one of them sends out some distinctive cry, the most heavily laden the loudest; and as there are thousands of these shouters continually in the streets, the aggregate uproar is deafening. Sedan-chairs form the mode of conveyance for all classes, from the Governor to the poor mulatto. Those belonging to private individuals are, of course, handsomer, and have bearers better dressed than those let out on hire. The churches are very numerous, with tall steeples, vast domes, and huge bells; most of which are generally clanging, apparently in the pious effort to drown the commercial clamor of the streets. Many of the churches are magnificently decorated, both without and within. The grandeur of the cathedral, as seen from the entrance, quite astonished us. We had read and heard of the splendor of Roman Catholic churches, but the reality far surpassed imagination. The first object which arrested our attention was an exquisitely carved image of the Saviour, immediately above the altar; on which stood massive candlesticks, as long as a tall man, with the other glittering paraphernalia of Popish worship. The pulpits are of solid marble, elaboately and tastefully carved. The side aisles and transepts are fitted up with confessionals, and the innumerable niches in the walls seemed occupied by the whole Pantheon of Popery. The roof looked like a broad firmament, curiously constellated with carven and gilded devices; the centre being an immense sun, surrounded by groups of angels. We could have spent hours in examining this grand work of art, the receptacle of so many smaller works of art, but felt little drawn to devotion.

"Thence to the market, where we found nothing so remarkable as the thousands of negroes, vending all manner of fruits, and gorgeous parrots, and other rare and lovely birds. Some were busily plaiting mats and sombreros. We went into two or three shops, one a perfumer's, luxuriously fitted up, with a variety of little elegances in glass-cases. On our way back, we passed through many crowded, narrow, squalid streets, some quite lined with palanquins, the bearers of which hustled us provokingly.

To escape this torture we were obliged to purchase the services of one of our tormentors; and so, for the first time, experienced the dignity of using men as beasts of burden. The dinner at the hotel comprised some fifty different dishes, consisting mainly of a vast variety of stews—stewed beef, stewed tongue, stewed beans, stewed peas, stewed everything; the most substantial dish was a fine turkey. For dessert came guava jelly, cheese-cakes, and piles of oranges and bananas. We had much noise and merriment, but no disorder or excess.

" We left Bahia with an ample supply of water and of oranges, and a store of pleasing recollections."

Whilst within the tropics they suffered almost as much from heat as, a few weeks before, from cold. They reached the English Channel on the 16th of August, and had their first view of the English coast in bright summer weather; and first "set foot" on British soil on the 19th of that month. This expression was true of both, as Mr. Powell had left his native land before he could walk or stand alone. So happily are we constituted by our *faithful Creator*, that all the weariness and anxiety of the voyage were lost sight of in a moment; its extremes of temperature, its crises of peril, its winter-passage of " the formidable Horn," its threatening storms, and scarcely less trying calms, all were as nothing now; and the journal closes, " after a long but *delightful* passage of four calendar months and eleven days."

CHAPTER VIII.

WE shall henceforward give but few extracts from
Mr. Powell's spiritual diary. Those which we have
already given have allowed a privileged access to his
inner life, and have opened the secret pathway to
the sources of his perennial kindness, integrity, and
usefulness. They have demonstrated that his secret
communion with God had stamped upon his brow
" the beauty of holiness," and that his sweetness
and benignity of character had only been attained
by severe, protracted, and strongly-contested struggles with his natural temper and disposition.

But there is a certain monotonousness inseparable
from a daily record of the alternations and vicissitudes of his Christian life. We are not to look for
graces of style or flowers of rhetoric in a spiritual
more than in a commercial day-book. To many
readers, too, there is such a dread of everything
which savors of cant, that they are suspicious of
even the simplest utterances of earnest godliness.
And yet the language of Canaan varies very little
throughout the tribes of Israel. How curious it is
to note that Miss Mitford, for example, when age
and sickness bring her face to face with death and

eternity, falls into the same phraseology of which she had made such graceful and good-natured sport, when used some twenty years before by a " Methodist " acquaintance, who ventured to manifest some interest in her soul, and which she had once regarded as the very *patois* of enthusiasm !

Our extracts must now, however, be of a different kind, presenting another phase of his well-rounded character. Every scene through which he passed was to him a field of observation. The journal, which took its rise from the sternest principle, became at length a passion and a necessity. He seemed as if resolved to arrest the evanescence of our mortal life, by sketching and fixing those features of each succeeding day which gave it individuality and meaning. Thus his journal became a strange miscellany. Some smart and fool-rebuking retort stands side by side with programmes of strenuous self-culture ; and comic photographs of odd situations alternate with the gravest notices of spiritual progress or recession. The aspect of his nature, which the present chapter specially reveals, is his exquisite sense of the ludicrous, his genuine love of fun, his keen appreciation of the grotesque element of human life, in fact, his broad geniality of nature. Mr. Butters, who knew him intimately from his conversion to his death, says, " that with all his earnestness and eagerness, he was the merriest fellow I ever met with in my life." Nor is this strange, or in any wise exceptional. The correspondence between him and the noble-natured Daniel Draper, overflows with lively drollery. For cheer-

fulness, like praise, is *comely to the upright.* Hence
earnest men are, in a double sense, *the best company
in the world.* A fixed heart is a light heart. " My
heart is fixed, O God, my heart is fixed : I will sing
and give praise."

Mr. and Mrs. Powell remained in England nearly
six months. The voyage, the marvels of his native
land, never seen till manhood, gazed at with childish
wonder and adult intelligence; the warm welcome
of relations of whom he had heard so much, but
seen nothing ; and, above all, the long vacation from
the daily strain and worry of business, told most
favorably upon his health. Although he had
passed through two winters in the twelvemonth, one
on either side of the globe, one on sea, and one on
land, yet, when he stepped on board the good ship
in Plymouth Sound, on the 5th of February, 1849,
he found himself a much haler and healthier man,
than when, ten months before, he had lost sight of
the Australian coast. He had accomplished the
main object of his visit, having obtained an introduction to some first-class houses in the iron trade.
He had also laid in a good stock of well-chosen
books. He was commencing another stage in his
heavenward pilgrimage. Like Jacob, he had gone
forth to visit the land of his race, his parents' country and kindred, which was to him, moreover, the
unremembered land of birth. Instead of four
hundred miles of desert, he had traversed twelve
thousand miles of ocean ; he had come not to find a
wife, but accompanied by his Tasmanian bride and
his sea-born son. Before he undertook that journey,

he had seen the ladder of light, and had heard, and
assented to, the gracious overtures of God. He had
set his seal to God's covenant, saying, " If God will
be with me, and keep me in the way which I go,
and give me bread to eat, and raiment to put on,
and bring me home in peace, then the Lord shall be
my God, and of all that Thou givest me, I will
surely give a tenth unto Thee."

The return voyage differed from the outward in
many points, besides the total change of course.
Our travellers were obliged to take a crowded emigrant ship, there being no other for Port Phillip
direct. She had on board two hundred and fifty
emigrants, and six saloon passengers, including Mr.
and Mrs. Powell, and the surgeon-superintendent.

I shall make a few extracts, which will suffice to
give continuity to the thread of our story, to illustrate Mr. Powell's unremitting self-culture and
thoughtful piety, in striking combination with a
vivid interest in all human matters. We also gain
amusing sketches of life on board an emigrant ship.

" Sunday, February 11th.—Many of the emigrants
deplorably ill. The doctor, after calling over their
names, was about to proceed with Divine service,
when he was hoisted from the poop by Mr. ——,
who demanded to know whether he meant to let the
sick people die for want of attention. A fine *fracas*
ensued, the altercation was violent; but after this
unseemly introduction, order being partially recovered, the service commenced, and continued in
spite of many interruptions. The sermon was from
the words, ' Come thou into the ark.' "

Judging from subsequent entries, which it is not expedient to print in full, the emigrant ship afforded as rich advantages for studying the natural history of the human species, as did Noah's structure for showing the instincts and habitudes of clean and unclean beasts.

"Monday, 12th.—Wind contrary. Storm in the saloon, in consequence of the doctor's forbidding the gentleman who interfered with his clerical functions yesterday any further intercourse with the emigrants."

"Tuesday, 13th.—At the tea-table was enabled by the grace of God to express my opinion of the practice of profane swearing, and trust that this awful habit will be checked. Our time is passing pleasantly; our little boy being a constant source of amusement. I am reading with great interest Alison's ' History of Europe.' May God still prosper us, and enable us to live to His glory ! "

A healthy baby on board ship is a blessing to the whole community ; every one in turn is a nurse and a playmate.

"14th.—One of the children died, and was committed to the deep. I was drawn to muse upon the glorious salvation which Christ has wrought for children dying in infancy, and to remind myself of the Lord's admonition, ' Be ye also ready.' Several of the emigrants in a pitiable plight. But those who are well amuse themselves in the evening with singing, dancing, and playing on the flute, violin, and clarionet."

"16th.—Read an instructive meditation on the difference between 'Knowledge and Wisdom.'"

"17th.—Favorable wind and weather, but half a gale between the captain and the doctor about the treatment of the poor sick emigrants. I read an essay on 'Inadequate Views of our Fallen Nature.' The sea superbly phosphorescent: a shoal of porpoises showed grand and grim, like a vision of monsters weltering in fire."

"Sunday, 18th.—Service this morning, and a prayer-meeting on deck this evening. Two of the emigrants offered prayer, and all seemed greatly pleased with the service."

"19th.—The trade-wind is rapidly bearing us into hot weather, but the oppressive days are richly compensated by the magnificently starry nights. We have made good way; as I have also in reading Alison. The doctor commenced a school; and I proposed a Sunday-school, and was accepted as a teacher."

"Wednesday, 21st.—We had Divine service at mid-day. The doctor read one of Burder's 'Village Sermons.'"

"24th.—Reading 'Protestantism in France, from 1584 to 1685.' Also, 'A Memoir of Thirza, a converted Jewess.' I feel my heart drawn to the Saviour of sinners."

"Sunday, 25th.—Near Brava and the volcanic island Fuego. Divine service as usual at eleven, and in the evening hymns and prayers. The two religious emigrants offered prayer. Read a part of 'Modern Jerusalem.' Also Wesley's sermon on

'Speak evil of no man.' Lord, ever remind me of this Thy benign command. Mr. —— threw one of the beds, placed on the poop to air, at the doctor, which struck him on the head so violently as to knock him down. This offended the passengers more than the doctor, who seems to have been so stunned by the blow as to think it an accident, or is so meek as to give it that interpretation."

" 27th.—Walking up the poop, after reading in my cabin this morning, I found the married men amongst the emigrants in a state of mild mutiny against the doctor, making threatening demonstrations, and clamoring to be transferred to the care of the captain. This added an alien responsibility the captain could not accept. The doctor only replied by reading the 'Regulations.' I fear this move will rather aggravate than relieve our disturbances."

"February 28th.—The heat overpowering. More troubles amongst the emigrants, who have much to try them. We have on board,—

" Married couples, 41................82
    Single—males, 40, females, 43....83
    Children—boys, 36, girls, 41......77
                                      ———
                                      242 "

"March 2d.—Having copied all my invoices, I installed Annie as my chief clerk. We checked them carefully; my clerk doing very well for a beginning; but when we came to certain articles of household furniture, her clerkship suddenly forgot her place, and insisted on appropriating several of them, not only for use, but also for ornament.

"The portion of Scripture read this morning was Rev. ii. The peculiar promise here is, '*To him that overcometh*.' What a breadth and urgency of application belong to these words! How much to be overcome daily everywhere, both by resistance and attack! Lord, increase my faith!"

"3d.—Notwithstanding the monotony of the voyage, the days seem to pass very quickly. We reach the end of the week before we are aware. Near the 'tween-decks at night it is like an oven. The emigrants endeavor to avoid the heat by sleeping in the boats, under the stairs, or anywhere they can find a little shelter."

"Sunday, 4th.—Another death this morning; a married woman. She was attacked suddenly last night. Another loud summons. 'Prepare to meet thy God.' She suffered fearfully from heat and thirst."

"6th.—Hotter and hotter. Many of the female emigrants unwell; the poop transformed into an hospital. Dispute between the captain and two of the saloon passengers, because he would not leave his duty to play cards."

"7th.—Making about a knot an hour. Was very much impressed in my Bible reading this morning with the truth that 'to obey is better than sacrifice,' from the fact that one so devout and zealous as the good King Josiah should have his useful life cut short in an engagement, entered upon in opposition to the express command of God."

" 8th.—Made only five miles in the last twenty-four hours. Lat. 4° 48'. The poop nearly full of emigrants ill with the heat. Another stormy debate between the colonel and the doctor, about the emigrants sleeping on the poop."

" 10th.—An examination held in the captain's cabin, on an emigrant who had committed an assault on another. Sentenced to appear before the police office, on arrival at Melbourne."

" Sunday, 11th.—Divine service sadly interrupted by the insubordination of the emigrants, over whom the surgeon-superintendent has lost all control and all influence, excepting to excite their ridicule. This lamentably spoils the peace and harmony of our little community. I employed my Sabbath morning in reading Ford's ' Laodicea,' and trust that the solemn and just arguments there employed to arouse Christians from their lethargy may not be lost on me. ' Save, Lord, or I perish ! ' "

" 12th.—Squally weather. Sharp disputes on board. Mr. —— interfering with the doctor, blaming him for frequent bleeding of an epileptic woman ; after that a comic, loud-voiced altercation between the doctor and some Irish girls, who had been reprimanded by him for their attentions to the first mate. The poor doctor had no chance with the arch Hibernians. He was ingloriously driven from the field by volleys of irresistible laughter. These quarrels, like the squalls, are unpleasant breaks in the monotony of our voyage. Spoke the ' James Gibbs,' emigrant ship. Her captain and doctor came on board, and our saloon passengers returned the visit.

We spent two hours on board the 'James Gibbs,' and were delighted with her discipline and cleanliness. Our doctor was so much impressed that we had scarcely regained our ship before he commenced a most vigorous reform, assuming a resolution and an energy altogether foreign to his character, and more grotesque than imposing. Having heard on board the 'James Gibbs' that an unruly emigrant had been put in irons, he was determined without delay to magnify his authority, and literally to *make* an example of some one or other. He went strutting about, threatening men and women in the most overbearing style. He tried to stop the dancing of the Irish girls, thrusting his lantern in their faces. Whereupon one of them made of him an improvised May-pole, dancing round him in the wildest glee. The doctor seemed to take to his new character remarkably well. He stood stock-still, as if stuck there for the very purpose. At every pause in the performance, the emigrants clapped and encored, and the music jangled all the while. The doctor did not recover from his fascination till the breathless girl sat down. He then became terrible, foaming with rage, and ordering her below, amidst derisive advices to put her in irons. To these marine theatricals we had an unpleasant afterpiece in the cuddy, the captain not caring to interfere."

"14th.—Four vessels in sight. All calm and bright, excepting another violent altercation between two female emigrants. In the evening had a pleasant conversation with the cuddy passengers on personal religion. Studying Cobbett's English

Grammar, feeling the necessity of understanding the principles of my mother-tongue better than I now do." This beginning at the beginning of self-education is characteristic and instructive.

"17th.—St. Patrick's Day. The Irish emigrants made some shamrocks. Crossed the Line. The captain waived his declared aversion to the usual ceremonies, but quietly advised the doctor to send the emigrants below, for fear the sailors might be too rough for some of them. The masquerade was not without a rude, good-natured humor. Neptune and Amphitrite were charioted on a gun-carriage, with classical attendants in masks, smeared with lamp-black, and guarded by a human-visaged lion, clothed like a false prophet, in sheep-skins. They demanded to initiate into the mysteries of the Equator those of the crew who had not before passed it. About half a dozen sailors were duly lathered with tar, grease, and turpentine, mixed with black paint, scraped with a key-hole saw, and plunged into a large tub. This operation they bore with infinite good-humor. But, of course, the doctor must play the principal part in the pantomime. To decoy him from the poop, Mrs. Neptune was suddenly seized with a fainting-fit. She fell heavily upon the deck; her attendants, with loyal alarm and tenderness, raised her in a state of helpless unconsciousness, and propped her up against the main-mast. The doctor's aid was anxiously implored. This time, no one could accuse him of negligence or want of sympathy. He hurried from the poop, and whilst bending over his mythological patient, was suddenly drenched with a bucket of salt water, —of course intended to revive the fainting goddess! At all events it had that effect, although absorbed by the doctor instead of the patient. The swooning immortal was instantly herself again, and her physician, finding that his services were no longer required, proceeded to withdraw; but her attendants kept him in an enchanted circle, until they had saturated him with libations of their monarch's element. The emigrants now joining in the play, and crowding round the leading figure, several buckets of salt water were distributed amongst them from the main-top. The scene closed very harmlessly, and accomplished its purpose,—an amusing change in the dreariness of a long voyage. About an hour afterwards we sighted a homeward-bound vessel, some seven miles ahead. We all forgot the frolic in thoughts of the friends we had left behind, and set briskly to work writing letters. They were conveyed to the stranger in the captain's boat. She put her sails aback, and received them on board. She proved to be the 'John Daniel,' from Batavia to Rotterdam. The captain, with injudicious generosity sent back to us several case-bottles of spirits, with almonds and cigars. The gift was unfortunate, as the doctor showed his forgiving spirit by not only dispensing the liquors, but by allowing a quantity of porter besides. The result was that the emigrants' steward, the third mate, and the carpenter, became mad drunk; and the two latter so violent, that the captain was obliged to confine one of them, and put handcuffs on the other, and bind him to the side of the vessel, where he kicked and cursed for hours, till completely exhausted. Thus miserably ended the entertainment of the day."

"Sunday, 18th.—All calm and peaceful, calcuculated to draw the mind to the Author of peace. All praise to Him for the blessed Sabbath and its holy services, so sweet and elevating even on the sea!"

"19th.—Still at Cobbett. My little boy this day said 'Papa.' Sweet sound to a father's ears!"

"20th.—One of the married female emigrants died. She caught a slight cold through the playful drenching three days ago. She complained a little on the next day, and died this morning at ten o'clock, shortly after taking a dose of turpentine administered by the doctor. The scene was heart-rending. Her *seven* children threw themselves down with the most piercing exclamations of grief. Her loss to them is irretrievable. She had brought them up respectably, and with great care. The captain did not intend to bury her till to-morrow, but the poor father, doubtless anxious to bury his dead out of his children's sight, requested that her body might be committed to the deep this afternoon. The colonel read the Burial Service, the emigrants mournfully gathered around. While the sad words were said, 'Man that is born of woman hath but a short time to live, and is full of misery,' how solemnly did they sink into my soul! I had heard them read over father, mother, brother, sister, friend, and child, but never did they speak so home to my heart as on that bright day, above that sparkling

5

sea, surrounded by that crowd of strangers and of pilgrims. I felt, as I had scarcely ever felt before, on what a precarious tenure life is held, and the momentousness of death, as fixing forever the character and the condition of the soul. When will this service be read over me? What will be my state when friends gather round my lifeless form? The case of our departed fellow-traveller is solemnly impressive. She was in high health three days ago, but now her dead body is left far behind us, beneath the mighty deep. Why are we spared who still voyage on? Mrs. C—— had no idea this morning that death was near. It was a most lovely evening when the corpse was borne on deck, stretched on the captain's bed, the British flag shrouding the body of one of Britain's daughters, who, six weeks before, had left her shores with the praiseworthy purpose of improving her children's prospects by leaving her own fatherland. The sun was just setting, with tropical suddenness and splendor, and seemed like hers to *go down while it was yet day*. A gorgeous equatorial sky was stretched above us, and reflected in the heaving deep. There was no sound but the deep-voiced, measured reading of our soldier-chaplain, the lapping waves, the creaking timbers, the smothered sobs, the sudden splash. May we not hope, as well as pray, that through faith in the precious blood of Christ, our end may be peace, and our *rest be glorious?* "

"Sunday, 25th.—Divine service and disgraceful bickerings, both as usual.'

"27th.—Finished Mungo Park's Travels. Wrote a letter to my old band-mate, Thomas Bonner."

"30th.—A child died."

"31st.—Amused myself by arranging 'What fairy-like Music' for the emigrants."

"Sunday, April 1st.—Heard some of the boys read the New Testament, and *questioned into* them the second chapter of Matthew."

"2d.—Arranged for the emigrants, 'Sound the loud Timbrel.'"

"3d.—Amused myself by arranging two hymn-tunes, which I hope to teach the emigrants. If we had but a piano, we should get on famously. At all events, singing and playing hymn-tunes will be a much better pastime than the poor emigrants are sometimes driven to by weariness and want of mental and spiritual resources,—such as women dressing themselves up in men's clothes."

"Contrary wind for the last four days. Very wearisome; perpetual tacking, but 'He holdeth the winds in His fist,' and we will thankfully acquiesce in His appointments. We have need of patience, and must ask for it."

"5th.—Read one of Wesley's Sermons, and studied a chapter of Cobbett's Grammar, in which I make slow progress, as we are making in our voyage." "Stopped by the elements," in both cases; to borrow one of Byron's puns.

"9th.—Commenced reading a second time Robertson's 'Charles V.' A great number of the emigrants ill. My dear wife and I are constantly hearing language of the most debasing kind May it drive us to pray to the holy God, whose Spirit alone can save us from the demoralizing influence of 'the filthy conversation of the wicked!'"

"13th.—Have been greatly interested in reading the Books of Samuel and Kings continuously, as I read Alison and Robertson, without regard to the division into chapters, or breaking up the history into a daily portion. The Bible, Cobbett, Robertson, Alison, Wesley, etc., stave off weariness. Without reading, how insupportable would be the tedium of a long voyage!"

"14th.—Copied several hymns, and composed a tune."

"Sunday, 15th.—Confined to bed in a high fever from a severe cold; but very happy from a sense of God's forbearing mercy towards me. Annie read to me one of Wesley's Sermons."

"16th.—Another death."

"18th.—Made a full statement of my affairs in my cash-book."

"20th.—Copied some more hymns."

"23d.—Finished Robertson the second time."

"24th.—Read Read's 'Discourse on Watchfulness,' and found in it quite sufficient to alarm me, and stir me up to earnest prayer."

"25th.—Read a discourse on 'Lukewarmness,' with much benefit. I find it good for the soul to be always employed in reading, writing, arranging music, or taking exercise—pacing up and down deck. As the novelty of voyaging wears off, I find that I can occupy my time to great advantage."

"Sunday, 29th.—The weather too squally for service on deck. Annie and I and two of the passengers held it in the cabin."

"May 2d.—Read the Life of Sir Francis Drake."

" 4th.—Making but slow progress. Some of the passengers relieve the monotony by the cruel diversion of shooting the albatross and other birds—restrained neither by the sailors' superstition, nor by Christian feeling."

" 5th.—Weather very cold, so that the schoolmaster was not able to teach the children on deck, great numbers having the hooping-cough. He wished to instruct them between decks, for which he was deprived of his office by the doctor. I drew up for him a statement and protest."

" Sunday, 6th.—Read H. Bonar, on ' The Blood of the Cross,' and Dr. Barth's ' History of the Church.' Was much quickened by perusing the account of the sufferings and heroism of the Christians, during the first three centuries. We are longing for a home-Sabbath."

" 7th.—One of our cabin-passengers used such coarse and impious language, that Mrs. Powell, who was seated next him, was obliged to retire to her own cabin. On my expostulating with him, far from apologizing, he threatened to *make* me hold my tongue. This, however, he found himself unable to accomplish. The captain never checks these frequent obscenities and blasphemies."

" 8th.—Annie employed herself in painting the poop. Saw a cape pigeon for the first time this voyage. A shoal of bottle-nosed whales passed us. Read several articles in Chambers' Journal—a capital book for a long voyage—the articles being short and varied."

"9th.—Read a Memoir of Louis Philippe."

"13th.—Another death."

"14th.—The father of the dead child demanded an inquiry into the cause of its death. An inquest was held in the captain's cabin. Witnesses examined, and the evidence taken down before the captain, Dr. ——, Mr. ——, and myself. The court sat for two hours and a half. Our finding was very unfavorable to one of the parties."

"15th.—Had a hard day's work copying the evidence taken yesterday. Have been able to take no observation of the sun for four days past, so that, having only our dead reckoning to rely on, we feel rather uncomfortable. We can, however, trust in Him, who neither 'slumbers by day, nor sleeps by night.'"

"18th.—Another married female emigrant died to-day."

"19th.—Poor Mrs. Sheehan committed to the deep. As she was a Roman Catholic, her husband would not allow the Burial Service to be read. Alas! the emigrants seem now quite as little impressed by a burial at sea, as by an ordinary funeral on land. The drowning of a cat would have created a greater sensation. She has left seven children."

"22d.—Commenced Bigland's 'Letters on History.'"

"Sunday, 27th.—Service in the cabin, the wind being squally and unfavorable. Read James on

'The Duty of Meditation.' Surely we shall make much of our Sabbaths on shore, if spared to enjoy them again."

" 28th.—My twenty-seventh birthday. My few days have been full of evil on my part. May 'the God of all grace' root out all evil from my heart before the day of death arrives! An infant severely hurt, and dangerously ill, through the narrowness of the berth where it and its parents sleep; only two feet nine inches wide!"

" June 2d.—Engaged in writing certificates for the captain."

" Sunday, 3d.—Service interrupted by a shower, and not resumed. Read Wesley's Sermon on ' The Witness of the Spirit.' "

" 4th.—At half-past three this morning, the captain informed us that Cape Otway light-house was visible. I immediately rose, dressed, and went on deck. The sun rose brilliantly, and the shores of Australia looked pleasant to our eyes. The emigrants forthwith began arranging their boxes. We caught a large number of barracoots. We were almost within the Heads; but the tide running out, the wind falling, to our sore disappointment, we were obliged to put to sea again."

" 5th.—Distant many miles from the Heads. Towards evening, made out the light-house again, and the wind yielding a little in our favor, we hope to get in to-morrow."

" 6th.—Entered the Heads this morning, had a beautiful run up the bay, and a very happy meeting with our friends, after nearly fourteen months' absence, more than eight of which we have passed at sea."

" 8th.—Occupied the whole of yesterday in passing the entry of my goods; to-day in looking for a house. Was much struck with the extension and improvement of the town. Its population is now estimated at 20,000."

Mr. Powell at once recommenced his Church activities.

" Sunday, 10th.—Visited the Melbourne Sunday-school; and attended Divine service."

" 30th.—This week has been mainly occupied in getting up two large sales, which have gone off remarkably well; so that, by the blessing of God, I hope to be soon able to discharge every obligation, and ' owe no man anything but love.' "

CHAPTER IX.

Mr. Powell had ventured his all, the reward of unremitting industry, and resolute frugality, in the endeavor to form a connection with some two or three leading firms in England. His maternal aunt had become responsible for the first shipment of goods. This generous guarantee represents all the help that Mr. Powell ever had in his life. He took a situation for a year, in order to start on his owr account unencumbered by debt. His principal introductions had been to houses in the iron trade. This led him to commence as an importer of hardware, at first, upon a very cautious scale. As clerk in an auctioneer's office he had no special acquaintance with any branch of business, but he possessed some invaluable elements of success—shrewdness, promptitude, punctuality, indomitable industry, a happy home, and trust in God. In connection with his wholesale warehouse, he opened a retail shop, " to weed off surplus stock." He expressed his resolution that if, after a fair trial, the undertaking did not promise success, he would retreat into a subordinate position, and content himself with that for life, unless Providence should make for him some clear opening out of it. He felt his way with

5*

great humility, wariness, and self-control. At first he had much toil with little profit. He observed the most rigid economy; never spending a shilling on luxury or self-indulgence. At the same time, he adhered to his plan of proportionate giving, and used hospitality without grudging, "being content with such things" as he had, and relying on the promise, "I will never leave thee, nor forsake thee."

At that date, Melbourne was a quiet though steadily thriving town. It had but two streets with any pretensions to regularity. Mr. Powell's was one of the few tall houses, surrounded by wooden huts, placed according to the convenience or fancy of the owners. But in 1851 the news burst upon its industrious tranquillity, that rich "gold-diggings" had been opened in the colony, within a hundred miles of the little capital.

Forthwith almost the whole population caught the "yellow fever," and the greater part of the males abandoned home and business, and rushed to the gold-fields. For a time trade was suspended, and Melbourne almost depopulated, and the entire social system of the colony disjointed. Then thousands streamed in from all parts of the world. For a while Melbourne seemed to be a magnet, drawing to itself all the loose population of the globe. Wastrels from Great Britain, "old lags" from Tasmania and New South Wales, superfluous Chinamen, Californian diggers precipitated themselves on Victoria, along with the more adventurous and sanguine of the industrious class. The worth of real estate was quadrupled; month by month necessities rose to the price of luxuries; the race for riches became reckless, almost rapid. People seemed to think that gold would forever grow under the spade. Mr. Powell however had the good sense to see that his diggings lay at home. Many hundred spades threw gold into his till, and many a score of pickaxes brought the coined metal over his counter before they struck upon the auriferous quartz. No one toiled harder at the diggings than he in his store. Clerks and servants all forsook him. *Every man his own clerk*, every lady her own housemaid, was the order of the day. Mr. Powell had been guided to a business singularly suited to meet the utterly unforeseen demand. Money poured in ; but sorrow came along with it. Two sons were born and buried in two years. The sudden and incessant influx of thousands a week, for whom there could be provided no adequate accommodation, generated insidious and malignant distempers. A sister of Mr. Powell died suddenly. A brother, to whom he was tenderly attached, and to forward whose interests he had recently made great exertions and sacrifices, was accidentally killed. Both brother and sister left large families unprovided for, the care and maintenance of most of whom Mr. Powell at once undertook. Scarlet fever and measles of an aggravated type attacked the family. Mr. Powell was suddenly seized with dangerous illness. Soon after his recovery he was called to give up his first-born son, his fourth-born into the land of the blessed. He had gone to Geelong, sixty miles from Melbourne, to attend the annual District Meeting, for the transaction of the financial business of the Methodist Churches in Victoria. He was to remain there from Wednesday until the Monday following. On the evening of Thursday a strong premonition fell upon him of some calamity impending over his household. He spent the greater part of the night in prayer. In the morning his foreboding deepened into certainty, and although the very business was in hand which his Church-offices required him to transact, and he had that day to bring in a special report, he left his document with the chairman, and immediately took the steamer home. Had he delayed he would never again have seen his child alive—our little voyager, who five years before had come into the world upon the high seas, off " the formidable Horn."

Nothing can require less intelligence than to sneer at phenomena, which are not of rare occurrence in the experience of the man of prayer, and nothing can betray a more uncandid stolidity, or a more grossly unscientific blinking of well-authenticated data, than to summarily discredit them. If science cannot explain these occurrences, let it honestly admit that there are undeniable facts which lie beyond its sphere. Why should it be thought a thing incredible that men who live in the constant and intense realization of the invisible world, should have experiences which never occur to men whose tastes and talents, explorations and acquisitions, are in quite another direction? And the spiritually-minded man of business is at least as likely to come upon such wonders as the caverned hermit. The Father of the Faithful was a grazier when God said, "Shall I hide from Abraham the thing which I do?" And it was the ploughman Elisha who said with wonder of an afflicted friend, "Her soul is vexed within her: and the Lord hath hid it from me, and hath not told me." Mr. Powell was no enthusiast. His was a manly faith. His piety was as sensible and practical as it was profound and all-pervading.

No fewer than eight deaths occurred in one branch or other of Mr. Powell's family during this one year. He attributed to the admonitions and consolations of the Holy Spirit accompanying this terrible but timely discipline his preservation from the intoxicating effects of sudden and rapid prosperity. The severe but gracious husbandry of Providence prevented thorns from springing up and choking the good seed. Meanwhile he in no wise relaxed his assiduous attention to business, perceiving that he worked beneath "the golden weather" of a brief and precarious harvest-time. He made judicious investments of his rapidly-increasing property, purchasing land, building stores in new neighborhoods, and extending his business connections. His habits of systematic beneficence and spontaneous generosity were strengthened, not impaired, by the sudden influx of success. His liberality never lagged behind his pecuniary prosperity.

The following letter shows in what spirit he received the loss of his first-born son.

"MELBOURNE SOUTH, Sunday afternoon.

"REV. AND DEAR SIR,

"That which I so greatly feared has come upon

me : my cup of bitterness is almost full ; my darling boy has just departed, and with him our brightest hopes on earth. I left him in health, and returned from Geelong to find him on the bed of death. May the Lord help us, for we have great need of Him!

"I have been pleading with God day and night to save him, but He saw good to take him. We have strong consolation in the certainty that he has entered into the joy of his Lord; and the terrible stroke says, 'Be ye also ready.'

"Such has been the nature of the disease, that we dare not keep him longer than a day, and we have again to solicit your attendance at the cemetery at half-past four to-morrow. May I trespass upon your kindness to choose me in the new ground one of the most lovely spots for my dear son, and may I request that sufficient ground may be marked out for a family vault? There is no one beside yourself whom we should like to bury our child. You have married us, baptized our child, and buried our two sons.

"Your greatly afflicted brother,
"WALTER POWELL."

The place he held in the "heart's just estimation" of those who were most closely connected with him in business, may be gathered from the subjoined testimony of a gentleman who was first his assistant, then manager of one of his businesses in Victoria, and at last his partner. He states:

"My acquaintance with Mr. Powell dates from

1849. At that time I was a lad, 'a stranger in a strange land,' having come to Melbourne to begin life, away from home and friends. The kindly welcome he gave me to his house, where I became a frequent visitor, has left an indelible impression on my memory: it forms one of the greenest spots in my past life. It is very plain to me that the kindly Christian anxiety on behalf of a young man entering life prompted his hospitality. I soon left Melbourne, and obtained a situation in IIobart Town; but the gold being discovered here, I hastened back, bent on going to the diggings, and was only prevented by the wise expostulations of Mr. Powell; and my idea of risking my health in this way was banished by his offer of employment.

"Thus my business connection with him began in what we look back upon as the 'busy times;' and I can picture him as he was then, full of energy, doing the work of three men, now serving customers, now buying gold, then snatching a few minutes to write letters, working hard early and late to keep his business under control; and, in the midst of all this activity, never forgetting the class-meeting or the Sabbath-school, and loving the public worship of the Lord's day. The trying ordeal he thus passed through, left his Christian character unchanged. IIe was the same genial friend when prosperous and immersed in business affairs, as when struggling and comparatively low. The crowd of occupation did not cause him to forget the intimacies of less stirring times. IIe loved old friends, and was graciously preserved from forgetfulness of the 'Friend that sticketh closer than a brother.' As his business prospered, he promptly recognized the claims of benevolence, and lent a ready hand to the various schemes then laid to meet the exigencies of the time."

The Rev. J. C. Symons, then one of the Wesleyan ministers in Melbourne, thus records his recollections: "Those who were in the colony at that time do not need any description of the marvellous change in Melbourne; those who have come since could not understand any description which might be given. Business at that time made terrible demands upon the energies. The rush of people was so sudden, its extent so unprecedented, and the whole of the circumstances so novel, that men in business were sorely taxed. Besides, the means and appliances for doing so suddenly extended a trade were not at hand. Mr. Powell felt this, and was fully aware of the spiritual peril to which he was exposed; but he sought strength from on high, and was preserved from that worldliness and greed of gain into which so many fell. Often did he remark to me, 'I am in this position, I must work as I do, or close up my business: there is no middle course. I would have more help if it were possible; but with such a press of business, and the small space in which to do it, additional hands would be only in the way, would, in fact, be hindrances rather than helps.' He was unable at this period to give all the personal service in the Church which he desired. 'I can't give you much time,' he would say to me; 'that is impossible; but if you will undertake the work, I will help you with money.' And well he fulfilled his promise, not only in the liberal contributions which he gave towards the erection of places of worship, and the various enterprises of the Church, but also in the large responsibilities which he, with other excellent men of that time, readily undertook, and without which the Methodist Church of Victoria could never have been in the position she is in to-day. He found time, however, even when thus pressed, to attend, and take part, in many public meetings, and thus to aid with his presence, as well as with his purse."

The Rev. W. Butters writes: "In 1851, when gold was discovered in Victoria, Mr. Powell was one among our most active office-bearers, and notwithstanding the urgent claims of business, he was but seldom absent from his post. No description that I could give would convey anything like an accurate and adequate idea of that state of confusion into which everything was then thrown, and of our utter inability to guess what would be on the morrow, or what new action sudden emergencies might require."

All this happened when business was yet new to him. The strain and pressure, both mental and physical, were excessive and unintermitted. One would not have been surprised if, in such circumstances, his spiritual life had scarcely found room to grow. But the good seed had fallen into good ground, well pulverized by deep conviction of sin, and softened by the warm showers of genuine repentance. His strenuous effort was to keep the passing world and the eternal world in their just relative positions. His guiding principle was still to "seek *first* the kingdom of God." And this was, after all, his highest and happiest success. This swift deluge of care, perplexity, and prosperity, utterly unforeseen, did not carry him off his feet. He still daily exercised himself unto godliness. This sudden summer of prosperity, after the long winter of anxiety, did not blight his kindly, generous sensibilities, but made them "blossom as the rose." He recognized the orphans, the widows, and the unfortunate, as the proper wards of the successful. He did not deem it an unreasonable expectation in his less prosperous relatives and friends, that they should be substantially the better for his rapid rise in wealth and in position. He learnt "first to show piety at home." In like manner the deep interest in the cause of God, which he had manifested in his straits, flourished vigorously in his successes. At the very last Quarterly Meeting of the Melbourne Circuit, before the news of the gold-fields broke upon the town, whilst from sensitive dread of debt he was scarcely allowing himself sufficient nourishment, he was one of twelve individuals who guaranteed $30 a-piece, towards the outfit and passage-money of two additional missionaries. Whilst the thirst for gold raged like an epidemic, and the wild hope of making a fortune in a few weeks was absorbing all the energies of the majority, leaving little room for a regard to public or eternal interests, half-emptying the places of worship, reducing the class-meetings to skeletons, and sweeping away "the greater number of the class-leaders and local preachers" to the huge scramble for the precious metal, and thus deranging all the evangelistic and educational machinery of the Church, Walter Powell kept faithfully to his post.

In 1855 Mr. Powell removed to Prahran, a rural suburb of Melbourne; for the Victorian merchants, like the British and American, have adopted the healthy custom of living out of town. This change was made in the hope of improving his own health and that of Mrs. Powell. We again quote Mr. Symons: "There, as leading the service of song, as a worker in the Sabbath-school, and as a class-leader, he did good service; service which is most gratefully remembered. It was very touching, on the Sabbath immediately following the intelligence of his death, at a love-feast held in the new church at Prahran, to hear one after another referring to him, testifying to the kindness and wisdom of his counsels on their first arrival in the colony, or to his having spoken to them and invited them to join the Church, or to the piety of his daily life. Such tributes are worth more than storied marble or than sculptured urn."

The following extracts from a letter to the Rev. W. Butters may not unfittingly close this chapter:

"MELBOURNE, *July* 17, 1855.

"MY DEAR MR. BUTTERS:

"The letters of Mrs. Butters and yourself reached us safely. I postponed a reply until business should permit me to make one comfortably; not that it is a task to write to an old and dear friend, but I like, when writing to one who has a place in our hearts, to give something more than a few hasty lines. . . . . .

" In the Methodist world little has been done of late. We have been wise enough to lie on our oars during the settling of the surging tide. I think now, however, commercially speaking, the efflux has nearly ceased; after which the reflux will commence. We seem at present to be just at that point where the waters do ' neither one nor t'other.'

" Methodists, you know, are no idle spectators of such matters. I must no longer make you to doubt by dealing in parables, but come to plain matter-of-fact detail. Stranded, then, lie first and foremost the Collins Street chapel and school-room. Fortunately, however, this is the only great difficulty we have, nearly all the other chapel debts being owed by Methodists to Methodists.

" Mr. Bickford continues to work quietly, but usefully and earnestly, at Brighton; and, being ' a good man and full of faith and of the Holy Ghost,' will undoubtedly be successful.

" At Collingwood a school-house is in course of erection, the foundation having been laid in consequence of some frail promises of help from the school board, which, having no money, cannot give any; wherefore the Collingwoodites have shrewdly determined to depend on themselves.

" I think our Church will, on the whole, be much improved and strengthened, both in numbers and spirituality, through the late trying scenes. It is time that pure religion and undefiled should begin to make its way ; and unless the Methodists lead, who will? As it is, the Papists, by their unremitting watchfulness, are fast taking up every post where their influence will be felt. I hope soon to break off many fetters thrown around me by the events of 1854, and again take an active part in the great work.

"Yours affectionately,

"WALTER POWELL."

CHAPTER X.

LOVE TO GOD MANIFESTING ITSELF IN CHRISTIAN
CHARITY.

It is the reproach of our age that among our
active business men, the rush, hurry, and pressure
of commercial life leaves no leisure for the contemplation of great truths and great principles; and
that in consequence the meditative spirit is dying
out; the reverential and thoughtful elements of our
nature have, it is said, no opportunity of development, except in those retired by-places where they
can exert no influence on the world of living active
men.

Yet here was a man who, in the words of one
who knew him most thoroughly, was for years so
energetic in business that he constantly did the work
of three men; who kept up to the demands of a
rapidly growing and most variable market, under
the most difficult circumstances; who endured
great and deep afflictions, the loss of children and
of near and dear relatives, sickness and sorrow upon
sorrow; a man on whose shoulders lay heavy burdens in the secular affairs of a Church which was
trying to expand itself to supply the spiritual needs
of a rapidly increasing population; a man whose
counsel and judgment were invaluable in matters of

Church and state ; and yet with all his cares, labors, burdens, and anxieties, he managed to find time for self-examination, for careful introspection, for the study of God's Word, and for that calm contemplation of the present and the future, which, amid the turmoil and confusion, the mad strife and roar of the waves of an excitement such as the world has seldom seen, kept him anchored safely and firmly " to that within the veil." How did he manage to combine these diverse, and as some would think, incompatible qualities, the highest activity, and the most profoundly contemplative spirit? Let the apostle answer for us : " he endured, as seeing Him who is invisible." In youth, in the time of poverty and illness, he had formed this habit of communion with God and his own soul, until it had grown to be his life, and now, in the time when he most needed it, this habit steadied him, and kept him above all earthly excitements and agitations, where his soul at every, even momentary, pause in business, flew upward, like the captive bird let loose from its cage, and sought its supremest joy in communion with God. If we sought for evidence of the rare abilities with which God had endowed his servant, where could we find those which would be so conclusive as this faculty of living in and yet above the world? of enjoying the full sunlight of heaven, while down in the murky depths of an all-engrossing commercial life ? With God, be it remembered, the humble, lowly, contemplative spirit which delights in His Word and His works, is far more highly esteemed than the most brilliant intellect, which in its proud self-reliance forgets the Creator who endowed it with such rich gifts.

No sooner did Mr. Powell find himself in possession of a moderate degree of ready money and of attainable leisure, than he began forthwith to secure that money and that leisure for the noblest conceivable objects. He did not say, "I shall wait till I am worth so much money, and can retire from business altogether, and then the Church shall *see my zeal for the Lord of hosts.*" Detecting the excursive tendencies of hoarded or even well-invested riches, he kept their wings well clipped; and seeing that leisure without some passionate pursuit is dull torture and insidious temptation, he resolved, more likely he intuitively felt, that he must cultivate an interest in movements which, whilst they benefited others, would bring into his own breast a rich return of God-like satisfaction.

The Rev. Mr. Butters has kindly furnished the subjoined list of the principal movements in which Mr. Powell took a principal part at this critical period of the religious history of Victoria:

" 1. Our Sunday-schools, which he was very ready to help both by personal service and by his purse.

" 2. Increased ministerial strength to overtake the rapidly growing wants of the community.

" 3. The establishment of the Wesleyan Immigrants' Home.

" 4. Additional Church accommodation for the thousands who were constantly pouring into the colony.

"5. Ministerial and Church provision for the gold-fields, which threatened, unless immediate and effective measures were taken, to deluge the colony with vice and crime.

"6. The formation of the Australian Wesleyan Mission Churches into a distinct and independent communion, with a Conference of its own.

"7. The establishment of a Book Depot in Melbourne.

"8. The erection and furnishing of Wesley College."

To all these objects he devoted earnest attention, and made large contributions. A just estimate will not be formed of the generosity, the public spirit, the quickness, keenness, and breadth of view, and the prompt recognition of responsibility displayed by Mr. Powell, amidst a state of things as unprecedented as it was unforeseen, unless we bear in mind the fact that these were the contributions, the plans, and the toils, of a hard-driven young man, who gave as fast as he got, and under the pressure of private anxieties lavished time, thought, and strength, as well as hard-earned money, upon the public service.

Of his Sunday-school labors we need not say more; and the urgent necessity of increased ministerial strength, in a city which sometimes witnessed a thousand new arrivals in a day, is too obvious to require comment. Of the other movements, it may be well to make a brief record.

1. *The establishment of the Wesleyan Immigrants' Home.* When tens of thousands a month

were streaming into the then comparatively small and ill-appointed town, nearly the whole even of the most respectable immigrants, however able and willing to pay for decent accommodation, could only find nightly shelter amidst physical and moral disorder and pollution which alike forbid and defy description. Individuals of the best character and of ample means were obliged to walk the streets of the city whole nights, not being able to " obtain accommodation of any kind, on any terms." Schoolrooms, vestries, even churches, were devoted to the charitable object of providing a place where bewildered strangers might lay their heads, who otherwise must have passed the night in the streets. During this state of things, July, 1852, a society meeting was called by the Rev. W. Butters, then Superintendent of the Circuit, " to devise means for obtaining additional ministers." Mr. Powell rose to speak under strong emotion, which he was for some time unable to repress. He stated that on that day, in passing along the street, he had observed a woman weeping, and apparently in deep distress. On inquiring the cause he learnt that she was a member of the Wesleyan Church, who had landed on the preceding day, having come from Tasmania to join her husband at the Ballaarat gold-diggings. She had been unable to obtain sleeping place or shelter, every available spot being crowded, and had been compelled to pass the night on the wharf with no other protection than that afforded by a cask. " He concluded his little narrative by asking, ' Why not have an Immigrants' Home of our own?' 'Why not?' was re-echoed from various parts of the chapel. 'I will give $250 towards it,' said the proposer. 'I will give $250,' said another. 'I will help,' said a third. 'I will give all the ready money I have,' said a fourth." The scheme thus incidentally started was promptly and vigorously carried out. A successful application was immediately made to the Government for the grant of a suitable piece of land; upwards of $3,500 were subscribed at a public meeting called for the furtherance of the object; and "in less than ten days" from the first suggestion of the movement, the arrangements for commencing the erection were complete. The site granted by His Excellency, C. J. Latrobe, Esq., was an eminence commanding a beautiful view, with an open square in front, and a reserve for public gardens at the rear. The word "HOME," in large capitals, greeted the wistful eye of the immigrant, when he first felt the heart of a stranger in a strange land. The object was not only to give a few nights' shelter away from the squalid discomfort and the moral and physical contaminations of the lairs called lodging-houses, but also "to save from utter apostasy those who might have suffered spiritual loss" during a long voyage, amidst a promiscuous and unimproving companionship, and to remind them, in the most kindly and telling manner, that their abandonment of country and kindred, in hope of finding a short cut to wealth and ease, did not lessen the importance and urgency of their eternal interests, or divest them of their Christian responsibilities. The effort was to assimilate all the internal arrangements and usages, as much as possible, to those of a happy Christian family. The immigrants were at once introduced into a hearty, loving, Christian society, and found themselves breathing a pure, bright, kindly, bracing, spiritual atmosphere. Family worship was solemnized morning and evening in the large room, where worship of the dear old home kind was held every Sabbath, and at least on one other evening in the week. Prayer-meetings and experience-meetings were also conducted, and most of the appliances of Methodism, for reviving and sustaining the spiritual life, and for making the members of its churches conscious of their common life, were in full operation. The building comprised one dining-room, accommodating two hundred persons, a sleeping-room for one hundred, one hospital for males, another for females, a library, and reading-room, and private apartments for the governor and matron. It had also a large store for immigrants' luggage, a kitchen, a servants' room, a wash-house, a bake-house, and a lavatory. The amount of bodily, mental and spiritual refreshment, solace and protection, which was thus afforded to thousands deprived of all their wonted supports and restraints, and many of them re-echoing the Prophet's cry, "Weep not for the dead, but weep sore for him that goeth away," cannot be estimated. Perhaps the true scriptural idea of hospitality—*i.e.*, *friendliness to strangers*—was never more effectively carried out on such a scale. Here was a home for the homeless, a welcome to the wanderer, a seat by the fireside, and an affectionate admission to the family circle for those who were cut off from kindred and from fatherland. Here was a sweet smile for the weather-beaten face, a warm clasp for the purseless hand, a gentle tone for the heart that yearned for loved voices far away, a home Church, a family altar, a clean bed, a soft pillow for the weary head, and an exceeding precious promise for the weary heart. Perhaps the venerable and almost obsolete virtue of hospitality—not friendliness to friends, but friendliness to strangers —which the patriarchal religion bequeaths to the elevated ethics of the Gospel, and which the simple manners of classical antiquity commend to our advanced Christian civilization, never received a more congenial entertainment. How much more deserving is this of the name of that antique duty of hospitality which Christianity has enrolled amongst its heavenly train of graces, than the luxurious companionship around the festive board, the round of parties by which familiar acquaintanceship is cemented or commenced, that now usurp the name!

Whilst the primary object of the Wesleyan Immigrants' Home was to make provision for the members of the Wesleyan Church, it was part of the originators' plan to extend the advantage of the institution without restriction to members of other Churches. These principles, prominently set forth at the commencement, have been strictly acted upon, as will be manifest from the following facts. During the first fifteen months of its existence, the number of persons accommodated in the Home was two thousand seven hundred and seventy-three. Fancy

what an aggregate of misery and temptation prevented, of immediate comfort and permanent benefit secured ! The proportions in which the various
denominations of Christendom contributed recipients
were as follows :

```
Wesleyans...............................1,335
Episcopalians...........................  813
Independents............................  184
Baptists................................  103
Presbyterians...........................  229
Lutherans...............................   18
Roman Catholics.........................   30
Friends.................................    4
Primitives, and other Methodist offshoots  50
Moravians...............................    2
Add to these Jews.......................    5
                                        -----
                                        2,773
```

In connection with the Home was a register
office, for supplying information to parties on their
arrival. The cost of the building was $17,500. Mr.
Powell subsequently contributed largely to the formation of a still more extensive institution, sustained
by the general public, whose tardier philanthropy
had been stimulated by the example of the Wesleyans. This was called the Immigrants' Aid Society.
It still exists, affording effective help to numbers who
have fallen into poverty. Of the affairs of this later society, Mr. Powell was one of the most active
administrators.

2. *Additional Church accommodation*, to meet the wants of the thousands who were pouring into the colony. Even before the rush into Victoria commenced, the Church accommodation was deplorably inadequate to the demands of the steadily growing population. The gold discoveries, which created the necessity for enormous Church extension, cast up the most formidable obstacles to the accomplishment of the very modest and cautious plans which had been already initiated. The price of labor and building materials rose in proportion to the demand for both. True, wealth increased, but a very small proportion of that wealth came into the hands of those who were laying to heart the spiritual necessities of the times. The chronic worldliness of the community had, by this sudden stimulus, been aggravated into delirium. As the love of money raged, the love of souls waxed cold in many hearts. For a while the decrease of religious earnestness in the Church was in proportion to the increase of intemperance, debauchery, and the frantic lust of gold. Only a few found time or heart to reflect that this was the crisis in the religious history of the colony. A severer testing-time to character can scarcely be conceived. It could not but become apparent then who really cared for the cause of God. The population of Melbourne had quadrupled in six months. It had already eighty thousand inhabitants, eight thousand of whom, unable to procure houses, were dwelling in tents. Every new cargo of colonists seemed to accelerate the progress of demoralization. In one twelvemonth hamlets had become towns,

and towns had swelled into vast commercial centres. New townships were springing up on every side. Soffala, "the canvas city," Ballaarat, with sixty thousand souls, Mount Alexander, Bendigo, etc., had started into existence. There was, besides, a vast moving multitude, who followed the rumor of some new gold-find. The comparatively few earnest, thoughtful Christians felt that the spiritual destinies of the colony were, to a very great extent, in their hands. And right nobly were they enabled to do their duty. At such a time not only money, but judgment was required, and, by the grace of God, both were forthcoming in a very remarkable measure. By universal and grateful admission, one of the largest contributors of both requisites was Mr. Powell. A gentleman of Melbourne writes: "To my knowledge, nearly every church, of every denomination, in and around Melbourne, secured the help of his purse. One transaction incidentally shows how his business abilities, as well as his business proceeds, were placed at the service of the Church. In consideration of the extravagant costliness, not only of labor, but also of the ordinary building materials, it was deemed expedient to resort to iron. Mr. Powell's acquaintance with the iron trade here stood the Church in good stead. A large shipment of galvanized and corrugated iron was obtained from England. On its receipt, however, the state of things had so far changed that it was not thought desirable to use the metal to the extent formerly contemplated. The surplus was sold at a profit of about $4,000, which was applied opportunely to the building fund for the erection of town and suburban chapels."

3. *Ministerial and Church provision for the gold-fields.* In 1852, at Mount Alexander alone, eighty miles from Melbourne, there were between twenty and thirty thousand persons digging for gold, among whom were hundreds of members of the Wesleyan Methodist societies, without a single Wesleyan minister. At Bendigo, the " rushes," the violent alternations of immigration and exodus, accumulation and dispersion, changed the statistics of population by twenty thousand in a month. The temptations to intemperance were tenfold greater than in England. Profligacy, and adventurous marriage after a few days' acquaintance, were generating all manner of social mischiefs. Hundreds proved to what a sad extent their religion and morality had depended on their surroundings. Both the one and the other, built upon the sand, fell, when home restraints and home supports were left behind. Besides all this, great numbers, like the young heir in the parable, had come " into a far country," for the very purpose of making the worst of themselves, without interference from a father's authority, or a mother's tears, or a public opinion leavened, in great part created, by long-working Christianity. They had sought the antipodes, eager both to make money and to spend it. These new towns became ghastly emporiums of sensuality and sin. *The diggings* became conservatories of vice, huge hotbeds, where moral weeds and poisons flourished in tropical luxuriance. Into this reeking

caldron of a corrupted Christian civilization, many thousands of Chinamen brought their obscene heathen habits. Whence could there come a louder call for a strong body of faithful evangelists?

4. *The formation of the Australian Wesleyan Mission Churches into a distinct and independent communion, with a Conference of its own.* It was never the design of British Methodism either to endow or control Australian Methodism in perpetuity. So soon as they found themselves in a fair way to provide for their own exigencies, and to manage their own affairs, the Australian Methodist Churches ceased to be dependencies, and became associated, or, as the more endearing and descriptive phrase is, "*Affiliated* Conferences." Indeed, they were allowed autonomy before they felt themselves quite ready for financial independence. The axiom of apostolic Christianity announced by St. Paul was thus illustrated by the maternal instincts of Methodism. "The children ought not to lay up for the parents, but the parents for the children." The desire of the Australian Methodists to sustain the responsibilities of manhood so soon as they were conscious of the energies of manhood, was creditable to them; whilst the readiness of the British Conference to recognize their ability, and to encourage their willingness, evidenced that sagacity which belongs to singleness of aim. As to the latter, it showed that the light of their council-fire did not burn dim. A huge Romanistic centralization is as opposed to the true idea of a Church as cerebral congestion is adverse to muscular and mental efficiency.

The difference between economy and parsimony or penuriousness is perhaps nowhere better illustrated than in Methodist missionary administration. The secret of its unparalleled extent and effectiveness, as compared with its resources, must not be sought in niggardly disbursement, but in lessons of self-help to its robust and numerous offspring. Mr. Powell's direct, practical intelligence, his manly trust in God, and his enterprising generosity, led him to enter heartily into this project.

5. *The establishment of a Wesleyan Book Depot in Melbourne.* Of this the Rev. J. C. Symons says: "The Wesleyan Book Depot, *if it does not owe its existence* to Mr. Powell, is at least largely indebted to him for its present position. In order to secure for it the premises in which its business is carried on, he gave $2,500." On the same subject, the Report of the Melbourne District Meeting, 1860, contains the following record: "Walter Powell, Esq., having presented to the Book Committee books of the value of nearly $750, on condition that the Wesleyans of Victoria would raise a similar amount, and having also engaged to present a still further supply to the former on the same condition, the very cordial thanks," etc.

Mr. Symons adds, "Though his conditions were not complied with, he gave his first contribution of books, but devoted the second $750 to the purchase of furniture for the book-steward's residence."

6. *The erection and furnishing of Wesley College.* On this point Mr. Symons testifies: "To no man is that noble institution, Wesley College, so

much indebted as to Mr. Powell. His gifts to its building fund exceeded $1,500, but he gave to it what money could not purchase, earnest personal service." From the first he acted as secretary to the College Committee.

Surely no one can contemplate without dismay the enormous growth of merely commercial colonies, on which but few and feeble influences, intellectual, moral, and spiritual, shall be brought to bear. A monster money-making England at the antipodes, *minus* English culture, Christianized public opinion, and religious services and agencies, would be a chaos and a curse. But it required men of deep minds and deep characters, like Daniel Draper, Walter Powell, and others who survive them, to realize the immediate exigency, and rouse themselves and the public to meet effectually the higher wants of the rapidly multiplying community.

The object of Wesley College was to provide a high-class Christian education for the general public of Victoria, and for the Wesleyans especially. The scheme was launched in 1853, Mr. Powell being chosen a member of the Committee of Management. Owing to the fluctuating condition of affairs, the violent oscillations of trade, and the outrageous price of labor and material, but slow progress was made at first. In the following year, the sum of $100,000 was voted by the Government for the establishment of grammar schools, and allotted to the various religious denominations in proportion to their numerical strength as indicated by the census. $13,847 fell to the share of the

Wesleyans, in two successive grants. Ten acres and a half of land, in a choice situation, were subsequently obtained from the Government, and a large and handsome, and every way suitable, building erected and furnished, at a cost of eighty-five thousand dollars. We shall have to recur to the two last-named enterprises in a later portion of our narrative.

But whilst Mr. Powell was so intent upon the accomplishment of the mission of Methodism in Australia Felix and the fulfilment of its duty to those strange and stirring times, he by no means confined either his liberality or his exertions within the boundary of that large and expanding community. We have seen that he contributed to almost every church in that rapidly-growing neighborhood, where churches were springing up on every hand, and that he was a munificent supporter and an active member of the General Emigrants' Aid Society. In the service of this philanthropic institution and of the Benevolent Asylum he labored day by day. He threw himself enthusiastically into all philanthropic plans, and all movements of public utility. He contributed a large sum towards the establishment of one of the daily newspapers of Melbourne, in which he had no pecuniary interest, moved by a pure conviction that a paper was needed which might call attention to many important social questions that were in danger of being overlooked. One instance of his generosity, which gives a glimpse of his nobility of character, must not be omitted. Learning that Mr. Hargreave, the discoverer of the

Australian gold-fields, was very little advantaged by a scientific revelation which had enriched so many thousands, Mr. Powell most gracefully sent to him anonymously, through the editor of the " Argus " newspaper, $1,250, as an acknowledgment of his own personal indebtedness, and his sense of Mr. Hargreave's claim on the public gratitude.*

But in a very short time the flood-tide of money-getting turned.   People had imagined that the gold-fields were as permanently productive as corn-lands or grazing farms.   They were soon undeceived. The richest gold-finds were soon exhausted.   The outrageous price of goods reached its maximum. The markets were overstocked.   The glut was followed by revulsion.   Commodities of various kinds which had before commanded fabulous sums became utterly unsalable.   Engagements made in sanguine good faith could not be met.   Blocks of half-finished stores and houses stood as mocking monuments of over-eager speculation.   Great snow-balls of quickly-gotten wealth had melted in a summer.   Hundreds elated by swift success had adapted their establishments and modes of living to an exceptional and ephemeral state of things, as if it were normal and perpetual.   Many reproduced the prophetic picture: " Greedy dogs that can never have enough—they all look to their own way, every one for his gain from his quarter.   Come ye, say they, I will fetch wine, and to-morrow shall be as this day, and much more abundant."   Not so Walter Powell.   The little cot-

* The Government voted Mr. Hargreave $2,500, as reimbursement of his travelling expenses.

tage at South Yarra, with its verandah festooned with honeysuckle and jasmine, was unchanged, excepting that a few pictures beautified the walls, and rather better furniture filled the rooms. The habits of the household were not appreciably altered. A friend who had known him in his youth, in giving an account of his impressions of Melbourne, said, "Pleased and astonished as I was with the growth and prosperity of the new city, nothing gratified me so much as to see Walter Powell, with his increased means, still the same." The truth is, the loss of his four children had, in its effect upon his character, counterbalanced all his pecuniary gains. This, with Divine grace, had subdued and chastened him, and corrected any disposition to extravagance. "O Lord, I know that the way of man is not in himself, it is not in man that walketh to direct his steps. O Lord, correct me, but with judgment; not in Thine anger, lest Thou bring me to nothing." Often, the only effective *di*rection is *cor*rection.

But, with all his care and judgment, Mr. Powell suffered very severely, mainly through his multifarious efforts to help others. Those efforts involved him in heavy solicitudes. He thus became obliged to accept the trusteeship and undertake the principal management of many estates. But he received the reward of his prudence and moderation, and his resolution always to keep his business well in hand, in the being enabled to stand firm amidst the general crash. Whilst devoting his leisure, his energy, and his practical ability to the interests of religion and philanthropy, he yet showed much meekness of

wisdom in the steady preference of the less prominent and more lowly walks of usefulness. He per-
sistently held out against repeated requisitions to
enter Parliament; nor would he so much as allow
his name to be placed upon the list of magistrates.
One reason for this retiring spirit was his sensitiveness as to the want of a thorough systematic education in early life; a want which he, however,
with surprising success, labored to supply. Meanwhile, he kept within the sphere for which he felt
himself most fitted. He earnestly devoted himself
to the formation of a fund for the support of aged
ministers and ministers' widows, and to the erection
of the large Wesley Church in Melbourne, said to
be " undeniably the finest church in Australasia," and
pronounced by Dr. Jobson to be " the noblest ecclesiastical edifice in Methodism, surpassing any in
England or America."   He was also an active member of the Committees of the Bible Society and the
Benevolent Asylum, and was especially interested
in the erection of a workshop, that the inmates might
be employed in tailoring, shoemaking, hat-making,
sewing, etc.   He undertook a week-night Bible-
class for the elder Sunday-scholars. He also labored
vigorously in the establishment of an Industrial
Home, and was, in short, " ready for every good
word and work."

All this was done under a solemn sense of responsibility, and from no pitiful ambition, as appears
from such records in his journal as the following:
" I must not be inert, or indefinite in action. By
the Providence of God I am placed in a most re-

sponsible position. *I must work!* work for the Church, and—should the way be made plain—for the State also. No more shrinking; no more self-indulgence; but earnest, sincere, decided effort for the glory of God and the good of man. The ambition is noble to do good and be abundantly useful. May God, the Source of all strength, give me grace and wisdom, and plainly indicate my path, and pardon my offences?" He endeavored, moreover, to animate others by his exhortations, as well as to provoke them by his example, to a course of Christian toil and sacrifice, and to earnest spiritual and mental cultivation. He kept an exact record of the daily disposal of his time, and noticed his progress in self-training. Neither his labors nor his givings were confined to Methodism. He accepted the presidency of the Melbourne Sunday School Union. As organist and choir-master he gave attention to practising the choir, and was extensively employed in drawing up reports on the state, the prospects, and the wisest management of the various Wesleyan institutions in Victoria. He took a statesmanly view of the duties and destinies of Methodism in the Australasian colonies.

In short, the story of Mr. Powell's Life, from this time onward, could it be exactly detailed, would form a continuous chronicle of schemes, sacrifices, and efforts for the public good and the extension of the kingdom of God, and of the " work of faith and labor of love." The simple statement of his benefactions would form a rich lesson on intelligent and conscientious charity. The discretion, discrimination, and judiciousness, by which his munificence was regulated, incalculably enhanced their permanent utility. Yet his givings were not all made in large lumps, or on great occasions. Except when it was necessary to provoke others to good works, his left hand never knew what his right hand did. Most of his donations were entered in no Report, but that which is kept on high.

CHAPTER XI.

In 1856 Mrs. Powell's health gave way so seriously that her medical advisers urged a voyage to England as the most promising remedial measure. This was regarded by Mr. Powell as a providential indication. He was also very anxious to see once more a sister in England who was slowly sinking under an incurable disease. Business had now become more settled, and he clearly saw that a second visit to his native land was necessary to the perfecting his relations with English firms and his general business arrangements. Above all he wished to study in the great centres of trade the principles of legitimate success. He was, however, wide awake to the danger of leaving a large business for a year and a half without its principal. He had recently written to Mr. Butters: "—— has returned from England. Such changes a few months have wrought that he seems to have *lost the run of things.* All the buoys have been taken up during his absence. He helplessly leaves all to ——, being obliged to keep his pilot on board. A warning this to any 'Successful Merchant' who contemplates a change!" But he had such well-founded confidence in the two young men whom he had selected, trained, tested, and taught to feel a personal interest in the business, that he felt quite justified in leaving them in charge, even for so long a time.

The following notices of this second trip to England, written for the amusement of friends, can scarcely fail to interest our readers. They still further illustrate his powers of observation, and his instinctive and indefatigable self-improvement. He also drew up a still more lively account for his little daughter, who accompanied her parents, and invited a large party of juveniles almost immediately on her return to Melbourne, to hear her read the history of her travels and "surprising adventures."

"MY SECOND VOYAGE TO ENGLAND.

" The romance associated with a voyage round the world in the days of Captain Cook is quite dispelled. Whether accomplished in steam-ship or sailing-vessel, nothing but disaster can invest it with the charms of adventure. With a lively remembrance of the dulness of the voyage in a sailing-vessel, I resolved that my next trip should be by steam, and ' by the Overland Route.' We left Melbourne in the ' Oneida,' a pioneer ship of a new company, the European and Australasian. She was a beautifully-appointed vessel, but, alas! soon proved herself unfit for her voyage. Our first run was to Nepean Bay, situated in the centre of Kangaroo Island. Here we were met by the ' Adelaide ' steamer, from whose deck we received mails, and several additional passengers. With scarce an hour's delay, onward we rushed to Albany, King George's Sound, a fine harbor in Western Australia. The vessel was detained here twelve hours for the purpose of coaling, an operation duly appreciated only by those who have had the privilege of witnessing it. No passenger is hardy enough to remain on board while coaling is proceeded with. Two huge barges are moored to the steamer, one on either side. Scores of begrimed figures commence shooting coals out of heavy bags into the vessel's hold; an impenetrable cloud of fine black dust arises, covering the deck, choking up the saloon, and filling the sleeping cabins like a London fog. We had used foresight enough to stow away every article damageable by coal-powder, and imagined that we had made our cabins coal-powder proof, by hanging up sheets and towels against the Venetian blinds; but as well might Pharaoh have tried to keep the vindictive vermin from his bedchamber.

"Coaling complete, we point the vessel's head towards Ceylon. This run should be accomplished in fourteen or fifteen days; but within forty-eight hours our machinery gave way, and our fine ship was utterly disabled. Many consultations are held as to what must be done; some eager to reach home propose to push on to Batavia, but as the ship proved almost helpless under sail, it was finally resolved to turn her head, and make for King George's Sound once more, and there await the next mail-steamer. This was more easily attempted than accomplished, with a vast unwieldly vessel, clogged by useless machinery and baffled by contrary winds. Day followed day, without bringing us any nearer to our desired harbor of refuge; but at length the engineer, who showed great skill and resource, succeeded in so patching up the engine that we could proceed at quarter-speed. We regained St. George's Sound in sixteen days, having retraced a distance previously passed in two. Our joy on reaching it was much tempered by the information that the mail-steamer, the 'Simla,' a magnificent ship, had left the harbor the day previously with a very moderate number of passengers. There was nothing for it but to wait here a month for the next mail. Albany is a small town, with not more than two or three hundred inhabitants; so the passengers insisted that the ship should be detained, and utilized as a floating hotel. Our detention, of course, was weary enough, but happily the weather was fine, the country charming, and the inhabitants obliging. Almost every day the passengers went on shore, the captain placing the ship's boats at their disposal, and made agreeable little explorations. The gentlemen found amusement in rabbit shooting, fishing, etc. The natives, too, afforded no little diversion. We were soon on very friendly terms with them. They readily danced the *corroborce*, dived, and threw their spears and boomerangs for our delectation. We visited the native school, and observed a higher type of intelligence amongst the aborigines of Western Australia than amongst those of Victoria. The children could read, write, and sew well; but we heard the same story here, as in the other colonies, that after a time they abscond to their native wilds, not being able to endure the thraldom of civilization. One incident, especially, served to break the monotony of our detention. One of our passengers, a squatter from Queensland, had fallen in love with a young lady on board. They turned our misfortune to good account by getting married at Albany. There was some little difficulty in procuring for the bride a sufficient *trousseau*, no provision having been made for the contingency of a wedding. The little town was ransacked for contributions to the lady's gear, and her bridal dress was at last the joint present of the passengers and townsfolk. One sad event, however, marred our merriment. The boatswain, firing a salute in honor of the event, shot off two of his fingers. A liberal subscription was immediately made for the poor man, who had a wife and family.

"After we had lost nearly seven weeks, the 'European' mail-steamer arrived. She was a noble ship, but had already almost her full complement of passengers; and pitiable was the disappointment and discomfort inflicted on them by the crowding in of some sixty new-comers. All was endured, however, with exemplary good feeling. Our voyage was now resumed in good earnest.

"On steamer, as on shore, there are ranks, orders, and degrees. The Englishman carries his reserve and taciturnity along with him to the ends of the earth and the uttermost parts of the sea. It may have been modified to some extent by the great freedom which prevails in colonial social life; but enough is always left to constitute a formidable bar-

rier to anything like a swiftly-formed acquaintance-
ship, even in our small ship-world. Meal-times afford the greatest facilities for fraternization. The
habit of feeding together is wonderfully equalizing
and uniting. The necessity for social amusement
perforce brings and binds for a time people together.
Here, as elsewhere, self-interest is the great bond of
union amongst average human beings. Even in our
little community, numberless, though vain, were the
efforts of the lower ranks to creep into the upper.
It is quite natural to depreciate and affect to despise
those who happen to be above us, but we soon re-
verse our prejudices if once admitted into the
charmed circle, and begin to wonder at the vulgar
pretensions of those whose society we once enjoyed.
Still, even in this ignoble tendency, the good pre-
dominates; the desire to improve our position puts
us on our good behavior, and thus improves our
manners. Our movements and conversation are
placed under a sensitive and rigid, though half-un-
conscious, self-inspection; and we gradually become
fitted to mingle, not ungracefully, with the higher
rank. Distinctions of rank would be less marked
on ship-board but for the presence of the ladies.
They are your true aristocrats, and will permit no
encroachment on what they regard as their own do-
main.

"The discipline to which one is subjected on ship-
board is, like all other discipline, less pleasant than
profitable. So closely packed together, brought
into close contact with people you never saw before,
cut off from those whom you have been accustomed

to associate with, thrown together, and shut up with
a society not one element of which is of your own
selection ; debarred from your usual employments,
you have need of patience. If you would pass your
time agreeably, you must rein your tongue and curb
your temper. You must learn to be calm and cheerful in circumstances tending to disturb and depress.
Those who will not learn these lessons expose themselves to constant punishment, and turn for themselves a steamer into a house of correction. If they
quarrel, there is no getting away from their opponents. There they are, and there are their enemies, in close and inevitable proximity. The proud
and scornful must learn to deport themselves with
humility and deference, or no quarter will be given
to their airs and imperiousness. Nor, in discussion,
will a vehement or dogmatic manner be tolerated
for an hour in the saloon of a first-class steamer, as
you are sure to find some one capable of casting a
chill upon your overheated self-importance. Then
you will assuredly be tried by annoyances inepara-
ble from your cramped position (having little space
for bodily exercise), squeamishness, and the rapid
change of climate. From a moderate temperature
you may be suddenly plunged into the tropical
summer. Prickly heat breaks out all over you, and
worries you for a week. These and other disagree-
ables, nameless and numberless, will find out your
less amiable peculiarities. Whatever may have been
a man's apparent character at the outset of a long
voyage, his real disposition and principles will disclose themselves before he lands. ' Do you know

7

so and so?' said a person to an old Scotchman. 'I canna say I ken the mon,' was his reply; 'I never lived with 'um.' On ship-board you *do live with* one another, and find it a shrewd test of character. All that was latent is there developed. You gain such a view of a man there, that your judgment is not likely to need any future correction. That passenger, so reserved and silent at the beginning of the voyage, is not at all unlikely to prove the most companionable and loquacious man on board. Yon dignified personage will probably turn out to have learnt little else but *deportment* (the weakest animals have some means of self-defence). Those who profess 'the broadest charity' and the 'broadest creed' soon convict themselves of narrowness in both. Some who have overwhelmed you with pitiless erudition, reveal in good time their unfathomable superficiality. We had an old gentleman on board, who for a while quite astounded us by his learning and originality. By and by we found that he was constantly priming himself on some particular subject, and *letting* himself off at the company. When his stock of books was exhausted, the fountain suddenly became dry. No duller or more unconversable man could be found amongst us than this accomplished individual! He was worthy of the talented young lady, who, having charmed an evening party with the brilliancy of her conversation on a variety of topics which she had herself introduced, was struck dumb by the incidental starting of a much simpler subject by another person. It turned out that she was reading through the 'Penny

Cyclopædia,' and having only waded as far as the letter G, was quite out of her depth on any theme which had the misfortune to bear an initial letter later in the alphabet.

" One of our fellow-passengers was at first remarkable for his exuberant and perennial flow of spirits. The prodigal soon wasted his substance. When disaster and delay came, he suddenly turned sour. Some—fortunately very few—endeavored to drown ennui in deep potations; but this unnatural resource proved a cup of bitterness to them all. They immediately lost caste in our community, and found themselves drafted off to a marine Coventry. And so, as we steam on, the mask falls off, or the veil is by degrees withdrawn, and the contour charms in many instances, but disgusts in others."

In few men were the educational advantages of travel more apparent than in Mr. Powell. To his long and frequent voyages were, doubtless, traceable not only much of his general *savoir faire*, but much also of his breadth of view, catholicity of sentiment, and the easy frankness of his bearing. Yet all this keen appreciation of external interests, and vivid insight into character, did not perceptibly diminish the deep undercurrent of religious earnestness, or interfere with his spirituality and inwardness of mind. Happily his profound personal experience of religion, the inward miracles which had left their abiding memorials on his own consciousness and character, formed an impregnable basis of certainty in all promiscuous discussions on religious questions. Yet he had enough to depress and disturb him, besides the vexatious prolongation of the voyage and his confinement in Albany for the term of one calendar month. The relieving steamer brought very bad commercial news from Victoria, calculated to awake intense anxiety as to the effect of his absence upon his own affairs. But his confidence in God rescued him from unavailing solicitudes.

We shall now recur to the journal.

"April 3d, 1857.—Sighted the light-house of Point de Galle, Ceylon. The harbor is small, and much exposed, and the swell greater than out at sea. The canoes (*catamarans*, as they are called) of the natives are very singular, and ingeniously adapted to the peculiarities of the harbor, being narrow and deep, and from twenty to thirty feet in length, and having an outrigger in the shape of a curved pole at each end, with a crescent-shaped log fastened at their points, which renders them peculiarly safe, though so fragile in appearance, and capable of withstanding the heaviest sea. The coast scenery is very beautiful; the surf bursts in most majestically. No sooner had we anchored than we were beset with native boats, soliciting the passengers to land, and asking us to let them have our clothes to wash. This they accomplish with great expedition. My wife gave out four dozen in the morning, and had them back by four P.M. exquisitely clean. But the natives are the greatest cheats I have yet met with, asking a sovereign for an article for which they would gladly take sixpence. The town is prettily situated, and the trees planted in the streets give it a very picturesque and Oriental appearance. The streets are beautifully gravelled and perfectly level, and the country roads are as straight and as smooth as a table. The houses are built of small stones, stuck together with mortar, and are roofed with burnt tiles. We proceeded to the Light-house Hotel, not without difficulty; for all the innkeepers have their noisy agents; and at the corner of every street, as in an English port, your hands are crammed with cards and placards from the various shops. At the hotel they required an hour and a half to prepare our breakfast. We took a one-horse vehicle, bearing some resemblance to a cab, and called on the Wesleyan missionary, Mr. Ripon. We were sorely tempted to purchase some of the beautiful ornamental articles manufactured here: work-boxes, etc., of tortoise and other shells and various woods, ebony elephants, etc. We drove out to Wachwalla, about five miles, and had a fine view of the country. The refreshing groves of cocoa-nut trees finely contrasted with the dark leafage of the mango. The indigenous flowers are strikingly beautiful, and grow wild in every direction. The roads are narrow, but so pleasantly shaded, that although in the latitude of five degrees we did not find the heat oppressive. We also saw the cinnamon plant, the nutmeg, and the lemongrass. After dining at the hotel, we had to run the gauntlet back to the jetty, and by dint of resolution managed, in spite of distracting vociferation, threatening, and abuse, to get all our luggage into one boat, and treated to a native song, with wild chorus, by the boatmen, reached the ship in safety at two o'clock in the morning.

"April 13th.—Aden. The dreariest and most desolate place imaginable. Went on shore in one of the Arab boats; not a tree or blade of grass to be discovered. Dark brown masses of lava, grotesquely sharp, and craggy, from a hundred to a thousand feet in height, and fortified in every available part. It is stated that upwards of a million sterling has been expended on the fortifications. You approach the town by a *pass* deeply cut through the volcanic rock, guarded by sentinels and bristling with cannon. The population consists of Armenians, Jews, Arabs, negroes, and Abyssinians. We managed to get a one-horse conveyance, capable of holding four passengers. The driver agreed to take us to the town and back for twelve shillings. Most of the passengers procured donkeys, some horses, and we made for the town pell-mell. Every donkey and horse was accompanied by its owner, holding on by the tail, or running alongside, belaboring the animal with a stick. Ever and anon the owner would pull up, and insist upon further payment, before he would allow the unfortunate rider to proceed. By dint of hard words and harder blows, our fellow-passengers cleared this difficulty.

"The negroes and Arabs appear capable of any amount of endurance; they run about without any covering to their heads, and with scarcely any to their bodies, apparently unaffected by the burning rays of the almost vertical sun. We met long strings of camels, troop of donkeys laden with water-skins,

and a flock of black and white long-haired sheep.
Three or four hundred wretched, dirty, flat-roofed
huts, a few shops, and an inn, compose the town,
which stands within the crater of an extinct volcano.
The shops are kept by Parsees with a strong Jewish
physiognomy. The whole scene seemed curse-
stricken; and we were glad enough to get away from
it."

On reaching England, Mr. Powell was distressed
to find that the "Oneida's" break-down had deprived him of the privilege of spending with his sister the last fortnight of her life. She had died five
weeks before his arrival. Mr. and Mrs. Powell
spent ten months in England, broken by a seven-
weeks' trip to the United States. But Mr. Powell
allowed himself very brief holiday. Almost the
whole time was devoted to strenuous business. He
made a complete tour of the manufacturing districts
of England and Scotland, making himself especially
familiar with the manufacture of all the goods in
which he traded, visiting all the iron-works of any
note, ascertaining which were the best firms, taking
notes and writing in his journal descriptions of the
most interesting and ingenious processes, and gathering useful information from every available source.
Almost the only recreation he allowed himself was
a visit to the Manchester Exhibition of Fine Arts.

CHAPTER XII.

MR. AND MRS. POWELL embarked for America
Sept. 26, 1857. The voyage was very pleasant, their
companion voyagers being many of them American
clergymen and Christian laymen who were returning from the Conference of the Evangelical Alliance
at Berlin. They passed through the skirts of the
cyclone in which the " Central America " steamship
foundered.*

They landed at Boston, and were " charmed with
the elegance of its public and private buildings, and
the loveliness of the surrounding scenery." After
visiting the neighboring places of historic interest,
they proceeded to New York, and found that all
they " had heard and read of the combined splendor
and comfort of American hotels and steamboats
rather fell short of than exaggerated the reality."

* Mr. Powell records a remarkable incident in connection with
this melancholy wreck. The captain of a vessel, hailing from
Havana, observed a small bird fluttering peculiarly and anxiously about his deck, flying back again repeatedly in the same
direction, and returning. He was so impressed with this as to
change his course in the direction taken by the bird, and at
length came in sight of a raft, to which several men were cling-
ing in the last stage of exhaustion.

While in New York, Mr. Powell devoted his mornings to business, having crossed the Atlantic mainly with the view of extending his commercial connections in America. The latter part of the day was given up to inspection of the city. Whilst there he received an impressive lesson on the evils of over-trading. The following extracts from letters record his American experiences:

"New York, October 23d and 24th, 1857.—On arriving here, I found myself in the midst of the most terrible financial panic which this great commercial city has ever experienced. In one day twenty of the fifty-two New York banks suspended payment, and the next day all the banks throughout the State followed their example. Firms of the most undoubted standing, and having three times as much in stock and property as they owed, had succumbed to the pressure, and been compelled either to become bankrupt, or, at least, to suspend payment. All this has come upon them in six weeks, and doubtless is owing to their having pushed their railways along too quickly, and to over-trading and general extravagance. I cannot help thinking, however, that they have frightened themselves more than was necessary, as they had very fine crops this season, and will have an enormous amount of breadstuffs to export besides their cotton. This must have a bad effect in England, if it do not cause a crisis. It will certainly occasion many failures and a stringent money market, for America trades with England to the extent of two hundred millions of dollars per annum. I scarcely think that Australia will soon be revisited

7*

by commercial crisis, unless the Government plunge into plans for making many railroads at once. This panic, passing under my immediate observation, teaches me that no man in business is safe who has many bills payable and a large discount account. As it is not at all unlikely that England may be severely tried with her Indian war and her American debtors, that the banks will tighten their strings and interest rule high, take care that the rebound does not hit you; for not America only, but France and Germany also, are at present in severe commercial distress. I need not say anything on the subject of remittances, as you will send all you can consistently with your own comfort and safety.

" As the panic increased, people sold for £14 or £16 discount. I declined to sell bills at such enormous loss, and therefore shall not buy until exchange is better. If, on my return to England, I find any order for American goods, I shall have it put in hand, if possible; for, although exchange to me may be charged at £5 or £6 loss, the scarcity of American goods in your market will bring this up. There are so many American ports from which they ship to Australia, that I cannot learn how many vessels are laid on. They must be very few, however; for the panic is so great that confidence is gone, and most people have to go to market with dollars down. Since they will not let me work in America, I intend to play; and while acquiring all the information I can, I mean also to see all I can. I came down to New York (from Boston) in one of their splendid river boats, which will accommodate a thousand people. Until you see them, you can have no conception what a vessel may be brought to. They have three decks, and saloons from one end to the other. They measure from three hundred to three hundred and fifty feet.

"The streets here, like ours, are mostly at right angles. The celebrated Broadway is not so broad as Melbourne streets, but is of great length. The buildings go up four or five stories, on walls only fourteen inches thick. They are, however, very handsome, many of the fronts being all of white marble. We stayed at an hotel where fourteen hundred people can be accommodated. We went by boat up the magnificent river Hudson, one hundred and fifty miles, then by rail to Niagara. We stood upon the Table Rock dressed like Esquimaux, and went under the great Horse-Shoe Fall, not nearly such a difficult or heroic undertaking as some represent it. We crossed to the opposite side in a little boat, which every moment seemed as if it must be overturned, yet was perfectly safe. We thought the rapids, as seen from Prospect Tower, quite as wonderful as the great Fall itself. All the arrangements for travelling are more perfect, methodical, and safe in America than in any other country. I paid six dollars and a quarter each for travelling the three hundred and fifty miles by rail, and only a dollar and a half each for going up the Hudson by steamer. But they are beginning to find out that they run a much lower rate than will pay. We saw Lakes Erie and Ontario. I give you but a skeleton report, but hope to clothe the skeleton on my return. I shall not be so prosy as to give you full descriptions of the places we have seen, thinking these things better said than sung.

" We intended to proceed to Montreal, but, as the lake steamer would not face a strong wind that was blowing, after three days' waiting, we got tired, and returned to New York. We went to Buffalo and to Rochester to see the Genesee Falls. They are very grand, but, passing through the town, have not the charm of the clear, pure waters of Niagara. We spent Sunday at Rochester, attended the Methodist chapel, and were shocked by the irregular behavior of the congregation, who were talking loudly until the service commenced.

" We found that, splendid as were the interior arrangements of the boat on Lake Ontario, she was in very bad condition ; so declined to commit our persons to her. We afterwards heard that she was lost that very day, and twenty persons drowned.

" I hope to discuss with you the Yankee mode of living, their churches, and preachers ; but you must neither expect a sound judgment nor a correct description, as I am only a flying traveller. With the country I am delighted, and do not wonder at the progress of the people ; but the prodigal gifts of Nature make the people prodigal in their expenditure. What a wonderfully happy nation they might be, if they did not live so fast ! What misery they are now passing through ! and the sufferings of the unemployed during the coming winter, no one can contemplate without deep commiseration. The present agony must surely teach them a valuable lesson ; and I have little doubt that their heavy losses will deter English capitalists from again trusting to anything so rotten as Yankee rail-roads."

Mr. Powell was characteristically interested in, and impressed by, the immense American Methodist " Book Concerns ; " and spent a considerable part of his time in visiting them. He had purposed spending a much longer period in America, but the panic compelled him to change his plans. The house on which he had letters of credit failed ; the apprehension of a commercial crisis in England, and the setting-in of the wet weather, induced his speedy return. He was in Wall Street on the day of the great rush upon the banks, and " saw money handed out of the doors and windows to the alarmed and excited crowds. The great stores were selling off, and elegantly-dressed ladies were seen in Broadway, hauling great packages of goods, purchased at immensely reduced prices."

Mr. and Mrs. Powell afterwards visited Philadelphia, and left America on the 28th, reaching Liverpool on the 9th of November. Mr. Powell spent the winter busily in London ; where, in February, 1858, a son was born to him. Unfavorable news of the state of trade in Victoria reached England by the February mail ; but owing to the judicious mode in which his business was conducted, " amid extensive failures," he " lost no more than £30 altogether ; " and taking everything into consideration, the profit was not only unexpected but unexampled.

In April, 1858, Mr. and Mrs. Powell commenced their return journey; spending two or three weeks in Paris, and a few days at Lyons, where their only British-born babe died of cholera; and a fortnight in Egypt, where they nearly lost their sole surviving child. From Galle to Melbourne the voyage was protracted and uncomfortable. They were several weeks without fresh meat, and the machinery was incessantly breaking down; "the Peninsular and Oriental Company not having then the monopoly of the route." He resolved, should he ever visit England again, not to return by the Overland Route. "It is a great risk to bring children that way."

On reaching Melbourne, a fortnight overdue, Mr. Powell found his business "quite snug," and at once gave its managers very substantial proof of his grateful appreciation of their services.

He was "received with overflowing cordiality," and two days after his arrival received a requisition to stand for the Upper House; but thought he could make a better investment of his time, until fitted by a regular course of study for such responsible duties. He was astonished at the progress which Melbourne had made during his absence; not only had it increased in size, but also in beauty and convenience; whilst "in the suburbs, or small municipalities, the opening of new roads had quite changed the character of the scenery." Four new railways had been commenced.

Mr. Powell took a house, overlooking the bay, three miles from town, but only eight minutes by rail. He at once recommenced his activities in the Church, and accepted "the post of organist in the Wesleyan Church at St. Kilda, and the superintendency of the Sunday-school." He at once prepared a definite plan for continuous self-education.

He writes in his diary, September 15, 1858: "I have now, what I never before possessed,—a large library, and a room for reading and study. Next month I take into partnership the two young men who managed my business so faithfully during my absence. I only work at the business now from ten to one o'clock, but the rest of my time is completely occupied by Church matters, attending committees, and by reading, etc.; in fact, I have no disposition to waste time." In less than a month, he reduced his attendance on business to two hours daily. Mr. Symons testifies that, at this period, "Mr. Powell gave up the greater portion of his time to the general weal, for which he labored incessantly and most usefully." In order that he might be at liberty for the service of the Church, he kept himself as free as possible not only from political, but also from commercial engagements extraneous to his own business, declining even to be a director of the National Bank. He, however, felt bound to perform the duties of citizenship, by serving as a city councillor. He also labored hard in the humblest departments of Christian charity. His diary contains entries like the following:

"February 27th, 1859.—Hearing of Mr. ——'s continued illness, I went over and stayed with him through the night."

The following was his plan of study at this period :

" Monday.—Mathematics, English history, music."

" Tuesday. Morning.—Grammar. Afternoon.— Music and ' M'Culloch's Dictionary.' "

" Wednesday.—Mathematics, English history, music."

" Thursday.—Grammar, English history, music."

" Friday.—Mathematics, English history, music."

" Saturday.—Set apart for preparing the ' Address to the Sunday-school children.' "

Thus he labored with conscientious steadiness to fit himself for the position in which Providence had placed him, and

> " Followed thus the ever-running year
> With profitable labor."

He, notwithstanding, found that the exigent claims of the Church and the secular community so consumed his time and strength as to baffle to a great extent his best-laid plans of personal cultivation. Besides this, the insidious disease, which a few years afterwards brought him to the grave in the high summer-tide of life, was beginning to check his energies ; and, since the truth must be told, his generosity had surrounded him with so many claimants on his pecuniary resources, who practically assumed that his beneficence gave them a vested interest in his property—a prescriptive right to fall back on him, whenever and from whatever cause, or for whatever purpose, they thought a little ready money might be of service to them, that like some stately tropical forest-tree, he was in danger of being dragged down by parasitical vegetation. He therefore resolved, early in 1860, to spend three years in England, to give his constitution a chance of recovery, and his mind the enrichment and enlargement which he believed that the responsibilities of his position required.

On the day of his embarkation, a number of gentlemen of Melbourne and its vicinity entertained him at a valedictory *déjeûner*, and presented him with an address, expressive of their high sense of his worth. The Hon. A. Fraser presided. The following paragraph appeared in the Melbourne " Wesleyan Chronicle," March, 1860 :

" Mr. Powell's departure from the colony is justly felt to be for many reasons a Connectional loss. He has been associated with all our public movements, and by his princely liberality and sagacious counsels greatly contributed to their success. We are glad to learn, however, that Mr. Powell purposes to return after the lapse of two or three years."

He again varied his route, coming by way of the Mauritius, where he had a two days' drive into the interior of the island, seeing all that is most remarkable. He was much struck by the beauty of the scenery and the vegetation, the goodness of the roads, the plenteousness of the markets, and the brilliant colors of the fish—" vivid blue, scarlet, green," etc.

On arriving in London Mr. Powell at once vigorously recommenced his course of study. His

diary records his humble, painstaking labors He
set apart six hours daily to this duty, and corresponded with Dr. Beard on the suggestions given in .
his work on Self-culture. In the autumn he visited
Dr. Guthrie's Ragged School in Edinburgh, and
took the opportunity of seeing the Scotch and English lakes.

He closed the year 1860 and began 1861 in what
can scarcely be called a *mood* of humble and all-
consecrating gratitude, since it was but the intensi-
fying by reflection of his habitual state of heart.
His entry for Christmas day runs thus : "I was
never more affected on any former Christmas than
I am on this by the innumerable benefits bestowed
upon me by my great Redeemer. My heart glows
with gratitude.   May the flame be never quenched!"
That for the last day of the year was as follows:
"Spent the evening alone, acknowledging the mercies of God during the past year, and deploring my
deficiencies as a Christian."

On the first of January, 1861, he entered into
partnership with Mr. Henry Reed, an Australian
merchant, by whose earnest and pointed discourses
as a lay-preacher in Tasmania he had been so much
benefited more than twenty years before, when he
was a young clerk in Tasmania. The offices were
at 6, Broad Street Buildings, since taken down to
make way for the Broad Street Terminus. Although he undertook the entire management of the
business, Mr. Reed having just lost his partner, Mr.
Hawley, and being himself advanced in life, Mr.
Powell had no doubt that he "should be able to

conduct it with facility," as it was based upon the self-same principles which he had years before adopted, and to which he was resolved to adhere, principles which, by regularity and moderation, saved a world of trouble and anxiety, and enabled him to carry on immense transactions with ease, comfort, and security. He wrote to the Rev. Daniel J. Draper, detailing the reasons which induced him to protract his stay in England, for so long a period as seven years, the term to which his partnership extended, and expressing an earnest hope that he might be yet spared to spend several years in Victoria, giving a sketch of the state of Methodism in London, and inquiring how he might best help the Church in Australia.

Thus the ambition of his boyhood was realized, and that by the most direct and honorable means, in fact, by God's blessing on the observance of God's own laws. He was now a London merchant, his office being within a few minutes' walk of that which his father had left more than forty years before.

In the summer of that year he had an enfeebling attack of scarlatina; recovering from which, he felt it necessary to take a month's tour in France, Switzerland, and Germany, attending the meeting of the Evangelical Alliance at Geneva, and returning by the Rhine "in the same boat with the King of Prussia." He embarked for England at Rotterdam, and reached home, feeling "fit for another twelve-month's wear and tear."

His record for January the 1st, 1862, is as follows: "Began the new year in Bayswater Chapel with joy. Reviewing the past year, I felt that I had every reason to thank God, and take courage. I dedicate myself to Thy service, O God! body, soul, and spirit. May the time past suffice wherein I have transgressed Thy law! May loving gratitude urge me onward to every good work! May I redeem the time; cast off 'the works of darkness,' and put on the whole armor of light!" In accordance with this renewed dedication to the service of God, he consented to undertake the superintendency of the Wesleyan Sunday-school, Denbigh Road, Bayswater.

He took full advantage of the great Exhibition of 1862, as an extraordinary opportunity of acquiring information in the most interesting and effective manner. For this he had special facilities, as he resided at Kensington, within easy reach of the great palace of Industry and Art. On the 25th of October, he writes to a friend in Melbourne: "I have been to take a last fond look, a melancholy farewell of the most beautiful and varied collection the world has ever seen. I must not indulge in descriptions, though I could write a volume of 'Personal Experiences in the Exhibition,' but inexorable business commands me to proceed to ordinary topics."

The record for January the 1st, 1863, is as follows: "Spent the last minutes of 1862 and the first of 1863 in communion with the God in whose hand my breath is and whose are all my ways."

On the 22d of December, 1863, he notified to his

young partners in Melbourne, an important change in his business relations in England: "Mr. Reed has proposed to retire from business, and make it over entirely to me. After due reflection and consultation with my friend Mr. William M'Arthur,* I have agreed, and the dissolution of partnership will take place at the end of this month."

The entry in his diary on January 1st, 1864, is, "May the God of all grace be honored by the new firm in all our transactions, His will done, and His blessing secured!"

* Now M.P. for Lambeth.

CHAPTER XIII.

HIS SINGLENESS OF PURPOSE AND CONSCIENTIOUS RE-GARD TO THE DIVINE COMMANDS.

WE have now reached that period in Mr. Powell's life in which it may be convenient to pause, and ascertain his business principles. Happily we have ample data for a correct and complete estimate. He was now conducting a large business in London, and, at the same time, directing other large businesses in Australia. All his letters were written in duplicate, and not on scattered sheets, but in prepared "Writing Copying Books." His entire business correspondence for the last ten years of his life is now in my possession. I have read it through again and again with keen enjoyment, and studied it with much moral and religious profit. The first, second, third, and last point which strikes one is—conscientiousness, simple regard for the will of God. He had, as already stated, carefully studied the principles of legitimate success in trade. He had also habituated himself to a heroic spiritual training, by means of which he kept in check the trading spirit, and maintained an internal isolation — the life and peace of spiritual-mindedness in the midst of brisk and arduous commerce.

Upon his conversion, he set before himself a

clear and definite life-purpose. That purpose was not bounded by the present world—it was not even based upon the present world. He began his new life in this world with the strong conviction and vivid realization of the life to come. Under the impression of a near view of eternity, calmly calculating the probabilities of the shortness of his own earthly existence, he deliberately laid his plans for a very long life—a life which death should not terminate, or even interrupt. He profoundly believed " in the life everlasting." Christ was " made to " him " wisdom," first, in those matters in which the keenest and shrewdest are oftenest in error. He saw that the life which now is, derives all its value and significance from that which is to come. Hence the sensitive and solicitous introspection, that self-scrutiny and self-severity, which marked the delicate and overworked young clerk. Doubtless, that severity was sometimes mistaken, and even morbid, but under its keen husbandry a true and noble character was shooting up. Sincerity was the root, consistency the stem, and benevolence the flower. Hence Mr. Powell's business life was not a something apart, or even distinct, from his spiritual life. Business was part of his religion, whilst religion was the whole of his business. His character was all of a piece—" woven from the top throughout." His exceptional success in business was not the great lesson of his life. He would have been as good and as exemplary a man if he had not succeeded, and yet his success was the natural sequence of his principles, qualities, and habits.

Prosperity in his case was a providential award to a trustworthy servant, according to the principle, "To him that hath shall be given, and he shall have abundance." Affluence was added unto him, as he was intently seeking "the kingdom of God and His righteousness." Though evidently born for business, and feeling in it the keen enjoyment and exhilaration of conscious power exercising itself in its native element—being in this sense *fervent in spirit*, whilst *not slothful in business*—he yet never allowed business to become with him a ruling passion. It was never—what with him *giving* always was—a dominant propensity, requiring to be kept in check. It was throughout a secondary and subordinate consideration. The charm of business to him was not the excitement of acquisition or the pride of possession, nor does he seem ever to have developed that genius for commerce which triumphs in driving a hard bargain, and exults in outwitting and outwilling all with whom trade brings one into contact. Business was to him simply a department of duty; success meant enlarged facilities for spiritual and mental cultivation, the means of helping the needy and deserving, and contributing to the material resources of the kingdom of God; and the speedier attainment of such an income as would justify his retiring from business, making way for younger men, and devoting himself to the humble offices of Christian philanthropy.

It is impossible to understand and correlate the business qualities of Mr. Powell without noting how they all grew out of this root—all radiated from this centre, *regard to the will of God and the interests of the eternal future*. It could not be justly said of him, " Mr. Powell is a very religious man, and very free with his money, *but* he certainly has a great talent for stealing a march upon you and beating you down in price, and he makes good use of it." All through life, he was not so much an auctioneer's clerk, or a warehouseman, or a commission agent, or a merchant, as a *doer of the Word*. Hence that conscientiousness and consistency, that *keeping*—to use an artist's phrase—and that roundness of character which impressed all who had the opportunity of watching him. Hence his character was as clear, translucent, and homogeneous as the object-glass of a great telescope; and for the same reason—it had been fused again and again in the white heat of affliction. He might well say with David, " Thy loving correction hath made me great." (Psalm xviii., Prayer Book version.) There was no incongruity, no distinction between his saintly and his secular life. His moral excellencies so shaded off into each other that it was impossible to trace the boundary-line between shrewdness and generosity, or to say where benevolence ended and cautiousness began. His estimable qualities did not seem to inhere in separate organs, but to be universally interfused. A keen observer of character remarked to the writer: " Mr. Powell seemed to me a rare exception to the general rule, ' The children of this world are in their generation wiser than the children of light;' for he brought into his religion all the acuteness, energy, and system which

8

distinguished him as a man of business."　An eminent Congregationalist minister, the Rev. Henry Allon, one of the editors of the "British Quarterly," gives the following testimony:

"In the whole of my acquaintance I know no one who impressed me with more perfect esteem for the reality, simplicity, and naturalness of his piety.　He walked with God, in the common ways of life, and with the natural gait of men; and made devout service of God not a separate thing of life, but life itself.　We hardly suspect how quickly quiet goodness like his comes upon us until we are called upon to estimate what we have lost."

Yet his spiritual-mindedness sat naturally upon him.　He never attempted a compromise between the interests of this world and the next.　No one could detect in him two interchangeable characters —a man of business and a religious man.　The whole mass of his secular dealings and duties was leavened by the spirit of his Christianity.　He had not one class of feelings and one economy of action for the Sabbath, and another for the six days. His Sabbath was the first day of the week, and not the last.　It did not just wipe off the shortcomings of the six days, but gave to them its own celestial tone, and imbued them with its sacred influence. He never accommodated himself to the conventional code of worldly morality, but witnessed against it by his whole spirit and conduct.

His business letters to his friends, with reference to the choice of *employés* or partners, and his lectures to young men, overflow with the conviction that Christian character is the only *sure* ground of trustworthiness in business, and that sound conversion to God is the only true basis of Christian character. To the Young Men's Mutual Improvement Society, Denbigh Road, Bayswater, he says: "All your labor will be in vain, unless you have first sought 'the kingdom of God and His righteousness.' Your first care must ever be to keep your hearts in a right relation to God. Having this peace, through Jesus Christ, you may then safely pray, 'Lord, increase my abilities.'"

Again, in his lecture on "Development," he reminds them, "Spiritual development must be first. Many excellencies you may acquire, by sheer industry, because you already possess their germ. But the power which is to change your heart comes not by nature. It must be obtained from God. Rejecting every other mode by which men seek it, throw yourself helpless before God, and ask, ask, never cease to ask, until He gives you His Holy Spirit. You will then stand in the relation to God of a loving child to a loving Father; and henceforth grow in grace, and in the knowledge of your Lord and Saviour."

To a friend in Australia, asking him to send out a managing clerk, he writes: "Religious principle is the only principle really to be relied on; although, as we know, Church membership is not an unfailing guarantee for its possession." To a young man whose temporal interests he was endeavoring to advance, he thus writes:

"I know not what views or feelings you entertain on the subject of religion. Let me say, it is the first requisite. It is the groundwork of all good conduct and duty. Without it you will fail in everything. With it you can conquer every difficulty. It will sustain you in every trial, sweeten all your toil, fill your heart with peace and joy. Without it the soul dies for want of food. It is a *power* which gives victory—the most glorious victory —over one's own passions, over sin of every kind. You *cannot* do without it. I do not wish to weary you on this topic, but if you *feel* an interest in the subject, I shall be glad to ask one of the many excellent Christian ministers I know in Victoria to invite you occasionally to his house, that by inquiry and conversation you may thoroughly inform yourself on this great subject. I should be glad indeed to see you nobly struggling, and eventually raising yourself to your right position."

His religion was as genial, cheerful, and indulgent as it was strict and earnest. This appears from the whole tone of his letters. In reply to a facetious epistle from a young correspondent, he says: "I am glad to see that you have not forgotten 'the little busy bee' of Dr. Watts. Even the pious Doctor was not so straight-laced as yourself. I am sure *he* would not have restrained the industrious insect from working on Sundays. Well, let all your fun and merriment be as harmless as this. I am sorry that —— is so great a fidget. I think the right way is to give business our attention, to work at it with manly energy, to do all honestly, and in the fear of God, but resolutely to avoid corroding care, and the perpetual scheming how to make a shilling out of ninepence; to cheerfully ask God's blessing on one's business, shunning everything on which His blessing cannot be confidently asked; and, withal, to let our business influence be for the good of others. As regards your 'old horse Theology,' I shall not quarrel with you. There is an infinite variety in the human mind. We cannot all think alike, even as to the teaching of the New Testament. Still, there are certain matters on which our Saviour *insists*, as essential qualifications for His kingdom. What about that total change of mind, represented under the name of the *new birth*—the 'being re-newed in the spirit of' our 'minds' and other kindred expressions? which assuredly imply something, and that so marked, that no one can be long in doubt as to whether such a change has ever passed upon him or not. No, there *is* a *higher* and *inner* life, which it is your privilege to enjoy, which you can only secure by making a complete surrender of yourself to Christ, and receiving His Spirit to work within you. The subject is too great to discuss in a few lines, but I recommend to your attention a little book, which I send you by post, written by one of the most earnest preachers of the time, an Episcopalian layman." *

His views on the non-essentials of religion were

---

* The correspondent was himself a Churchman.

in accordance with the following quaint paraphrase
of

ROMANS XIV. 6.

Some Christians to the Lord regard a day,
  And others to the Lord regard it not :
Now, though these seem to choose a different way,
  Yet both at last to the same point are brought.

He that regards the day will reason thus :
  This glorious day, our Saviour and our King
Performed some mighty act of love for us ;
  Observe the *time* in memory of the *thing*.

Thus he to Jesus points his kind intent,
  And offers prayers and praises in His name :
As to the Lord alone his love is meant,
  The Lord accepts it, and who dares to blame ?

For though the outward shell be not the meat,
  'Tis not rejected when the meat's within ;
Though superstition is a vain conceit,
  Commemoration, surely, is no sin.

He also that to days pays no regard,
  The shadow only for the substance quits,
Towards the Saviour's presence presses hard,
  And outward things through eagerness omits.

For warmly to himself he thus reflects :
  My Lord alone I count my chiefest good,
All empty forms my craving soul rejects,
  And seeks the solid riches of His blood.

All days and times I place my sole delight
  In Him, the only object of my care ;
External shows for His dear sake I slight,
  Lest aught with Jesus my respect should share.

> Let not the observer therefore entertain
>   Against his brother any secret grudge,
> Nor let the non-observer call him vain,
>   But use his freedom, and forbear to judge.
>
> Thus both may bring their motives to the test,
>   Our condescending Lord will both approve ;
> Let each pursue the way he thinks the best;
>   He cannot walk amiss that walks in love.

To a young friend who had been unsuccessful :

"Nothing is lost whilst honor and virtue are retained. I believe you will pay to the uttermost farthing. If it leave you penniless, you have wife and children, good health, and the prime of life. You are living in a young and energetic country, where men who go down can, by good conduct, readily rise again. Wife and children are worth every struggle that can be made for them. Besides, there is a God who cares for you, though you may not have thought enough of Him. He may, in mercy, have placed you in this extremity, to drive you to seek His aid, and to give Him your heart, and to learn that religion is not a round of ceremonies, but life, comfort, and love—' *the love of God* shed abroad' in your heart by the Holy Ghost. You have not besought God in the only *practical* way—*by Christ.* In your distress try the plan that has never failed me in my affliction, distress, and *poverty.* Cry unto God, and say you will not rest until He accepts you for the sake of your Saviour. You *must* have the Holy Spirit to make you a new creature, or you will perish. Beg and entreat of Him that He will give you faith—power to trust

Him wholly. If you act thus, God will accept you as His son, and you will be able really to call Him *Father.* You will gain peace, will find that you have only just begun to live. There is no difficulty in persuading God to be reconciled to you. *He* is already 'reconciled by the death' of your Redeemer. The only reconciliation now wanting is on your part; and if once you, with a broken heart, tell Him you are willing to be His for time and eternity, you will find by the hitherto unknown peace and joy springing in your heart, that you have become a child of God. I have talked thus on religion, and given you a few directions that never have been known to fail, because there is no other comfort or ease for a distressed mind. God requires heart-service ; and real temporal good, and, of course, all spiritual good, depends upon our hearts being in a right relation to God. There is no other foundation on which to build true and abiding honor, virtue, truth, and love. Make the Scriptures your constant study. Establish family prayer in your house, if you have it not. Conduct the prayers yourself, extempore. You will soon find yourself in a right relation to God, and obtain all the comfort from the promises which sustain every true Christian in the time of calamity. Think you that the eternal God, whose name is Love, who feeds the young ravens, who gave His adorable Son for you, regards you, your wife, and your little ones with unconcern ? No! He may, in love, by this unfavorable turn in your affairs, be drawing you to seek Him, so that your whole future life may be gladness. 'Seek *first* the kingdom of God and His righteousness.' You have, heretofore, begun at the wrong end; and, of course, failed. Seize hold of the precious opportunity now afforded by your afflictions, and henceforth let secular things be engaged in, in view of your new relation to God as His child. I am satisfied that sound piety will give you the steadiness, peace, and contentment, so essential for guiding temporal matters with discretion, besides the indescribable comfort of knowing that the God of all power and love has a *direct* interest in all your affairs, and will guide you with His eye. Pray earnestly for direction as to what step to take; the best path then will soon appear." Then follow *suggestions* as to the wisest course. "Do not go among a small community. If you want to do business, get to one of the centres of population. Do not trouble about my account. Pay me only when you can afford it; and should you get into extremity use the enclosed $500 draft. Do without it if you can, as I have plenty to do.

"Until a man recognizes God as his father, and is reconciled to Him, all will go wrong with him, and worse, every day he lives. The first duty is to be reconciled to God."

There is, then, no incongruity between business and devotion. Daniel, recording his sublime intercessions and subsequent revelations, simply adds, "Then I arose, and went about the King's *business*." And Christianity gives to commerce its own special consecration. The Forerunner, when asked by the tax-farmers, "What shall we do?" quietly replies, "Exact no more than is appointed you." To the

8*

commercial Corinthians, St. Paul writes : "Let every man abide in the same calling wherein he was called." And, again, "Brethren, let every man, wherein he is called, therein abide with God."

CHAPTER XIV.

WE have seen that Mr. Powell's social and commercial virtues grew out of his duteous regard to the will of God, that his civic character was the natural product of his religious convictions, and that his convictions were derived from his creed, that creed not being a lifeless tradition, but a substantial verity which he was "persuaded of and embraced." His creed, again, though initially derived, of course, from the religious teaching under which he was providentially brought at the turning-point of his spiritual history, was carefully compared with and checked by Divine revelation. He was a spiritually-minded man of business, who did *abide* in God's *tabernacle;* cultivating daily communion with God, and finding the home of his heart in the realized presence of the Invisible. He possessed, in a high degree, the cardinal virtues of Christian commercial ethics,—integrity, industry, benevolence, truthfulness; but all these divinely-human attributes, which should, like God's glory, fill both heaven and earth, had their root in *holiness.* And *holiness* is harmony with the sympathies and antipathies of God. Hence, Mr. Powell could never be charged with that selfish absorption in his own spiritual solace and security which Coleridge so truly calls, "other-worldliness;" nor with that infirm sentimentality of benevolence which the same acute writer terms, "not goodness, but goodyness."

It was not in his nature (renewed as it had been by the grace of God) to obtain an advantage over a competitor in trade by any of those mean, unworthy acts which are the constant resort of small and tricky souls to draw away from others the customers they have fairly and honestly gained. He had no "leading articles" sold at cost to tempt unwary buyers. He would not stoop to deception, nor allow any of his employés to practise it. He would never permit, for example, goods of German manufacture to be stamped as if made in England, nor let a bronzed figure be mistaken for real bronze. On the other hand, he did not hold up his Australian hardware establishment, which was for several years the largest in that country, as a great philanthropic institution erected simply for the supply of the public with "the best and cheapest agricultural and mining instruments," etc. His direct object was to acquire an honest competence, which would both entitle and enable him to retire from business as early as possible, and devote his leisure, his property, and his unspent mental and bodily energies to the service of Christ and of humanity. But, meanwhile, he felt himself to be responsible to God for fidelity to man. He held that the man of business, as well as the statesman, the poet, or the preacher, must *serve* "his own generation by the will of God."

His directions to his managers show that the rate

at which goods were sold was carefully calculated upon a fixed principle of fair and permanent remuneration, "not to be deviated from by any salesman." He writes, "I have full faith in our mode of business, and am convinced that it could not be done lower and done honestly." He had not two consciences,—a buying conscience, and a selling conscience.

In his vocabulary, salableness was a synonym for serviceableness: *e.g.*, "I have picked out a large variety of patterns of paraffin lamps, as I am persuaded that if you push the trade, by advertising, etc., it will be large and profitable, because, Firstly, the principle of the lamp is simple, involving no trouble. Secondly, the light is brilliant, putting gas into the shade, as proved by experiment here. Thirdly, because of the wonderful cheapness both of lamps and oil, especially the latter, etc.; so I hope you will push the trade with spirit." His reliance was on the superiority of his goods, and not on any species of humbug or deception. For the same purpose, we find him writing to his managers, "I shall keep to the —— brand (of iron) only. I think by this means we shall secure a splendid iron trade."

But it must not be forgotten that Mr. Powell's minute and sensitive commercial integrity was the outflow of his spiritual-mindedness. A sentence with which he concludes a letter to his managers in Australia is strikingly expressive of that principle of fidelity to the interests and objects of an absent master, on which he himself strove to act towards his unseen Lord, in matters not literally defined in the written word. "As many things will arise which I cannot possibly advise upon at this distance, in all such cases act as you believe I should act were I present. Whatever the consequence, I shall be satisfied."

This sensitive integrity Mr. Powell earnestly impressed upon his friends and co-religionists. In his letters one meets with such sentences as this: "It is not just to settle property on your wife, children, or others, when your capital is barely sufficient to maintain your credit."

All this, it may be said, *is very well. Truthfulness, integrity, and fairness are very fine qualities, no doubt; but the merchant or shopkeeper who relies for success wholly on these virtues, backed by industry, prudence, caution, and frugality, is not likely to have much to give away.* Certainly not, unless some rich uncle should die and leave him a large fortune. Other qualities must be bracketed with these, of which they form the necessary counterpart. Thus conscientiousness must be coupled with shrewdness; fairness linked to wariness, frugality to generosity, and cautiousness to energy. And it is the rare combination of these qualities which makes Mr. Powell's character so well worth study. Let us now look at the obverse of the medal. Let us note what may be called the supplemental virtues of business—shrewdness, astuteness, firmness, energy, and push. Mr. Powell evidently possessed these qualities in a high degree, but they were always under the control of conscientiousness. He applied to his business transactions and relations the mingled admonition and direction given by our Lord to his disciples : " Be ye wise as serpents and harmless as doves." One need scarcely say that it is not open to the Christian to sin, though it be in self-defence. There may be, and doubtless have been, places and periods in which for a time "he that departeth from evil maketh himself a prey." Circumstances will occur in the life of most men of business in which the alternative is to do wrong or suffer loss. A man may have to make his election between the being the victim of fraud or a rival in fraud. In such a case, the Christian tradesman's course is clear: he will rather suffer wrong, and " commit " himself " to Him that judgeth righteously." But there is neither good sense nor charity in loving one's neighbor better than one's self. It is not only admissible, but right, to meet effrontery by self-possession, and wiliness by wariness. When stupid, unyielding, and evermore exacting selfishness dreams that it has brilliantly outwitted plodding conscientiousness, and finds the tables turned, it is a very edifying discovery. To take advantage of a neighbor's innocent ignorance, or pitiable necessity, is a very different thing from using an unjust and unfair man's unskilful, overreaching avarice as the means of its own defeat.

In studying closely Mr. Powell's modes of conducting business, I have found that whatever might from some points of view wear the appearance of hardness or keenness, resulted from the determination to secure the fair and full advantage of prompt payment and large orders. In accomplishing this both for himself and those who had intrusted him with their commissions, he certainly exhibited great acuteness and persistence. But he only labored to secure the terms which would make continuous business transactions equally favorable to both parties. His object in his second visit to England was, as we have seen, to make such arrangements with manufacturers and agents as "could not be improved," and need not be disturbed. He resolutely objected to terms which placed him at disadvantage in competition. He did not hesitate to use pressure, to "put the screw on," when he perceived that such a process was necessary to bring a house to an equitable arrangement. Of course, he would not deal with a firm on conditions less favorable than those which had been readily conceded to him by some of the highest in the trade. Himself rigidly punctual and exact, he was correspondingly severe with others, keeping them up to his own mark. He would not allow parties who had inflicted on him the anxiety and annoyance resulting from the non-fulfilment of an engagement, through negligence or preference of others, to impose upon him, in addition to anxiety and annoyance, the loss entailed by the late arrival of goods to an overstocked market. He found that respectable houses, acting on the principle of *caveat emptor*, would permit him to forego certain advantages, if he seemed comparatively indifferent about them. In short, he had to make his own terms in accordance with the dictates of his conscience and judgment, and the best information as to the usages of the best houses. His principle was that, not an *equal*, but an *equable* remuneration (in proportion to promptitude of payment and extent of order) was the only *equitable* arrangement. He laid it down as a principle, "No one has a right to trade on my capital."

He writes, " I have never, I trust, made any claim which I do not conscientiously believe to be strictly honest." And he kept as sharp a lookout upon the consciences of those with whom he had to deal as upon his own. He would not allow others to take an advantage over him which his principles did not permit him to take over them. He manifested an instinctive *wide-awakeness*. He would neither over-reach nor be overreached. Of course, his firmness and exactness were inconvenient, and often irritating to persons whose business habits were not like his ; and were regarded by them as unamiable and an-noying qualities. When he *would* be exact, they thought him exacting. But this could not be helped. Business cannot be adjusted to the comfort of un-business-like people. Thus Mr. Powell writes to his manager : " ——— is evidently not much in love with you, but he is a man who has to be dealt with firmly. Show lenity, if there is a fair prospect ; but I am afraid his case is incurable." This firm-ness on his part was sometimes the commercial sal-vation of less resolute men. To his manager he writes again : " ———'s matter must have given you much trouble, but it is a great satisfaction that it is brought to such a close. I hope he will duly ac-knowledge the obligation of being saved from de-struction ; and, as to ———, if he get extricated,

he ought to be chiefly on his knees with thankfulness,
all the rest of his life."

He found that he must not only master " the art
and trade," but also the " mystery" of an importer
of hardware. Hence, he resolved "to acquire as
many secrets of the trade as would keep" him " going for many years to come." As in obtaining this
information, and securing these terms, he had incurred great trouble and expense, he was wisely
careful that competing houses in Australia should
not gain gratuitously, and in a few minutes, the information which had cost him so much travelling
by sea and land, and such a large outlay of time,
strength, and money. That would be allowing
others to acquire hardly-won knowledge at his expense, and to his detriment. Hence he would not
let even salesmen see his invoices. In short, he was
not easily over-seen, and therefore not readily overreached. Few things annoyed him so much as the
" scattering information obtained at great toil and
cost." The knowledge thus acquired, he said, is as
much " my property as anything else procured by
great expenditure of thought, time, and money."
It was by the sagacious use of this hardly-acquired
information, and, by purchasing " largely and regularly from the same houses," that he gained influence and became " master of the position." He
saved over $8,000 a year by the more advantageous
arrangements secured during his brief stay. His
tone in negotiating terms gave the just impression
that if the party applied to would not accept the
proposed terms, some other party would.

He writes : " None of the salesmen ought to see the invoices. If they should, they may gratuitously hand over in an hour knowledge to our competitors which it has cost us and our allies many arduous years to attain. The art of buying well in England takes a lifetime to acquire. Let, therefore, this precious knowledge be carefully guarded. Let the invoice-books be kept under lock and key."

One thing, however, is apparent in studying Mr. Powell's business letters. He experienced a natural pleasure in the discovery that his promptitude had baffled those who, with self-complacent cleverness and twinkling fore-exultation, had come with eager purpose to forestall him—*a day after the fair !* But the exhilaration was perfectly boyish and innocent. " In malice " he was a child; " howbeit, in understanding " he was a man. In his letters to his manager, one meets with communications like this: " ——— has been buzzing about ——— and ———, saying that he wants —— tons of——. But it will take ——— and ——— four months to get it together, so I do not think you need fear a great glut of the article, and I hope we shall checkmate him." *He took good care that his competitors should not distance him by virtue of higher mental and moral qualities.* He strove to meet, or even to anticipate, the public taste, as well as the public necessities. *Quick payment and large orders entitle to favorable terms. The nimble ninepence is better than the slow shilling.* These were his maxims in dealing with manufacturers and merchants. " I hope I shall receive such splendid remittances from you " (his managers) "during the summer, that I shall be in a position to dictate rather than submit to terms." His capital, bearing an unusually large proportion to the extent of his business, enabled him to make "splendid arrangements with the best houses in the worst states of the money-market," and to "take high ground" with firms which required "keeping in check."

His mode of dealing with defaulters was a judicious combination of firmness and consideration. He never resisted the cry, "Have patience with me, and I will pay thee all;" but he insisted on regular and regulated payments, at a ratio adjusted to the ascertained means of the debtor.

A few extracts may suffice for illustration:

"We pay cash for our purchases every week, and give our correspondents the benefit of every penny that ready money will command. If we once began to purchase on credit, we should be on a level with other people. We should have delays in getting goods from the makers, and quotations of prices would be higher. Now we possess all the advantages a cash system can give. Manufacturers are most anxious for our orders; they know that when we ask for a quotation, they are placed in competition with several makers of the same article, all eager to supply us for cash, and that they must cut it fine to secure our order; while their anxiety to get ready money always acts as an incentive in getting goods quickly out of their hand, whilst those who buy on credit have to wait.

"I am glad you go so particularly into all apparent discrepancies, and point out where you think we have not done so well. It enables us to keep a vigilant eye upon the manufacturers, and if you are in error you are all the more satisfied when you have the explanation." Thus the misunderstandings of merchants are the renewals of confidence.—" Bear in mind that it is equally important that we should know when the goods please you ; when you consider them well bought, and of the right kind, it enables us to go with confidence to the same makers. We know whom to trust. Let me know, also, of the arrival of each shipment, and in what condition it turns out of the ship. It is a check upon the vessels, and gives us something to guide us during the ensuing year."

Our friend was religiously strict as to the good conduct of all his servants and *employés*. He writes to his manager:

" I think there is no alternative but to send ———— away, and I authorize you to do so, unless he remain perfectly sober, industrious, and obedient. Because, to keep him in employment, while he continues to drink, is only to find him the means of gratifying his evil propensities, besides setting such a shocking example to all your subordinates. Our duty is plain, though painful. No hope is there for *him*, even temporally, while he remains unconverted; and the only thing likely to lead to reflection, which might thus issue, is—*suffering !* " *

He clearly saw that many a good man's prospects,

* Mr. Powell greatly befriended this man's family, when left destitute.

family influence, and religious reputation, have been ruined by a want of firmness.

"I was exceedingly grieved to hear of ———'s failure. He is the victim of his own good-nature, for a more gentle and guileless creature I believe there is not."

"I think that friendship in business should not go beyond this,—preference when your friend supplies as cheaply as another. If he will not, you must leave in self-defence, or your customers would soon leave you. To purchase well is a necessity."

" You must keep in mind the necessity of coming to a plain and *written* agreement with ———'s agent as to the future of ——— warehouse. This must be effected at least twelve months before the lease expires; so that if he ask too high a rate, you can go elsewhere, and also shut up the place six months before you leave it, and thus destroy the connection."

CHAPTER XV.

MR. POWELL was as exact in guarding his own interests as those of his customers. Thus he writes about "Starkey's patent beam:" "The pivots work on the finest balance without wearing. It is desirable for every one that wishes an exact article. I have ordered him to make a very good counter machine for warehouse use, to prevent the men weighing small quantities of goods on the large platform scale, by which process I think we lose considerably. I wish you would test a small quantity of nails, weighed first on the platform scale, and afterwards in a finer counter scale."

He judged that if salaries had been raised during a period of exceptional prosperity, a reduction of salary was right when such exceptional prosperity was succeeded by a time of corresponding depression. As at such seasons rents fall, and the price of most commodities is lowered, he held that wages should not be kept up. His idea was that *employés* should sympathize with and share in both the prosperity and the adversity of their principals. We have seen how honorably he acted upon this maxim when he was yet a servant.

To what extent the very conspicuous qualities of

Mr. Powell's personality on which we have touched were traceable to temperament and early history, it would not be easy to determine. Certainly, they were not due to constitutional vigor, or exuberant health, since he was a perpetual invalid, and, to use his own words, was always " creaking." In his boyhood, these essential elements of success grew out of his noble ambition to retrieve the fortunes of his family ; during his later years of clerkship they were sustained by fidelity to his employer, and a thorough, genial interest in his employer's success. In his earlier career in Melbourne, necessity might be the mother of industry as well as of invention. During the prevalence of the gold mania, the stimulus of a passing season of unparalleled prosperity might keep him up to the highest pitch of effort and endurance; but the self-same, all-conquering industry distinguished him as principal of a large mercantile establishment. He had no idea of relaxation but as the preparation for intenser work. His periods of sojourn in his native country seemed sacred to hard work. A few days with his maternal relatives at Worcester, a day at Oxford, and an evening at the Crystal Palace, indulging his musical taste by hearing the " Messiah," were almost the only breaks in months of strenuous toil, amid countless inducements to, and ample facilities for, the gratification of his lively sensibility to manifold enjoyment. Incidental evidence of this high-strung activity is abundant throughout his enormous business correspondence. To give detailed proof would be to publish a record of his daily life. An example or two may suffice:

"London, December 11th, 1857.—It is now twelve days since the 'Emeu's' mail was delivered, and six since that of the 'Simla.' R. and II.'s order was in their hands the day after the arrival of each mail. I have spent three days in railway carriages, two days in Sheffield, and four in Birmingham, etc.; had two Sundays, and the remaining day was occupied in writing and placing orders. I went with M.'s buyer to every house in Sheffield, London, Birmingham, Dudley, and Willenhall, in many cases placed goods at lower rates, obtained better discounts, and promise of increased attention to the orders."

He justly required his *employés* to emulate his own energy and painstaking. He writes, "I am not sorry you have got rid of —— : I expect you will have to pack —— after him, unless he gets smarter." It must be admitted that his own laboriousness was sometimes carried to excess. Always at the highest pitch of activity which his strength could fairly sustain, in times of extraordinary pressure he went beyond due bounds in unrelieved continuity of toil, working not only "like a slave," but as no humane man would allow a slave to work ; in his anxiety that the work should be done well, and that no interest should suffer.

Another secret of his success was *concentration*. In lectures and letters, he insists on Lord Brougham's axiom, " Be a whole man to one thing at a time." To a friend he writes, " I have reasons for not going into business in England, but rather than be checkmated for the want of good agents, I would turn to and try myself." To another: "I am glad you retain your disgust of politics. Let others 'frustrate their knavish tricks,' but stick you to the warehouse, and tell the 'patriots' that you will live and learn, and perhaps take a seat at the Council Board at the mature age of fifty; hoping by that time to have your children settled, and to be yourself retired from business with a rent of $15,000. Then you can afford to talk, now you must work. The 'orators' will upbraid you. 'Can you stand coolly by and see your country' (namely, the stump orators) 'drifting to ruin?' To this you must calmly reply, 'It will be a happy clearance for the country when all the stumps are stubbed out.'"

To another.—"I am sorry you have had so much worry with the railway matters. These secular trusteeships are unthankful offices. I hope you will soon be clear of them, and stick solely to your own business. With a large retail business you will have enough to do."

Again.—"I am sorry that —— is in a bad way. If he *will* affect the learned man and the philosopher, rather than the shopkeeper, it must needs go hard with him in such pinching times."

Once more.—"It is only by close watching and comparison that a business can be consolidated and improved. Now your attention is not distracted by other affairs, you will be continually discovering modes of developing the business, and of working it in the most economical manner."

Mr. Powell knew that a day would come when his Lord would command the "servants to be called unto Him to whom He had given money, that He might know how much every man had *gained by trading.*" By *trading,* not by cheating ; for trading is not cheating, and cheating is not trading. *Gained by* trading,—the very object of trade is gain, and gain implies skill as well as toil, and this makes trading an intellectual exercise.   Mr. Powell's strong sense of responsibility, his acute feeling of a sacred trusteeship in all the honorable gains of a conscientiously conducted business, would not allow him to be indifferent as to his just claims on others. So much conceded to the exacting, unyielding, or shuffling selfishness of others, was so much taken from the poor, or from the exigencies of the Church of Christ. "If —— will not pay quietly, he must be made to pay," he writes of one who tried to evade a clear obligation. He saw, too, that his duty as a servant of the public required him to make the best terms he could with the manufacturers, since such terms enabled him to put a lower price upon the articles which he procured from the latter to meet the wants of the former ; *e.g.,* "You would be surprised at the advantage we derive for our customers, in very many cases, by placing the manufacturers in competition with each other, and getting special quotations." "Went to —— and Co. but could not get them to alter their prices one penny. After a desperate battle of two hours, I had to threaten them with withdrawing my orders. I succeeded in getting a further reduction of two and a half per cent."

"The date of my return will depend entirely upon your reports and remittances. If both be favorable, I shall not return till April next year; if unfavorable, I shall come next November. It would never do for me to remain in England with small remittances coming forward. I should have ——, ——, and ——, all down on me; but if thoroughly well sustained, I shall be able to take high ground.

"—— do not select their goods, but leave it to the manufacturer. In such cases you are sure to suffer, as they put in goods they cannot sell themselves." "I find that —— has no buyer here, no one to select his patterns or keep the makers in check. This alone is five to seven and a half per cent. out of his pocket."

"My practice is, on the arrival of the mail, to go through the indents, and see what freights I shall want for the ensuing month, and then go round to all the agents who have good vessels, and make the cheapest bargain I can. I sometimes make a good one with a vessel that wants a few tons to fill up."

"I told —— my business would be five times its present amount if they would *cut it fine*. They, however, say they prefer a smaller business with greater profits. I am afraid they will live to repent their policy. At any rate I shall not do much with them."

"Instead of allowing cash discounts, the interest is to commence at three months from date of invoice, which will allow me a uniform rate of discount. On any invoice where the cash discount is allowed, the interest, of course, commences from date of shipment. They will not send direct, but through ——. As a kind of check on them, however, I made them consent to draw for only four-fifths of each invoice; the other fifth you are regularly to remit direct to them, three months after arrival of the goods; so on arrival of the vessel, let it be entered on your bill-book as a regular engagement. The remaining four-fifths of each invoice they will always draw for through —— at four months. I have cut them down, you will at once perceive, considerably. A clear three and a half per cent. is saved by the new arrangement."

"I see this cunning gentleman has outwitted you. We must use as much ingenuity as himself, and I hope a little more." If he thought that any unfair advantage was gained over him by a competing house, in dealing with manufacturers, he would complain frankly; but if complaint were unavailing, he would defend himself by a "change of tactics," and could play "a very cautious game;" always keeping, however, clearly within the bounds of truth and honor.

He could make a "stir" about an injustice, and give "battle for long hours" with obstinate unfairness.

"They have deceived me often in dealing with them. Trust nothing but facts."

"Remember that we had considerable breakage in one of ——'s invoices. In estimating the damage, take into consideration the expense we were at in sending and receiving back machines, also the smiths' wages while repairing, and the difference in value between a repaired machine and a sound one. Let the claim be fair, and at the same time fully cover the loss sustained. I think they will entertain it; at any rate I shall get something."

"I hope by this time you have quite subdued the great ——. If he will not submit to your directions, let him go. Do not fail to keep him up to the mark."

"We must not be too timid with the bank; a good, bold course is the best way to get properly served by them."

He had great faith in the virtues of advertising. He says: "With our facilities and valuable stock, our name ought to be before the public every day."

"Get —— to allow the overcharge. If they will not, and the iron does not suit you, throw it on their hands, as it was shipped contrary to instructions."

"If we are to look for development in our trade, we must increase the means of showing our goods, and have premises worthy the stock we could display."

Answers to applications for orders:

"I shall be glad to have your best terms of business stated, so that I may see whether you can offer any advantages I do not at present possess, that might induce me to place some orders with you."

"I wish to know before I call whether you are prepared to meet me on the above stated terms.

They are what I can obtain to the amount of my requirements; it would be folly for me to give more."

" To MESSRS. ———.

" As my object in coming to England was to improve my business arrangements, and place them on a footing that could not be disturbed by competing parties, I have, of course, had my attention drawn to the commission charged by you on ———'s iron, and before addressing you on that subject, resolved privately, and without alluding to my arrangement with you, to inquire from two influential houses in London the commission they would charge for exactly similar business.   One house asked five per cent., the other four, the latter house having also the advantage of being better known. You will please bear in mind that these offers are spontaneous.   I have not screwed them down one penny, and I am so well known to both that they are content to give me three months' credit in the colony without the slightest security.

" I must, of course, go to the cheapest market, but am quite willing to give you the preference, provided you are as cheap as others.   I leave the matter for your consideration and reply."

Mr. Powell's promptitude was one very main element in his success.   By getting his orders placed first, he gained more than a month's start in the Melbourne market.   Whatever his hand or his brain found to do he did with his might.

" It will be two months before those I first ordered are ready.   I coaxed ——— out of seventy dozen he had ready, which will come at once, and come in nicely for summer orders."

"I placed the order for the Vieille Montagne zinc immediately on the arrival of the mail. It rose twenty shillings per ton the next week.

"The greatest force of steam has been put on with your orders, per 'Simla.' You are aware that —— required five or six months to get out an order for nails. I adopted a move worthy of ——. Expecting an order, I sent to —— a week before the 'Simla' came, and placed an order for five hundred kegs. By this means I got placed on the books before twenty orders that came by post. I then wrote to —— to go to the agent in London, who keeps a stock for his London customers, and buy all the sizes he had in stock, of the sort we wanted. He managed to secure about twenty tons. As they are scarce in Melbourne, I should think you will sell them without difficulty. Remit me well, so as to keep me independent."

"You will find that goods come rapidly forward since I have been in England. I have quite stirred —— up. He was half asleep, and thought nothing of letting a month or so elapse before he put an order in hand. I have taught him that a week's delay is dangerous. I think he is now quite alive. I shall make them *all* ship in good vessels. The difference of ten shillings per ton is nothing compared with the advantage gained by speed."

Not slothful in business, fervent in spirit, serving the Lord.—I can give no truer description of Mr. Powell's business habits than that which is supplied by Valpy's comment on this text: "*Minime ignavi—i.e.*, Non cunctantes, sed prompti, ne tarditate nostra pereat opportunitas. *Ferventes spiritu —i.e.*, Summo animi ardore ad exsequendum ea quæ officii vestri sunt. *Domino servientes*—Omnia quidem officia complectitur, at hic non docet Paulus *quid* sit agendum, sed *quomodò*, nempe ex animo, sincerè, apertè, candidè, tanquam Domino Jesu Christo, qui omnia videt, qui renes et corda scrutatur, servientes."

Which, for those who prefer plain English to the best nineteenth-century Latin, may be thus rendered: "*Not in the least slow, i.e.*, not faltering or fumbling, but prompt, lest the chance should slip away through our own unreadiness. *With energy at boiling point—i.e.*, with the highest ardor of soul towards the thorough completion of all the details of your duty. *Serving the Lord*—This certainly embraces the whole of business; yet here Paul is not teaching *what* is to be done, but *how*, namely, from the very soul, frankly, openly, handsomely, even as befits those who are in the service of the Lord Jesus Christ, Who sees all things and scrutinizes the reins and the heart."

What Cicero says with regard to the orator is scarcely less true of the merchant—*There is no kind of knowledge which may not, at some time or other, be more or less useful to him.* Mr. Powell brought a high general intelligence, and the results of assiduous self-culture, to bear on the details of his trade; and was, consequently, very happy in his commercial forecasts. He was sagacious in estimating the effect of events upon the market. This is apparent in his business correspondence: *e.g.*,—

"September 4th, 1857.—Gunpowder is likely to rise, in consequence of the war in India. Great part of our saltpetre comes from that country, and the war has cut off most of the supplies. I therefore placed an order for five hundred quarter barrels, in anticipation of your order. By this I saved two shillings and threepence a keg. It rose the very next day nine shillings the hundredweight."

"I am glad you have adhered to sending me bank-drafts. Victoria being a new country, and its success depending on good government, English people are very difficult to persuade that the investment in Victoria debentures is good. You will have to watch the effect of the news of this mail. I do not think that matters are particularly healthy in Victoria. I fear there is a good deal of speculation in land going on, and this, of course, absorbs much money otherwise engaged in commerce."

Business, as he went about it, was a fine, intellectual exercise, as well as a strict moral and spiritual discipline. He made a perfect war-map of the department of commerce in which he was engaged; and knew the ins and outs of it as well as the Prussian army knew the cross-roads in the neighborhood of Paris. He acquired the "Open Sesame" to all the labyrinths of business. He studied manufacturers, agents, merchants. With him business was not only a system, but a science. This, of course, was not accomplished without great expenditure of time and brain-power. He writes, during his second visit to England : "I wish to get the business into a first-rate position.   This cannot be done under twelve months' stay in England.   I shall, of course, come sooner, if you think it desirable.   Be plain with me on this point.   My coming to England has not been altogether fruitless.   I have already saved more than $8,000 a year."

"My chief business here is to look out for any-thing that is likely to be of service."

"I wish you to give me, in a brief, business-like manner, all your views that will tend to settle the question, that I may get any papers prepared that may be required, should there be a change.   Be rea-sonable in your views, and it will facilitate matters."

His letters to his managers put them in possession of his own broad, general ideas ; *e.g.*,—

"September 24th, 1860.—No one can tell how Continental affairs will go next year.   Should Gari-baldi aim at Venice, there will be a pretty general Continental *scrimmage*.   England, I am glad to say, is actively preparing in every way for defence—building ships of war and fortifications, as well as training men—and, I have no doubt, will be ready, should the trial come, which may come amidst the universal ferment.   The efficiency she is gaining by the constant training of so many thousands of rifle-men gives great confidence and stability to every pursuit, especially commerce, which heretofore has been constantly taking alarm at the slightest move-ment of France.   I hope the rifle corps in Victoria will become as permanent an institution there as it is likely to become here."

"I hope Queensland will turn her attention to cotton, if on ever such a small scale. The government should try a model cotton farm, with coolie labor, and see if it would answer. The coolies would be a better breed than the Chinese to introduce. The cotton shown in the Exhibition from Queensland is beautiful, and valued at eighty-eight cents! Supposing in ordinary times it is worth only half that amount, one would think it would pay well at that.

"Victoria at last makes a most creditable show in the Exhibition; the goods, through arriving late, are scattered about, but still the effect is good, and her position secure."

"July 20th, 1866.—On the whole, the prices of manufactured goods will never be much lower than they are, as wages have *permanently* advanced, and since the gold discoveries, prices, though fluctuating, have risen steadily. In nearly every instance in which workmen have struck for wages they have gained the day. Five dollars will hardly go as far now as three dollars would before the gold discoveries."

"I shall from time to time make many remarks upon good makers, and hope you will cull from my letters all that is valuable upon this subject, and have it copied into a book, the observations placed opposite each article they refer to, as the information is being obtained at great cost and trouble, and I hope will be of value for many years."

"Our harvest is not likely to be a good one; unless we have drier weather in August large quantities of produce will be destroyed. This will, however, benefit the Australian farmer, as we shall perhaps require the surplus grain of America, and you will be saved to that extent from Californian shipments."

"I do not think your present Government will last a month. I am afraid their appointment will not have a good effect on Victorian debentures, especially when more are issued. Italy is not likely to fight this year; she will wait until she grows stronger. We shall soon know what is about to be done in America, as the new President takes the reins on the 4th of March, and is known to be a determined man."

"What Victoria most wants now is rest from politics, and that some intelligent ministry should hold office for at least three years. Anything is better than mob government."

"There is every reason to believe we shall have peace, in which case there will be a reaction upwards; but should the war go on, it will stimulate many manufacturers in England, since Germany made large quantities of goods for the Yankee market, which will in that case be made in England."

"I think that Yankee goods will go up instead of down in your market. If the dreadful panic here should spread to New York, goods may somewhat decline there; but high wages are being paid in America, and that frequently keeps up prices in spite of commercial depression."

"If the government of Victoria knew how to

turn events to profit, they would try to direct the tide of emigration just now turned from America to their own shores. All the Australian colonies should awake and make this terrible war their flood-tide of fortune."

"No one knows when the war on the Continent may begin, and if begun, when it may end; the result of suspense to commerce is almost as bad as if the fight were going on. I hope and pray that God in His infinite mercy may spare us the punishment of a war of such tremendous magnitude as that which is threatening."

"I hope the dissolution of your Parliament will result in a strong and respectable government that may last two or three years. This, with emigration, is all you want to make the colony prosperous. Since we must be ruled, let our rulers have brains and education, at any rate, and if possible, position."

"I advise you when this reaches you to make up a good order for cutlery; things are flat at Sheffield, owing to the American war, and, I think, will be as low as they well can be in about four months' time."

"The steady shipments of gold are gradually but surely raising the value of everything, especially labor, which more materially affects our trade."

"One great disadvantage of direct shipment from manufacturers is that, when trade is brisk, such orders are sure not to receive attention till the ready-money customers are served; they will fall back upon such orders when things are dull. All the manufacturers are aware that we *pay on de-mand*, and have a strong motive for executing our orders speedily."

"—— is now shipping all he can by the Black Ball line. The difference is fifteen shillings per ton; but, I think, taking into consideration the time a London vessel is filling up, the slow passage generally made, and the delay in discharging at Melbourne, making about two months in favor of a Black Ball vessel, we save money by always getting first in the market. Ship by good vessels. The difference of cost is nothing in comparison with the advantage gained by speed."

"Send by a good clipper-ship, as there is some speculation going on there which will probably raise the price."

"You must report what progress —— makes with his shop, at ——. We must not despise it because it is a little place. He may sell cheap for all that."

"Find out what prices other shops sell at. You must not be higher. Rapid sales at light profits bring the best return in the end. The larger your business the cheaper you can sell, hence the folly of your keeping too small a stock. Bear in mind the telegraph, if your stock gets small. The results of turning stock quickly are quite startling."

He held that, *as a general rule*, it was foolish for a shopkeeper to be also a manufacturer. " It works best to buy ready made-articles of the workmen. If they find you are a steady purchaser, you will always be able to buy articles at a fair rate. You know then what an article costs you, and instead of having a lot of raw material constantly on hand, you will have all your capital invested in your show-room and your shop. The largest and most successful dealers in London do not employ a single maker *exclusively*. Every week one little maker promises them a few of one class of articles, another a few of a different description.

"A good book-keeper is of vital importance,—of the *first necessity* to a business. Double entry is an unerring fault-finder, correcting mistakes which a less perfect system would never discover. Without it your affairs, in course of time, will assimilate to ——'s, who muddled himself and half Melbourne." Another business axiom was that returns and stock should be so managed that three hundred and fifty thousand dollars capital should be turned over three times a year. He insisted on the immense importance of turning stock quickly. "The results of a quick account are quite startling."

"The chief point that influences our judgment is the rapidity with which an account is turned over in proportion to the credit. We expect it to turn over once a year at least, while the interest is at eight per cent. If you wish the interest to be reduced, the account, of course, must revolve more rapidly. The way you must look at an account is, What return does a person get for the money he has advanced you? It is by ordering largely and regularly from one house that we gain influence and obtain better terms. If we so split up our orders that they are no larger than those a house gets elsewhere, we cannot expect better treatment."

"To buy on credit, and wait for remittances, is a dear plan. The manufacturers always stick it on, and when busy, always serve their cash customers first."

"I wish you would turn your attention to the value of wool as a remittance. True, it is a speculative article, and occasionally you may lose, but I find that our customers who remit in wool, on an average of years, not only save exchanges, but make a profit besides. You would, of course, have to employ a shrewd judge of wool, otherwise the broker might *sell you*."

Mr. Powell deemed it of importance to have not only a full-sized show-room, but also some strikingly handsome goods ; even of a class for which there was no very large demand, as being attractive to customers. For, to gratify the general taste for beauty in an open, honest manner, available to every one in the trade, differs widely in its moral quality from the trick of decoying customers by acting deceptively upon their blind eagerness for a wonderfully cheap article. With the same view he would have beautiful models of the larger machines disposed about the show-room. An attractive appearance in business premises, and in arrangement of goods, gives a fair vantage ground in competition.

To a friend in another line of business :

"I am determined before I leave England to find out the cheapest market for your goods as well as for my own. I am going to Stoke, in Staffordshire, to see an earthenware manufacturer, who makes most beautiful fancy flower-pots. As flowers are getting such a rage at Melbourne, I shall select a crate for you, as they come to little money, and afford an enormous profit. They will prove a great attraction, and draw fresh customers to your warehouse."

" I shall be glad to have all the quotations of the prices merchants are getting for our leading goods. It will be a guide to me. Let me have as full a report as possible of the goods you open, whether suitable or not, dear or cheap. Give me makers' names, and the ship by which you had them. All the small miscellaneous information you can cram into your letters will be acceptable, but do not let me overtax you."

" To insure against war risk will be no loss, as all the leading houses are insuring, and you must all advance the prices of your goods."

" It is better to sell before the railway is opened. Anticipation generally exceeds reality, and I am convinced it will be so in this instance. But whatever you do be in earnest about it."

CHAPTER XVI.

OTHER BUSINESS CHARACTERISTICS ILLUSTRATED—PRU-
DENCE, CAUTION, WATCHFULNESS, AND SOUND JUDG-
MENT.

PRUDENCE in business matters is an essential trait
of morality and therefore of natural religion.
There is as much of moral principle as of sound
common-sense in the declaration of Solomon, " He
that is surety for a stranger shall smart for it, but
he that hateth suretyship is sure."   Mr. Powell had
learned prudence in these matters, not only from
the Scriptures but also from sharp experience.   He
was capable of the very chivalry of friendship.   A
gentleman writes: " He often advanced me very large
sums, as much as \$350,000 at once, with no security
whatever but my honor."   And this, though an extreme, was by no means a solitary case.   He confesses to a friend : " I have been in great misery,
wholly owing to my having allowed my various
correspondents to exceed their cash credits.   I am
now finally resolved to keep them within limits ; for
if I allot the whole of my capital amongst my
friends in the colonies, what right have they to expect me to run into debt on their account?   Yet
this is the case exactly to the extent that the retail
cash credits are exceeded."

"Why in the world should I be so foolish as to fill my mind with cares and troubles, when I might live in peace ? My resolution is taken, my correspondents must keep to their agreements with me, or give up their accounts."

Perhaps the best mode of showing how Mr. Powell exemplified the great commercial virtue of caution will be to gather from his correspondence some of his prudential principles and maxims, as well as his advice and incidental observations to his friends, by whom he was largely consulted :

"Your account, though a poor one this year, is quite satisfactory, as you are steadily reducing stock and expenses, and this, I am persuaded, will shortly enable you to send better orders and remittances."

"You draw interest on your capital when your business is making a loss. Is this wise ? Get your book-debts into a narrow compass."

"To carry on a business by drawing against bills of lading at eight and a half per cent., will not pay."

"Strike off all retail customers who will not steadily pay up monthly. Keep strictly to this rule. Apply the pruning-knife, if you want a healthy business. Our friends in the hardware line remit monthly with the regularity of clock-work. Remitting a regular sum monthly can be no worse for either party than remitting large sums occasionally. You lose people and custom when they get into your debt."

"Keep the bank credit down."

"Gradually reduce your discount, etc. Try by

keeping a fourth of your bills back for collection, at first, and gradually increasing the number, to reach as soon as possible the point where you will have no bills under discount, but all for collection."

He saw that a commercial glut will be succeeded by a revulsion, as certainly as one oscillation of the pendulum is balanced by another in the opposite direction. "Those who play the fine gentleman in good times, will have to change their costume in bad ones." "I expect you will have great speculation, now the money-market is easy with you. Keep *close-hauled*. Hard times will follow the easy times. Let those commit themselves to the stream who like to do so. I have been down quite far enough, and have had a good deal of trouble to get back. One struggle like 1854 is enough for a lifetime."

And yet bankers, when money is abundant, will sometimes lure on to their confusion and undoing ambitious traders, by the offer of most tempting advances. "Don't stop for want of money." Then when the leaders themselves become alarmed, a sudden demand is mercilessly made. In vain the victim cries, "Have patience with me." His prospects and his religious influence fall together.

But to resume:

"I have never (since the disasters of 1854) engaged in any project unconnected with my own legitimate business, which, being large and multifarious, requires all the supervision and watchfulness which my managers can bestow upon it in my absence." "Although you may think it a simple matter to discount a bill for $—,000, it, in fact, deprives me of so much capital, since my arrangement with the bank is to have a certain amount of discount during my absence, an amount only sufficient for my own purposes. Why do you not build and furnish gradually? Your profits would soon supply you with the balance without extraneous assistance."

"———— Store.—I think the profit shown by this establishment is more apparent than real, for I look with great suspicion at the large stock that has accumulated there. You must put the pruning-knife vigorously to work. Half the stock would be ample, so accessible as the place is now both in summer and winter. The monthly returns are wretchedly small for such a stock and premises. I look anxiously for a speedy reduction."

His conscientious common-sense kept him clear of those seductive illusions which so easily beset eager, sanguine natures. Some tradesmen take pleasure in beguiling themselves into an exaggerated estimate of their prosperity by calculating their stock at figures not much below selling price, thus almost leaving out of the account the incalculable risks of business and the working expenses of the establishment.

" Stock-taking.—Let nothing but real value appear in the balance-sheet, under rather than over value; the latter will prove ' vanity and vexation of spirit.' Heavy stocks do not increase sales as clearly as they increase expenses. Light stocks, combined with light expenses, will win the day. Take stock twice a year."

" Better be understocked and weak-handed than have too much of either. The many failures amongst the strongest houses here, in the course of only three weeks, must instruct us still further to contract our liabilities, and keep all *snug*. So many of the *knowing ones* have been nipped, I think there will be a chance for the prudent ones."

Mr. Powell held that, in the main, the great natural law—*survival of the fittest*—obtained in the business world.

His caution was specially directed against the overstraining credit. He was careful not to invest capital before it was created. He had a religious dread of " inflation."

" I suspect that now speculators have been fairly knocked down, some of them forever, you will see a very marked improvement in all goods held in the colony."

" I read that —— is going to build ; if so, he must not owe us much."

" I do not like sending goods on speculation, as I have certain and profitable employment for all my capital."

" Do not, for the sake of sustaining me well with remittances, for one moment endanger your home position by drawing too close upon your cash credit. Leave a margin for bad bills or other contingencies."

" Your shipments are not heavy enough to entitle you to take your own risk. I hope that the sad losses you have experienced will prove the richest gain. In other words, let them make you doubly cautious and attentive, and break you of the terribly evil habit, which has cost me thousands of pounds, of deciding too quickly. When an important matter is pressed upon you, say that you will think it carefully over, and give an answer the next day. But never let your courage give way; always 'thank God and take courage.'"

It is evident that for his exemplary prudence he was largely indebted to the discipline of experience.

"Live near your business until you have firmly established it."

"We have only half furnished our house, and do not intend furnishing the other half, till things mend in Australia."

"Your not writing places me in an unpleasant position, owing to ———'s having made a shipment to you. They came round to me and said that the shipment exceeded the amount of the guarantee, and they were unwilling to forward the goods unless I extended the amount. I consented to do so, on condition that the bill of lading was made to order, and forwarded to my firm at ———. I adopted this course, because your position was uncertain; and I felt sure you would not wish to involve me beyond the heavy amount for which I am already responsible. I have requested ——— to give you up the bill of lading, on your giving an acceptance at three months, with five per cent. added, and satisfying him that your position is sound. Let me beg you, for your own sake, not to accept the bill unless your position is undoubted. What I have done was at a risk without profit, and you will not intentionally

injure me. —— will keep the matter quite private,
so that your credit will not be injured in any way.
But keep up a good heart. Trust in God, and do
what is right, and you will be helped."

" I hear that a benefit club is started, and that you
are one of the trustees. Mind that you are not let
in by bad management and loose book-keeping.
The benefit club might ' go squash ' some day, and
the depositors come down upon the trustees. Let
your partnership-deed in future exempt you from
such engagements."

" I was astonished at the action of the banks in
raising the interest; but if the blow be aimed at
over-trading, we may not complain."

" December 16th, 1857.—All the world has been
going too fast. Although many of the kites flown
were strong and handsome, and the strings long and
stout, the gale has been too severe. Nothing but
money down is believed in now."

In his view, a little risk outweighed a great profit.

" By buying myself, without an agent, I might
save $20,000 or $25,000 a year, but with risk; and,
therefore, I shall not undertake it unless compelled."

" Now it is believed that America will get overstocked. There a most speculative trade has been
going on since the war closed. Prices there are
very high. Exchange has been tumbling down the
last few weeks, and they will have enough to do to
avoid a panic in the foreign market. It is well,
therefore, that you are not ordering largely, and getting English goods at from ten to thirty-three per
cent. above their usual price. We may escape a

10

panic ; but we shall have a reaction in a few months
without fail. I only hope the good demand for
wool will continue, as it will help the colonies
amazingly. But it is a risky thing, never safe till
sold."

"May 16th, 1866.—We have experienced one of
the most wonderful panics ever witnessed in London.
It was like a hurricane for severity and brevity. On
the Stock Exchange things had been tending towards a panic, owing to the general expectation of
a European war. Matters culminated last week
through the failure of Overend, Gurney, and Co.,
for twelve millions. The next day people went
mad, and were only brought to their senses by the
suspension of the Bank Charter, by which move-
ment the Bank of England was able to issue five millions of notes extra. This short storm swept down
several large houses, and during its three days' continuance advances could not be obtained on the first
securities."

"May 20th, 1866.—If you had seen London last
week, you would have been amazed at the madness
that can seize people about money. It would have
been a life-lesson for you—not to spread your arms
too wide. One large house was knocked over because it could not get an advance upon some of the
best bills in London. If war break out on the Continent, I hardly know what times we shall see. By
the *dread* of war, thousands will be ruined before
the crisis is over."

"I hope the crisis will have the effect of stopping
speculative shipments to the colonies, so as to give

all legitimate importers a better chance.   No doubt the panic here will cause the banks on your side to draw in; so I hope you will keep tight hold of the reins, and not have too many local bills.   Take every advantage of the rising tide, and be found with light stocks when it again ebbs."

" My affairs are in close compass, so that although business will be dull for the next two mails—as usual in the winter—they will be able to send very fair remittances, in consequence of the very moderate engagements on the spot."

" Seize the right time for modifying your business with advantage."

" I have frequently felt that I ought not to be in such a position as makes me dependent to so great an extent on your life and health, for the guidance of my large business in the colony.   If you were taken away, we should have to depend on others for the practical working of the business, and that would not suit us; whereas, if the thing were in a moderate and compact compass, I could with judicious assistance manage it with ease and profit. But even for your immediate advantage, it is important that an alteration should take place."

He saw clearly that valor was sometimes the better part of discretion, and that a retreat often requires as much courage as an advance, and displays as good generalship.

" I wish you to take the bold step of gradually reducing stock at Warehouse No. ——, by selling at prices which will move the goods in large quantities, so as to bring it as nearly as possible to a point

by the time the lease is out. Furnish —— and
—— with lists of your surplus stock. They doubtless could work off some. I think this branch of
the business may be very well relinquished. Many
of the articles, especially the great staples of the
stock, are so operated in by merchants, and form, at
all times, such favorite articles of consignment, that
very little is got out of them. —— store too must
be brought to an end."

"The premises I would be prepared to sell, on
long credit, and at a moderate figure. The closing
of these two stores will give you $200,000. The
immediate advantage will be saving interest on the
amount, rents of the two premises, wages, etc. You
should not largely increase stock in the —— store,
in face of the approaching completion of the railway, when carriage will be so much reduced."

"Let the benefit to accrue from the vigorous use
of the pruning-knife sustain you. I know it will
come out all right in the end. But do not fall into
the error of selling too cheaply in the *retail ;* ——'s
get full fifty to seventy-five per cent. *net profit*, on
all they sell. The secret is to have a well-assorted
stock; but have your price. Retail terms in London are much higher than with you, and yet competition is greater and expenses less."

" You had better buy small supplies on the spot,
as wanted, rather than incur the danger of getting
too heavy a stock. Keep a moderate stock by ordering lightly, and buying a little in the market when
you run short. But better run out than have a
heavy stock, paying interest. Your safety and wis-

dom is in sticking to the retail. In it the profits have been chiefly made, and will continue to be, while the mental relief will be incalculable."

"Spare nothing that will make the retail complete. Retail prices can generally be kept up. At any rate, in this old London, prices are as high as in Melbourne."

"Begin reduction and retrenchment in good time, that you may do it gradually, and not excite public attention to the fact. At all events, now take the sensible and honest resolve to economize, although it gives pain to carry it out."

"Have nothing that would plague you in times of panic. You will look upon business with new eyes when it is robbed of its risks, and consequently its anxieties. Credit customers insidiously begin with buying hundreds, and end with thousands. When an account is opened, ask the parties to what extent they wish to go, and keep them to the amount agreed upon, which, with their name, should be entered in the ledger. Divide your risks as the insurance people do; so that, in case of a failure, you will not be much hurt. Your last year's balance-sheet shows that a business one half the extent of that which you are doing, conducted with strict economy, would have paid well, while the unwieldly business with heavy expenses leaves a loss."

"I dare not take your order, lest it should injure both you and me."

"Retrenchment was a necessity, a duty, and therefore to be done fearless of consequences. You must look at the whole thing without shrinking.

How every part of the business pays should be sifted with the greatest nicety."

"You must take off your jacket and go to the retail. You ask, 'what will the public think of it?' The public thinks of nothing but its own interest."

"In order to make business pay, there is nothing for it but to have moderate stock and small expenses."

"I am master of the position here. My business does not occasion much anxiety. I only deal with undoubted houses; and, as we pay all cash for our goods, no crisis can seriously affect us."

"We open no more accounts than our capital will warrant, and I shall not deviate from my fixed rule of having good evidence of the means of a party before I take him up. We always have a statement of affairs from each of our correspondents once a year. To this you will not object, as I am sure yours are satisfactory. There must be mutual confidence in trade, and in order to this, mutual candor."

"Inability to remit with regularity results from extending business beyond the competence of your capital, or ordering particular goods in quantities beyond the requirements of the market. You thus bury money in unsalable stock, whilst you load yourself with excessive interest. To extricate yourself from the penalties of these two errors, you must dispose of your branch stores, and adjust your orders as closely as possible to the state of the market. All speculative business must be abandoned at once. Your business will, of course, not be so large, but it will be more lucrative. With half your past business done safely, you would have been better off. What is the use of doing a large business that will not pay? Let me urge you once for all, if you desire to prosper, resolutely refuse business, unless it is safe. Get things well in hand for the storm; all your prudence will be required. Get your business into such a form that you can handle it with ease. Large stocks have been the bane of most trades in Australia. Now you have such rapid communication with England, you certainly need not keep so many months' supply."

"The banks here are very cautious, so we have the comfort of knowing that there is not much inflation."

"You are wise in resolving not to have a heavy stock, but rather a business that can be kept well in hand. With sufficient capital at command, and a business that can be easily handled, your progress will be safer and happier than with an immense stock and apparently large profits. Business in Australia can only be conducted successfully with great economy. More may be made now in the colonies by cutting off expenses than by doing an immense business."

"I have requested —— not to make such large shipments in one vessel; for should the cargo get damaged, we should be in a pretty mess with fifteen or twenty thousand dollars' worth of damaged goods on which we could not claim."

To his junior partners:
"As an incentive to you to proceed with great

vigor in bringing our business into a more compact compass, I have resolved to bear all the loss incurred in winding up the —— store and warehouse No. ——, and will consider such loss as so much in reduction of my capital, as if you had remitted drafts for the amount. The tide will be turned before the end of the year, and you will be under easy sail. I am not afraid of a temporary loss, when I believe that a greater subsequent preponderating gain will be the result. Do not let any fear of loss stand in the way of rapid realization. This is the only way in which you can speedily get the business within due bounds. What is left will be quite enough for you to manage profitably. You must look this boldly in the face. We soon made an end of the timber business, when we set about it."

"I must concentrate my forces before I spread them again."

"You must look out and have only moderate stocks in 1863; 'times will be tight.'"

"Take the bold step of gradually reducing stock."

To a correspondent:

"I can readily imagine your anxiety while your business grew so rapidly beyond your capital. Whilst you were worrying yourself about remittances, I got into a fever, because I could not execute your orders so quickly as I wished. I think the present time needs special caution. Goods are getting very dear both here and in America. I think there will be a reaction before the end of the year; and, in such a case, it would be a pity for you to have your shelves filled with dear goods."

" The longer I live the more I am convinced that a compact, economically managed business is the most profitable. You are wise in getting your business into such a form that you can handle it with ease. Large stocks have been the bane of most firms in Australia, but now you have such rapid communication with England you certainly need not keep so many months' supply as formerly. Could you not make use of the telegraph wire from Galle when goods run scarce? Surely, it would be to your advantage to get nearly a month's start."

" Our salesmen and porters, do they do a good day's work? Is punctuality the order of the day? Economy must be practised by every man doing his work. Is it requisite to keep so large a staff, now business is likely to be dull for many months?"

" Have your business thoroughly under control, by keeping light stocks. Light stocks, with light expenses, will win the day."

" It showed great shallowness on the part of ——— to be ready to rush into such a speculation. If he do a few more such things, he will get on his back."

" We open no more accounts than agrees with our capital."

" I am sorry ——— required a renewal. In all such cases I stipulate or plead for the reduction of one half."

" I wish to do without letters of credit."

" I shall only send a few; for I know the difficulty of selling with a new name."

[1860.]—" I do not desire to commence buying here on my own account. It is rather dangerous work; for if a crisis overtake the colony, or a mail were to be a month overdue, how could I meet the current bills?"

"I do not think ———'s system of doing business will stand. You may depend upon it they have been buying too heavily, and must have suffered to a corresponding degree. They give bills to the manufacturers at six months, trusting to remittances to meet them. The bank *don't like* their paper, and when the manufacturers find it won't melt readily, they will be chary of taking it, unless they charge great prices. Get your business more compact; you have only to bide your time."

"The ——— Bank has a curious directory, and offers ——— per cent.! for a sufficient reason—in time following the ———. Another evidence of its weakness is, that one or two of the trustees are likewise directors: as *Winkle* would say, 'Suspicious! very!'"

"I have stopped furnishing my house, and shall not complete it till times are better."

" London, 6, Broad Street Buildings,

" *October* 23d, 1861.

" I know you are naturally prudent, and that your efforts have been for some time to get things well in hand for the storm. I think all your prudence will be required in the future, for it is the opinion of sagacious men here that Victoria will have to pass through a crisis to which all others that have been will seem as nothing. It is argued that when you have to *pay* $2,500,000 interest for your debt, instead of *receiving* upwards of $5,000,000 per annum by the sale of your debentures, when by the railways being completed thousands of persons are thrown out of employment, then it will require master spirits to get you through the storm.

" It is thought that a good deal of this pressure will come upon you next winter. These surmises may not be realized to their full extent ; but you must admit there is a good deal of truth in them. To be forewarned is to be forearmed. All I can say is, keep your accounts well in hand ; watch them with increased vigilance ; have *no* engagements in the colonies ; order merely for your wants ; keep only a moderate stock. Then you will have an advantage over your competitors. For although business in the aggregate should materially decrease, yet yours will receive a fresh impetus from there being less competition. Some great houses will collapse or withdraw with the pressure, as many little ones have already."

Answer to an application to open an account with a trader in a new settlement :

" We are quite willing to open an account with you, believing that in time it will be valuable to both you and us ; but we are quite averse to commencing in a large way, such as consigning you a ship. It is wiser for you to proceed gradually, strengthening your connection among the settlers, until you could rely on their support. In the interim you should send an order, at first for about five hundred pounds' worth of goods, and repeat it in six months. We could then increase your credit as your business advances.

"Let me know whether you have a bank that would discount any bills you might draw on us against wool by hypothecating the bill of lading. I should like also to have a chart of your port, and, in fact, every particular that you can think of, *e.g.*, if you have had any vessels direct, or is it usual for vessels first to touch at another port? But, our fear is, that sending you a ship at once would give you a premature start. Eight months' residence would hardly give you sufficient influence to load a vessel. You had better let the thing grow for a year.

" In the mean time, you might ascertain and send us word, by return mail, what quantity of wool will be grown in your neighborhood; whether any of the settlers would support you if a ship were sent; and to what extent and what advance they require on their wool. (The rule is, I believe, if wool is worth one shilling and sixpence, to advance one shilling.) If you took a tour amongst the settlers, you could soon ascertain all that I have written about. Many of them probably would be inclined to support you if there were a probability of your getting a vessel direct. I should advise you to draw up two indents—one for us to execute under any circumstances, the other in the event of a ship coming direct to you, as, in the latter case, you would order bulky articles for the purpose of influencing a consignment. Keep to useful, every-day goods, and you cannot be hurt. We buy goods of every description, and are conversant with the best markets. We buy wholly for cash, giving our correspondents all the discounts we obtain. You may depend upon the interest being moderate, and such as would enable you to compete with your neighbors."

He saw that push and energy on the one hand, and caution and judgment on the other, might be thoroughly harmonized. But he never regarded himself as having attained perfection in this matter. He writes to his manager: "I do not wish you to relax your caution, but the satisfaction you manifest as to our style of doing business, may, I think, with safety be abated. Our business is not a model business. Although presenting some good features, it is capable of great expansion with push and energy. There is danger in being too satisfied with things as they are. When this is the case, little progress can be made. Do not fall into the error of thinking that our business is perfect."

CHAPTER XVII.

BUSINESS CHARACTERISTICS, CONTINUED.— FRUGALITY,
FAIRNESS, CONTENTMENT, AND MODERATION.

Mr. Powell acted on the principle that an un-
selfish frugality is noble.   Before marriage, notwithstanding the smallness of his income, and his systematic liberality, he had saved enough money to
purchase the house in which he lived, and to have
laid by what in his position amounted to a very considerable sum.   The like virtue he insisted on in
the case of every one in whose prospects he took
especial interest.   For example, he writes to a young
man: "I will add $250 to every $500 you have
saved by the time you are twenty-eight; but if you
do not depend upon yourself, you shall not depend
upon me.   That would destroy all your energy and
make you worthless."

Frugality was with him a matter of personal
honor and self-respect as well as of common morality.   His maxim was, "Whoever exceeds his income
is a thief."   But he resolutely kept within his income.   He confesses, "The *feeling* of being *hard
up* I never could stand."

For the first three years of married life Mr. and
Mrs. Powell lived on $750 a year.

On this subject he writes to a young friend:

"You must not only keep out of debt, but must

resolve to save.   Put something by every year, however small a sum.   You will then find how pleasant it is to have something of your own."

"If the being a volunteer lead you into expenses which you cannot afford, you must give up being a volunteer."

But his fairness was scrupulous and sensitive. He detested what he calls "the abominable cut-throat system."   He was wont to take the most trustworthy and impartial advice within his reach as to the fairest mode of adjusting claims, and was careful to start with terms which would not need future alterations or discussions—a great saving of time and friction this.   He brought an unsophisticated conscience as well as a keen intelligence to the study of business relations.   His was not "the rigid right that hardens into wrong;" *e.g.*, "I will not go into the indirect loss the laying out of so large an amount has caused me."   "As to the disputed point of commission, I shall yield it in your favor—not to your arguments, the force of which I cannot recognize, but because trade has been against you.   But you should not endeavor to evade reasonable charges by fallacious arguments."

"In consideration of your last hard year we will reduce the interest."

"I am very glad you have settled amicably with ——.   He was much to blame, but I did not like to quarrel with such an old acquaintance."

"I shall simply put you on the faith of honest Christian men to do justice to me in these valuations. I do not wish a third party to intervene."

His thoughtfulness and consideration towards his *employés* were beautiful. To his managers: "I fear you have been sadly overworked; however, I know that you have a cheerful spirit and plenty of pluck." He laid down this rule, and adhered to it throughout: "Make your *employés* comfortable from the first. It is this that gains their affections, and devotes them to your service." It is refreshing to observe the relations of perfect friendship which subsisted between him and the two highly estimable young men who managed his various businesses in Victoria, and subsequently became his partners. There was a familiarity which did not breed contempt, which did not destroy or even dilute the due respect of subordinates for their principal. His voluminous letters to them, dealing with the minutest details of business, are as confidential and cordial as if they were his brothers, as affectionate and regardful as if they were his own sons that served him. "I write to both of you, as this makes the correspondence more pleasing and definite; so you must read each other's letters, and each reply to his own." Nor did he let kind words serve instead of kind acts. He gave them very handsome *substantial* proofs of his appreciation of their ability, fidelity, and good-will. And he had his reward. To a friend: "My business is being managed in first-rate style during my absence, and I expect will pay a large profit during this year." To his managers: "The very full reports you send me enable me very accurately to judge of the business. You may be sure nothing escapes me." In short, the fine relations between him and those whom he employed were highly creditable to both parties. The following letter to a friend casts light upon his own procedure. "Do as I have done. Train up one or two young men of sound moral and religious principles to your business, give them a small share of your profits, and let them know that their prospects in life depend upon their good conduct. Let them feel the responsibility of the business while you are there, so that you do not leave untried men behind you. Why, I have half a dozen deserving young men now in my —— establishment that I would not hesitate at once to take in as partners, provided I required them. They all know that I feel an interest in them, and they feel an interest in me. This plan would wonderfully relieve you; it would take off the pressure from yourself, and they would take delight in their new powers. If you have no one you can trust, let me name two in my —— firm that would serve you admirably. They would be diligent, conscientious, and honest as the day; and after two years' training would take the entire work off your hands, and leave you a free man. You will find that the great pleasure of business is, the not being a slave to it. Be a master, and have authority over those that can do all the work."

To a young man the prospect of making altogether his own, in a few years, a business which has cost an immensity of thought and labor to get together, is no light matter.

For all Mr. Powell's dealings with those in his employ, I know no term so applicable as the word *handsome.* Sentences like the following occur in minute and lengthy business letters: " Mrs. —— writes that —— is growing weak, and his appetite failing. Perhaps his present situation is too confining; could you not place him at ——?" Yet his gentleness never degenerated into weakness; *e.g.*, " —— will require kind and patient treatment. But if remonstrances fail, there is no alternative but to let him go."

He would moderate the application to business of those whom he saw to be in danger, either from temperament, or desire of promotion, of overworking themselves in his service.

His fairness and moderation were universal—to his *employés*, to manufacturers, to customers, to everybody. We have seen that he would insist upon every clear claim which his large orders and prompt payments gave him on prosperous firms. He knew that not only "he that oppresseth the poor to increase his riches," but also "he that giveth to the rich shall surely come to want." (Prov. xxii. 16.) To forego trade-rights in favor of money-making houses, would have brought upon him this personal guilt and providential liability. On this matter he was positive and pertinacious. He did not regard business transactions with well-to-do gentlemen as the true sphere for generosity. Hence, some thought him hard and unyielding. But all this was only a part of his clear-headed conscientiousness.

" I find —— intend coolly throwing us over, after having availed themselves of our advice. We thought we had to wait too long for our remittances, and having proposed that they should remit more sharply, they are now trying to do without us. We have no feeling in the matter, beyond a determination to protect our own interests in such cases. In fact, we think they have only acted without sufficient reflection, as they have previously always behaved in the most honorable and gentlemanly manner.

"As to doing business with you to the amount of $125,000 per annum, I am unwilling to bind myself down to any sum; but am willing that it should be understood, that if in twelve months from the time that terms are agreed on, it is the wish of either party that business relations between us should cease, a notice to that effect shall be sufficient. I think also, that since my London agents give me credit for the fifteen per cent. allowed upon insurance, you should do the same. Should you see fit to consent to these alterations in your proposed terms, please to state the terms (so altered) distinctly in your reply, and note that the eight per cent. mentioned in your former letter is eight per cent. *per annum.*"

As instances of Mr. Powell's moderation and fairness, I may give the following extracts from his correspondence:

Answer to an application from a friend to select and send out an agent to Australia :

"As regards any trouble you may give in commissions of this kind, that I do not think of. I am well pleased to do anything that may promote your interest or comfort. What I do *not* like is the *responsibility.* If I send out a man who does not suit you, it is harder for the man than for you, if I take him away from a situation which he fills with satisfaction to his employers, and where his chance of promotion is good. In such a case you are annoyed, but *he* has his prospects in life clouded. It is a hard matter for both of you. I am willing, however, to proceed, if you are prepared to run all risks. Now, as to the young man whose credentials I sent you. He is now in a good situation. If I engage him, he intends to get married. Here he at once incurs two grave responsibilities; and how would he feel, if on arriving he found he did not suit? Clever men are as scarce here as in the colony. Muffs are to be had in countless thousands. There is as brilliant a field for a man of real ability here as anywhere."

" The requisite qualifications in a good and ready salesman are, in addition to a thorough knowledge of the business, insight into character, cool temper, activity, obligingness, and plenty of tact and push, and, above all, high honor and sound religious principles, and consequently sobriety. With such a man you will not grudge an extra $250."

" You must remember it takes some time to develop a man's energies in a new position. Men are not thrown on their own resources in England as in the colony ; there is so much division of labor in England, that the administrative faculties are not brought out. A good managing man is consequently as highly valued here as in the colony."

" Your names have been favorably mentioned to

me, but I thought the fact of your services being so largely devoted to —— would prevent your serving a competing house. I am afraid our interests would clash, and should be sorry to be brought into collision with a firm I so highly respect."

"Your orders are put in hand with the greatest celerity; but order no more than you want. I had rather your account paid me badly than that you should fill up your shelves with dear stock."

"I am desirous that you should be cognizant of every penny we make out of your account.

"You are aware that when you opened your account I was to charge you five per cent. on all the goods you ordered. I have not done so up to the present, as the goods have come to a bad market.

"I am unwilling that I should guarantee the account, whilst —— have all the profit. I do not wish to deprive them of any business, but I think my view of the case a fair one."

Mr. Powell never attempted to injure a competitor, though he did strive to distance all in efficient service of the public. He writes: "Fiery little —— is disposed to lose a few hundreds, all for the honor and glory of driving ——'s article out of the field. I shall not make a penny difference."

One of Mr. Powell's finest and rarest business qualities, when viewed in connection with his energy and astuteness, was his *moderation* in the pursuit of wealth. He was as little depressed by a break in the continuity of his success as over-elated by a long run of prosperity.

In reply to the intelligence of an unfavorable

stock-taking he writes: "After I saw the amount of the expenses chargeable to the business, I judged they would exceed the very low profits you have been compelled to accept. It is of no use to be downhearted, or to attribute the result to causes not clearly apparent; enough has been shown to prove where the real evil exists. You must attack the evil with courage and patience. To place the business on such a basis as will require no further alteration is worth all the energy and ability you can throw into the fight." He then writes to the Rev. D. J. Draper: "As I have no profits out of which to give, I must see what I can afford, notwithstanding my losses."

To another correspondent:

"$2,500 a year with peace is better than $50,000 with care. I want to keep body and soul clear of care, that I may the better prepare for my eternal home."

Mr. Powell's moderation was, humanly speaking, his mercantile salvation. The times when prosperity began to flow in upon him were abnormal and seductive. The immediate demand was immense, the profits of trade were proportionately large. His distance from his base, so to speak, seriously endangered his position. Before an order upon firms in England, no larger than the then present and pressing public wants would justify, or even necessitate, could be executed at Melbourne, the demand might suddenly contract, so as to throw upon his hands a huge shipment of unsalable goods.

Several of his compeers and competitors were thus sacrificed to sudden success.

Another branch of Mr. Powell's wise moderation was his contenting himself with his own proper business, and never dabbling in what he did not understand, or committing himself to any of those costly and precarious undertakings which ruin ten families to enrich one. He thus secured for himself the full advantage of experience. Many a clever and honest-hearted man has *pierced himself through with many sorrows*, by distracting his attention and dissipating his energies. Security should be the paramount consideration with a Christian in the investment of his money ; to this, largeness of return should be distinctly secondary.

Mr. Powell denounced all risky speculations on the part of his friends with stern fidelity and cutting conciseness ; *e.g.*—

" You thought you knew a ready way to get rich, and launched into the destructive sea of speculation. How could I trust or respect one who gambles, staking his all : dissatisfied with the slow but sure way of succeeding ? ' *He that maketh haste to be rich shall not be innocent.*' The greatest mercy that God has shown you is that He has taken from you the means of gambling, or you might, had you succeeded, have been a gambler all your days. The money that is best earned will do you most good. If you are dissatisfied with such rewards as God gives to the patiently industrious, and are seeking some rapid mode of acquiring wealth, you must take the consequence—probably disgrace and poverty. You have nothing left now but to repent. You cannot serve God and Mammon : you cannot, without blasphemous falsehood, call yourself a Christian, if you conduct business on the principles of heathenism."

To another friend :

"Extending your business too rapidly occasions you all this trouble, anxiety, harass, and annoyance. It redoubles your work, and after all issues rather in loss than profit. What can be the use of business of this kind ? It allows no time for reading or recreation, and sets up and keeps up a restless excitement, that wears out body and mind before the time. Let me urge you to reflect and act reasonably. Do not lose your courage or your cheerfulness. Put your whole trust in God, and ask for the assistance of His Spirit through Christ; but resolve, at the same time, to bring your business within the limits of your capital."

Mr. Powell believed and acted on the belief that —leaving out of view cases of very exceptional calamity—the laws of success in business are as fixed and reliable as any other laws. He records his deliberate conviction that, "No man can conduct a business *well*, without succeeding in the long run."

His success was in the face of strong competition. He writes in 1857 :

"There are now twenty-two ironmongers in Melbourne, but although the number has greatly increased this year, my business not only keeps up, but shows at the end of the half year nearly $7,500 more than at the same period last ——. This is something to say in the face of ——, who are importing at the rate of $50,000 to $60,000 a month."

To know *when* to retire from business, and *how* to retire, requires great judgment. It is as grave a blunder to retreat too soon as to hold on too long; to withdraw too suddenly as to linger too tenaciously. Unless warned away from business by declining health, or drawn by such a love of Christian toil as amounts to a "call," it is a serious mistake to retire on a bare competence. It is well to retreat from business "before we yet discern life's evening star," if two main points are secured: first, ample resources for a rate of giving, proportioned to the *style* of living adopted, and the position occupied; second, some healthy and useful occupation, which can be followed *con amore*. If the former proviso be neglected, the necessarily small contributions of the *independent gentleman* will tend to lower the standard of giving in his church and neighborhood. If the latter be lost sight of, the misery ensues which Cowper has so well depicted:

> "'Tis easy to resign a toilsome place,
> But not to manage leisure with a grace;
> Absence of occupation is not rest,
> A mind quite vacant is a mind distress'd.—
> He proves—
> A life of ease a difficult pursuit."

As Mr. Powell died in the prime of life, his views on this subject can only be gathered from his letters to his friends:

"Suppose you closed your business, you would find that twelve or eighteen months' travelling would give you a surfeit, and you would miss your old occupation. But, by training a couple of young men thoroughly, which could be done in eighteen months, you would be free to see all Europe and America, and then you would return with great zest. The yoke having been on your partners for so long a period, you could lead a very comfortable life, having simply to give oversight and advice. Give these suggestions careful thought, and get free from the notion that held me in chains for many years— that I must do everything myself. Gradually place the weight on other shoulders. The secret of finding good partners is *training them;* and letting them have a large share of the management, whilst you are on the spot. You will then see if they are up to the mark; and if they work well then, they will not disappoint you when your back is turned. As an additional precaution, when you leave for your grand tour, you might give any old and tried friend a power of attorney, to be used judiciously in case of emergency. The knowledge that a third party had power to interfere if anything went wrong would exercise a salutary restraint."

"If I were you, I should let the full weight of management fall upon your two intended partners some months before you leave, that they may get trained to the work under your own eye."

To a friend who consulted him as to the propriety of retiring from business:

"You cannot too carefully weigh this question, nor too earnestly ask the wisdom which cometh from above. If you are fully satisfied that under all contingencies you have ample means, and are convinced that you can fill up your leisure life usefully, I think you wise in getting rid of your burden."

To another friend, who proposed a premature retirement from business, he gives the following advice:

"In commercial life you have as many opportunities of doing good as in other spheres; and we are neither of us young enough to serve an apprenticeship to anything else, and yet we cannot be idle. I should strenuously recommend you not to wind up your —— business, but do as I have done, train up young men to relieve you gradually."

"Taking in a *thoroughly good* partner affords incalculable relief. It also prevents the sudden and complete break-up of a business in the event of death. To take in a partner with power of dismissal is a duty you owe to your family; for, if death should overtake you, your business would be closed."

To a friend whose worldly position had been lowered by the misconduct of others:

"I feel very sorry such misfortune has fallen to your lot; but am heartily glad you have had the sense to face your difficulties manfully, and hope your courage will bring you through. Struggles such as you are undergoing are the best cement for married life, and will more attach you to each other, if you help each other, than if you had lived from the commencement to the end in the greatest luxury. Now you have commenced the business, go thoroughly into it. Do not be ashamed of an honest business that is supporting you. And make it honorable by your Christian conduct. Acknowledge God in all your ways, and He will direct your steps. Be more than ever a man of prayer, and your way will open."

What a noble thing is trade, when conducted by a noble man, in a noble way, and for noble ends! What a sphere does it throw open to intelligence, energy, and Christian virtue! What a fine pursuit is commerce—business—*money-making* in the hands of a sensible, conscientious, and believing man! How contemptibly inert are the flutterings of fashion, the forced and feeble excitements of pleasure-*seeking*, compared with the brisk, resolute, patient, wakeful activity of a thorough business man! Such a man was he whose characteristics I have sketched. The sedulous boy-clerk, in high-toned health, abandoning his forest freedom, and chained by a generous purpose to his desk, in a dim and dingy office; the ailing young man, with shattered constitution and small salary, devoting himself steadily to his master's interest, slaving, saving, "hoping all things, enduring all things;" the young husband, resolved to make one bold, but well-considered effort for the independence and comfort of his wife and children, giving up his situation, selling his house, spending all his savings, to secure what he saw was his only chance of ultimate success—a connection with some first-class firm at the other side of the globe; the single-handed store-keeper in a crude township, straining all his energies day after day to support those who were dependent upon him, achieving "social success in his shirt-sleeves," till inundated with an unimaginable influx of custom through the rush to the gold-fields; the large importer, selecting and training and attaching to his interest and his personal character agents to whom he could quietly confide his business for a year and a half, whilst he was making himself master of the art and mystery of British trading, and visiting America with the view of establishing safe and profitable relations with some honorable house in its great commercial centres; the London merchant, *the city man*, the principal of a large mercantile establishment, conducting its wide-spread and multifarious details vigorously, honorably, and successfully, yet, with head and heart above the world, living in the region of unseen and eternal realities, putting the interests of Christ's kingdom in the forefront of his commercial calculations, not waiting till he had made his fortune, but giving thousands of pounds, year by year, in quiet alms-deeds, and to bold evangelistic and educational enterprises, sedulously cultivating his mental powers, fitting himself for service in the Church and in the secular society, accepting Church cares, and discharging Church duties, keenly interested in all human affairs, yet proving that "to be spiritually-minded is life and peace." Surely such a man vindicates the nobility and sanctity of trade!

CHAPTER XVIII.

HIS CONSECRATION OF HIS WEALTH TO CHRISTIAN BENEVOLENCE.

THE man who dedicates to God that which he has obtained by covetous practices, by double dealing, untruthfulness, trickery, bad bargaining, a cruel use of capital, gambling and God-tempting speculation, or an eager pursuit of wealth to the neglect of spiritual, mental, and bodily health, is offering God the reward of iniquity, the wages of unrighteousness, or casting into the Lord's treasury the price of blood. The Popish princes, who founded abbeys and endowed churches with the acquisitions of rapine and of murder, were but endeavoring to make God an accomplice, or accessory after the fact, to the violation of His own holiest laws—and how much better is the Protestant merchant or banker, who builds churches or chapels, founds and endows colleges and seminaries, or hands over to evangelical enterprises sums acquired by unchristian practices. In order to the hallowing of trade, two things at least are indispensable:

1. That the pursuit of property be entirely subordinate and subservient to the pursuit of piety, and that all our commercial virtues flow out of spiritual-mindedness, and a regard to the will of God.

2. That in the acquisition of property, absolute truthfulness and unfaltering fairness and moderation be religiously maintained.

Both these conditions Mr. Powell had fulfilled, and could therefore rightfully dedicate his substance to the Lord.

Immediately upon his conversion, he felt it to be his duty to take upon himself Jacob's vow—"Of all that Thou shalt give me I will surely give the tenth unto Thee." This resolution was strengthened shortly afterwards by reading Dr. Harris's "Mammon." He strictly adhered year after year to proportionate giving through all fluctuations of his fortune. But the tenth was not the maximum of his yearly contributions to religious and charitable objects; it was the minimum. It was not the limit beyond which, but below which, he would not go. His systematic giving did not check his spontaneous generosity. He did not make the freest and noblest of the graces—charity—a mere matter of the book of arithmetic. We have seen him, when but a clerk with five hundred a year, with "frank-hearted thriftlessness" give $50 to meet the difficulties of one poor man. The tenth was not in his case hush-money to conscience, or quit-rent to God— a discharge in full of all obligations to the great cause of religion and humanity. Nor was it a kind of insurance-payment to Providence. But he found this principle—*the tenth, to begin with, is sacred to religion and philanthropy*—very helpful towards a wise adjustment of the concurrent claims of business, culture, home-comfort and the amenities of social life. He found it necessary in his position, and with his reputation for liberality, and his relations to Christian enterprise—metropolitan, connectional, and antipodal—to extend to his beneficence the like regularity and exactness which presided over his commercial affairs.

The following extract from a letter to a friend in Melbourne explains his principle in his own words:

"LONDON, *March* 21*st*, 1866.

"I have for years adopted a systematic plan of giving. It is better to give on a recognized plan than by fitful impulse. In the latter way you neither give so much nor so well. But setting aside in your ledger a tithe of all your gains as God's portion, you can periodically, and as a faithful steward, decide how that portion shall be distributed."

But his liberality was none the less spontaneous because it was systematic. His generosity, though like all his other virtues, an offshoot of his fidelity to God, and restrained and regulated by the sense of responsibility, was not rigid or geometrically ruled, but graceful and luxuriant as a branch that runs over the wall. Side by side with his munificence to great Church undertakings there flourished much private generosity. We have already noticed a very characteristic instance of what might be regarded as an almost eccentric liberality in one so conscientious and so calculating even in his givings, and so committed to great Church schemes—his anonymous donation of $1,250 to Mr. Hargreaves, the discoverer of the Australian gold-fields. This was accompanied by a graceful letter representing the donation as a scant offering of simple justice. The reply of Mr. Hargreaves to his unknown admirer, through the same channel, was equally tasteful and honorable. It was Mr. Powell's very conscientiousness, his sense of fairness, that prompted an act, which, had it been imitated by all who derived benefit, directly, or, like Mr. Powell, indirectly, from the gold discoveries, would have made the discoverer a millionnaire. It brought into play a principle, which, if universally acted upon, would redeem the world from the disgrace and guilt of neglecting its greatest benefactors.

When he saw a worthy tradesman "under the weather," he would nobly "come to the rescue," and both man and steer the commercial life-boat by heading a private list of subscriptions.

Another fine and exemplary instance of Mr. Powell's conscientious liberality was his persistent endeavors to raise the stipends of Christ's ministers to a point which would enable them to live comfortably and *respectably*, without pinching, and free from anxieties which tend to distract the mind from the great work of saving souls. Protestants, who cannot insist on the celibacy of the clergy, are bound to put pastors and their families into a position of comfort.

The sustentation of the ministers of Christ on such a scale of liberality as shall place them in a position of frugal competence—not of luxury, but

11*

of plenty, not of ostentation, but of seemliness—is represented in prophecy as one main result and direction of Christianized commerce: " Her merchandise and her hire shall be holiness unto the Lord: it shall not be treasured nor laid up; for her merchandise shall be for them that dwell before the Lord, to eat sufficiently, and for durable clothing."

Our friend paid the difference between the rent of a small and ill-situated cottage and that of a good-sized house in a pleasant locality for the minister by whose instrumentality he had been brought to the vital knowledge of the truth.

He thus expresses his convictions in a letter to a friend:

" LONDON, August 17th, 1857.

" I do not think that the Wesleyan Church occupies nearly so influential a position in England as in the Colonies. One great drawback to her progress is that many of her ministers have their energies damped and their courage broken by the pecuniary straits incident to their insufficient allowances. Having witnessed the blighting influence which this exerts on the cause of God, I shall more strongly than ever advocate in the colony that our ministers be fairly salaried, and that such a provision be made for their old age as may permit them to look forward to it without anxiety."

In a most delicate manner, he would supplement the income of ministers who had little or no private property, so as to carry it somewhat beyond the

point which the Quarterly Meeting thought sufficient.

He loved to give some elegant and substantial
tribute to acts of kindness and consideration in
others, *e.g.*,—

"My dear ——, I have chosen a very pretty pic-
colo piano for you, of a nice tone and touch, which
I beg you will accept as a small token of the estimation I have for the generous kindness you have
shown to ——."

This was always done in the most graceful manner :

"I know how delicate and high-principled you
are, especially as to money matters, but you must
not allow that to prevent your accepting what is
really your *right;* and remember, it comes from an
old friend."

One of his guiding axioms was : "Some of our
good deeds should be performed publicly, for example's sake, but the greater part quietly. The right
hand should not be always shouting to the left, 'Ho!
don't you see, I'm putting up chapels here, there,
and everywhere.' "

As might be expected, his generosity sometimes
drew him into difficulties and perplexities and manifold awkwardnesses, the extricating himself from
which brought out finely his idiosyncrasies of adroit
goodness—the exquisite combination of firmness and
decision with judiciousness and gentleness. Of all
this his correspondence affords ample, but unquota-
ble, evidence.

The pleasure he felt in parting with money when

his judgment gave him leave was of great service to him in his business, rescuing him from that penny wisdom, which is proverbially pound folly: *e.g.*, " Give the mate of the —— $30, if the mirrors arrive with *few* breakages."

" There is some pleasure in paying the P. and O., they do their work so well."

He had a deep conviction that giving was an essential part of a religious education.   To an Australian minister :

" The Church must not neglect to cultivate the hearts of the youth of the colony, so that they may have true sympathy with and generous impulses toward every agency that will improve mankind. Children must be trained to give, or they will give little when they become men.   Giving is waging a successful war with the great enemy of the human soul—covetousness."

A strong instance of Mr. Powell's good sense was that he had rather give than bequeath.   He had no idea of giving with the dead hand (*mortmain*). He held, with Sir Isaac Newton, that " those who give nothing till they die never give at all."

One would fain linger on a subject so pleasant as this.   In fact there are few aspects of the Church in the present day so hopeful as the revived spirit and heightened scale of Christian liberality.   So strongly has the grace of giving grown up amongst us, that an attempt is made to systematize it into a science.   But in determining the due *proportions* of giving, the *principles* of Christian liberality must not be lost sight of.   The beneficence of the Church must never become a mere matter of tariff. Christ Himself must be the motive, the model, and the measure of our giving. Grace itself is generosity, —" the very prodigality of heaven ; " but steward-ship implies order as well as kindliness, an economical and discriminating, as well as a diffusive munificence. It was this judicious liberality that gave completeness to Mr. Powell's character. Humility was its base, an energetic conscientiousness its shaft, and a well-poised charity its Corinthian capital. When he had but little, he did his diligence to give of that little, and ever as his resources grew, *to his power, yea, and beyond his power, he was willing of himself.* Whilst his beneficence was systematic in degree and direction, its *quality* was *not strained.* With him giving was not only a principle, but also a pleasure and a passion. He gave to indulge the God-like propensity and *penchant* of his renewed nature. It was not a duty to which he felt bound to work and wind himself up, but a luxury of feeling which he was bent upon enjoying to the full extent which conscience would allow. It was, in fact, the only luxury in which he indulged. He was " given to " giving. Generosity had obtained a real and effective mastery over him, so that he was incessantly either gratifying his passion, or laying plans for its gratification, *devising liberal things.* It was a kind of gracious besetment, which had to be placed under the strict guardianship of propriety and prudence. It required vigorous self-control to keep his bounty within bounds. He had *a bountiful eye.* In fact, he was " one of those rare men in whom the desire to relieve distress assumes the form of a master-passion."

He was always trying to stimulate the less ardent benevolence of others, challenging them to a bolder strain of benevolence, provoking them to love and good works. Like Saint Paul, he would not hesitate to pique the well-to-do by contrast with the enthusiastic beneficence of the comparatively poor. It is a not uncommon complaint of individuals who have no need to be under any personal alarm of catching the contagion of generosity, that appeal is sometimes made to a principle of emulation, a passion of rivalry in endeavoring to excite Christian people to a large-hearted liberality. Yet is not this precisely the point of the apostolic appeal to the Corinthians (2 Cor. ix. 1–4)? It is as if he had said, "You commercial and cultivated Corinthians will hardly let yourselves be distanced in the glorious race of generosity, by the poverty-stricken peasantry of Philippi." Emulation in that which is good is a healthy and honorable, and may be a hallowed passion. It is as salutary in its influence upon individual character as it is beneficial in its effects upon society at large.

The subject of this memoir loved to make his giving all the more productive by making it, as much as possible, provocative of generosity in others. He belonged to that happy and increasing class whose epitaph on earth might be, as their record on high doubtless is—*Your zeal hath provoked very many.* It is impossible to estimate the indebtedness of Victorian Methodism to the man who, at the be-

ginning of its history, set before it such a high
standard and such an inspiring example of well-
applied beneficence, and did so much towards the
creation of a just public opinion on the subject of
Christian liberality.

Wealth only becomes "the mammon of unrighteousness" when it is ill-gotten or ill-applied. Then
only does Proudhon's dictum, "Property is robbery,"
hold good. *Gathered by* serviceable *labor*, consecrated to Christian objects, *merchandise and hire* are
holiness to the Lord. Accumulation has been
called "the crucible of character." Mr. Powell
stood the test.

Nor was it only by direct donation of solid sums
of money that his generosity indulged itself. Like
Gaius, he was the "host of the whole Church."
His liberality, though methodical, was not mechani-
cal; it was systematic, but not stereotyped. He
was always brooding over some new scheme of
benevolence, and asking himself how he might
give in proportion to the magnitude and urgency of
the enterprise. Thus he became "rich toward
God." Despite his feeble health, life was to him *a
continual feast.*

Mr. Powell learnt first to show piety at home.
His conduct to his less successful relatives was
nothing less than munificent. He laid it down as a
principle, "It is not only natural but just that members of my family should derive benefit from my
success." Several sudden deaths having occurred
in his family, many orphan nephews and nieces
were left unprovided for. These he at once accept

ed as his providential wards; and, for the last sixteen years of his life, he supported, clothed, and educated them. For a succession of years the sums he spent on them amounted to nearly $6,000 a year, and in his will he left a very considerable charge upon his estate for their advantage. During the decade 1850–1860, his books show that he had expended on the average $8,000 a year on private benefactions to individuals. His fidelity and tenderness towards his young relatives were exquisite. On the 26th of February, he wrote to his little nephew N——, asking him what he would like to be, and giving him a wide range of choice, encouraged him to pursue especially those studies which he had the keenest relish for, and asked him to request his master to allow him to pursue any study he had a taste for, besides the ordinary course of school teaching. Yet with all this fatherly indulgence, he exercised the most resolute firmness and discrimination. He knew *how to give good gifts*. He challenged their confidence, and wrote pages at a time of fatherly counsel, gently and piquantly correcting their juvenile misconceptions. "As to 'defying competition,' I hope you will *defy* nobody and nothing but sin, and become 'a star of the first magnitude' as to truth and virtue, and then, if God will, as to wealth."

Having come into possession of considerable property through the death of a relative (who died intestate), and thinking it probable that had the deceased made a will, the property would have been bequeathed to more necessitous relations, Mr.

Powell devoted the whole to the maintenance and education of some young relatives, supplementing the amount by handsome allowances from his own mercantile profits ; and that in such a way as gave them the superadded advantage of his commercial position and experience. The expenditure of feeling, the wear and tear of heart and brain voluntarily undertaken by him on behalf of others, whilst his own business was so severely drawing upon his bodily, mental, and spiritual strength, inspires one with an admiration, not unmixed with pity, and even tinctured with some degree of blame. His self-imposed, or rather love-imposed, toils and anxieties for others told terribly on his health.

He was, in short, almost a martyr to benevolence, being obliged to admit, " The large number of pensioners I have depending upon me is beginning to make me prematurely old."

And whilst thus mindful of the claims of kin, he was to the poor most pitiful and considerate. He ever and again sent directions from London for the relief of necessitous individuals in Melbourne. " I am sorry for poor ——'s accident ; do not let them starve." " I give you authority to do anything for —— that you think right to be done." He was wont to bestow on all such cases thought as well as money; *e.g.*, " Give a little help to —— from time to time, but judiciously, as —— is not a good manager, and must be taken care of." In his diary one meets with such records as these :

" July 22d, 1865.—Went to Islington (from Bayswater) to call on a woman who had come to me for relief; found her case a deserving one; sick husband and three small children."

"August 1st, 1858.—Wrote to Mr. —— to allow Mrs. —— $5 a week, until she can get a living for herself."

"August 23d, 1859.—Wrote to ——, promising to lend him $150, for six months, without interest."

"September 30th, 1859.—Wrote to Mr. ——, offering to send his two nieces to school next year, provided he would assist."

"December 22d, 1859.—Wrote to Mrs. ——, sending her $25, and telling her that, in future, I should allow her $25 dollars a month."

He writes, "I reckon the widow and the fatherless are as good an investment as a man can make."

Advising a lady (who had no claim on him but that which rested on a knowledge of her difficulties and the admirable character of her family) that he had remitted $400 to a New York firm, to pay her passage to Australia, and to furnish necessaries for the voyage, he adds the following suggestions: "Whether you go by the Cape of Good Hope or by Cape Horn, take all the light and all the warm clothing you can get together, as you will be sure to meet with extremes of heat and cold, whichever route you choose. I should also advise you to take a small stock of useful medicines, as these are often required at sea, and it is a favor to get them; also, a few *medical comforts*, as port wine, sago, brandy, arrowroot, and, if you can meet with it, preserved milk in tins. A good supply of gingerbread you will find useful for the children, also some biscuits.

A few candles and matches, some oatmeal, and rice, as you will not get vegetables or milk on board. These few hints may enable you to escape much suffering at sea.—London, June 15th, 1857."

His whole arduous correspondence with his friends yields a beautiful manifestation of his "good and honest heart." We have seen that one well competent to judge can only account for its laboriousness on the ground of his all-pervading conscientiousness. With all his caution and shrewdness there was an element of the heroic in his friendship. A gentleman testifies: "I know full well that my present successful position is in a great measure attributable to his energy and judgment, added to his generosity and confidence in intrusting me with so large a portion of his capital. I do not forget that he also saved my life. I got out of my depth at the Cataracts before I had learned to swim, and was sinking for the third time, when he plunged in and brought me safe to shore." The same gentleman also describes the delicacy with which Mr. Powell, having the opportunity and the intention of purchasing a very lucrative business, on learning that his friend had set his heart upon it, at once retired from the field. The same gentleman adds: "One sentiment pervaded his life and his letters to me. I have just been reading one in which he says, 'Be sure to keep in view the fact that the only thing that has substance in it is to get good and do good. Let you and me be thankful that it is in our power to give, for it has been given to us. It is God that giveth thee power to get wealth. He has given us the talents which lead to riches, and we shall one day give our account as to how they have been employed. This should check our pride in thinking of any success with which we have been favored. A little reflection will convince us that " it is more blessed to give than to receive," since not only is it pleasing to God when done with a true motive, but it has the very best effect upon our own hearts, teaching us not to live to ourselves or harden our hearts, but to keep soft and sympathetic. 'To do good and to distribute forget not : for with such sacrifices God is well pleased.'" Thus did he animate his friends by word and by example to devotion and philanthropy. He never felt that he had done enough for his friends. He thus apologizes for the letters on which they set so much store : "So much business correspondence spoils one for the descriptive detail which makes a private letter interesting. The drudgery of the mail takes all the finer flights of imagination out of a man, and leaves the correspondence of friendship to be ' performed ' as the undertakers do a funeral." Yet he manifested the utmost leniency and indulgence to the epistolary shortcomings of others : " You, we hardly expect to write, unless you are obliged, as I know it is a task to you."

He loved to encourage others to similar acts of generosity ; *e.g.*, "I saw —— the other day. She was in raptures at some kindness you had done for her, and showed me some useful articles she had been able to procure in consequence—a clock, etc."

His attention to the interests of his friends was

indefatigable. He is not content with giving English news to his Australian acquaintances, but appends such pregnant postscripts as the following: "If you or —— want any commission executed, I will take the greatest pains to get things for you good and cheap. Music, furniture, ornaments, clothing, in short, whatever you state. It may save you a few pounds, and would be a pleasure to me." Mr. Powell did not hold himself acquitted by giving money freely. He felt bound to exercise the like discretion in the disbursement of the sums set apart for charity to that which he employed in the management of his business. We have seen that he would undertake a journey across London to verify a tale of woe. Like Job, he could say, "I was a father to the poor, and *the cause that I knew not I searched out.*" He writes with reference to some young people whom he was wishful to help: "I should only do them harm were I to assist them beyond £——, for none are so helpless, wretched, and dissatisfied as the habitually dependent. I therefore, etc. In the event of my death, regard this as an 'instruction to my executors.'" "To help many I have been economical with all." "I will not give money to support persons in idleness, which brings ruin on earth, and involves, if persisted in, eternal destruction."

His liberality was as practical and business-like as it was unconstrained. He took good care that his charity was well laid out. He gave to the needy not only money, but also that which was far more precious, time, thought, and attention. He was one of those to whom the King shall say, " I was sick, and ye *visited* Me."

· He would not allow himself to be imposed upon. " I would be the last man to distress you, whilst you are doing your best." " The party who confers a benefit has the right to determine the conditions, not the one who receives it."

" I have written a very plain letter, telling him that any endeavor on my part to help him will be useless, unless he thoroughly forsake his evil habit. If he is sober, and in distress, try to give him some employment; but if he drink, to give him money will only be destroying him."

" I will serve you to the utmost of my power, so long as you deserve it."

Yet, it must be confessed that much of his caution in charity as well as in business was learned from bitter experience. In 1858, after describing how a party whom he had lavishly helped, had deliberately robbed him of $500, he writes : " Whilst I must not close my heart or purse to real objects of charity, I confess that I am getting tired of clamorous greediness. I think I shall now start afresh, and quite put down any whining imposture."

Another very characteristic excellence of Mr. Powell's was carefulness not to hand over to another a troublesome case of unhelpable helplessness : *e.g.*—

" To break up ——'s bad associations, the best course will perhaps be to send him to —— : but *don't give him an introduction* to ——, or *even his address*, since I do not wish to afflict my friends, as they sometimes afflict me."

"—— is a thorough begging vagabond. I have frequently relieved him. He persuaded a minister to give him an introduction to me some months ago, and has stuck to me ever since. The last time he applied I warned him off. If he cannot support himself and family, he must make friends with the 'Union.' If he come again after you have warned him—which he is almost sure to do—threaten him with the police."

Our friend deemed that the conditions of success in Church enterprises and in secular business were identical. Against burdening a religious enterprise with debt, he writes concerning Polynesian missions:

"MELBOURNE, *September 29th*, 1858.

"To REV. JOHN EGGLESTON.

"You are not obliged to send more men than the fund can support, nor are the men, when sent, required, either by the Committee or their Great Master, to do more work than they are equal to. What is the use of preachers, any more than tradesmen, trying to do a large business with a small capital? That can only end in disaster. Let the missionaries do what work they are equal to. If they attempt more, they will accomplish so much less. I imagine that the island preachers proceed much on the same system as their Australian brethren, viz., endeavor to take up more ground than they can profitably work. I see a preacher has been sent to the Samoan Group. Why seek this new field, when the old ones are not properly attended to? Admitting the importance of the Samoan case, had it not better be left until our resources, and our staff of missionaries, will enable and entitle us to work it? I see that New Zealand absorbs a large amount of our Fund. This ought to be carefully looked into. It is a downright shame that this station, which ought to be self-sustaining, should swallow up the lion's share of the funds. The 'John Wesley,' if managed in a business-like way, would, I imagine, nearly pay her own expenses."

"Grammar School and Wesley Church:—Be very vigilant as regards the Grammar School money. See that it is not loaned for Church purposes, and that Wesley Church repays her debt with good interest when the railway is complete. Mind you remain one of the treasurers of the fund, and, please, in your next give me a statement of its present position."

Answer to application for subscription to new chapel in Victoria:

"My dear Mr.——,

"As to your new chapel. In January, D.V., I will go closely into my engagements, and send you an order for what I can afford. I hope it may be $2,500; possibly it may not be half that sum, as the claims upon me are large in proportion to my income; but I thank God heartily for giving me anything to spare, and any disposition to give. I will do what is just and right, in consideration of my other engagements."

"At present I am engaged with a few other friends in our Circuit in getting up a chapel in a destitute part of London, where ten years ago there were not five hundred people, but now from twenty-five thousand to thirty thousand. They belong chiefly to the laboring classes, few of whom attend any place of worship. London would appall you by its rapid growth and its spiritual destitution. Vast exertions are being made by all denominations; but to overtake the *annual* increase of population, requires fifty to sixty new places of worship. The pressure to give from every quarter is wonderful. Deputations, collectors, letters, reports, collections, etc., a man who has anything to give is now flooded with, so that a systematic plan is one's only relief and safety."

"March 26th, 1866.

"To Rev. John Eggleston.

"Chapel debts must become things of the past. They are now held in abomination in England, and I hope will be in the colony. I have lately been interested in getting the means together of raising a chapel to seat three hundred, in a poor neighborhood. I made a good heading to the subscription list, on condition that all the money required, $8,000, should be promised before the building was commenced. This has been accomplished through the zeal and activity of our superintendent, the Rev. G. Maunder, and we hope to begin next week.

"I am obliged to all the friends who said such kind things of me at the College breakfast, and thankful you had a good start. The Grammar School will, doubtless, do well under good management. Mind that the profits, after you get out of debt, are devoted to making the establishment most complete, improving the property, collecting a library, and, lastly, founding scholarships. Not a penny of the profits must be diverted from the College. I am glad to learn that you are so heartily engaged in the greatest work of all, the work of God, whether in erecting chapels and schools, or preaching Christ.

"I have quite made up my mind never again to subscribe to a chapel which will have a debt upon it or its accessories. This condition secured, I give you authority to pay to the treasurers $2,500, a promise binding on my executors in the event of my death before the money is paid. Do not propose any relaxation of the principle—*no debt*. From the blessings which flow from offering to God a house as a free sacrifice, and the curse that I have seen upon chapels involved in debt, my mind is made up on the subject. The congregation with which I worship have erected two buildings in five years, for *other* congregations, at a cost of $40,000, free."

Answer to an application for a loan:

"July 3d, 1862.—It occasions me much pain *not* to accede to such an application as yours. To grant it, however, would place me in precisely your position, that of borrowing—and to that I cannot submit. My whole experience is against loans. They rarely effect the object designed, in most cases only postponing the evil day, and not unfrequently exciting hard thoughts with reference to the lender, and, at the end, leaving the borrower, after a weary struggle, in a worse position than when he first took the loan.

"Whatever help I afford you in future, I have resolved it shall take the form of gift.

"It is certainly your duty to try to avert the painful sacrifices to which you allude, and I throw out the suggestion whether it would not be wiser to seek permanent relief from your debts by raising the money as gifts among your friends.

"Carrying out my principle of *gift*, not *loan*, I would promise to make one of fifteen at $50 each, so as to raise the entire amount of your liabilities. *Less* than that result I could not recognize. With kind regards, yours, etc."

To a correspondent who had been sneering at the dishonesty of some large givers, he quietly replies: "The chaff will cling to the wheat, but it is a comfort to know that the bulk of those who subscribe to charities are still the salt of the earth."

But our friend's caution never got the better of his compassion,—*e. g.*, "—— is a poor, weakly creature, and has been in misery ever since. It is true that this allowance ($50 a month) may make them less inclined to work, but I could not bear to think of my own affluence and her penury, and will incline to mercy—much as you may preach to me. I have warned her that if this is diverted from its proper object, the support of herself and child, it will be withheld."

CHAPTER XIX.

ONE of Mr. Powell's most marked and exemplary peculiarities was his conscientious intellectual culture. He evidently regarded the enlarging and enriching of his mind by assiduous and systematic study as an essential part of his duty to God and man. That his steady pursuit of solid information, his indefatigable self-training, was not the mere indulgence of a taste for intellectual occupation, or a desire to shine in society, is plain from the humble thoroughness and plodding consecutiveness of his life-long self-schooling. " Thou shalt love the Lord thy God with all thy heart and with all thy *mind*." This, our friend felt to be the first and great commandment. We have seen that the only schooling he received in youth was that which his mother could find time to give him, in the mud mansion of a pioneer settler, and that even this did not extend to his thirteenth birthday, before which period he became clerk to an auctioneer in what was then a bustling, thriving, colonial seaport. His acquirements could not have stretched much beyond the point of bare competency to keep his master's accounts with passable correctness. But conversion made the young Tasmanian clerk a student. He forthwith developed what Wordsworth calls "a strong book-mindedness." This was one main object of his laborious journal-keeping. He lays down for himself this standing order: "All suggestions struck out in conversation, or come upon in reading, and all your own reflections that strike you as worthy of retention, and likely to be of use, register *at once*, as they occur. The rain that is not stored up in reservoirs wastes away, till it is absorbed in the sand, or lost in the ocean, leaving the ground parched and barren; but if husbanded in tanks, it may, by irrigation, fertilize and beautify the land with a thousand rills, even in the drought of summer; so our good thoughts suggested by Him who created the mind, unless retained, and turned to practical purpose, pass away, and leave us none the better. By careful diligent culture our minds will bring forth, according to natural capacity—'some thirty, some sixty, some an hundred fold,' but in every case amply repaying all the cost and husbandry." No wonder that the man who thus traced true thought to its real source should estimate its responsibilities. We have seen also that he took advantage of the enforced leisure of his first return voyage to Australia, for supplying the deficiencies of his education, and for general mental enrichment. The first use he made of his prosperity, after copiously contributing to the religious, philanthropic, and social interests of the place which was so rapidly rising from a village into a capital, and the district which was changing from a desert to a province, was to "ease off" from business, confiding it more

and more to the excellent young men whom he had
selected, trained, and trusted; devoting his mornings to study, his afternoons to business, and his
evenings to the service of the community and the
Church. This scheme of study was often baffled,
but never relinquished. In a letter to a friend he
thus states the object of his third visit to England
—"Health, schooling, information." The leisure
he had contrived to secure from his large business
had been to a great extent absorbed by Church
affairs, and philanthropic efforts. On the one hand
he had found that his resolutely formed plans of
self-improvement were frustrated by the importunate claims of a country and a Church laying the
foundations of their future greatness; and, on the
other, he felt that he could not efficiently, and therefore could not conscientiously, accept the position which his imminent wealth would thrust upon
him without some previous education. His good
sense and singleness of purpose taught him that he
must *begin* at the *beginning;* with the grammar of
his own tongue. He saw that to make haste to be
learned is as foolish and unchristian as to make
haste to be rich. Being already familiar with Cobbett's "Grammar," he set himself to the study of
more recent elementary works, and in his fortieth
year passed through a course of grammar exercises,
and the school-boy drudgery of "Spelling and Meanings." His mode of pursuing the latter department
of sound English education, was "to go carefully
through a copious dictionary" (M'Culloch's was the
one selected), "to write out all the words you do not

understand, with their meanings." He then went on to English history; taking, contemporaneously, " the Bible studied with chronological consecutiveness, making an analysis of each book, and ascertaining the condition of the world at the date of its writing, or of the events it records." His next step was to familiarize himself with " some of the great masters of the English language, making frequent extracts, especially from Shakespeare." Then he went on to study the *principles* of arithmetic, being already sufficiently versed in the art for all business purposes; the elements of geometry, Euclid, and algebra. He would never pass on from an earlier stage of any acquirement until he was " perfectly at home in it." He thus gained, to a remarkable degree, a gift he most earnestly coveted, " correctness and readiness of expression," and confidence that " his speaking and writing were in harmony with the best English models." He also studied " the Constitution of Methodism," " The Laws of Health," " The Duties of Magistrates," and acquired a fair general knowledge of English law. * " All articles in the various Encyclopædias on the subject of education " he eagerly perused. Next he took up the grammars of the Latin and French languages. Is not this, *in the main*, a striking anticipation of Professor Seeley's scheme for the groundwork of a thorough education? He laid down for himself helpful rules, such as the following: " Write out all Latin and French words and phrases of frequent

---

* Stevens's " Commentaries " was his text-book.

occurrence." "Carefully examine your common-place book, when about to write or speak on any subject." "Inquire into the special objects of prayer and the nature of the faith with which we ought to approach God through Christ."

The above is a part of his plan of study, laid down in 1860. He maintained the eager pursuit of knowledge, without discouragement from the slowness of his progress and the vastness of the field, by such considerations as these, appended to his "plan of study:" "Superior abilities are acquired by long application." "Successful plans of usefulness commence on a small scale, which can be enlarged as experience dictates. Too much attempted at one time ends in failure." "The acquisition of knowledge will form one delightful occupation in heaven, where we shall enjoy an unlimited sphere with ever-enlarging powers of mind." To secure time for these pursuits, he made a point of rising at six o'clock, and was very severe upon himself in his journal when he overslept that point.

His recreations were the study of music, for which he had both taste and talent, and rendering into verse choice portions of Scripture.

His high estimate of sound mental culture, as an auxiliary to true vital godliness and as a means of advancing the kingdom of Christ, was shown by the efforts and sacrifices he made for the establishment and efficiency of the two great educational and literary institutions of Victorian Methodism, Wesley College, and the Melbourne Book Depot. He writes (London, September 25th, 1860), "I am determined, all well, to keep in view the Grammar School and Book Depot, and, if spared to return, make them both efficient; for I am convinced that on these two agencies rest the future intelligence and strength of Methodism." This conviction, or rather passion, manifests itself ever and again in his letters, especially to the young. Thus he concludes a business letter to his junior clerk (London, July 17th, 1860): "As you are, I know, a bit of a student, I may tell you that there are works now published well adapted to direct you in self-culture. Dr. Beard's 'Manual' on this subject prescribes the regular course to be pursued by private students in their leisure moments. If you want this or any other books, I should be glad to select them for you." In his extensive juvenile correspondence (one of his special departments of usefulness) such urgent incentives as the following incessantly recur: "Be sure you cultivate a taste for reading; it will insensibly teach you how to think." "Study will find you a most delightful employment. 'An idle brain is the devil's workshop.'"

The religious light in which he regarded intellectual cultivation is strongly shown in the introduction to his paper on "Self-Development," read to the Young Men's Mutual Improvement Society, Denbigh Road, Bayswater:

The improvement of the mind is a subject on which the greatest men have spoken and written. You may, perhaps, wonder then that I should have the rashness to attempt such a theme. My boldness, I hope, however, may be excused, when I say that my sole object is to help you in carrying out your noble resolve to become more intelligent. I bear in mind that many of the members of this Society have had but few educational advantages, and are desirous of educating themselves; that they want a few simple and practical directions how to proceed, as well as warnings with regard to some dangers into which they might fall.

I have had long experience of the path on which you have begun to travel. At the age of twelve, I took a situation, knowing, of course, nothing beyond the barest rudiments of education; and, having ever since been engaged in business, have had to depend on personal efforts in spare hours for any progress in self-culture.

Many a time have I felt the need of some such suggestions as those I now intend giving you. I speak only to those who, feeling great need of help, are willing to avail themselves of the humblest hints. I am a mere finger-post, pointing to others who will teach you how to make the best use of your time, and how to proceed straight to your object. They will never weary of your questions. Had I met them earlier in life, I should have made much greater progress, and should have been saved much misdirected labor, and much irrecoverable time.

The thought has often occurred to me—How few Christians are well qualified to help the Church! The want of a trained capacity unfits the majority for the places which a minister would wish them to fill. The intellect of the greater number is left undeveloped, notwithstanding the express commandment of our Lord, "Occupy, till I come!" Most are content with such knowledge as may enable them to gain the places and profits of this world. They undervalue acquirements which will not yield "material" advantages, and therefore remain profoundly ignorant of the better parts of knowledge. I regard this Society as instituted for the purpose of making war on your own individual ignorance, and developing the talents which God has given you.

That development is best which is gradual. The animals and vegetables longest in attaining maturity are the longest lived : the gourd which grew up in a night, perished in a night. If your desire for knowledge be so eager as to make you impatient of the first steps, it will prevent your acquiring any knowledge worth having. The greatest minds have climbed the mountain of knowledge by slow, successive steps. The members on whom this Society will eventually bestow the reward of merit are the steady ones who have already the wisdom not to be in a hurry ; who will thoroughly know A before they go on to B ; whose attainments—as far as they go—are sound, and fully to be relied on. Successful students are those who did not make feverish haste, but were content to learn each day a little *well*—not disheartened by the small progress made, if each day they knew that they were wiser and better than the day before. Learning became part of their daily duty, and sweetened and lightened all other toil. Their minds opened imperceptibly, their faculties *grew ;* and, at the end of a few months, they were astonished at the facility with which knowledge was acquired. As the leaves of a flower open, one by one, successively, yet simultaneously, so one branch of learning led naturally to another; and thus, in the course of years, all their powers received culture and bore fruit. Learning in this gradual way, we discover our capabilities. We should not, however, neglect to make occasional experiments upon ourselves. We should thus find that we possess talents, of the existence of which we had no suspicion. Since the formation of this Society, have not many of you accomplished what previously you scarcely deemed possible? The successful attempts of some acted as a stimulus to the rest. You were seized with an impulse to read, to speak, to write. Never neglect such impulses. The powers within you are struggling to get free, to develop themselves by exercise. Be wise, and give them the opportunity they crave. Do not repress them by lethargy, or strangle them by pride under the guise of modesty.

Latent talent may be detected by the discernment of others. There is a touching preface to J. S. Mill's work on Liberty, dedicated to his deceased wife, in which he acknowledges that it is to her discernment of that for which he was specially fitted which induced him to attempt his great work on Political Economy. Last year, when at Spa, in Belgium, I called upon a doctor, who, seeing me look at some pretty water-color drawings, said, "Those are from my own pencil. Two years ago I knew nothing of the art, but, watching a landscape painter, I resolved to try whether I had any talent for drawing. I set to work with a will, and can now sketch from nature, and find it a most delightful occupation." These few instances show that we may have great undiscovered resources.

Those are not virtuous students whose object is to shine before the more ignorant. Such men are always talking of being "up to the age" of "progress," and "the march of intellect," with that self-confidence which ignorance confers. To such Thackeray's advice may be useful: "I would certainly wish that you associate with your superiors, rather than your inferiors. There is no more dangerous or stupefying position for a man in life, than to be a cock of swell society. It prevents his ideas growing, and renders him intolerably conceited." No! we must love knowledge, because in acquiring it we are obeying and glorifying God, and may apply it to the advantage of our fellow-men. These are the only motives becoming intelligent creatures, whose pursuit of knowledge, *beginning only* in this world, will be continued through eternity. For some beautiful thoughts on the true motives for self-culture, read the opening chapters in Craik's "Pursuit of Knowledge," from which let me quote the following passage for our encouragement: "Everything that is known has been found out by some person or other, without the aid of an instructor. There is no species of learning, therefore, which even self-education may not overtake, for there is none which it has not actually overtaken."

But what is the order of procedure? Well, what are your most pressing wants? Begin with supplying them. The knowledge required for a successful pursuit of your calling has the first claim. A lad resolved to be a carpenter will be none the worse for obtaining the best work on carpentry, and studying it until he is familiar with all his tools and their uses; but how foolish would he be to limit his knowledge to that one particular! We can only converse sensibly on what we know; therefore our friend the carpenter, if only gifted with a thorough knowledge of his trade, would be no companion for an intellectual tailor. A knowledge of the grammar of one's mother-tongue is the first requisite after a knowledge of one's vocation. Some attention to Cobbett's most amusing grammar (written by a self-educated man) would prevent your playing tricks with the English language.

Our time in this world is too short to admit of our learning many things well; but we have plenty of time to study some thoroughly, and to attain a slight acquaintance with many others. At the risk of repeating myself, I urge upon you this rule, *Whatever you take in hand, begin at the foundation: whatever you know, know well.* If you read at random, whether on science or history, you will destroy your power of orderly thinking. All will be confusion. Happily, experience teaches the self-educator that the right and sure way to make sound progress is also the most pleasant. Resolve to pursue one particular subject. Let that have your chief attention. Do something at it every day, but never weary yourself over it. Shut the book the moment you find your attention flagging, but never relinquish the book until you understand it from beginning to end.

But while intent on mastering the one subject, you are not to keep to that exclusively. You wish to be familiar with the history of your own country. Whilst pursuing that, you may acquire a little geography, by referring to a gazetteer for the places mentioned, and glance at the contemporaneous history of other countries, always making those collateral subjects subordinate to your English history.

You may wish to accumulate facts relating to subjects which you have not time to enter into thoroughly. This you may readily do with the assistance of the admirable little handbooks published by Chambers, Cassell, and others. They give an outline amply sufficient for the beginner. More would only confuse and distract. If you get very interested in a subject, and wish to go more thoroughly into it, a larger work may then be procured. But the handbook lays the foundation, the superstructure will rise almost without effort, by subsequent reading, conversation, and reflection. Get the catalogues of W. R. Chambers and Cassell; you will then see that a few shillings well laid out will procure you books sufficient for many years to come. Chambers's "Introduction to the Sciences" none of you should be without. It is a small book, which you may read through in a few hours; but what a field will it open to your view! Having mastered these handbooks, you need not be dumb in conversation, since you know at least the facts on which a science rests. Professing to know no more than you actually do know, people will respect you, and will gladly add to your stock of information. Hugh Miller and Dr. Kitto did not complain of want of time or lack of opportunity. I believe that both of them were more unfavorably circumstanced in youth than any of you. The Doctor hungered for books, and, while in the workhouse, contrived to raise a few shillings to purchase some, and, step by step, rose to be one of the first Biblical scholars of the day.

No obstacles can prevent a man's making daily acquisitions who is animated by a love of knowledge. Eyes are given us for the purpose of observation. Have you educated them? Houdin, the French conjuror, used to get his audience to exhibit a number of articles at once for a few seconds, and upon their withdrawal his son would state their exact number and describe them one by one. On collecting the articles, it was found that the boy's enumeration and descriptions were correct. Houdin trained him to accomplish this feat in the streets. In passing a shop window, they would walk slowly and try to outvie each other in recollecting the number of articles they had seen, until the lad could, almost at a glance, name all the contents of a shop window. Some people's eyes are so uneducated, that they can walk through the fields, or upon the seashore, without seeing any object they can specially recall. Their walk would have had other results had their attention been roused by previous reading in botany and natural history. "When you travel," says Johnson, "take knowledge with you, if you wish to bring any back." "The works of the Lord are great, sought out of all them *that have pleasure therein.*"

Our adult want of observation is rebuked by little children who are always making observations and incessantly asking, "What is that?" "Why is it so?" Why should we leave off our intelligent inquiries, and cause a full-grown brain to be more lethargic and less capable every day we live? St. Pierre, whilst residing in Paris, had one day his attention drawn to a strawberry plant growing in a pot. For advantage of light and air, he had placed it near an open window. Presently some small winged insects settled upon it, which he describes. Some of them shone like gold, others like silver or brass; some were spotted, some striped, others blue, green, brown, chequered. The heads of some were round, like a turban, others conical. Here seemed to be a tuft of black velvet, there a sparkling ruby. He dwells on the beauty of their wings, the way in which they were disposed, and the wonderful mechanism by which they were propelled. He watched the plant at intervals, and found that in the course of three weeks thirty-seven different species of these insects had visited it. He describes the structure of their eyes, shows how much more they could see in an object than a man with the most powerful microscope. This led him to examine his plant with a lens. He found the leaves divided into compartments, hedged about with bristles and divided by canals. The compartments appeared like large verdant inclosures, the bristles seemed to resemble curious kinds of vegetables, some forked, others hollowed into tubes, from the extremities of which a liquor distilled, whilst the canals seemed filled with a brilliant fluid. He then reflects on the varieties of the strawberry plant, remarking that we cultivate but twelve kinds, whilst there are several hundred, and that the plant is found in almost all climates. I have but glanced at his paper, which is of amazing beauty. He concludes with the observation, that "a complete history of the strawberry plant would give ample employment to all the naturalists in the world."

What fear is there, then, of our ever exhausting nature, as a source of instruction, if one common plant be such a world of wonders! "O Lord, how manifold are Thy works! In wisdom hast Thou made them all: the earth is full of Thy riches!" Should not such wisdom humble us, revealing to us the insignificance of our knowledge? Should not our cheeks flush with shame, when we remember how puffed up we have been through our profound ignorance?

> Knowledge makes humble; ignorance is proud:
> Knowledge speaks lowly; ignorance is loud.

Cultivate a sympathy with the brute creation. The more you know about them, the more you will admire the wisdom of the Creator, and will learn to treat them with consideration and kindness. Their instincts, their reasoning powers, are marvellous. Captain Hall tells that the snow-huts, so admirably adapted to the Arctic regions, are copied by the Greenlanders from the seal. He also mentions the cunning of the bear, who, when he finds a walrus or a seal, sleeping under a cliff, carefully climbs to the summit, and kills his unsuspecting victim, by rolling down great stones.

An early formed habit, the cultivation of which he earnestly recommended to others, was to "store the memory with wholesome sayings, and let them act as a spur or a check whenever applicable."

CHAPTER XX.

WE have seen with what humility, self-abnegation, and industry, Mr. Powell, from the date of his conversion, devoted himself to the lowliest duties of the simplest departments of Church work—those of the prayer-leader, Sunday-school teacher, and exhorter, and how highly he estimated the responsibilities attaching to these offices. We have also seen how readily he consecrated his musical talents, vocal and instrumental, to the cause of God. As wealth, leisure, and intelligence increased, he still in the same spirit of unobtrusive fidelity dedicated all to Christ. We have already touched upon some of the schemes of Christian philanthropy on which his heart was set; but it is worth while to give a few extracts from his correspondence with regard to two of these objects—Wesley College, Melbourne, and the Book Depot; showing that he devoted mind as well as money to the enterprises of the Church.

To the Rev. W. Butters he writes:

I am heartily glad you have filled up the subscription list for Wesley College; but I hope all the subscribers have paid. I suppose there is now every chance of the College making a good financial return. If so, I hope the wish I expressed at its commencement will have the attention of the Committee, viz., that all the profits should be devoted to the general improvement of the establishment. I suppose, however, that the Committee share my views in this respect. The ground, the building, the interior arrangements for the physical comfort of the pupils, as well as their mental advancement, should be constantly improved until all is done that is essential.

The Methodists appear to have lost their old fire in giving their energy in carrying out objects. Long experience has taught me that a willing heart is more wanted than means. Some of the subscriptions to the Grammar School surprised and annoyed me; others were more than I could have expected from the individuals.

On another occasion he wrote:

I am glad to learn the great success which has already attended the opening of the College. When it gets into fair working order, it will have still greater success. I should be delighted to see the formation of a good library, and the school rendered each year more and more efficient. Dr. Corrigan must aim at making it the best school in the colony, and the Committee must second all his efforts to accomplish this.

Not content with the gift of $7,500 to that one object, he devoted to it invaluable time, and an incalculable outlay of mental and bodily strength. I quote the following letters to show how all his business qualities were made available for the service of the Church:

To his Managers in Melbourne, about the Grammar School Bazaar.

Woncooton, *July 0th*, 1857.

I forward you original invoices of all the goods that have

been shipped, a very attractive lot. I have spent nearly three weeks over this matter, and hunted through most of the foreign houses to select fancy goods. I was at heavy travelling and hotel expenses, besides employing ——'s buyer, for which, of course, I had to pay. I think it would serve the bazaar, if a good advertisement were inserted two or three weeks beforehand, stating the various goods as selected from the manufacturers of England, France, Germany, and Switzerland. I think every article ought to be marked at fair value, in plain figures, to prevent mistakes. I think your best plan would be to engage a good-sized room, and as you mark off, repack the goods, and send them to the bazaar in their cases. I wish you and —— to superintend this. With some goods Mrs. Draper * and Mrs. Bell might materially aid you in fixing the value. I should like a committee of gentlemen formed, to carry out all the arrangements of the bazaar several weeks prior to its opening; so that a complete code of rules may be drawn up, and strictly carried out. This would prevent all confusion. It will be worth all the trouble bestowed, as I anticipate such a beautiful assortment of goods, collected with much care and labor from the finest warehouses in England, will prove a wonderful attraction to the Victorians, and with such aid as I believe the ladies will give, will realize something like $15,000. I shall send, next mail, a list of all those who have contributed in England,† with their addresses, that their contributions may be acknowledged by the Bazaar Committee. Give bazaar credit for my contribution of $2,500, and mind you get payment for balance *out of bazaar* proceeds.

One advantage of a bazaar, or "sale of work," is, that it enables persons to contribute skill and labor as well as money in aid of the pecuniary exigencies of the kingdom of God. It also interests them, and

---

* Wife of Rev. D. J. Draper, who was lost in the "London."
† On his own application.

unites them in the religious or philanthropic objects to which the proceeds are dedicated. It should not, however, be a frequent expedient, for reasons indicated by Mr. Powell: "I do not think it right to hold bazaars for Church purposes often, as that would injuriously interfere with small shopkeepers in the fancy trade."

To the Rev. D. J. Draper.

LONDON, *February* 11*th*, 1858.

The plan broached by some of our leading friends of making the Grammar School a joint-stock business, raising the money by shares, is a fallacy. In the first place, I do not believe that half the money required could be raised by shares; and in the next, I want to know what security you could offer the shareholders, since neither the building nor the ground will be theirs, but will belong to the Methodist Connexion? Government has also recognized the fact that to build grammar schools subsidies are required. Some seem to think that we are lowering the character of the school by "descending" to a bazaar, as that will fix on it the stigma of having been raised by charitable contributions. But the bazaar you are about to hold will not be an affair of charity: people will get value for all the money they lay out. Should the school prove a profitable one, there will be no difficulty in disposing of the profits. For the next twenty years, all that we can raise in that way will be absorbed in securing efficient apparatus and a good library, and improving the property. But had the school belonged to a proprietary, who might insist on dividends, no improvements could be made. No! Let us (if possible) raise the school free from obligations; and if subscribers want any return, let them have it in the privilege of sending one or more scholars—free—for a certain period.

I hope you will adopt the same system as you did in building your chapels, viz., give a premium for the best plan. Let us have a school which will do the Wesleyans credit a century hence; and let us rather wait for funds than spoil so important a structure for want of capital.

To the Rev. J. S. Waugh, President of Wesley College, Melbourne.

LONDON, ST. DUNSTAN'S BUILDINGS,
January 24th, 1866.

MY DEAR SIR,

I address you as to one or two matters connected with the Institution to which you have been appointed President, which have arisen through the foundering of the ill-fated "London." I saw much of our dear friends, the Drapers, while in England, they having stayed at my house for a fortnight, and spent Christmas day with me. Mrs. Powell and myself were the last persons they bade adieu to in London. We saw them depart from the Paddington station to Plymouth, on the first inst. My last conversation with him was in reference to Wesley College. I was anxious that an effort should be made to place the Institution in a good position before he left Melbourne. He replied, that he would make it his first business on landing, to see what could be done; adding, that he intended giving $1,000 himself, and should endeavor to get four friends to join in making up $5,000, and then, by a general subscription, raising a total of $7,500, so as to secure my $5,000 within the stipulated time. With the "London" was lost the stock of books which Dr. Corrigan and I selected. Fortunately, I had insured them, and will, if possible, send you a duplicate list by "Great Britain."

It is very consoling in the midst of our distress to know that Mr. Draper's faith did not fail him in the hour of trial, and that for twenty-four hours before the vessel went down, he labored incessantly for the salvation of the passengers.

Mind that the profits, after you are out of debt, are all devoted to making the establishment most complete—improving the property, founding a library, and *scholarships*. Not a penny of College profits must be diverted. I am glad to learn

that you are so heartily engaged in the greatest work of all
—the work of God—whether in erecting chapels and schools,
or preaching *Christ*.

To the Rev. P. Wells.

(Extract.)   LONDON, *February* 19*th*, 1861.

I AM most anxious for the prosperity of this institution
(the Book Depot), and would give to any orders you may
forward (for books) double the attention I should bestow on
an ordinary business transaction.

It is an object near my heart to promote the sale of religious
publications in Victoria, for the public good.

To the Rev. W. L. Binks.

LONDON, 6, BROAD STREET BUILDINGS,

(Extract.)   *May* 25*th*, 1861.

MY DEAR MR. BINKS.

Your appointment to the office of book steward has
delighted me, and I cannot but congratulate the Conference
on their choice. I think you are aware, from painful experience, that flattery is not my forte. But, in common justice
I will say, that you have the requisite qualities to make the
Book Room a great success. It is a noble task that you have
undertaken. There is not a finer field in Victoria than the
one you have entered upon for the exercise of the best qualities of the head and heart; but the work is great; it will demand your whole energies for "the six days;" and I do
hope you will be *set apart* for it. It is impossible to estimate the influence of such a concern in promoting the piety and
intelligence of the whole Church in Victoria, and I do hope
that the Wesleyan Church will gradually awake to the value
of such an auxiliary as the Book Depot, and that both ministers and laymen will strengthen and encourage you to the
utmost. I hope you will adopt a wise and liberal policy—
that your main object will be the good of the people, that you
will sell at a very moderate rate of profit, and that you will
advertise and circulate your books to the widest extent. Do

not weaken your central depot by scattering its contents into little lots in the various Circuits ; thus keeping your shelves empty. That plan will serve when you have more stock than you require. *At present*, always keep a good stock in Melbourne. It will soon get wind throughout the country and the surrounding colonies that you have a well-assorted stock, that they can always rely on getting an order supplied at the central depot, and your connection will be large and steady. Sell only for cash, and for all who want to sell again have a uniform rate of discount, no matter if the applicant be heretic, Turk, or Jew. Your business is to sell, and let the Word have " free course." I will write to the New York " Concern " and get you their catalogues. I promise for the first two years to make you a present of $250 in books, and shall select them from all the publishers that I think will do you service. I have written to Mr. Whitney, requesting him to grant you a loan, *at any time*, to the extent of $500, without interest.

To the Rev. W. L. Binks.

(Extract.) LONDON, *June 9th*, 1861.

My anxiety to give you all the information I possess, and to make every suggestion that might promote the best interests of the institution of which you have charge, must be my apology for the formidable dimensions my letters have assumed. What I have done to give the Depot a fair start, has drawn heavily upon my time, which, with a business of the magnitude of the one I now manage, is of great value ; and when I tell you that I have from thirty to forty other correspondents, you will admit that I have made some sacrifice. It is not to procure such an admission that I allude to it ; I only wish to prove that Victorian interests are still precious to me, and, by acts, convince old friends that I have not forgotten them. I may, perhaps, have gone beyond your wishes in some things. Should this be the case, I am quite willing to receive your corrections along with your suggestions as to how I can serve you better. That you should have a wide and varied choice appeared to me essential. I have therefore not only procured you catalogues, but have selected a little over $500 worth of samples from various sources. It is impossible for you to form a correct idea of books, etc., from catalogues—the samples will at once throw a flood of light upon the matter, and will enable you with great facility to make up your future orders. I enclose an order on my firm for $125 additional towards *shelving*, etc. I think this ought to be done in a nice manner. The fact that the profits of the institution are eventually destined to the worn-out ministers, ought to induce some effort. Why not invite to a social tea-meeting all those likely to sympathize with such an object? You might then state what you hoped to accomplish with the Book Depot, and urge the claims of the old preachers upon the gratitude of those to whom they have devoted their best days. You might also urge the necessity of creating a small capital to give stability and insure success to your new enterprise. You might take advantage of the same meeting to distribute the lists of books sent by this mail among them, and then endeavor to secure subscribers for magazines, newspapers, etc., stating that you would at all times be ready to send for any religious works required.

What are you going to do with regard to tracts? You ought to have a good supply. Of all religious publications you should have such a stock on hand, and so well-sustained by quarterly importations, that every Methodist shall have the conviction that most of his wants of that kind can be supplied from your Depot. Aim at making your establishment perfect; watch your stock carefully; and, if possible, guard against running out of *essential* works.

As some publications will pay a larger profit than others, the *business* members of Committee must aid you on this point, as it requires discretion and *experience* to regulate prices. Some books *must* be sold at almost cost price.

To arrive at the exact cost of your books, you must calculate the charges on every shipment, to ascertain the proportion

they bear to the *net* value of the books ; and, of course, add
the proportion to the net cost. In the charges you must not
only reckon freight, insurance, commission, and other items
connected with the transit, but also the cost of the cases and
packing, and then add to the whole twelve months' interest
at eight per cent. When your first shipment arrives, get Mr.
Whitney to assist you. On every book and packet I should
mark the cost and wholesale price in private letters, and the
retail price in plain figures. I think it will be quite legitimate for your Depot to sell all kinds of sacred music. I have
sent you Novello's catalogue; and if you wish to encourage
the sale of music, I will send you R. Cocks and Co.'s catalogue. I have selected you a few examples of anthems,
chants, and tune-books : you will see how you get on with
them. With regard to publishers,—

1. Gall and Inglis, Edinburgh, lay themselves out for
such works as Sunday-schools require. I send you one of
their catalogues, with the trade prices marked. They will
allow a further discount for cash, of at least ten per cent.

2. Glass and Duncan, Glasgow, publish small reward books,
tickets, and a " Child's Monthly Newspaper." I shall forward samples.

3. Varty and Co. get up many nice works for children and
schools, but only allow —— discount. I send their catalogue.

4. Tract Society and Conference Office. —— you know
well.

5. Society for Promoting Christian Knowledge. This is a
well-managed institution. It is a treat to go to their great
depository. I hope you will look as well when your shelves
are arranged and the counters up. This Society publishes
many admirable books for children. I have made you a
selection from all their new things. Their picture-tickets
and picture-cards are very beautiful. Of these I send an
ample supply. They allow a liberal discount, forty per
cent.

6. Sunday-school Union.—Only order from the Union such

works as they publish.　Go to the fountain head for all you want.

7. Groombridge and Son publish many useful works.　I have selected a few.

8. Darton and Son devote themselves to juvenile publications.　I have made a large selection.　Their catalogue will repay perusal.

9. Hayman Brothers have published two or three cheap tune-books, of which I send a few that I think will serve you.

To Rev. D. J. Draper.

(Extract.)　　　　　　　　LONDON, *December 3d,* 1860.

I must burden my gift with three conditions, which I hope you will not think unreasonable: that Mr. B.'s appointment to the Book Depot be for at least two years; that the trustees will never again impose any rent on the Book Depot; and that they exempt me from all further obligations in the debts of Wesley Church.　With the exception of Mr. B.'s appointment, the other matters are, I think, proposed by yourself.　I am most anxious about the Depot.　The attempt to burden it with a rent when there were no funds but what I had supplied, was not fair!　I am determined, as far as I can, to protect it, until it has some strength.　I have told —— to hand you bills to the amount of $2,500; and also that he is to double any amount raised for the St. Kilda Church, not exceeding $2,500.

It is not well to clog a gift with conditions.　Mr. Powell felt this; but he would not throw away money on badly-managed institutions, or give money for one urgent object which he saw would inevitably be drawn to the relief of another and much less pressing affair.

To the Rev. D. J. Draper.

(Extract.)　　　　　　　　　*June* 19*th,* 1861.

MY DEAR MR. DRAPER,

I do not wish to make this matter a difficulty; my desire

being to afford real, not sham help. While I wish to help
the Trustees of Wesley Church, my chief sympathy is, as you
are aware, with the Book Depot. I wish to see it firmly
established; and, since it is weak, and I feel much interest
in it, I must insist upon my conditions, merely requiring that
which is easy. I think, to the success of this institution, the
reappointment of Mr. Binks is necessary. To remove the
manager of *any* business so shortly after his appointment
would be destructive. I have a right to look well to this
matter, being the only one who has *given* anything to insure
its success.

Mr. Butters' arrival in Victoria looks like a preparation for
your voyage to England, since I can hardly imagine that
the Church can afford two men of your experience in one district.

To Rev. W. T. Binks.

(Extract.) *June* 19*th*, 1861.

MY DEAR MR. BINKS,

You have done well in boldly ordering a good stock of
books. Your keeping shop comparatively without stock was
ridiculous, and would speedily have insured the failure of
your enterprise. You must not be higher in your prices, but
on the whole, lower for *religious* works. While the Book
Depot is made to pay a moderate profit, forget not that the
grand object is to spread truth and convert souls. I shall be
glad of Church news.

To Rev. D. J. Draper.

October 22*d*, 1861.

MY DEAR MR. DRAPER,

It gives me great satisfaction that the Trustees of Wesley
Church have placed themselves in a position to receive my
$2,500. I have heard that those gifts are of the greatest
value that cause some self-denial on the part of the donor.
When I tell you—for your own eye and *ear* only—that my
drawing-room remains unfurnished this year in consequence

of the help I have sent to St. Kilda, you will admit some sacrifice has been made. I hope, however, to realize such a love to Him who had "not where to lay His head," as to do much "greater things than these" before "the pitcher is broken at the fountain." It is pleasing to find that Robinson is devoting himself to the work in such a noble way. You certainly have made the $2,500 grow to very respectable dimensions. As regards the Book Room, business to succeed must be done in a business-like manner. I have heard in public meetings Methodism praised more than Christ—the scaffolding attracting more attention than the Architect! I have been placed on the Committee of the Metropolitan Building Fund, but not having contributed—could not, at present—I would not go to vote away the money of others.

To the Rev. W. T. Binks.

LONDON, 6, BROAD STREET BUILDINGS,
June 13*th*, 1861.

MY DEAR MR. BINKS,

The office that has been assigned you, I am persuaded, is one of the most responsible you have ever been intrusted with. I believe that the influence of the Depot for good will be in proportion to the exertions of yourself and the Committee, and that, rightly exercised, it will be such a lever in raising Methodist piety and intelligence in Australia, as your Church little dreams of. You must, however, be wise and liberal upon the broadest basis. You must be willing to welcome publications from every source, provided they are *good* and *cheap.* Setting out on such a free-trade track, you will win the respect and gratitude of the Victorian population, and have substantial proofs of their favor in the large and profitable trade the Depot will soon be doing.

I have spared no pains since the last mail left to make a selection from various publishers of books suitable for your Depot. In selecting the newest and most attractive things that have been recently published I have spent days.

To the Rev. W. T. Binks.

LONDON, 1861.

MY DEAR MR. BINKS,

It is vain to think that the concern will succeed if you are not *set apart* to it. To attempt the duties of a Circuit in connection with the Depot would be ruin to the Depot. I am now an old hand at business, and know that it requires undivided attention. If you be not set apart for the work, give it up. If not, sorrow is in store for you. Why should you not be set apart for this work? You could still preach on Sundays, and the importance of developing so mighty an agency of good may well be set against all you could accomplish in a Circuit.

To prophesy failure of a concern that has not yet been fully tried is the mark of a feeble mind, or else of envious opposition. To strengthen your hands I enclose an additional order upon my firm. You may be sure I have plenty to do with all my spare money: still, I cannot spend my money better. "Wisdom and knowledge" should be "the stability" of the times, and preaching alone will never give this. People to be steadfast must read. Take care of yourself, and may God preserve you to the Depot.

The amount of his subscriptions to the Book Depot up to the end of 1861 was $3,875.

October 11th, 1866.

I am sorry to learn that your Book Room only pays expenses. Would the "Chronicle" be more attractive in a newspaper form? Must you have so much space taken up with accounts of local meetings? These might be noticed; but the speeches of John Jones and Timothy Snooks, on the affecting occasion of presenting their ministers with a teapot, are not sufficiently instructive, or even amusing, to be reported in full.

He then recommends that a considerable portion

of the "Chronicle" should consist of "extracts from works of the greatest celebrity and in the highest style of composition;" and that the "Poet's Corner" should not be "filled with the effusions of every *gusher*," to the exclusion of the beautiful compositions of our standard poets. "Those trashy local effusions—smite them hip and thigh with the weapon that forms the distinctive part of their author's own development. 'Clear your minds of cant,' was an axiom of Dr. Johnson—in my opinion, a healthy one." After all, he admits that such information "as" . . . "is much needed to promote a sympathetic feeling among the various Circuits."

He drew up an elaborate report on the best constitution for the Committee of Management and the mode of conducting its business.

When Mr. Powell found himself fairly settled down in London, he devoted himself to the service of the Church there as unweariedly as he had done in Melbourne.

A noble Christian simplicity breathes through the following extract from a letter to a friend in Melbourne :

LONDON, *November* 21*st*, 1862.

My work at present is in a Sabbath-school. I occasionally address the children and teachers, and now I have begun intend to embrace such opportunities as may present themselves to speak at public meetings on religious subjects, so as to attain greater efficiency. You think I "may sit down in the House of Commons." That is not my vocation, at any rate not my taste. My desire is after giving up business to devote myself completely to religious and philanthropic movements. I hope I may be spared to labor abundantly in this way before my Lord calls me hence. Let every one glorify God in the way he is best fitted for.

Throughout he acted on the motto of Lord Somers, "*Prodesse quàm conspici;*" he had rather be serviceable than conspicuous. Yet he aimed at the highest efficiency. On finding himself summoned to usefulness upon the platform, he put himself through a regular course of training under a professional elocutionist. He was incessantly urging his friends to work as well as to give; *e. g.*, "Do not give way to frivolous pleasures, even if you can defend them and prove them innocent. You can employ your time better and more nobly. I hope if you have been duly presented with a license as a lay reader in the Church, that you will throw yourself into the work. You will soon find whether God has called you to it. Mr. Butters tells me that through earnest application and sincere devotion C. H. G. has become a most acceptable preacher. He was in circumstances similar to yours. Work while it is day in whatever sphere of usefulness you may find yourself: if not, listlessness will grow into a settled habit, and spoil all your plans of usefulness."

To friends in Melbourne and Tasmania:

January, 1866.

My course is just the same as when you were here. I work at business and for the Church, and am now engaged about a small chapel we wish to erect near Bayswater. It is in a very destitute part of London, where ten years ago there were not five hundred people, but now a population of from twenty-five thousand to thirty thousand. They belong chiefly

to the laboring classes; few of them attend a place of worship.
London would appal you in many parts with its rapid growth
and spiritual destitution. Vast exertions are being made by
all denominations; but to barely overtake the increase requires fifty or sixty new places of worship every year. The
pressure upon one from every quarter to give is wonderful—
deputations, collectors, letters, reports, etc., a man who has
anything to give is now flooded with, so that a systematic
plan is one's only relief and safety.

We have a good plan in our Circuit of inviting our congre-
gations once a year to tea. We then address them on various
matters, urging them to duty and decision and anything else
that will make them better and happier. The tract-distrib-
utors get up annually a similar meeting, inviting chiefly the
poor among whom they labor, and urging them to accept the
Gospel. Our Sunday-school superintendents also give an
annual tea to the parents of the children who attend our
schools. The teachers call upon the parents individually.
They are thus brought into personal contact, which establishes
a sympathy between them. Our Parents' Tea Meeting is a
grand event. They are addressed by ministers and laymen
on their responsibilities and duties as parents. It is shown
them that these can only be discharged by the grace of God.
Those who are not *living* members of the Church are then
urged to become so. Such meetings as these develop the best
feelings of the heart. They afford scope for the talent of
many excellent people who but for such meetings would never
know their own gifts. They create also that kindly sympathy which is the golden link between the poor and their
brethren who are "better off," instead of the gnawing envy
which forms an impassable gulf. I hope that if you have
none of these periodical gatherings you will try to promote
them in Launceston.

Is it not instructive that one so given to self-an-
alysis should yet be so healthily *outward* and vigorously objective? It is clear that his sensitive and

searching introspection did neither overstrain nor distort his mental vision.

How well it was for Melbourne that, in the formative period of its history, it developed so many intelligent, energetic, high-principled, and God-honoring citizens! Mr. Powell was almost to the last a Melbourne man, regarding London as only his temporary residence. He writes: "I cannot help sighing for Australia." And again in 1861: "What I have done and intend doing in Australia necessarily limits my giving in England. This you may suppose is painful, since I am constantly solicited. I must do the best I can and leave the rest with God."

13*

CHAPTER XXI.

A YOUNG Irishman, preaching from the text,
"Perfecting holiness in the fear of God," instructed
his audience quite as much as he startled them by
his introductory sentence: "The first thing I have
to say about *holiness*, brethren, is, There's nothing
shabby in it." If there had been, it would have
been strangely out of keeping with the character of
Walter Powell, whose

> " Eye, when turned on empty space,
> Beamed keen with honor."

A very inadequate and even misleading idea of
Mr. Powell's personality would be given without
those minor traits which may be regarded as the
filling in of a true portraiture. Though his character had a bold contour, with pronounced features,
yet it bore no hardness or sharpness of outlines. He
was no smooth model of a man, but presented a
strongly-marked individuality. In committee he
was often eager, and almost overbearing, when intent on carrying, against the inertness or timidity of
others, some scheme, of the utility, importance, and
urgency of which he was deeply convinced. In

society he was chatty, communicative; fond of trotting out hobbies, and showing their best paces; full of anecdotes and apologues; a strange combination of earnestness and *abandon.*

His overflowing humor, and his keen sense of the ludicrous, were, nevertheless, in perfect harmony with his rare business ability, his intense sensitiveness of conscience and his earnest devotion. His pleasantries were but the outgushings of a spirit, which had caught its cheerful tones from the songs of the seraphs. His laugh had in it the ring of a Christmas chorus:

> " Peace and good-will, good-will and peace ;
> Peace and good-will to all mankind."

In his journal he sets down smart replies and happy hits in common conversation. Of course, there is very little quotable in this bubbling of good-natured mother-wit. But our sketch would be incomplete without a dash of his light-hearted playfulness. In his confidential letters he would burst out into madcap rhyme.

To Mrs. Powell.

(Extract.)   HYDE PARK SQUARE, *August 5th,* 1861.

Well! shall we do the grand? Must we fall back on Upper Hyde Park, with its huge rent and bumptious pretensions? What are two poor Methodists to do? However, I shall confer with A——, and see what mischief he is desirous of getting me into.—So chapel and church—We'll leave in the lurch ;—And as for the schools !—Let the young grow up fools.—For mind, my dear honey—We haven't the money— To waste in this way—It really don't pay—We want all our

cash—To lavish on trash.—We must furnish a mansion—In
all its expansion—With everything elegant, wondrous, and
fine—In painting, and music, and th' crockery line. What
style would you like for a drawing-room fender?—On the
subject of fire-irons, I know you are tender.—As an emblem
of trade, on the whole, p'rhaps the best—We could paint on
our carriage for family crest!

Even in his business letters he could not suppress
his humor.

He concludes thus a mock-heroic denunciation of
the Conference for a financial policy of which he
disapproved:

"But perhaps it is better to be like the local
preacher from whom I once bought gold in Melbourne. Said I, ' If you get digging it up in these
quantities, you will soon depreciate its value in England.' ' Ah, sir,' replied he, with a wise shake of
the head, ' there are men in our Conference there
who would *never allow* that.' "

Mr. Powell's acute susceptibility to all kinds of
merry-wisdom was shown in conversation, correspondence, lectures to young men, and even in his
grave diary, where, amidst records of his reading
and religious struggles and successes, he notes serviceable retorts and sensible repartees. Though he
was neither a wit nor a professed punster, he yet
displayed in a quiet, easy way, genuine humor in
most of its forms; "pat allusion to a known story,
seasonable application of a trivial saying, play on
words and phrases, taking advantage from the am-
biguity of their sense or the affinity of their sound,
an odd similitude, a sly question, a smart answer, a

quirkish reason, a shrewd intimation, a tart irony, a lusty hyperbole, a startling metaphor, an acute non-sense, a scenical representation of persons or things, a counterfeit speech, a mimical look or gesture, an affected simplicity."

Our friend also studied "whatsoever things are lovely," entering carefully in his journal fine though slight traits of goodness, and small instructive incidents; *e.g.*,—

"March 15th, 1860.—I saw a beautiful sight in one of the crowded thoroughfares of London. A well-dressed lady had just crossed the street, when she met a poor, blind beggar-man, who was trying to find his way to the side from which she had just come, groping with a stick, and in great danger from the horses and carriages on every side. The lady, without a moment's hesitation, took hold of his hand, and led him across, and then returned, and went her way. But her act of love was silently recorded."

Resolute as Mr. Powell was by habit, and irritable as he was by temperament, and strongly as he thought, spoke, and acted, he was very relenting, and always tried to soften the effect of too energetic expressions, by healing and explanatory post-scripts: *e.g.*, "Having read this over, I am afraid its tendency is to depress you."

To a young friend just setting up in business:

"One essential element of success in business is *uniform* politeness and kindness. It does one's self good as well as those towards whom it is exercised. It acts wonderfully on assistants. I should insist on their treating *all* persons not obsequiously, but courteously. I have no faith in your burly brutes, who pride themselves on their bluntness, and think themselves thereby licensed to wound the feelings of all they come in contact with. I regard a written sneer as a detestable thing."

Mr. Powell's prosperity was clearly not the prosperity of a fool; it had no perceptibly injurious effect upon his character. He seemed at least as humble and submissive when a merchant in London as when a clerk in Tasmania; when the most liberal, active, and influential member of a prosperous colonial Church, as when a young convert trembling under the responsibilities of a prayer-leader and Sunday-school teacher. At any rate, his journal records with perfect acquiescence his Church humiliations as well as his Church labors and successes.

"Melbourne, September 27th, 1859.—Attended the leaders' meeting from seven till ten P.M. The meeting finally arrived at a resolution to the following effect: 'It is cause for regret that the matters in dispute between Messrs. —— and Powell were not brought before the Church prior to resorting to an action at law. That both the brethren are in the wrong: Mr. —— for giving occasion for legal proceedings; Mr. Powell for not bringing the affair before the Church court in the first instance.' The leaders also expressed their conviction that my claim on Mr. —— was, nevertheless, perfectly just, and he signified his willingness to admit it. The matter is thus brought to a satisfactory conclusion."

"September 28th.—The Rev. Mr. —— called on me, with Mr. ——, and showed me a receipt from my lawyer for the debt which I had recovered from him. I returned him £——."

Perfectly good-humored submission to the formal and recorded strictures of a Church court, composed for the most part of individuals of inferior social position, is not the easiest virtue to a man who has rapidly risen in wealth and in consideration, occupying a forefront station both in the Church and in the secular community.

After all, the loveliest phase of Mr. Powell's character must remain unsketched—his fireside graces and " all the sweet civilities of life."

But such entries as the following are very significant :

"August 12th, 1860.—Gave Laura a lesson on Christ the Example for the young, and, after commending her to the blessing and protection of the Almighty during our absence, took her back to school."

The very extravagance of his language was often obviously intended to be self-correcting by its comic exaggeration :

" Such a mode of carrying on business is enough to make one dance with rage."

At other times it was serious enough :

" I would rather throw the money into the sea, than give him a farthing of that to which he makes an unrighteous claim, or yield to his greediness. Idleness seems to have eaten into his heart's core. So he had better cease from worrying, in the vain hope of inducing me to give way. I must raise my voice against sin. You say —— has been put out of his situation. He put himself out by negligence and carelessness."

Yet it must be confessed that he was at times too impetuous, too impatient of the prejudices, the leanings, and likings, and habitudes of others, in his ardent pursuit of a good object. He evidently had a difficulty in making due allowance for the temperament and inveterate notions, and, if one may so say, the natural history, of his opponents in committee or negotiation. This fault of his was, doubtless, to a great extent, not only constitutional, but the result of insidious, and at last fatal, physical disease. It cost him deep sorrow. He was one of that very exceptional class who find a difficulty in seeing a matter from an opponent's point of view, or giving a large margin of indulgence for a Christian brother's state of health or business, or domestic relations, or spiritual conflicts. Yet he himself was conscious of needing such allowance. He was built upon the high-pressure principle, and there was always danger of becoming overheated. His greatest mistake was in not making due concessions to the fixed habits and the helpless irritability of old age; *e.g.*, "They plead ——'s old age; but I ask, Is an offender to be dealt with more leniently because he is an *old* offender?" But that such explosive sentences were, on his side, the indications of excited exhaustion, is perfectly plain; the very next sentence being, "I am knocked up with business;

so pray excuse more. I have been writing until head and hands refuse to do more."

It was his nature and his habit to speak, as well as to think, feel, and act, strongly and straight out. Writing in relation to a friend's affairs: "Those banks destroy the colonies, sucking the very blood out of the trading community for the sake of a lazy proprietary."

Mr. Powell did not shrink from that highest and most arduous act of true friendship, earnest remonstrance. His affectionate frankness and unflinching thoroughness in pointing out any serious defect in the character of a friend, and warning against any weakness or thoughtlessness which had the appearance and the effect of a breach of the golden rule, was one of his rarest excellencies. "Faithful are the wounds of a friend." It was, perhaps, in the band-meeting that he acquired this Christian accomplishment—fidelity in reproof. To an old friend, on the proposal to renew a suspended correspondence:

"I am not surprised to find you lamenting that any interruption should have occurred in our friendship. It is difficult to renew a correspondence with thorough heartiness; *difficult*, but, happily, not impossible. I have no desire to recur to the past, by charging you with faults, which, if they existed, ought at once to have been pointed out by me. It would scarcely be seemly to 'say out' now what should have been spoken years ago. I therefore accept, with all heartiness and sincerity, your proposal to proclaim a mutual amnesty for the past. And let us resolve, by God's grace, since nothing else is strong, that our renewed friendship shall be based on the utmost simplicity, candor, and truth.

" The longer I live, the more I see the necessity of bending before the one fountain of truth—the Scriptures ; endeavoring to drink in those clear disclosures, by which our duty to God and to our neighbor is made plain. All other ' remedies ' fail to heal. But this not only heals, but gives Divine power to contend daily with the world, ourselves, and Satan, which, unless opposed by Divine energy, will assuredly prove our destruction."

Expostulating with a friend who had inconsiderately placed him in a very annoying and perilous situation :

" No doubt your position was one of difficulty, but I am afraid you did not give my interests as much consideration as they deserved, after the very plain way in which I wrote on the matter. It has caused me much mental suffering for the last few months. I, however, cordially accept your assurance that you did not think it would at all injure me."

Again :

" I spoke plainly, as having your interests at heart. You must remember that remarks in writing always appear more severe than those made vocally, having none of the qualifications of tone and manner. The only way of getting right again is to repent, *i.e.* to see that the wrong is in yourself, your own foolishness, and not in others. Let us be faithful to each other. Our friendship is based on mutual faithfulness. Of yours I have the firmest conviction, and you must not have less confidence in mine, even when I point out errors."

It must be admitted that our friend was not " a smooth man." He was much more like the cocoa-nut than the peach. His character was rather firm and strong than pulpy and downy. To some he might sometimes seem to have a hard shell, and a rough though serviceable coating; yet he had withal a large heart and a profusion of the richest milk of human kindness. His very vehemence was the milk of human kindness boiling over. In such moments Thackeray would have called him " beneviolent."

One of the most marked characteristics was his love of children. This is strikingly illustrated in his correspondence ; *e.g.*, to a friend in Victoria :

London, St. Dunstan's Buildings,
April 26th, 1866.

I have sent a small case addressed to you,--a few toys for your poor child to amuse her during her wearisome affliction. The toys are of a substantial character, but among them is a nice little china tea-set. Tea-sets always have a great reputation among children.

His correspondence with young people was very large. I can only give a specimen.

To a little niece at school :

London, 79, Lancaster Gate,
October 10th, 1866.

(Extract.)

My dear ——,

You must throw all your energies into your studies. It is a noble thing to resolve, as the catechism says, "to learn and labor truly to get my own living."

I am sorry to learn that you have a bad temper; but it is wise to acknowledge it, since "confession is half way to amendment." I can give you an infallible recipe for its cure. Try secret, earnest prayer. "The grace of God brings salvation," not only salvation after we are dead, but salvation while we are living. Jesus Christ came to save us *from* our sins. Now bad temper is a sin, and your heavenly Father is waiting to save you from it and from all sins, if you would ask Him. God is faithful Who promises. He always keeps His promise. Well, He promises to give His Holy Spirit to those who ask Him. Now, remember, that where God's Holy Spirit dwells, evil cannot triumph. Have you made prayer your delight as well as your duty? Formal prayers will never profit you much. Prayer should be the pouring out of your heart to God, telling Him earnestly all you need, and entreating Him to help you, begging Him to supply your wants. Do you want a sympathizing, loving friend? Jesus is your Saviour, Brother, Friend. Now, after this little sermon, let me beg you to go to God, believe that He will keep His promise; pray and expect to receive the Holy Spirit to abide with you. When *He* comes you will find your bad temper cured; and then cheerfulness and thankfulness will be the constant state of your mind. Now I have witnessed this cure in so many hundreds of cases, that I speak with confidence when I recommend it.

Your drawing will always be a delight to you, especially when you learn to sketch from nature. You must read all the well-written books you can meet with; they will improve your knowledge and your style. When you meet with a good author, examine attentively how the sentences are framed. If you like me to write in this way, I shall be happy to open a steady correspondence with you.

I remain, yours affectionately,
WALTER POWELL.

Another form which our friend's kindliness assumed was his love of "personal talk."

To one of his partners in Melbourne :

My dear Chambers,

The news that most interests me is what does not appear in the public prints, *i.e.*, the doings of all I have any knowledge of—their advance or decline, their removals, selling off, etc., marriages, births, and deaths. We already have a summary of the latter, still I miss many. How does —— —— prosper ? Has a public garden yet been opened ? Where have they decided to make the terminus at Castlemaine ? What are the Wesleyan ministers about ? Have you been to see the Book Depot, and what is it like ? These, and a hundred other small things constantly occurring, are what I want to know. For, strange to say, these small items of intelligence are of the most value to us here.

Then follows good-natured gossip about Australians in England, full of quiet humor—as if England were just a place to which Australians might come for purposes of recreation and trade—finishing with—

I hope to hear that your parliamentary struggle is settled. Better have a strong government that does not quite please you, than be in the state you have lately been in.

The following testimonies from highly competent men cast further light on some fine traits in Mr. Powell's character. The Rev. B. Cocker, LL.D., now Professor of Moral Philosophy in the University of Michigan, writes :

My first introduction to Mr. Powell was in the early part of the memorable '52, when the gold excitement was at its height. I called upon him at the store, corner of Great

Collins and Swanston Streets, and presented a note of introduction. Sixteen years, spent mostly in other lands, crowded with great changes and stirring events, have since swept over me; and yet, to-day, the companionship of Mr. Powell seems the most vivid of all my remembrances.

My first interview left a somewhat unfavorable impression on my mind. He was exceedingly busy. There seemed a touch of reserve in his manner, and an air of abstraction on his countenance, which indicated that his mind was pre-occupied with responsibilities. A further acquaintance dispelled the apparent reserve; the air of abstraction melted away. I got through the outer crust of him, and approached his heart. I learned to love him with a brother's love. It was my happiness to be thrown a great deal into his society, in matters of business, in public colonial affairs, in social life, in enterprises of benevolence, in Church relations and communings, and my attachment was daily strengthened. New revelations of goodness, of nobleness, of purity of intention, were continually unfolding. I never saw him perform an act, never heard him speak one word, which diminished my affection for him; on the contrary, it ever grew deeper and stronger.

Those memorable years '52 to '56, tried men's characters, and put men's principles and resources to the severest test. The delirious excitement of the gold discovery carried men off their feet, and turned their heads. A great many became moral, and some mental, wrecks. But amid all this excitement and wild perplexity, Mr. Powell retained his self-control, his calmness of spirit, his inward life of communion with God. He stood like a rock amid the billows. He seemed almost the only calm and self-possessed man, in a great community run mad. With clear-sighted and far-sighted sagacity he saw that, to manage well his own business, to avoid rash speculation, and wait for calmer weather, was the surer way to wealth. And the course of events soon justified his prudence. For when the tide began to recede, and a commercial crisis arose, and swept like a tornado over the

colony, and probably two-thirds of the commercial houses in
Melbourne were driven on a lee-shore and wrecked, he went
through the storm securely; his losses were small, and he
came out with an ample fortune. During these exciting
times he was faithful to his duties as an officer of the Church,
and he longed and labored to bring up the Church to the responsibilities and duties of the hour. And, above all, he
was inexorable in his determination to secure time for the
culture of his heart, for closet prayer, and for the study of
the Word of God. Here was the secret of his calmness and
strength. He went forth into the noise and bustle of the
world in that repose and peace of soul which communion with
God supplies. His soul was "stayed on" God. He was
anchored in the calm of the Infinite presence. He walked
with God in holy communion, as he sold merchandise in the
store, and conversed on business in the streets. And because
he did everything in the fear of God, he did *right*. There
never was breathed a doubt as to his integrity or honor, and
his word was never questioned. In the business circles of the
colony he left a spotless name.

During these three years there was no true social life in the
colony. The masses went there to make their fortune, and
then return to England. Even the children born in Australia were taught to speak of England as their *home*. No one
cared to make a home in the colony. The chief concern was
to make money; and, for the rest, they barely "lodged"
and "boarded." The amenities of life—literature, music,
art, intellectual converse, the love and joy of friendship—
could there find no congenial place. The heart of Mr. Powell
sighed for these, and in his last letter to me from London he
assigns this as one chief reason for his return to England.
But he made the most of the little rills of joy which trickled
here and there amid the arid sands of that social desert. His
house at Prahran was an oasis in the wilderness. A well-
stocked library, and the refreshing strains of sacred music,
made his house a home. Never can I forget my walks with
him across the open country towards Prahran, the commun-

ion of spirit we enjoyed, the deep and serious converse of "the things of God." And then the joyous welcome of his wife, the sunshine of her face, as she met him at the door; and the music—he at the harmonium, and Mrs. Powell at the piano—accompanied by the richer melody of his voice! We seemed to dwell for an hour or two in a better world. He had a few chosen friends in whose society he took delight. When these were gathered round him, there was the radiancy of joy—the hearty laugh, the merry twinkle of his eye.

I am asked to indicate the weaknesses I detected in him. I must at once avow my blindness to his defects! He came nearer to my ideal of "a perfect man" than any other human being it has been my lot to know. *Behold an Israelite indeed, in whom there was no guile!* If for a moment, a day, perhaps a week, I doubted the wisdom of his conduct, or suspected him to be slightly blinded to the exact claim of right towards myself or others, a few more days or weeks sufficed to convince me he was right.

He had a sound judgment, an intuitive perception of the just and true, a tender conscience, a warm and loving heart. He was full of compassion. He conceived noble plans, had great executive ability, and a persistence which carried his plans to completion. His intellectual powers were of no mean order. He was at all times a good speaker: occasionally eloquent, always persuasive and convincing. A scholastic education would have fitted him for distinction in science or literature. But he was in his place. God's cause wants large-hearted, noble Christians in business, to conduct trade on Bible principles, to grow rich by industry and integrity, and to be faithful in the use of wealth. Mr. Powell was all this. He served his own generation by the will of God.

The great rush to the gold-fields was in 1852, after the intelligence had reached England and America. People were landing in Hobson's Bay at the rate of ten thousand a week. Mr. Powell had then erected his large wholesale warehouse in Swanston Street, and he threw open the upper room to accommodate the homeless, shelterless emigrants.

The Church Extension Society (afterwards called the "Church Building Loan Fund") was greatly indebted to his earnest advocacy and his liberal contributions. The friends in the colony cannot have forgotten the meeting in Collins Street Church, when, after one of his characteristic addresses, he offered *twenty-five per cent., additional* on all the subscriptions of that year throughout the colony. I can now see him as he stood on the floor, with his hands clasped, quietly but earnestly arguing the imperative need of immediate action: "We must struggle to overtake, and keep alongside with, the vast influx of immigration, or we shall sink into barbarism, and re-enact the outrages of California.....Christianity is the only lever which can save us from moral putridity." With such words as these he urged the Church to be equal, by God's help, to the great emergency; and then, by one of his strokes of native sagacity, he made his proposal. Some $15,000 were subscribed on the spot. And, at the end of the year, his check was drawn for the twenty-five per cent. additional on all contributions.

The Rev. William Arthur, M.A., states:

" My knowledge of Mr. Walter Powell extended over a good many years, and was such as to give me many opportunities, and some special ones, of judging of his character. The impression left upon me was that of uncommon integrity and high religious excellence; especially a deeply conscientious regard for duty, a simple and humble spirit, great generosity, and steady attention to departments of labor for which he made himself responsible. From private intercourse I knew that the humiliation of his spirit before God was touchingly deep, and his spirit towards fellow-laborers in the Lord's work gentle and considerate. During the time of my acquaintance with him, I never knew anything in his walk that I could justly blame, and saw enough of amiability and large-mindedness to secure unaffected regard; enough of Christian graces to make one feel that, in his soul, the Lord had wrought a work of grace little displayed in profession, but more than ordinarily well attested in spirit and life.

Mr. Powell's junior London partner says :

SPENCER VILLAS, NIGHTINGALE ROAD, CLAPTON.

THOSE characteristics which most impressed themselves upon my recollection, were,—

1. His quick decision.

Free from the vanity which would seek to conceal an imperfect acquaintance with the subject requiring discussion, he freely inquired into those points on which he was not fully informed.   Having thus obtained a clear view of the matter, his course of action was at once determined.

With the details fairly before him, he arrived with unusual celerity at the solution of the problem, often as if by intuition; and rarely did it happen that his conclusions needed reconsideration.

2. His persistence, perseverance, and tenacity of purpose.

These, I think, contributed greatly to his having achieved so much.   Instances have occurred, when travelling alone, of his being attacked by indisposition, such as, had he been an ordinary man, would have sent him by the first available conveyance to the comforts of home, which he could have reached in a few hours ; but he pressed on, in trying weather, through his self-allotted task, never swerving until the last place of business had been visited, and his purpose was fully accomplished.

3. His talent for organization.

Avoiding the occupation of his time with attention to mere details, he preferred leaving these to others, after laying down principles, or giving clear directions for their guidance.

It was thus that while the responsibility of extensive commercial transactions, involving interests of no little magnitude, were depending upon him, he was able, by devoting only a few hours each day, to keep his business well in hand, and find time for benevolent and philanthropic objects.

If an instance of mismanagement occurred, it was not his custom to seek out the author of it and take him to task, but rather to consider how and why the error had originated. He would then provide such safeguards, or alterations of system, as would prevent its recurrence. For sheer carelessness he made no excuse. He would frequently say, "Business neglected is business lost."

In many instances his correspondents abroad derived much advantage from his friendly counsel; and one who was exceedingly successful, said that he owed it greatly to the manner in which Mr. Powell had conducted the business which he had intrusted to him.

4. His regard for trifles.

Any new invention or article of merchandise, if it had merits, although insignificant in cost, he would take care to introduce to those likely to appreciate it.

He was not in danger of the fate predicted for those who "despise small things," though often engaged in arranging for whole cargoes from distant ports, the trade of which his own enterprise had done much to develop.

5. Order and punctuality.

These were prominent features of his character. Five minutes before an appointment, rather than one minute after, was his rule. However much of business—confusion or disorder in his own arrangements or surroundings was unknown. His task well considered, and judiciously provided for, was usually completed before the time prescribed.

6. His high character and principle.

While watching closely and keenly the interests of a large circle of colonial correspondents, he carefully avoided the taking of any undue advantage, either on their behalf or his own. His career, in short, affords one more proof that it is still possible for Christian principle to achieve commercial success.

7. Delicacy of feeling and kindness.

These were natural to him. He shrank from roughly reproving even those by whose failures in duty he suffered.

If he thought a clerk in his office did not seem contented and comfortable, he would inquire, indirectly, what was the cause, and, if possible, remove it. The Saturday half-holiday and early-closing movement had his sanction and support.

After visiting the International Exhibitions of London in 1862, and Paris in 1867, he provided that those who served him should share in the gratification he had himself experienced; and for this purpose ample time and means were specially afforded to each member of his staff, on both of those occasions.

8. His cheerful and genial temper.

Rarely did it happen that he parted with those who came to transact business before some pertinent anecdote or illustration, drawn from his large experience of men and manners, had cheered and enlivened the interview. Frequently he would wind up with some humorous sally that sent his visitor away with smiling face and " merry heart."

This is the result of my own experience, extending over several years.

J. TERRY.

These testimonies to Mr. Powell's kindliness might easily be multiplied, and countless illustrative incidents recorded, such as his lending a friend in straits $9,000, and on his almost immediate failure, paying his passage to America; and his sending an accomplished but obscure and necessitous teacher of music $125, to enable her to give a concert to make her talents known. But enough has been said to prove that with all his dexterity, regularity, and energy as a business man, and all his strictness and fervor in the cultivation of spiritual-mindedness, there was as little in his character of the gaunt and hard as of the censorious or the mystical.

CHAPTER XXII.

Mr. Powell's constitution had never fully recovered from the shock of the severe injury received in his youth. For years he had been subject to severe attacks of sickness, and whenever he was subjected to any great or long-continued strain upon his physical or mental powers, a long and trying illness was sure to follow. Latterly he had more than once had intimations that there were symptoms of that terrible disease which for the past twenty years has proved so fatal to energetic professional and business men—Albuminuria. This had led him to endeavor to keep his business within moderate bounds. In September, 1865, he wrote to a friend: "By the present mail, I am refusing good business orders to the extent of $150,000 a year, from wealthy parties. I have just retired from the Melbourne firm, because I wish to concentrate my thoughts on the London business, and keep everything in a compact compass." To the same friend under date of "April 26th, 1866," he thus states his reason for not immediately giving up business altogether: "I have not been strong the last twelve months, having been frequently under the doctor's care. The weight of the large business is wearing. I indulge sometimes in dreams of retiring, which I check by the reflection that I am more useful where I am, at any rate for the present." His Church cares also weighed heavily on him.

Although he was still at heart an Australian, confessing, " I cannot help sighing for Australia," and cherishing a hope that he should yet return and devote a few more years to Victoria ; although he felt that in England he was " a stranger in a strange land," looking at everything with the eye and the heart of a colonist; yet he threw himself with his characteristic ardor into the religious activities and responsibilities of his new though native sphere. Even in London he could not lose himself in the crowd; and, whilst still caring, saving, scheming, spending for his loved Victoria, he felt the claims of a city to which a Melbourne was being added every few years.

He had not been long settled in London, when he wrote to a friend in Victoria a long report on the religious state of London, from which I give a brief extract :

To A. S. Palmer, Esq.

6, BROAD STREET BUILDINGS,
November 21*st*, 1862.

MY DEAR PALMER,

Nothing gives me greater pleasure than communication with old friends. I manage, notwithstanding the tyrannous demands of business, to keep up a constant fire with all I most esteem. I promised you some account of what is going on in the religious world of London. It was an imprudent promise, one I am incapable of redeeming in any way worthy of the great subject. London is so vast, so utterly unfathomable, that the longer you live in it the more profound it seems to become. I need not tell you of ordinary religious life; that would be only a repetition of what you see and hear daily in Victoria. The Independents, Churchmen, Methodists, Baptists, are much the same here as there, save in one or two particulars. The Methodists are not so great a power, in proportion, here as in the colony. "The Church"—Episcopalian—has a high vantage-ground in her immense endowments and her status as the Church of England. These draw to her the wealth, fashion, and intelligence of the nation. A man inevitably loses caste who is not an Episcopalian. The Methodists, weakened by their long contest with "the Reformers," have made little progress for the last few years; but now, I think, are beginning to stir themselves, having recently raised a Metropolitan Fund of $100,000, besides paying off numerous chapel debts. A strong feeling has set in against chapel debts,—a healthy sign. The Revs. W. Arthur and W. M. Punshon are the most influential preachers. The latter can stir any audience to its depths. He is devoted to the service of God. His imagination is of oriental magnificence. He is aided by a memory most capacious, which enables him to adorn every discourse or speech with flowers culled from every literary garden. How he has found time to read no one knows.

The Independents are a great power in London; they have numerous and well-built chapels, and their pulpits are occupied, as a rule, by clever, hard-working, pious men. Their having such good chapels, in such good sites, is chiefly owing to their having established a Chapel Fund several years ago, on the same principle as that which I vainly endeavored to initiate in Melbourne. Methodism, now it has its Metropolitan Fund, can do little on account of the enormous increase in the value of land. The Establishment betrays elements of weakness in its divisions. Some leaders of the *Broad Church* party are engaged in the awful enterprise of shaking the faith of thousands. The more earnest evangelicals work anywhere and everywhere, and form a humble, devoted, self-denying band. They preach in the streets, theatres, concert-rooms, and private houses. There is but one drawback to their usefulness: they do not like to work with members of other denominations. Still there are many exceptions.

Then, as to the laymen. The way in which vital religion is working among the upper classes is one of the wonders of the age. I hear of several families among the nobility who hold religious meetings in their houses, and pray for the conversion of the ungodly with the same fervor, simplicity, and earnestness, that used to characterize our Launceston prayer-meetings. I was at a meeting held in the house of Dr. Forbes Winslow. About eighty persons assembled in the Doctor's drawing-room. After singing and prayer, the Doctor called on any one who had witnessed good results in the theatres, concert-rooms, and parks, to state what they had seen. Persons of all classes were present. A scene something like those we have witnessed in the Launceston school-room presented itself. The most stirring narratives were given of the progress of the work of God. In one theatre alone three hundred were known to have been converted. A peculiar feature of the laymen's preaching is, that they address themselves solely to the great subject—repentance towards God, and faith in our Lord Jesus Christ; Christ, a present means of escape from the thraldom of sin; and the Holy Ghost, our Regenerator, giving light, power, and love. They do not advocate the special views of any sect. They have what is wanted in these days of cold infidelity—great simplicity and earnestness. The question with them is, "Are you converted? If not, you are in the thraldom of the devil." God blesses this style of proclaiming the truth; it is practical and plain; there is no getting away from it; sinners yield more readily to its power than if attacked in the most learned and logical form. As of old, the greatest success is with those who lead a holy life, who are instant in prayer, and have a deep acquaintance with the Word of God. Is not this "Word a hammer that breaketh the rock in pieces"?

Mr. Brownlow North, brother of Lord North, preaches with singular power and originality. He speaks just like one who has escaped from the horrible pit and the miry clay. I heard him on Ephesians ii. 1–5—most startling and vivid.

Mrs. Powell and I attended an evening party, for "Christian conference and prayer," at a gentleman's house. Nearly all were Episcopalians. About fifty assembled in the drawing-room. It was a time of refreshing from the presence of the Lord.

Think of four hundred city missionaries; the Strangers' Friend Society, numbering three hundred unpaid visitors! But, as the Apostle says, when recounting the heroes of the faith, "time would fail" to speak of the numerous agencies for spreading the knowledge of salvation. Yet the laborers are too few. One of the most earnest said to me the other day, "The tide of wickedness is so vast, that our efforts are puny in comparison." Still the signs of the times are decidedly in favor of the Church of Christ; the people gladly flocking to hear any one who is *in earnest.*

In the spring of 1864, Mr. Powell visited the iron districts of Belgium and Germany, for the purpose of extending the trade of his Melbourne firm in that direction. This was almost wholly in the interests of his young partners there, as his connection with the Victorian business was to terminate in 1865.

On the 16th of November, 1865, the Rev. D. J. Draper and Mrs. Draper visited Mr. Powell, staying at his house a fortnight. They also spent Christmas there, and Mr. and Mrs. Powell were the last friends they saw in London, being accompanied by them to the train which conveyed them from Paddington to Plymouth, on New Year's Day, 1866. On the 17th of January, Mr. Powell wrote in his diary:

14*

"'The first thing I read this morning was the foundering of the steamship 'London,' with two hundred and seventy-six persons, and amongst them our dear friends, Mr. and Mrs. Draper. 'Precious in the sight of the Lord is the death of His saints.'" On the 22d, he writes to Melbourne, "I am sure their death will fill the colonial Churches with mourning. Mrs. Powell and I are deeply cut, although our grief is mitigated by the reflection that he died nobly, discharging his duty, and that God, in His all-wise providence, permitted him to embark in that vessel in order that he might preach salvation to those who went down with him. The last words I had with him were about the Grammar School. I said, 'I hope you will take this matter vigorously in hand when you arrive at Melbourne.' He replied, 'It is my intention to do so.' In the midst of our distress, it is consoling to know that Mr. Draper's faith did not fail him in the trial, and that for twenty-four hours before the vessel sank, he labored incessantly for the perishing passengers."

"It is to be hoped that he was the means, under God, of bringing all who went down, to repentance and faith in our blessed Lord. Who, then, would have prevented his going to sea in 'The London'? The conduct of Captain Martin and of Mr. Draper are amongst the finest examples of heroic duty in modern times. They have left behind a testimony which will have its effect on millions of minds. Our dear friend was just the man for such an emergency. God gave him grace and courage for his solemn and terrible task. It is also stated that Mrs.

Draper, with characteristic thoughtfulness, kindness, and care, gave to one of the seamen who escaped, her shawl to wrap round him in the boat. I have got the artist who photographed Mr. and Mrs. Draper only a few weeks since, to prepare a lot of their *cartes-de-visite*, which I have sent by book-post. Will you be good enough to distribute them? I have also advised the photographer to send you a packet for disposal at the Book Room."

"I think the idea of a scholarship in memory of Mr. Draper a very happy one."

Mr. Powell's first strong symptoms of failing health appeared on Sunday, the 18th of September, 1864. On that day he opened the Sunday-school of which he was superintendent, at half-past nine A.M. At the close of the morning school, he attended the public service of two hours' length in Denbigh Road Chapel. At half-past three P.M., he conducted the Sunday-school teachers' prayer-meeting, and in the evening attended the public service again, leading its service of song. On the way home, he was taken ill, and was laid up for ten days. He attributed his extreme exhaustion to the want of ventilation in the chapel. Doubtless that may have expedited and aggravated the crisis; but this was not the first time he had spent two hours in a thronged and imperfectly ventilated building. The fact is, years of mental and bodily exertion, always up to, and often quite beyond, his strength, were working their inevitable results. Whilst regular, temperate, and conscientiously careful of his health, he had notwithstanding failed to apply with sufficient strictness to his expenditure of strength the judicious principles which he had worked so steadily and happily in all his commercial transactions. He had not limited his exertions to his capital of constitutional energy. He had mistaken spirit for strength; more correctly speaking, the strength that spends itself too soon for the strength which, having ascertained its limit, husbands itself and holds on. He was not so cautious and frugal in his investments of cerebral and nervous energy as in his pecuniary outlay. He did not in this matter "take stock twice a year," or "always live a little within his income." Like an improvident general, he had no reserves. His was the intense force, the *vis vivida*, which only becomes aware of its limitations by collapse. Few men of his temperament adopt the sagacious policy, by which the Oxford oarsmen won the day from their smart American rivals, contenting themselves during the earlier part of the course with a buoyant pleasurable forth-putting of strength, without over-straining or distress, reserving the extreme expenditure of power to the last decisive agony of competition. It is true that Mr. Powell resolved not to overwork himself, and believed that he could and should carry out his resolution; but he had no adequate reserve-fund of physical energy to meet an unexpected emergency. He writes from London, October, 1862: "Business progresses satisfactorily. I have as much as I care to do, not wishing to work myself into the grave by over-application." Early in 1866, he tells an Australian friend, "I have been so busy and anxious for the last two months, through the failure of the health of my book-keeper, and getting into our new offices." And in the spring of the same year, " I have been on the rack for the last six months, and felt inclined at times to *give up*."

Then came the terrible commercial crisis of 1866, when *all faces gathered blackness*, a monetary cyclone, during which no prudent captain, whatever his confidence in his abilities or his ship, dared for a moment to leave the deck.

He writes : " The money-market has given us a *drilling* the last half year, both in high rates and tightness. There has been an enormous break up in confidence ; everybody and everything is regarded with suspicion. How people have managed with less capital than I have I do not know."

On the 16th of May, he writes : " During the last three months I have been low in health and depressed in spirits, and have been laid up several times with feverish attacks and sore-throat. All this, my physician tells me, proceeds from general debility, and my only chance is to get away from the anxiety of business, for at least two or three months. I have therefore got all business affairs into very excellent trim. All orders are well in hand, and everything will be efficiently cared for, as if I were on the spot. I can, therefore, leave with great comfort."

But soon he has to write, " The critical condition of commercial affairs warns me to put off my continental trip for a few days."

Early in June, Mr. Powell went to Aix-la-Chapelle. On the 8th, he writes from that city : " I expect most of the banks here will fail. Two have gone within the last fortnight. I can only get my circular notes cashed, as a favor, by the landlord of the hotel; the banks will not look at them, having heard of the bank failures in London. The people are in great distress about the war. Most of the families here have had one member taken away to swell the ranks of the Prussian army; and, in many cases, the means of support have gone with the father, brother, or uncle claimed by the war. The doctor here is putting me through a course of bathing."

Again, on the 16th: "The Prussian towns get more miserable every day. Banks break, mills stop, trade stagnates. Nearly all the mills here are quiet."

"I am prevented making my contemplated tour, by the daily expectation of the commencement of hostilities. I am, therefore, staying here, hoping to derive some benefit from the waters. I am thankful that the first blow has not yet been struck, but all parties have gone too far to recede without a fight. Nearly two millions of men are under arms. I expect, if the powers hesitate, Garibaldi will precipitate matters. There will be slaughter on the American scale."

"Change of air and relaxation have already done me some good. I am suffering from a tendency to congestion of the brain, and my physician insisted on my forsaking business for a month or two, that my head may rest. In London we work, as a rule, too hard; but business, to be done well, must have minute attention."

On the 26th: " We can learn very little here as to

the details and progress of the war. The Government suppresses intelligence as much as possible. Only what they approve appears in the German papers, and French and Belgic papers are prohibited. There will, doubtless, be a heavy battle this week, otherwise people will think that Austria is afraid of her opponents."

Even here he could not give his brain the rest it needed. To his young partner he writes : "I hope you will not delay any matter, because you do not wish to trouble me now."

Early in June he removed to Spa, Belgium, " the waters of which are celebrated for curing disorders of the digestive organs." On the 25th, he writes: " I am much better than when I left London, and expect, in three weeks, to return to business in good condition."

July 28th.—" Since I last wrote the war has not only begun, but seems nearly finished. New complications may arise, but I think it quite possible that peace may be proclaimed before the (Australian) mail leaves. The breech-loaders, backed by the skill and energy of the Prussians, carry all before them. The Prussians, though victorious, have suffered greatly in the stagnation of their trade and the drain upon their population, whilst the blow has shaken the Austrian Empire to its foundations."

From this place he wrote :

To the Rev. G. Maunder.

(Extract.)　　　　　Spa, Belgium, *July 27th,* 1866.

It is gratifying to me that I have in any degree been of service to you during your ministry in Bayswater. It is true I have most thoroughly sympathized with you and your work, but the weak state of my health has rendered all my service so spasmodic and uncertain, that I have often grieved at the little help I have afforded you. To have won your affectionate regard is, however, great gain. Long may you be spared in your quiet but active work, which effects much greater results than the noisy popular style. Whatever may be our opinion of *fine talking* at an earlier period of our lives, we are brought as we advance in years to recognize most keenly the truth—that only those can accomplish any real good who have God's Spirit working in them—that only those can speak with power and demonstration of the Spirit, who renew their strength by waiting upon God in secret. A vivid perception of this truth only comes to us after we have proved the vanity of all efforts apart from God. And what a mighty unbelief it discovers in us that we try everything apart from God, before we will really submit ourselves to His teaching! I wish it were our habit (with all reverence) to cultivate a deep personal attachment to the Great Redeemer : to have Him associated with all our plans, arrangements, duties, as our nearest and dearest Friend. If Christians were, generally, thus to view the Son of God, I am persuaded we should see signs and wonders. If we were so convinced of His complete sympathy with our individual welfare, what a different view should we have of His cause! The notions of true religion, even amongst very earnest professors, are too *general ;* and hence, at least two-thirds of the energy and zeal of the Church is never developed. It is a *deep, personal attachment*, that draws out every power, such as the Apostles had. We want more self-abnegation.

But what a fit of moralizing has come upon me ! I was much pleased to hear that the laying of the Foundation Stone was successful. After all, no work we can undertake has less alloy in it, or gives such profound satisfaction, as rearing a place of worship. The Gospel is for the "healing of the nations." I hope that healing will come to that very sore part of Bayswater.*

"Spa, August 3d.—We find the day too short when the weather is fine, and only just long enough when the weather is bad. What with books, music, chess, newspapers, bath, and meals, we have always plenty to do. Beautiful trout-streams abound in this neighborhood, which is as hilly as Wales. Our health continues to improve, and we do not cease to regret our long stay at Aix, with this delightful place so near. We should have liked to stay here a fortnight longer, but my partner must have his holidays the first fortnight in September, and our office cannot be left without one partner, as every hour documents have to be signed, for which only a principal's signature will serve."

Mr. Powell returned to London so far recruited as to be able to attend to business for some six months, when a sharp disease of the kidneys so reduced him, that he was "obliged to flee for life." In June, 1867, he resorted to Schwalbach, in Germany, from which place he wrote:

"July 23d, 1867.—I am advised by the best medical authorities that my only chance of permanent recovery is to abstain from all mental exertion for

---

* See pp. 295, 296. Starch Green, now called Bassein Park. In reference to this the Rev. S. Cox states, "Mr. Powell took the liveliest interest in the Home Mission under my care, and was not only the largest subscriber to the Bassein Park Chapel, but ever watched the growth of that infant Church. His last public service was presiding at one of the social gatherings there. In him lofty and sustained spirituality was united, in singularly beautiful harmony, with keen, energetic, successful commercial enterprise. Simplicity and sincerity were inwrought with his nature."

several months, and for the next two years to be very moderate in my work. I have been here for a month, doing nothing but taking the baths and drinking the steel-waters. I do not suffer such intense pain as I did in London, but otherwise my progress is very slight."

Thus begins an anxious and able business letter, of four and a half folio pages, accompanying another of two and a half pages, bearing the same date. His old friend, the Rev. J. Eggleston, of Australia, was with him here for a short time. To him he wrote, on the 24th of July,—

" I hope you will, by care, retain the health and cheerfulness you picked up here. I have not got on well since you left. My loss of appetite and sleep has returned, with the usual catalogue of aches and pains. I am, however, thankful to say, that I have more strength to bear these troubles than when in London."

He then plunges into the affairs of the Book Room in Melbourne, going thoroughly into its financial position (to improve which he had advanced nearly $1,500), and making minute and well-weighed suggestions as to its efficient working.

*To the Secretary of Young Men's Mutual Improvement
Association, Denbigh Road.*

(Extract.)   SCHWALBACH, GERMANY,
                                      July 30th, 1867.

According to my promise, I send you list of a few books that will be very useful to the young men of your Society who are in earnest to make up their lack of education. In this list you will find Dr. Beard's "Self Culture," and Paxton Hood's "Self Formation." The first of these contains whole lists of books suitable for various kinds of students, and therefore is invaluable; while the latter refers in his book to many excellent works. The young men should get and study well these two first; they will then discover the kind of books they will require for further researches. Pycroft's book gives some capital suggestions, and, for the more advanced, "Abercrombie on the Intellectual Powers" gives advice that should be written in letters of gold. Chambers' "Introduction to the Sciences" contains wonderful information for its size. It is a book for a child or a man, and as charming to read as a romance.

Any desirous to attain the first principles of the French language, will find "Coutanseau's First Step" a gem of a book. But all the books in the small list I send are well worth having.

It would be well for any who want a larger choice of books, to get the General Catalogues of W. and R. Chambers, of Paternoster Row; Bell and Daldy (late Bohn), Covent Garden; and that of Cassell and Galpin in Ludgate Hill.

Then follows the list.

Next month he removed to Heiden, in the Canton Appenzell, Switzerland. Even in this out-of-the-way place, he could not wholly escape from business, thanks to the perfection of postal arrangements. Here, however, he derived perceptible benefit, by "drinking the Swiss goats' milk."

From Heiden he went in September to Munich, then to Dresden; whence, on the 1st of October, he again betook himself to Spa. Here he wrote on the 18th of October:

(Extract.)   SPA, BELGIUM, *October* 18*th*, 1867.

MY DEAR ———,

Thank you for the sympathy you have expressed with regard to my health. I shall return to London in a fortnight, and once more resume my duties; though whether I can continue them remains to be seen. I shall husband my strength all I can, mainly directing the principal parts, and leaving the details wholly to Mr. Terry.

On coming from Paris I was so bad, that I resolved to have the best medical advice, and was directed to a physician of great celebrity. He, for the first time, and at once, told me the nature of my complaint—disease of the kidneys. This, by causing me great loss of albumen, was weakening me like consumption; so that when I took up my pen to answer the June letters, I found I was utterly helpless, and like a person about to faint from loss of blood. The physicians consulted together, and ordered me without delay to the Continent, as the best remedy, to drink the Springs, which are strongly impregnated with iron. The relief I at once experienced was surprising. To cut the tale short, my general health has improved, but the disease is not cured; nor, say the physicians, will be, under the most favorable circumstances, in less than two years. They are of opinion that I shall have to leave England for two winters, the cold being likely to strengthen the complaint.

From the same place he wrote:

"Victorians should visit Continental watering-places, to see how beautiful towns can be made by the judicious planting of trees. With the water supply you will shortly command in Victoria, tree-planting should be vigorously commenced. Why should you not have beech, chestnut, oak, and lime trees, and the magnificent firs of the Mediterranean? They would grow wherever they could have a regular supply of water, and afford the delicious shade so wanted in all hot countries. In your ' picnic country,' shade would be doubly valuable. "

Even here, and in this state, he could not escape the harass of business.

To a friend : " From the tone of your remarks, I see that it is necessary I should apologize for being ill. I know it is a very disgraceful thing, and that a man is looked upon as a sorry vagabond when sickness overtakes him. The great Johnson observed, that ' every sick man ' was ' a kind of rascal.' No wonder, then, that you, casting about for a reason, should only be able to account for my illness on the supposition that there must be some dark, mysterious secret weighing upon my inmost soul. My crime is that I have tried to do too much. I have wrought in my business and in the Church like a strong man, when I ought rather to have nursed myself. I could not believe my doctors that I was killing myself, till one day head and hand refused to work for me any more. *That* convinced me that I *must* relinquish all my offices in the Church, and set about repairing myself. I hope, in future, *moderation in all things* will be my motto. With regard to business, you have my sympathy and support."

The interests of the Victorian Book Depot still pressed on him. To a friend at Melbourne he writes: "I would make a dead stand against the debt's getting one penny larger." He then insists in the strongest terms on the "immorality of getting into debt."

Of this closing period of Mr. Powell's life the Rev. D. C. Ingram (then of Bayswater, now of Cardiff) writes:

Mr. Powell's deep and practical concern for the stability and growth of the Church of Christ was also very noteworthy. I cannot better illustrate this than by giving you an extract from a truly characteristic letter written to me in May, 1866: "The Church of Christ is having a hard time of it now. The devil is playing a very bold game in our day, and needs casting down; for his agents use language now that is only consistent with great success. I am afraid he is making havoc in the Churches, since there is a wonderful increase within the last few years of Rationalism, Ritualism, and Materialism. We get confounded in these days by the specious reasons that are advanced for the decline of the success of the Church; but the time would be better spent by crying out as in days of yore, 'Lord, increase our faith; O Lord, revive thy work.' The lack of success is, after all, occasioned by the ancient cause—*unbelief*. I hope, in the deadly struggle that is now going on between the Church and the world, that our preachers will give themselves only to plain, earnest preaching. We want no gentle pruning of the branches, but the axe laid to the root of the tree. In these days we want men of the type of John the Baptist. I see that those who preach the truth without mincing matters are listened to with the greatest respect, and have the greatest influence."

I am grateful for my acquaintance with Mr. Powell, and for the stimulating influence of his character upon me. I think of him as a choice specimen of simple and beautiful Christian life, and of earnest, self-denying Christian labor; as the model of a high-principled Christian merchant, and as a pattern Christian gentleman. I pray God to give to Methodism, and to His Church at large, many, many, more such.

I have been impressed with his *tenderness of conscience in business matters ;* and many things that many respectable men do—and even some *good* men can do—in commerce, without qualms of conscience, Walter Powell evidently *could* not, *did* not do. Would to God that there were a higher tone of Christian morality in our land among business men, members of the Church! Then would the Church "put on" her "beautiful garments," and go forth lovely and attractive in the sight of the people.

The Rev. G. Maunder says:

His modesty and unobtrusiveness were striking features in his character. Indeed, considering his social standing, and his deep and intense longing to promote the welfare of his fellows, he was remarkably retiring. Who ever heard him in official or Church meetings with loud voice, or pertinacious doggedness, press his points? For a man having very decided views and a strong will, such as he had, he was one of the most practicable and pleasant men to work with I ever knew.

Mr. Powell returned to England in damaged health; he was for several years past but the wreck of his former self. Consequently, he did not take that prominent position in Church matters here which he did in Melbourne. But I can bear my testimony as his pastor for three years, that he was a worker, a hard worker, for Christ, and a liberal giver to His cause. In the welfare of the Circuit in which he resided he took a deep interest, spending time, toil, and money in endeavoring to improve the psalmody in its principal place of worship—Denbigh Road Chapel. He was the indefatigable, prudent, painstaking, and kind superintendent of the Sunday-school for several years. He was, for the usual term, the Circuit Steward, and managed the financial affairs of this Circuit with discretion and success. He supported liberally all our institutions.

The Rev. J. D. Brocklehurst says:

On my appointment to the Bayswater Circuit, August, 1867, I received from Mr. Powell, then in Switzerland, a long and deeply interesting letter. Its sympathy with each part of the Circuit, and every department of the work of God therein, was most cheering. How tenderly he cared for "the poor of Christ's flock!" What warm love glowed in his heart toward "little children!"

When Mr. Powell returned home, I feared the worst as soon as I saw the traces of suffering and weakness. But his eye was not dim; it sparkled with intelligence and kindliness. There was a sustained blitheness about him. When so weak that he could only bear a short interview, he inquired, as it might be a father concerning his children, about each officer, and the welfare of the work of God in each part of the Circuit.

I had one special opportunity of seeing him as his end drew nigh. That season of "holy communion" may never be forgotten. I was slowly retiring, when he drew back the curtain and signalled me to stay. It was to give me a thank-offering to be dispersed to the poor; a characteristic close to a life of singular love to God and to his neighbor.

In the beginning of 1868, fatal symptoms rapidly developed. During the few weeks of final conflict the reality and depth of his Christianity became blessedly apparent. Mr. Maunder, who attended him to the last, gives the following details:

GRASPING me by the hand, as I sat by his bedside, he said: "I have not to go to heaven to be with Christ; He is here;" (laying his hand upon his heart;) "*He is here*—it is Christ *in you*—heaven within. I have Him here."

Some beautiful expressions fell from his lips during his illness, which were noted down. "O mamma," said he one morning, addressing his wife, "such a glorious night! Such a baptism of love! Christ is in me, the hope of glory! I have always had a divided heart; now I have given it *all* to Him, and He in return has revealed to me the treasures of His kingdom."

When some flowers were brought to him, he said, "Put them near me, that I may admire the works of God. If ever I see the spring again, how I shall enjoy the beautiful trees and quiet walks among them! I have never appreciated as I ought to have done, God's beautiful works; they all glorify Him."

To Mrs. Powell he said, "If any one says to you that I have been patient, or have done anything during my life, say 'No.' I have deserved hell. It is all Christ."

Speaking of a friend, he said, "Hers is the right religion; it makes her happy."

"I shall leave you and Laura" (said he, speaking in reference to his beloved and only child) "in perfect confidence, knowing that you will soon follow me."

On another occasion he said, "If God spare me, I shall be very happy to work a little longer for Him; but if not, I shall depart, and be with Christ, which is far better." From time to time he would exclaim, "How I am surrounded by mercies! So many comforts that others are deprived of; nursed with such tender care; so many kind friends! Thank all who inquire after me." "Satan has tried hard to have me, but Christ has won the victory." On being told that "his was the happiest room in the house," "Of course it is," he replied, with a smile, "because Christ is here." To the Rev. R. W. Forrest, Chaplain of the Lock Hospital, he said, "I have loved and served my Saviour for more than five-and-twenty years; but I have never known such happiness as during this week, in this room." Even when his mind wandered, his words and broken sentences were illustrative of his loving character and Christian devotedness, as well as of the purity of his mind.

To the servants he spoke kindly and affectionately, blessing and praying for them, and referring to their faithful services.

Mrs. Powell records the following as amongst his last words: "Tell your father and dear Willy that

15

I bless them all, and that a great change has been wrought in me almost without my seeking. Tell Mr. Forrest how precious was the little communion." "My precious wife, I give you endless trouble, but love makes it all happiness."

He died on the 21st of January, 1868, at his residence, 79, Lancaster Gate. His medical attendant said, " I have attended men of rank and men of genius, men who have made a stir and noise in the world; but no man ever so impressed me as that man. Occupied as I am, the remembrance of his holy expression of countenance and his beautiful character is continually before me."

On the day of his death the subjoined lines were written :

BANK OF VICTORIA, 3, THREADNEEDLE STREET,
January 21st, 1868.

POOR POWELL ! I deeply grieve that all hope is now gone. He has been, in the truest sense, a good man—religious, without hypocrisy; charitable, without ostentation; bearing his riches without arrogance; in all his actions consistent. I greatly respected him.

A. H. LAYARD.

Dean Milman truly says: " What is wanted is a Christianity—not for a few monks or monk-like men —but for men of the world (not of *this* world); but men who ever feel that their present sphere of duty, of virtue, of usefulness to mankind, lies in this world on their way to a higher and better—men of intelligence, activity, of exemplary and wide-working goodness—men of faith, yet men of truth, to whom truth is of God."

Such was he whose character and career I have imperfectly sketched.

Mr. Powell was interred in the Marylebone Cemetery, Finchley. Impressive sermons, since published, were preached, in improvement of his death, at Bayswater, by the Rev. George Maunder; and by the Rev. J. C. Symons, at Melbourne, where, notwithstanding his long absence, his death was felt to be a public calamity.

CHAPTER XXIII.

THE LESSONS OF HIS LIFE.

We have endeavored to set Mr. Powell before our readers as he was; not a perfect man (for there are none upon earth who, in the sight of an infinitely holy and just God, can claim to be perfect in all their life and conduct, and Walter Powell would have disclaimed with all his energy the assumption that he was a perfect being), but a man with like passions with ourselves, tempted in all points as we are, who yet for a period of twenty-five years of an extraordinarily busy and laborious life, maintained a close communion and constant intercourse with his Saviour, and amid all the cares of business walked with God; and though in the world, and actively engaged in worldly enterprises, was yet not of this world, but rejoiced in being a citizen of the Jerusalem which is above.

Such a life is in most respects a model for our imitation, an example which we may wisely copy; and the lessons it affords should not be lost upon us. There are in our country thousands of professedly Christian young men, entering upon a business life, many of them under far more favorable circumstances than those which surrounded Walter Powell, when he first entered upon his Christian course;

could they be induced to follow Christ as he did, to make it their first and great concern to live and work for Christ, how much might they accomplish for the Church and for a perishing world! All might not, and probably would not, be endowed with his remarkable business capacities; but there are none who could not, if they would, follow Christ as he had followed Him, and thus prove themselves sons of God, without reproach, lights in the world, the glory and joy of the Church of God, and radiant jewels in the Saviour's crown.

There are, too, thousands more of Christian men, who have already entered upon a business life, and some of whom have begun to attain success and to accumulate wealth by their activity and enterprise; not a few of these, we are glad to say, earnestly desire to consecrate themselves and their earnings to the cause of Christ, and at times, under the influence of a holy zeal, resolve " to attempt great things for God." To such the example of Walter Powell's systematic and wide-reaching Christian beneficence, and his comprehensive survey of the wide fields for its exercise, will be of great benefit. They will learn that the charity which is to be effective for the overthrow of the powers of evil and the upbuilding of Christ's kingdom, must not depend upon impulse, but have for its foundation a full understanding of the vastness of the work to be accomplished, of the necessity for it, and an unfaltering persistency in pushing it steadily forward, till the topmost stone shall have been placed upon the noble structure, amid the acclamations of a rejoicing universe.

Let us then seek out the lessons taught us by this noble life, and endeavor to apply them to the benefit of those who, amid the cares and toils of a business life, are seeking to do the will of the Master, as well as those who, though hitherto careless, may be incited to Christian activity by his holy example.

I. We learn the importance of *self-culture* and *self-scrutiny,* not only at the beginning, but at every stage of the Christian course. Many of our young Christian business men have begun active life with a much more thorough education than the scanty training which Walter Powell received from his mother's lips on the Macquarie plains, or that which he afterward acquired in the auctioneer's store at Launceston; but no amount of early education can supply the place of a rigid and thorough self-culture such as that to which he subjected himself. The power of expressing his thoughts with freedom and force, the habit of thoughtful meditation on what he had heard and read, and above all, the constant, thorough, and critical study of the Scriptures—these were elements of the success which followed his subsequent efforts in laboring for Christ. For it is not, after all, so much in its quantity as in its quality, that the learning acquired in the schools fails to fit a man for the highest usefulness. It must be a culture of the spiritual nature, a sanctified learning, a knowledge of the works, the will, and the law of God, which shall pervade the soul and lift it above the sordid considerations of earthly gain into the purer atmosphere of heaven. Let all who would be, like him, "diligent in business, fervent in spirit, serving the Lord," learn this habit of self-culture, and they will find not only their spiritual strength, but their enjoyment, greatly increased thereby. To the thoughtful, prayerful, and earnest student of the Divine Word, there are constantly opened new and precious truths, so full of delight and instruction, so wonderful in their beauty, that he seems to himself never before to have discerned its preciousness, and he comprehends in its fulness what David meant when he said, "How sweet are Thy words unto my taste! Yea, sweeter than honey to my mouth!" "Thy word is very pure, therefore Thy servant loveth it."

And then, as really a part of this self-culture, comes the *self-scrutiny* or *self-examination*. It was the wisest of the Grecian philosophers who laid it down as a maxim for each of his pupils, "Know thyself;" but it was a wiser than he, an inspired prophet and teacher, who uttered the prayer, "Search me, O God, and know my heart; try me and know my thoughts; and see if there be any wicked way in me, and lead me in the way everlasting."

The advantages of a prayerful self-scrutiny are many and great: it enables us to detect and abandon our errors and faults; it tends to keep us humble, and to make us think of ourselves as we ought to think, and not as our vain hearts would lead us to think.

There may be weak and despondent souls, who, adopting Walter Powell's rigid and severe habits of self-examination and self-accusation, would be driven to despair; but if there are any such, we commend to them David's prayer, which we have quoted above, as commingling with a scrutiny more severe than his, a prayer for Divine support and guidance. But there is no possibility of rearing a character of consistent piety and Christian activity without laying its foundations broad and deep, in the knowledge of the weakness and sinfulness of our own hearts, their special defects and besetting sins; a strong and unfaltering faith in God, and that decided Christian culture which sanctifies all the faculties of the mind and soul, and consecrates them to the service of God.

II. In Mr. Powell's case, as in that of every man who like him has successfully combined the Christian life with the highest business activity, there was *a perfect harmony of spiritual and secular life.* His religion was not of that sort which expends itself in Sabbath-day observances, and is laid off like the Sunday clothing, at their close, not to be resumed till the succeeding Sabbath; it was not a religion which permitted during the days of the week, double-dealing, falsehood, commercial frauds and tricks, sharp bargains, and undue advantages over a customer. On the contrary his Christian principle was carried into his business; it permeated his secular life, and the first question which occurred to him in relation to any transaction was: Is this right? Will it be just and honest toward my neighbor? or Will it bring dishonor on the cause of Christ? We do not mean to say that in all cases he lived up to the highest spirit of these questions, but whenever he had departed from them ever so slightly, and the instances were rare in which he did so, his habit of rigid self-examination at once convinced him of his error, and he at once confessed it, and made ample amends. The instance in which he had prosecuted a claim he held against a brother before a court, and when convinced of his error, promptly made reparation, relinquishing a part of his just dues to promote reconciliation, is a case in point. His conscience was very sensitive on this matter. He was known after he had become wealthy, as a close buyer, but he never resorted to any unfair or dishonorable methods to obtain goods at less than their value, and while he would submit to no trickery, or double-dealing on the part of others, he always kept his own conscience free from stain. To his customers his course was eminently fair and just. He made a living profit on his goods, as it was his duty to do; but he would have no leading articles, and any advantages which his purchasing for ready money gave him or which arose from his skill as a buyer, were turned to the benefit of his customers. From them in return he required prompt payment, and reciprocally fair dealing; but if they met with misfortunes, he was first and readiest to help them to their feet again. There was no cant or hypocrisy in his composition, and hence his business conversation and correspondence was not overloaded with scriptural or religious phrases, as is too often the case with those who seek to make a gain of godliness; but the Christian principle which prompted them was obvious in all his business transactions.

Is it said, that all we have stated of his business
15*

intercourse with buyers and sellers, might with truth be said of some men who make no profession of piety? we admit it, but with a difference. To those who are prompted by no higher principle than a love of fair and honest dealing, there is yet a something wanting, hardly to be described, but readily perceptible by the dullest comprehension; a radiance like that which illumined the face of Moses when he came down from the Mount. Of one of these noble Christian men of business now living, we once heard this remark made by an irreligious man: "I know Mr. C. is a Christian. He never said anything about religion to me, and he did no better by me than Messrs. —— (a highly honorable but not religious house) would have done; but there was something in his way, that made me feel that he was doing business on Christian principles; and I could almost see his face shine." It is the "beauty of holiness" that thus illuminates the Christian life.

III. This same Christian principle made him, a man naturally imperious and exacting, the most *considerate and thoughtful of men toward his employés*. Very beautiful was his relation to these. He was ever regardful of their interests, solicitous for their health, and by judicious training and accustoming them to responsibility and care, and his affectionate and fraternal correspondence with them, he very soon fitted them to become managers and partners in his business, or procured for them other situations where they could be in the high road to advancement. He was also always watchful over their spiritual interests.

This is a matter of more importance than some are disposed to think. We have known some otherwise excellent Christian business men, whose treatment of their employés was a dishonor to their religious profession. They seemed only solicitous to obtain from them an amount of work which they assumed to be commensurate with the not very liberal wages. or salaries they paid them, and manifested no more interest in their physical, intellectual, or spiritual welfare than if they were mere brutes. There was no inducement to work in the hope of future promotion or partnership; no appreciation of acts of faithful service; no solicitude for their moral or physical health; no admission to any social privileges; it was only so much work for so much pay, and if an application was made, after years of patient and conscientious service, for an advance, they were very coolly told that if they were dissatisfied with their pay, there were plenty of others who would be glad to take their places. Now this course is not only unchristian, but it is unwise, as a mere matter of policy. In this matter, as in all others, the highest development of Christian principle is really the wisest human policy. The merchant or banker who makes the welfare of his employés his personal interest, who seeks to attach them to him by a generous policy and a solicitude for their physical, intellectual, and moral well-being, who protects them from the snares and temptations which beset young persons in all large towns, by a wise regard for their social condition, and recognizes with kindly thankfulness their efforts to serve him conscientiously, and who encourages their fidelity by timely and judicious promotion, will be served more faithfully and profitably, and by more loving hands, than the man who takes no interest in his employés; and in any time of disaster or peril, he will find that he has a corps of attached and willing clerks ready to do all in their power for him, while the coldly selfish employer will be either deserted or robbed by those who have ceased to feel any interest in one who evidently did not care for them.

But to the Christian merchant or banker there are other and higher considerations which should make him the kindest and most thoughtful of employers. God has placed these young persons under his care, and if he neglects their spiritual as well as their temporal welfare, he must give an account to God for his neglect, and if they through his disregard of their interests, are led astray and finally perish, their blood will be found on his skirts. Apart from this, there is no obligation resting on him in regard to those with whom he is called to deal which has not a tenfold stronger application to the case of his employés, and fidelity to God, and to his duties to his neighbor, require of him the fulfilment of his plain duty to those dependent upon him.

IV. We learn from Mr. Powell's life a lesson of the *necessity of spiritual activity in Church relationship*, to the full development of the Christian life. In the hurry and bustle of business, the on-rushing tide of commerce, and the absorbing interest of great financial operations, there is a strong tendency, on the part of really pious business men, to compromise for a neglect of active participation in Church duties, by the giving of money. They have not time to attend the prayer and conference meetings, to take a class in the Sabbath-school, to lead a praying circle, to visit the sick saints, or to aid in some city mission, which is sadly in need of help; but if pecuniary assistance will answer the purpose, they are ready to give that.

This is not the Scriptural rule. With the rich as well as the poor, the busy as well as the unemployed, the *prayers* and alms must go up together. Mr. Powell was in this matter a model Christian disciple. At a time when from the rush to the gold regions, and the impossibility of obtaining capable assistance, he was doing the work of three men, and giving very largely to every benevolent cause, he yet maintained his position as a prayer-leader, class-leader, and, for a part of the time, as an exhorter. Beyond this he was also active and zealous in the secular affairs of the Church, providing for its missions and the supply of the means of grace in the crowded mining districts, devising means of aiding homeless and friendless emigrants, and extending in every way the influences of Christianity over the communities, which, but for his energetic efforts, would have been " without God and without hope in the world." And in England, while in failing health, with the cares of a vast business on his hands, and still constantly thoughtful and active in promoting the spiritual interests of his Australian home, he yet took charge of a large Sabbath-school in one of the destitute districts of London, and succeeded in establishing there a chapel, and collecting a large congregation; and meanwhile was active in similar efforts in other parts of the great metropolis.

V. We learn from Mr. Powell's life lessons of great importance and value in regard to *the best methods of exercising a comprehensive benevolence.* Walter Powell's was too large-hearted and grand a nature, to be confined within narrow or circumscribed limits in his giving. He gave because it was a pleasure and delight to him to give; when he was poor, he gave freely and largely from his poverty; when he became rich, his wealth increased not only the amount but the proportion of his giving.

Yet this bounteous giving was only spontaneous in that it proceeded from a liberal, generous heart. It was like all his religious life, conducted on a systematic and well-ordered plan. In the very beginning of his Christian life, when his scanty income was hardly sufficient to support his little household, and he felt bound to economize to the utmost to avoid debt, he devoted the tenth of his income to the cause of religion and philanthropy; as his circumstances became more prosperous, he laid down the principle that the tenth should be the *minimum* of his yearly contribution, and while his *maximum* was subsequently a fifth, a fourth, or in some cases, the half of his almost princely income, the tenth remained as the measure below which under no circumstances he would fall. In one of those disastrous years, to which commerce is so liable, he wrote to a friend, " As I have no profits out of which to give, I must see what I can afford, notwithstanding my losses." At another time in answer to an application to aid in the erection of a new chapel in Victoria, he wrote : " In January, D.V., I will go closely into my engagements, and send you an order for what I can afford. I hope it may be $2,500, possibly it may not be half that sum, as the claims upon me are large in proportion to my income ; but I thank God heartily for giving me anything to spare, and any disposition to give." The order sent was for the $2,500. The principle with him was not, " How little can I give and yet satisfy my conscience?" but, " How much can I spare from my business without embarrassing it, for the cause of God?" And this is as it should be. A rigid adherence to the rule of giving a tenth of the income may work hardship in some cases, while in others it is not a fair proportion of the income for God's service. Let us illustrate this: A. has an income of $1,000 obtained by his daily labor, and has no reserve. On this sum he must support his family. If he consecrates one tenth of this = $100, to the cause of benevolence, he must in so doing deprive himself and family of some articles of food, clothing, or household need, or at all events of something which, if not of prime necessity, would minister greatly to their comfort. For him, situated as he is, the tenth is too large a proportion.

B. has an income also derived from his labor of hand or brain of $5,000, but little or no reserve. He gives the tenth = $500, and in so doing deprives his family of no article of necessity or of comfort ; but if misfortune comes upon him, if he is disabled by disease or taken away, this rate of giving must necessarily cease, and worldly wisdom may blame him for having given so much. This is a case where perhaps the rule of the tenth is a fair and just one.

C. has an income of $10,000 and a comfortable reserve. If he gives but the tenth = $1,000, he has still $9,000 left, and the certainty that his family will not be left to want. IIis giving a tenth deprives his family of no necessary food, clothing, or comfort, not indeed of any ordinary luxury, and if he doubled the amount he would still have an income ample for their use. IIere the tenth does not seem to be the just maximum of benevolent contribution.

Where the income is still larger, say $20,000, $30,000, $50,000, or $100,000, and accompanied by a reserved fortune, the intelligent and conscientious Christian disciple will feel that as God's steward his duty is not fully performed when he has given a tenth, a fifth, or even a third of his income to the cause of benevolence. He has an abundance, and more than an abundance, left for his own and his family's needs, and he will feel, as David did, " Of Thy own have we given Thee." It is one of the best indications of the increasing spirit of consecration among those whom God has blessed with wealth, at the present day, that so many are devoting the riches which IIe has given them to the promotion of those causes which will elevate humanity, diffuse the light of the gospel, and glorify God. In no period of the world's history has wealth been so freely consecrated to philanthropic and religious purposes as now, and never has human enlightenment and Christian knowledge, the culture of the intellect and the illumination of the soul, made such glorious progress. If this consecration of the gold and silver of the earth to the promotion of God's work shall continue and increase for the next hundred years in the same ratio in which it has done for the last fifty, we may indeed look forward with hope and joy to the speedy coming of the time when "the knowledge of the Lord shall cover the earth as the waters do the sea;" when "the kingdoms of this world shall become the kingdoms of our Lord and His Christ; and he shall reign forever and ever." The gifts of money alone will not achieve this glorious consummation; but money sanctified and made effective by the personal consecration of its possessors, and given to the service of the Master, will speedily accomplish it through God's blessing.

But Mr. Powell was also *discriminating in his beneficence.* He did not lavish all his gifts on one object or one class of objects; he did not give largely when only small sums were needed; nor a mere pittance when thousands were necessary; he gave on conditions where he deemed it needful to stimulate the liberality of others; and without conditions when he could, by so doing, accomplish the better, desirable ends. The larger part of his giving was in secret, not letting his left hand know what his right hand did, but where his example would produce emulation in others, he would allow his gifts to be made public. In his gifts to friends, dependents, and the unfortunate, he was very careful not to give in such a way as to pauperize the recipients of his bounty ; and his gifts were often based on their exerting themselves to earn an equal sum, or in some way manifesting their willingness to help themselves. The bold, brazen, importunate beggar was his special abhorrence, and if he sometimes gave to such a one, as who does not, it was always with a protest that he would not do so again, and an apology for his misplaced tenderness.

In all these particulars his benevolence seems to us a fitting model for our imitation. If, according to the old proverb, "he gives twice, who gives quickly," he doubles the value of his gifts who bestows them with discrimination and judgment.

Another excellent feature of his beneficence was *his fixed determination to be his own executor*, and giving what he had to give while in life, to see, in person, that his gifts were not misapplied. Too many excuse themselves from acts of wise beneficence during life on the ground that they have remembered such and such causes in their wills. But how few of these bequests ever reach the objects for which they were intended. "The dead hand," says a quaint old English writer, "has very little power." It is proverbially easier to break a will than to make one, and the cases are rare where some one does not appear to contest a bequest to any object of benevolence. Then, too, there are those who, holding on with a miser's grasp to their money during life, seem determined not to let go their hold of it till years after they are dead, and then reluctantly bestow earnings which they did not live to make, upon the cause of God.

In contrast with these reluctant and uncertain givers, how admirable does that system of giving appear which searches out its appropriate objects, gives wisely and discriminatingly to each, and watches carefully the effects of its beneficence, adding, if needful, to this, and diminishing the portion of the other, as it approaches the point of self-support, or, from the bounty of others, requires a smaller proportion. This is the very highest degree of Christian beneficence, watchful ever to make every dollar accomplish the greatest possible amount of good.

VI. Another trait of Walter Powell's character, well worthy of our imitation, was his *Christian cheerfulness.* In very many minds the idea of a true Christian is that of a man of severe and stern aspect, who seldom or never smiles or laughs, who looks upon all amusement and cheerfulness as downright sin, and who is never so happy as when bemoaning his own sins or those of his neighbors.

We need hardly say that such a picture represents, even at the best, a very imperfect, one-sided Christian, who has scarcely learned the alphabet of true Christianity; oftener it represents a long-faced, sanctimonious hypocrite, who has made his outward seriousness a cloak for inward iniquity. No! the true Christian is cheerful and joyous, and why should he not be? At peace with God and man, rejoicing in the sense of pardon and of a Saviour's love, he has nothing to sadden his heart except the deep regret that all the world do not know the sweet experience of pardoned sin.

Here was a man of earnest, ardent temper, an almost constant sufferer from disease after his eighteenth year, given through life to rigid, and some would say an almost morbid, self-examination; a man who in early life had known what grinding poverty was, and later had received stroke after stroke of affliction, losing eight near relatives in a single year, and burying in a few years six children; overworked almost constantly, and with a load of care in his business, in ecclesiastical matters, in the promotion of institutions for the public weal, in providing for the numerous dependents upon his bounty; and yet, amid all these carking cares, he maintained a constant cheerfulness, a buoyancy of spirit which never yielded to despondency. He could thoroughly enjoy the pleasant things of earth because he enjoyed so completely the light of heaven in his soul, and his sources of delight were so unfading.

We might go on to particularize other admirable traits of character in this Christian business man— such as his moderation in prosperity, his unflinching integrity, his wise foresight, his tenderness for the poor, the orphan, and the stranger in a strange land; but his life is so full of lessons for good, that we should be in danger of extending this little volume beyond due limits, were we to attempt to enforce them all. We can only counsel the young Christian who is commencing a business life to follow Walter Powell's example, so far as he followed Christ.

> "So shall his walk be close with God,
>   Calm and serene his frame;
> So purer light shall mark the road,
>   That leads him to the Lamb."